Auger's Touchstone

or

The Wrong Side of Contemporary History

Book Four
THE BLESSINGS OF GAIA QUARTET

Robert Balmanno

A Caveat Lector Book

REGENT PRESS
Berkeley, California

ISBN 13: 978-1-58790-536-0
ISBN 10: 1-58790-536-1

Library of Congress Cataloging-in-Publication Data

Names: Balmanno, Robert, author.
Title: Auger's touchstone : or the wrong side of contemporary history /
  Robert Balmanno.
Description: First edition. | Berkeley, California : Regent Press, [2021] |
  Series: The blessings of Gaia quartet ; book 4 | "A Caveat Lector book."
  | Summary: "Beyond dystopia ... After a millennium of cultural eclipse,
  the Earth's human inhabitants have resurrected civilization and
  rekindled high tech. But immense challenges loom. The Outer World
  remains caught up in barbarism. A tech-enriched plutocracy runs the
  Inner World. Prosperity is commonplace, but so is poverty and
  inequality. Schisms roil the Gaia faith as ancient artifacts come to
  light. And scientists struggle to convince the public that an errant
  asteroid could bring earthly extinction, and thus for humanity the end
  of the line, if not repelled. Set in Silicon Valley 27 centuries hence,
  Auger's Touchstone is a tale of historians, astronomers, techno-elites,
  agrarians, believers, dissidents, nihilists, a bruja, and a brilliant
  young couple living by their wits and trying to make sense of it all.
  It's a world much different from ours, but also surprisingly familiar.
  Ideas and adventures abound"-- Provided by publisher.
Identifiers: LCCN 2020037629 | ISBN 9781587905360 (trade paperback) | ISBN
  1587905361 (trade paperback)
Subjects: GSAFD: Science fiction. | Dystopias. | LCGFT: Novels.
Classification: LCC PS3602.A626 A95 2021 | DDC 813/.6--dc23
LC record available at https://lccn.loc.gov/2020037629

First Edition

0 1 2 3 4 5 6 7 8 9 10

Cover design/photos by S. R. Hinrichs

Closing poem *The Invention of Fire* by Christopher Bernard

Manufactured in the United States of America
REGENT PRESS
Berkeley, California
www.regentpress.net
regentpress@mindspring.com

Auger's Touchstone

This book is dedicated to the memory of Zoia Horn,
born 1918, died 2014. She was the first U.S. librarian fired,
jailed, and blackballed for withholding library records and refusing
to testify against dissidents; out of conscience.

With special thanks to my publisher Mark Weiman, editor Ethan Place, proofreader Fatima Ojeda, cover designer Scott Hinrichs, poet Christopher Bernard, nephews Alexander and Phillip Balmanno who read parts of my manuscript before I brought it to my editor, and above all Adele Horwitz, who edited the first three of my four books, and who at the age of 98, is still my mentor.

"For of the wise man, as of the fool, there is no enduring remembrance, seeing that in the days to come, all will be forgotten."
— ECCLESIASTES

Chapter One

And in the Year Gaia 2662 A.G.
City of Eccles

THE TWO YOUNG HISTORIANS Auger and Pius were turning old. Of course that wasn't so, they just *thought* they were turning old. They were turning twenty-eight, but they were argumentative, cantankerous, and courageous.

Yet untested in the physical sphere. Not their fault. They hadn't faced a circumstance where their mettle needed testing. But in the realm of responsibility for consequences of mental fortitude, cerebral insight, dedication to vocation, they were brave.

They awaited the decision. While it was being hand-delivered they stared at each other, amusing themselves with a *Westernized* Version of an Upanishads' Peloponnesian War whoop. "Harrrumgh!" they shouted. "Harrrrrrumgh!" They shouted again, more intensely.

Fast forwarding 3,000 years after the time of the Olympian gods, they then pretended to act like Prussian military officers, minus boots, medallions, gleaming epaulets, a mockery of a skit their boss had watched them perform and condescendingly smiled upon as an "exemplary show of manly behavior."

With slapstick comedy and boisterous horseplay, they struggled to outdo each other.

It was a last gasp effort at humor. It failed. After all, their goal

was to lighten the edginess of their nervousness, not heighten its
arousal. Their waiting game had gone on too long, for that reason
alone, they were reverting back—temporarily—to a state of ado-
lescent immaturity. With one last war whoop and a chortled battle
cry, they decided they needn't succumb to yet another attempt at
tension-relieving frivolity.

So they braced themselves.

The onslaught came in the form of a three-and-a-half inch long
aluminum-tipped folded paper, scented with lilac and ambrosia. The
note was placed in Auger's hand. He flipped it over. With disdain,
he sniffed at it (lilac, ambrosia, the boss? Of course.) Auger broke
the seal. He scanned the contents carefully and crumbled the paper.
Looking up, he didn't have to explain to his colleague the nature of
the message. His pumped fist and expression of joy confirmed it all.

Clicking heels, (again in mockery of their boss), unable to sup-
press a brief titter of laughter, they glided past desks, each cradling a
BIG BOX, containing data. On either side of the boxy gadget were
heaps of paper, print lit docs, physical copies of hand-written antiquity hagiographies, paper-trailed classical and neoclassical analytica,
ink, inkpots, ink-staunches, the normative scriveners' fare. Books
were heaped two or three feet high on the floorboards, arranged
in lines or short stacks, they were hoping this would be their long
awaited "moving day."

Auger and Pius stepped out from behind their desks and occupied the center of the room. Ceremoniously they bowed to each
other, sarcastically mimicking yet another detested mannerism of
their Prussia-obsessed boss.

A moment passed. They stepped forward. Without pomp,
they smiled. They flung their arms around each other and held the
embrace. For how long? Ten seconds? Fifteen seconds? But when
tears began to well up in their eyes, embarrassed, they broke off.

Stepping back, dabbing their eyes with tissue and noisily blowing their noses, they gaped at each other. Was it really happening?
They had been waiting three and a half years, facing a gauntlet of

procrastinations, postponements, and last minute delays. The Chair of the World History Department, Ubaar Suwiot, an obnoxious, on-again, off-again bully, had at last capitulated. Their long-awaited, joint promotions were at last official.

Using their right fists they punched each other into the folds of each other's left bicep, cross punching simultaneously, activating a Dark Age spiritual "brotherly re-enforcement tonic," in the city of Eccles an ever popular inspirational charm.

The 91-year-old Ubaar Suwiot had been deeply indebted to his youthful charges. For twelve years Auger and Pius successfully executed their boss's wishes by faithfully conducting his research. Whatever Ubaar demanded, they provided. It was Auger who unearthed the 5,500-year-old meme of a Hellenic-Spartan War Whoop. It was Pius who dug up a Prussian officer dress code, circa 1700 A.D., which he found by accident while searching for honor codes relating to medieval knights' chivalries—filling a lacuna, a missing dot, in the 3,000 to 5,500-year-old Period of the *Westernized* Version of the Upanishads.

Ubaar was embittered. He was being forced to depart the next day. The head of the university, Provost Kite, had issued a diktat declaring that Ubaar Suwiot must retire within the span of three dawns or face a public scolding and a brutal firing.

It was debated whether, in spite of Ubaar's alleged agility to juggle hundreds of thousands of facts in his head simultaneously, he understood anything about history prior to the "Great Machine Re-innovation Time," when the coal ship (*steamship*), via-phone (*telegraph*), fussers (*air & water turbines*), occurred. However, he was superbly adept on the subject of science and technology developments, notably with regards to military applications of technological breakthroughs, hence his notorious nickname Prussian Ubaar.

He was useless at politics, philosophy, and religion. He was a drooling idiot at SOC, Social/Organ of ancestor transmission/Cultural study. He had no understanding of Imaar's theory of *Primitive Man In Darkness*. He understood nothing about the millennia of

darkness, when 95 percent of the people lived in a state of darkness.
And what about pre A.G.? The time *before* the fall? The time *of*
the fall? Forget it. Even worse.

Ubaar had been Auger and Pius's controversial advisor for what
seemed to them like an eternity. The two historians seethed dispirit-
edly under their boss's repressive grip. On the eve of Ubaar's retirement—as figuratively the barrel of a gun was pointed directly at his
cranium—he uttered words of encouragement and seemed to support the youthful historians' aspirations, making the announcement
in a previous day's news conference.

The message was directed out to the larger community on a
live feed. The first-class *'posted citizens'* and second-class *'job-holding
non-citizen residents'* alike didn't care, or if they did care, didn't care
enough to watch the news—too eagerly engaged were they with their
heads tilted down, poring over displays on 'little boxes,' i.e., hand-
held electronic contrivances, lit up, sometimes with an accompanying vibrating alert-buzzer. Or they were fixated on the big-screen
announcement boards above The Exchange, city hall, the Tri-Tower
building, the tops of the eighteen pleasure gates of Pleasure Park,
at the base of the 214-story Galetar building and spiral—the iconic
symbol of TECH for the entire world. The spiral boasted an his-
torically accurate enlarged hologram of an Apple iPad, which a year
before replaced a hologram of an AMD microchip, which two years
before replaced a hologram of a piece of Egyptian papyrus, which
three years before replaced a hologram of a baked-clay shard of Babylonian cuneiform, which four years before replaced a hologram of a
1395 A.G. jewel-embossed, teak-covered copy of THE BLESSINGS
OF GAIA DOCUMENT, preserved in age-resisting tannic solution,
(oldest survivor of the original text, published in 553 A.G.), which
five years before replaced a hologram of a florally displayed exotica,
(among young people in general and 17 to 45-year-old mothers in
particular,) popular Gaia-Hope-Love-Peace meme-chime.

All the splendor of Auger and Pius's electronic community was
in the city of Eccles, mother of shape, manner, and form of electrical

gadgetry—flippers, dippers, and wedgies—the whole gamut of popular technology.

There'd been multitude instances of experiments gone awry. Voice-activated holograms (so perfectly human-scaled and lifelike, folks were afraid to walk through them because they feared they were real flesh-and-blood human beings); fake identity goggles and gloves (confusing everyone, including the users); body and implant shills and detectors, (electronically-triggered health improvement apparatuses), some of which eventually worked, but only after a gazillion bugs had been worked out.

Hundreds of products, over a vast panoply of applications, using milder molds or saner designs, components that had been more thoroughly vetted, tested, and retested.

Eccles! *Electricity! Home to Invention! Home to Powerful Imagination! Home to the mightiest Electrical Grid in the World:* more potent and complicated than at any other time devised by man: more dynamic and ecologically, environmentally pure than anything in the world. And for the first time, after nearly 2,800 years, Hail Tesla (alternating current), or 2,800 years before...hail the other guy, Edison (direct current). A world made electric.

Electrification was the key of course, but even that took on a new dimension with the near-monopolistic omniscience of the 364 (200 exclusively cyber-driven in nature) products of Gatetar Industries—producing, at least in the Inner World, a weird configuration of consumption.

The two historians had been shuttered in their office for eighteen hours, with around-the-clock guards posted to prevent communication with the outside world, as a sort of, paradoxically, semi-vicious, semi-heart-warming, intradepartmental prank.

The hubbub? This announcement in Eccles didn't involve news regarding a large or small acquisition by the all-conquering, all-devouring Gatetar Industries, or a *warble* from the Gaia religion

world, or a news-brief from the political world, or a puff-piece from
the entertainment world, or a new cloth arrangement displayed in
the fashion world, or a statistical result from the sports world. How
much fuss could there be over something so prosaic, *so manifestly
uneventful*, as an academic promotion? How much had changed?

Plenty.

That is, if you were an academic, or you had a more-than-passive
interest in the comings and goings of the University, then, at least
plenty.

The Chair of World History had only 75 years before been called
the gender-specific Patriarch's Chair for Gaia History. But that old
fuddy-duddy way of looking at things was gone. Just as the chair,
facing a sped-up retirement, was gone. The reforms at U. Presbyr in
2652 A.G. nailed down the long overdue, almost exclusively secular approach to the organization and exploration of knowledge. In
2150 A.G., out of 100 books published, 70 were devoted to Gaia
theology. One hundred and fifty years later, publishing of empirical
data had far outstripped spiritual wit and what passed for liturgical
doctrine. A century after that, theological binge-writing was in huge
decline. In 2600 A.G., out of 100 books published that year, only
one religious book, a thin volume issued more as a catechism than a
thrust into Gaia's relationship to the universe, was released.

Pius thought once of trying his hand at a spiritual tract himself,
but decided against it. After all, had he anything of worth to add to
the sacred canon? More importantly, wasn't something original in
the field of theology risky business? Or, in the eyes of the hidebound
archconservatives of his religious order, even dangerous?

As Auger was fond of saying: "Gaia theology is geology-like.
It's geological in nature. *Rock...right?* No, rock of rocks. Over time,
it requires a million gusts of wind, eons of pelting rain, to wear it
down. In a lifetime, it can't be altered by your weak, reedy voice, my
scraping pen, Ubaar's jabbing pencil, or some scholar's super box."

It was no accident Pius's chosen field of study was history, not
theology. He was a member of the ultraconservative—also, from

time to time, whenever necessary, defender against "*The Defilers of Our Blessed Purity*"—Majestic and Sacred Obsidian Order.

For the orthodox and the traditionalist alike, the Obsidian Order had been the gatekeeper for the Gaia religion, dating back more than 1,800 years.

Yet no reversals were possible, at least not from the point of view of Auger and Pius.

Everybody in the university, indeed, everybody in the community at large, knew there was no going back to the status quo ante. The sweeping changes meant that the old was out, the new was firmly in place. More than anything, the promotion of Auger and Pius solidified that change, making it a benchmark moment.

U. Presbyr was the most distinguished institution of higher learning, albeit *not* in the fields of Global Security, Science, Applied Technology, Medicine, Health Studies, Engineering, Space Studies, Public Safety Maintenance Studies, Economics, Political Economics, and Bureau Management. There were more distinguished centers of study for these, especially the Winnebet Center for Science and the Zesbos Institute for Economics. U. Presbyr was also little concerned with Gaia Religion and Earth Theology, the university's twin bedrock departments, which over a period of 400 years had come to wither. Now the university specialized in the upstarts: World History, Rhetoric, Philosophy and Fine Arts, Post-Humanoid Studies, Social/Organ of Ancestor Transmission/Cultural—SOC, and Post-Oral, Post-Writing Critical Theory.

The Department of World History represented a central facet of a new academic world that dovetailed with a Liberal/Humanities/ Social Critique dimensional breed of thought, otherwise known, in the words of the Department of World History's second most brilliant scholar, Pius: "The Enlightenment Project." The name occurred to him on his 21st birthday, his "Celebrate Gaia Day," as he stood on the edge of a cliff overlooking the Pacific Ocean, above one of the 30 most important Gaia Rock outcrops, beneath him waves, pounding and crashing, then retreating with a hiss on the slippery slips of sand, all the while on the edge of the cliff above, he was in a near ecstatic state. He peered out and levitated onto the optical boundaries of the farthest extension of the watery horizon, at which point "Enlightenment Project" popped into his head.

Then and there Pius decided he'd dedicate himself to *enlightenment*—a view of history, the future of humanity, and the future of the world that returned man to the center of the world.

This sparked the decision to promote the Enlightenment papers, which in turn turned the key for the enormously generous grant given to the two young and aspiring historians.

In this endeavor they were on the cusp of becoming stars of a whole new generation.

As co-chairs of the World History Department, Auger and Pius would have no bosses except for the rarely intervening Provost Ernest Kite, who spent the majority of his time on the 200th through 210th floors of the Gatetar Tower at the *Gatetar Multi-Center for the Education of Superior Cyber-Manipulating Children,* at which at any time there were approximately 2,500 participants, known pejoratively by subversives in the Rhetoric Department as "Zone of the Zombies," "Perch of the Walleyes," or "Kingdom of the Real-World Dead But Cyber Alive Memory-Eaters."

In their late 20's, Auger and Pius were the youngest stars to have been named in the 400 year history of the 'geriatricly hobbled' World History Department. Their youngest predecessor—Ringwald, 95 years before—had been a youthful 57. The typical chair was age 60 to 64, and served for a minimum of 15 years. Ubaar had served from the age of 60 to 91.

A revolution? No. Certainly a significant change. But what were they studying? Things they weren't permitted to study before, even just as recently as ten years before, when the new reforms kicked in: the period of 1914 to 2051. A.D., 2,662 years to 2,800 years in the past.

"Before the Fall, and of course, the Fall itself," Pius put it. He was referring to history leading up to the loa. Now only the years 2052

A.D. (2 A.G.) to 2133 (82 A.G.), the loa itself, were still on the proscribed list.

"Wouldn't it be grand if they permitted us to snoop at Two A.G.? At 82 A.G.? And all the years in between?" Auger's eyes gleamed with hope. "One shoe's fallen. Why not the other?"

Pius nodded, but the look in his eyes was disheartening. "Provisos against penetrating the loa, Auger, I'll remind you, are difficult. Our predecessors thought the ban would never be lifted at all. Are we on the cusp of a new future?"

With the arrival of the extraordinary news, Auger and Pius realized this was going to be the last time they'd be forced to occupy the same office. They weren't going to allow any time for nostalgia to set in.

"It's all politics you know," Pius murmured in a low voice, packing up his books. "It always was. Always will be. They had to bring somebody along with you who represented the ghost of the old order, in my case, a membership in the Obsidian Order. I am that strange, mythic, Unicorn-like figure, the combination modernist *and* traditionalist. I, I am certain, was the default candidate for the administration's bridge-building purpose. A sop to the old order. Let's face it, Auger. You're the star. You'll always be the magnet. You deserve the honor."

"Don't sound too pleased," Auger offered in a disappointed-sounding voice.

"'Course I'm pleased," Pius shot back immediately. "Better than that. Happy. I'm a diehard believer in the old faith, but also, first and foremost, a historian. I'm pleased."

"Good. And thinking along those lines, your paper, excuse me, your book, is going to be original, it's going to be one of a kind," Auger said. "It's going to be brilliant. I envy you. No, I know you don't believe it, but I do. And although SOC polling shows that religious attendance has sunk to an all-time low in the Inner World, in the Outer World, at least, in many places thereof, a crude and rough adherence to the original Gaia faith is still at an all time high."

"By crude and rough you're humoring me, what you really mean is boring, primitive, and superstitious," Pius said. "My world will never be the same again. The world of our grandparents and our great-grandparents is gone forever. What matters in the Outer World? The Outer World is wrapped in darkness, a state of chaos, or, at best, a state of fragmentation. In contrast, the Inner World is increasingly a place where people hold no conviction of any kind, good or bad. We've become a sinkhole of lowest-common-denominator relativism and entropy—representing a downward spiral in manners, morality, the mangled way we tilt at truth. A state of affairs aided by you ultra-modern humanistic secularists! Humanistic Secularists! As if all you had to do was release yourself from the dead hand of an oppressive past. Plus the odd assortment of cranks, rhetoric-besotted trolls, epistemology chaos gadget carvers, but my favorite of them all, youthful tricksters."

"A rogue's gallery indeed," Auger said. "I hate it when you weigh in with one of your contra-modern screeds. Target? Everyone from the unworthy to the non-repentant. Youthful tricksters? Why them? Nobody cares about them. They'd roil in ecstasy if you paid them the least bit of attention. Why do they engage in schemes that too often morph into thoughtless acts? For what purpose? To seek attention! Brief, split-second notoriety. Then they slither back down into purposelessness, into insignificance, driven back down into oblivion. I have better. We're historians. Why bother with the here and now. Stick with what we know, stick with history, right?"

"Eh?" Pius asked. He looked uncertain. He wore a thin smile. It was as if he was trying to hide something. Sadness? Longing? Pain?

"You'll receive more accolades and credit when it's all over than I shall ever receive," Auger added, completely misjudging Pius's thoughts and concerns. "You'll see."

Pius thought: Can we change things? Not by studying history, especially the lore of ancients. Let Auger chase the hobgoblins of futile dreams and doppelgangers of laughably hopeless hopes. That's what humanistic secularists gear themselves up to believe in—as if *fairytales* they've retold themselves could *still* be believed in—as if the previous 3,000 years were a mirage.

But instead Pius decided to put his best game-face on. "Yes. Gave us eight years to complete. Poring over sections of the past, which we were never given permission to study before, although we've been secretly studying this during the previous ten years. Imagine that! We'll see."

The two had a habit of arguing with each other, sometimes passionately, other times less bracingly, either way, lasting for days, often weeks. Their gestures of disputation reached back all the way to a time when they first met. They were nine. Young! They'd been randomly selected to be partners in a biology class, assigned to dissect fish (no longer possible to cut up frogs, 2,500 years extinct.) How quickly they tried to size each other up. They soon learned they cared more about the human record than they cared about fish or frogs. They both aspired to be historians of humanity. For much of their youth they acted as if they were older than they were; it was all part of a resolution *to grow orderly, to act efficiently.* They couldn't wait to put their childhood behind them, looking forward to a world of agency and adulthood.

There was one difference between them. Pius was extremely devout and religious. Auger was the exact opposite, a non-believer, perhaps even an atheist. But in 2662 A.G., if there ever was a time one might have been allowed to come out of the closet of out-and-out atheism, it was now.

"Pius, you should have been the premier grant-receiver," Auger continued, "not I. You're the one who came up with the *Enlightenment Project.* It has nothing to do with your religious order or the vows you've taken, you're a first-rate, first-class historian. You are my equal in every way. And this is coming from somebody who disagrees with you about nearly everything!"

Pius exploded. "1914! I insist on 1914!" Auger and Pius sometimes talked in this manner, acting like two sounding boards, which
they called a 'writing-by-dialectical-speech' trope.

"1914 A.D.!" Pius said. "Insist! The Great Transformation. I
believe in what 1914 can reveal about *everything*. When everything
collapsed."

"Darkness," Auger said. "You're drawn to the dark time. Before
the *real* collapse. But I get it. Without a World War, no Lenin, no
Mussolini, no Stalin, no Hitler, no Franco, no Mao, no fascism, no
communism, no second World War, no Cold War, no arms race, no
threat of thermonuclear war, stretching over 76 years. I get it. A lost
century, *but before the truly lost century*. Before the beginnings of the
true unraveling, before the beginnings of the global environmental
catastrophe. Okay. So you want to start early. Fine by me. But don't
call the first Great War *the* transforming event."

This was the kind of intellectual hair-splitting and verbal sparring
Auger and Pius loved to engage in, carefully worded and painstak-
ingly thought—arguments that outsiders found well-nigh incomprehensible. Still, the closely reasoned thinking of these two was helping
to clarify the ancient past.

"I bet it wasn't minor to those who lived it," Pius said. "Strange
world. We're assigned the task of reconstructing the tale of what
happened in the lead up to the collapse of 2051 A.D. You know
what I think was most important—the events of 2040 to 2051
A.D., the Eleven-Years-War. One and a half billion humans died, the
equivalence of the entire population of the world today. Darkness
fell a thousand different ways on hundreds of different communities
and nations. But one must include in one's analysis the events of
World War I, The Great War, The War To End All Wars. After the
Eleven-Years-War, they renamed it the first European War. You can't
understand the events of the Eleven-Years-War without understanding the earlier madness. You might call it fulcrum and crucible. Of
modernity! Of despairing modernity. If I weren't so prudent in my
rubrics, I'd be tempted to call the old age: Age of Twisted Boxes of

Metal and Steel: Cars, Trucks, Trains, Jets, circa 1914—2051. Bigger in scale than anything since the pyramids."

"Sounds like an Art Nouveau project by wannabe subversive visionaries," Auger said. "Strictly Rhetoric Department. Remember last spring? At the shrine? The behavior! Something our drooling, 91-year-old Ubaar Suwiot would have suppressed. Rhetoric Department oldsters being too weak and condescendingly appeasing for their own good. Couldn't you see it now? Ubaar waving his fist, like a maddened marionette. The last-ditch effort to purify the impure?"

As Auger watched his otherwise dour and reserved colleague laughing, he felt a wave of satisfaction come over him. But the laughter, having risen, quickly subsided.

"Why not call it the Twisted Boxes of Metal and Steel Age?" Pius asked. "No...seriously. All you have to do is scrape into a metal bone yard to unearth something."

"There were dozens of them found in isolated underground car parks," Pius continued, "buried beneath tree-and-foliage covered ghost cities in the Outer World, ancient, crude hulks of mangled cars, almost all of them buried after 2045 A.D., a tiny handful of which have been gorgeously if inaccurately reconstituted. There is a folk museum in Eccles donated by Gatetar Industries that houses a reconstructed 1918 double-decker bus, a 1920s-era biplane, a 1933 freight car, autos—from 1907, 1965, 2025, a 1960s-era jet, a 2060s-era helioplane, and a Gaia-Dome electric bubble car from 2097! The Ford Motor Company was churning out cars like crazy, a business building cars on assembly lines that lasted 130 years. In order to see the artifacts, Auger, all you have to do is walk four miles to the Gatetar tower, walk another half mile in the direction of Pleasure Park, there you have it, The Gatetar Technology and Science Museum. All right, I've said my piece. I'll shut up. *Now* you may respond."

"I love it," Auger said. "And I approve. Though you hardly need approval, to be sure. I just think it makes more sense to start later. From 1984 to that fateful day on September 23rd, 2051, marking the beginning of our calendar, the beginning of The Age of

Gaia. My study will take place over 67 years. Half your timeline. Why do I insist on that approach? It certainly has nothing to do with the so-called Cold War. Or the name of that utterly and preposterously unfathomable book that was entitled Nineteen Eighty-Four. No, 1984 was when the earliest climate-change scientists set up the baseline for the beginning of the climate-change scenario. Carbon level in the atmosphere was a relatively safe 350, but not for long. And I grant you, the Eleven-Years-War, speeded up the climate change process. Just before it went tipping point runaway. Minus a huge, devastating world-wide war, global warming might have moved at a slower pace, postponing the collapse for several decades. Would 2076 have been better than 2051? Looking at it from 2,662 years in the future, a foreshortened perspective is required. However, though the war wasn't the result of a single group's action, or an individual's action, it was as if the whole of humanity had surrendered itself to a nihilistically-driven, end-of-civilization, death wish."

"How would it had looked at the time?" Pius asked. "In 2051? That's the part we can't know. Without the benefit of hindsight, what could they have known. But also, what were people thinking at the time, when they were going about their everyday business, loving, raising a family, keeping an eye on the near, on the home? Walking the treadmill, walking it, walking it, walking it, the treadmill, then..."

"The-Eleven-Years-War *was* the swinging door of history," Auger interrupted. "No? There was destruction of the ozone layer. But allow me to be more precise, the human inhabitants, not to mention mammals in general, many life-forms in fact, were imperiled. There were creatures, too many of them to name—hundred of species of butterflies for example—and they were NOT mythological creatures. Like frogs and toads were NOT figments of a fantasist's dream. We all know now the Earth had all the time in the universe to bounce back, whenever it decided it'd choose to. So there! All the wars combined, over the vast surface of the Earth during that time, didn't add up to the negative changes that occurred because of what the carbon energy base *created*. Then the whole thing *collapsed!*"

Grinning ear to ear, Pius smiled.

"From the year September Snow turned 39 in 2062 A.D.," Auger said, "there was a 2,400 year period, even allowing for a 175-year hiatus of false dawn relative calm, in a few places, in the Colorado Basin, for example, between 550 and 725 A.G. This resulted in a deeply disturbing flux, called, from our more distant point-of-view of retrospect: The Deep Spasms Of The Dark Time."

"Then there was a 450-year period of speed-forward, bursting-at-the-seams science and technology renaissance, ushering in an array of technological innovations and discoveries. Promising a peaceful, non-bellicose world, allowing for sensible and sustainable population stability, eradicating not all but many diseases, establishing four-star, five-star, even six-star health care systems. The air was kept clear of human-caused pollutants. Ecologically-friendly water-recovery-and-delivery systems were built. Kimmel's rediscovery of Tesla-Edison's original discovery of the powers of electricity, combined with safe and reliable energy for heavy industry, were capped with a dozen unmanned, and two dozen manned space flights to the moon and beyond."

Auger continued. "How many ways is our world similar to 2,600 years ago? Swimming in a sewer-like river of Gaia-Dome ur-texts, compiled and catalogued in 2200 A.G.: double-entry accountancy charts, commissarial lists, hierarchy organizational columns, fiscal ledgers, corrupt code begetting corrupt code, a long winding sheet of historical necromancy. For what? Of course we have THE BLESSINGS OF GAIA DOCUMENT to rely on, don't we, Pius? Bequeathed to us by our primitive ancestors. That alternative fountain of truth?"

Auger's dinging of the accuracy of the "historical record" aroused in Pius pity and fury.

"At it again," Pius said. "At it again! All fuzzy. All diatribe. Always environment, never war, never politics. Your weakness. Loss of the ozone layer could have been attributed to one culprit. The Eleven-Years-War. *Not* your constant bugbear, human-caused climate change. Two giant threats to human survival converged, the military and the environmental, in other words, the Eleven-Years-War. They could feel, touch, experience the immediate effects, they couldn't know the longer term effects, the more profound effects. The Collapse of 2051 is important to us, as important to human history as the Big Bang is to the history of the universe. Why else are we studying it? No other event is so central, so important. It's the beginning. You're correct in pursuing what you are pursuing, but..."

"Yes, I understand," Auger interrupted, nodding back. "You tend to overemphasize the effects of the Eleven-Years-War, I underemphasize its effects, we've gone over this a thousand times, maybe we'll get it right some day. Yes, we have our own built-in biases. But as you so strongly implied, things happened after the Eleven-Years-War that were horrible. Worse. Human-caused climate modifiers, raised the temperature five or six degrees Fahrenheit in all places, twice that in some places, three times in other places. We both know from that time forward, there was a galloping, out-of-control global warming and climate change phenomenon which lasted for centuries. We both know the reasons why we refuse to study events after 2052 A.D. Why don't we go over that, since we're having a grand, old time, having an argument and disputation which we always love to share?"

Now Pius knew he had Auger over a barrel. "You said the Earth had all the time in the universe to bounce back, *whenever it decided it'd choose to*. I'm quoting you. You're exact words. Yet you insist on seeing the Earth as NOT being a sentient being. You insist on doubting the essential tenant of the Gaian religion. Where does life begin? Where does life end? You don't know!"

Auger more or less gave up, knowing he had been semi-foiled. He saw at least one, maybe two, chinks in Pius's intellectual armor, but he decided not to take aim. "Let's agree to disagree. But there's one thing we can agree on. We can't trust the documents of what happened from 2052 A.D. to 2133 A.D., right? Unless THE BLESSINGS OF GAIA DOCUMENT is a reliable source? Right?"

"We agree on that," Pius said. "We agree."

"Blasphemy," Auger said. "You've just committed blasphemy. And religious treachery. Here you are a member of the Obsidian Order. Look at you. You should be ashamed of yourself."

Auger watched Pius squirm. He enjoyed taunting him. But in the spirit of brotherly love and friendship, he changed the subject. "Explain the change?"

"Now what?" Pius asked with a note of exasperation and suspicion. "What change? *Whaaat?*" Pius feared Auger was setting another trap. "You mean Eccles? You mean the story?"

"Yes. The story. The city of Eccles story. Newfield, Job, Blake, Milton into Ecclesiastes. The story of the name. Why the name? Why Ecclesiastes?"

"Again?"

"Not too long ago my wife and I were residing in Job. You were renewing your vows at the Obsidian Monastery on Clotus Hill. Newfield in the south had a population of 1,300,000, Job 800,000, Blake 800,000, Milton, long, slender Milton, 30 kilometers long, five and a half kilometers wide, half a million. All cities bursting at the seams. They say they may have to open parts of the San Francisco Game Reserve."

It was a mystery to Auger why Andromenus, at the time head of Gaia's Obsidian Order, named all of those cities Ecclesiastes.

"Before his death Andromenus was having fitful dreams," Pius said. "These dreams made him fearful, perhaps even paranoid. I served as his number two acolyte for five years, his number one acolyte for one year leading up to his death. Usually Andromenus confided in me. Not this time. All Andromenus was willing to reveal to me was that he was honoring his namesake Andromenus. I'll remind you Andromenus presided over the Obsidian Order, a long time ago."

"1000 years ago?" Auger asked.

"Auger, your knowledge of Gaian ecclesiastical history is as scanty as your beard. You're ridiculous. Not that one. Wrong AGAIN! I'm talking about Andromenus. *The Andromenus!* The one from 2,000 years ago."

"Okay, okay," Auger said, "but why the name? Ecclesiastes is not Gaian. Maybe the old man was suffering from geriatric vacuity, or dementia. Why Ecclesiastes?"

"Don't know," Pius said. "Eccles? Shortened version isn't bad." Pius's eyes brightened. "Young people didn't like the original. Some people thought Ecclesiastes meant death. But the abbreviated? Eccles? No space between cities. Twenty-storied buildings between Newfield and Job, ten-storied buildings between Job and Blake, no open fields between Blake and Milton, staring at each other, across the street from each another, and one transportation system connecting all. Solution? Call it one. It's been a dream. Eccles. Don't you like it? I do."

"But what does it mean?" Auger asked.

"It comes from the earliest version of the *Westernized* Trope of the Upanishads. Words taken from an early, the earliest in fact, of the three Abrahamic religions. I don't know if Eccles is an improvement on Newfield, I know it's an improvement on Job, Blake, Milton. Andromenus's thinking? Maybe it was a bit of whimsy or caprice. Maybe the authorities let Andromenus have his way because he was so old."

"But the Obsidian Order doesn't do whimsy or caprice," Auger said. He liked to see Pius squirm. He began to say something even more obnoxious, but before he got the words out the mood had changed.

Pius flew into a rage. "All right!" he said. "Enough! To answer your question, no. Satisfied? Obsidian Order doesn't do caprice or whimsy. Satisfied? Now, at last, may I finish packing my stuff? My books? My Big Box? Leave *your* office, right?"

No matter how severe the wounding, no matter how deep the cut, a rift between the two old friends rarely lasted long.

"When is your wife expecting to deliver?" Pius asked, just before he exited the room.

"In seven weeks time."

"There you go. Announcement of your advancement has been perfect timing."

Chapter Two

WAS IT BAD? Rornar was calm, but anxious. Her condition involved more that just "premature maturation of the embryo's position."

Twelve days after Auger gave his pregnant wife the news of his promotion, she awoke early. She had been taken violently out of her sleep. She cursed beneath her breath, then added sheepishly, "Yes, but not yet."

Lying next to his wife, Auger murmured with a start, "What?" He was still very drowsy.

This was followed by a powerful jerk and a massive sob on the part of Rornar. Auger was now fully awake and more or less aware of what was happening.

The couple had been warned in advance by the maternity experts that the delivery could be problematic. So when the contraction came, Auger was concerned, but he forced himself to remain calm. He jumped out of bed and, without putting on a robe, made preparations for accompanying his wife to the hospital. After making calls to the hospital and the Express, he dressed hurriedly. In the mean time, Rornar, taking her time, dressed more slowly.

Auger grabbed his coat, grabbed his wife's coat, and grabbed her 'waiting bag,' which contained a change in clothing, a two-inch wide mirror, a hairbrush, a teeth-cleaning twig, cold medicine, two knitting needles, a ball of yellow-colored yarn, and a piece of very light reading.

"This is too early," Auger said. "None of the doctors saw this coming."

"When do they get anything right," Rornar said. "How to anticipate the unknown? How many weeks, tell me, how many weeks has it been? How many days?" Not getting an immediate response, Rornar shouted, "Come on!" She snapped her fingers. "Auger!"

For a moment, Auger looked lost.

"Come to think of it, before you answer, you're lousy," Rornar said smiling. "How many days? Can you count? No. History? Gold star. But numbers? Like you're still in short pants, class idiot. First class I ever attended with you. Remember it?"

Auger couldn't figure out why Rornar chose that *particular* moment to bring up the fact he nearly flunked math once, only surviving because of the intervention of Rornar's tutoring! But, of course, under the circumstances, Auger intended to let his wife vent freely to her heart's content. Could he see the justification of his wife's tone, after all, what did his near failure in math have to do with anything?

"Five weeks," Auger said. "Thirty-five days."

Auger remembered Rornar sneering: "I do street-smarts, you have pretence to book-wisdom. Which of the two do you think contributes most to the team effort?"

Auger had never been placed in doubt as to the answer to that question.

An arm akimbo, another dangling, tousled hair, body pushed forward, Rornar struck the pose of a Babylonian wanton-woman. Auger was familiar with *that pose*. Rornar's advanced stage of pregnancy made the look more tender and surreal. He loved Rornar's wise-cracking, propriety-attacking contrariness. That's why he was devoted to her, in awe of her, and so in love with her.

Before leading with another rebuke, the pain in Rornar's abdomen interrupted.

"Oh," Rornar moaned. "Oh Auger. Dear me. At last. She wants out. Now!"

Rornar closed her eyes. She twisted her hips, trying to rest. But once she managed to re-gather her strength, knowing that now was not the right time to push, she tried to channel her mind away from the surge. "I confessed to my *engineer* father, who lived and died by numbers. When you were dating me, I felt obliged to explain to him you were lousy at it. Math. Nearly flunked it. Did he care? No."

"Your father liked me," Auger said. "He also cared for something more. Cared you'd be happy. You got me. Look what you got?"

The shuttle arrived from the Express. They got in quickly.

At first Auger didn't know what to do. Then he took Rornar in his arms. He placed her head down softly so she could use his lap as a pillow. He held her. He cuddled her. He stroked her face and her hair. "Think," Auger said. "I can peel potatoes, whip up a stew. Can I make salmon pie? Your favorite dish. I can. Can I hunt? Dress a kill?" Auger looked helpless and struggling. "Is any of this working? Yes? No? Tell me."

When they had been calculating the urgency, Rornar admitted that Auger had made the right choice requesting 'chauffeur-driven' over 'auto-driven' at the Express. He was glad he selected the more expensive choice.

Rornar's grimacing concerned Auger, but in equal measure he was inspired by his wife's calm. The intervals between contractions grew shorter.

"Yeah?" Rornar asked. "Oh, Auger, you're not going to trash talk me, like you do Pius...when you babble, *babble, babble, babble*—on, oh dear me, my favorite...Babylon! Auger and Pius's talking about times when men dragged their knuckles on the ground as women kept the home fires burning...what has changed since then?"

Auger remembered Rornar saying, six months earlier: "Christians, ruling the roost, for 2,000 years, but all the time buried in the belly, interred in their own internal Babylon. 2,662 years later, people of Gaia, captured by the same illusion, dreaming of redeemers. *Ancients we celebrate excite mystification.* I'm quoting you now Auger. Brave words. But I have better. Gaia unfolding in a dream-like factory, run by Gatetar's Superior Cyber-Manipulating Children, all the while—there, in the muck, there is Babylon, even if they're high up in the tower, gazing down, on mud bricks, dung-spattered fields, low scudding clouds. Oh, climate scientists say it'll take up to 200,000 years, and maybe *much* longer, before all the darkness clears from every corner of the Earth. Are they being too optimistic?"

"Babylonian astrology, Babylonian numerology, Babylonian astronomy," Auger said, reciting words out loud to take his mind off the impending. "Apsu, god of fresh water. Tiamat, god of salt water. They created everything. Tiamat's body became Earth, sky. If you see Babylon as successor state *and* avatar to Ur, *and* the even earlier, Uruk, 6,500 years ago? Not even close. Just focus on Uruk. What do you get? The beginning was more than 8,500 years ago."

"Is that what Pius and you were arguing about?" Rornar asked with a mock-terrified expression on her face. (Auger was glad Rornar's mind had been—even if only for a minute, redirected.) "Your competing date lines? Two thousand years apart! Ancient history! 14,000 years ago, or thereabouts, they planted the seeds of agriculture. Whoop-de-do! *If it's more than 150 years old, it's a long time ago. I've tried to explain this to you so many times, with all your talk of ancient history!*"

When the van arrived at the hospital, Auger tipped the driver generously for having taken, whenever they were available, the speedier emergency lanes, shaving a good five minutes off the trip.

Gurney waiting at the curbside, Rornar was immediately wheeled into emergency.

Eight hours later, due to an obstruction of the birth canal, Rornar's condition deteriorated. She had *placenta previa*—which may have developed only in the previous few weeks. *Placenta previa* is a complication that involves the growth of the placenta toward the lower end of the uterus. In the worst case it covers the neck of the womb, thus impeding the baby's exit during birth. But Rornar also had an onset of *pre-eclampsia*, making her case worse. It delayed the decision to do the caesarean. But then she had a heart attack.

After the cardiac arrest, the doctors couldn't revive her.

Technically, Rornar died *before* childbirth. But an emergency caesarean saved her daughter.

Honoring Rornar's wish, Auger named the baby Zoia. The name had been in Rornar's family for generations, and the couple had known months before that the fetus was going to be a girl.

Even at four pounds, eight ounces, Zoia's condition was apparently stable. Seemingly unharmed by the obstructed birth and by the mother's heart attack, she was born premature but without any apparent complications. But she would have to remain in an incubator for at least two weeks.

After serving the eight-hour vigil leading up to Rornar's death, Auger manically extended his stay into a third day. He wanted to make sure his daughter was absolutely in the clear, even though the baby's condition was stable. During this time, he took 45-minute power naps and shorter snatches of sleep, using his light coat as a pillow and stretching himself out on one of the three divans arranged to form a circle in the waiting room. Upon the medical staff's recommendation, which turned into a mandatory decree, he was told to leave the hospital.

"Go home," the doctor said. "What happened to your wife is not happening to the baby. Stop conflating the two. We're sorry for your loss."

Auger had just turned 28. But he had no intention of celebrating his birthday.

It was an hour and a half after sunset. For reasons obscure even to Auger himself, he had decided to walk home, even though it was quite a long distance. Auger took an even longer and more circuitous route.

He passed through one of the eighteen gates of Pleasure Park.

Once inside the park he turned so he could see the menagerie of extinct animals, extinct plant life, extinct human tribes, 5,000, 8,000, and 25,000 years in the past. There was also a dinosaur and related flora and fauna. They were all holograms. Finally Auger traversed through a part of the city once called Job, a journey of 22 kilometers altogether. He arrived home utterly exhausted. But he was gladdened by the walk, every step taken, every breath taken between steps, seeming to signify something.

Auger entered his house. He was alone. He ascended the narrow stairs and entered the bedroom with its yellow-flower patterned wallpaper where Rornar had slept beside him a few nights before. Auger took Rornar's undergarments from beneath her pillow. He hugged them to his face. The smell was of two-day-old cut flowers and over-ripened pears. He breathed in. He broke down. He cried. Auger would have gladly welcomed sleep.

Auger, in grief, with dips into black despair, had become father and widower simultaneously in a very brief moment of time. Such a joy. Such a sorrow. Twisted together into a knot.

Was it trauma? "An experience of survival exceeding the grasp of the person who survived." Auger remembered reading the definition of trauma weeks before when he was killing time, marooned in a hospital waiting room, waiting for his wife to return from a routine medical check-up. Did the modern angle have an advantage over the old? The primal keening of a shaman? The image was in the forefront of his thoughts. Had not Auger seen a hologram of a shaman-death-lamenter before? Of course, in Pleasure Park, in a hologram display (so life-like!). Auger remembered the hologram of a Pleistocene shaman hovering over another man, supposedly 25,000 years ago, his eyes piercing—ancient brute or semi-noble-savage?—his piglet eyes searching, following. The shaman perhaps an avatar of Pius? Was there a superstitious belief buried beneath the clever posing of "modernity." Too many phantoms were colliding in Auger's mind. Maybe the image of the shaman signified progress toward his recovery from his grief.

Auger began to identify with the shaman-death-lamenter in earnest, not the other man in the display. *What had been the cause of the afflicted man's anguish? Had he lost a loved one? Auger was thinking. Then Auger wailed himself. Identification was complete.*

Auger shouted, "Rornar! Don't you see I'm burning? But you gave me Zoia."

Uttering these words, terrifying as they were, allowed Auger to fall asleep.

Having been out of town for three days Pius arrived at the hospital, but he was too late. Auger had already departed. Pius went to see him the next morning.

Pius's intention was to keep Auger company, and hopefully rally him.

Pius knew exactly where the door key was, and let himself in. He had been a frequent guest at the home.

Without asking permission, he prepared his friend's breakfast, then brought it up to Auger and Rornar's bedroom on a serving tray. Pius wept briefly at the sight of his dear friend, pausing between sobs only long enough to say, "You got to eat. You need your strength."

Pius pulled a piece of bread from the plate. He bit into it. "See? Good. Coffee? Good. Bacon? Good. Come on. Dig in. What's the matter with you? You want it."

When Auger didn't reply, Pius waited a minute. Then he commanded Auger to eat. "If you don't follow my instructions, you'll regret it." Pius took two more bites of bread and set it back down on Auger's plate.

So, in a mechanical way, just to appease his friend, Auger started in. He ate a little more. Then more. Finally, enthusiastically, he tucked in. With each mouthful, he realized he was hungry. He had not eaten a full meal in more than a day.

After that, even after Pius prepared Auger's lunch, and after he'd prepared Auger's dinner, no words passed between them. This was strange. Under normal circumstances, when it came to talking, they could not be stopped.

But Pius, in spite of his friend's perfectly understandable reticence, could sense that Auger was showing improvement. He had apparently gone through the inevitable process of diverse and sometimes contradictory emotional responses.

In light of this, Pius had to ask himself: Where was Auger's state of mind? Before the evening had concluded, Pius sensed that Auger had become himself. Auger had enough presence of mind to thank his friend for preparing the three meals. Pius reminded Auger it was standard Obsidian Order ritual to offer three meals to all mourners. Pius also reminded Auger he was a vegetarian and hated the smell of bacon. Auger assured Pius in a confident voice he would be perfectly capable of preparing his own meals from now on. "I'll cook alone." Only after that had been determined, and Auger had reestablished his sense of humor, did Pius feel that he could leave his friend alone.

"I was never good at humor," Auger said. He had a faraway look in his eyes. "I was the straight man. Rornar was the comic. I miss her humor..."

"Yeah," Pius said. "We miss Rornar. We'll miss her. We'll miss her humor. You know there's going to be a big hole in your life when it comes to that. Rornar used to refer to my religious order as the 'odor.' She mispronounced the word deliberately. She'd say: 'Obsidian *odor* this... The Obsidian *odor* that...' The expression was always conveyed with an arching of one of her eyebrows. Can you resist that? I couldn't."

Auger nodded. "Yeah."

"You know," Pius said, "consolation, does it mean anything at all?"

After waiting a quarter of a minute, the interval filled with thought, Auger sat bolt upright and replied, "Doesn't mean *anything*? Why do you say that?"

"The word, 'consolation,'" Pius repeated. "If it provided an understanding or meaning for the existence of suffering or death, that something we might call a bad thing, it wouldn't be called 'consolation.'"

"I don't know what you're talking about," Auger said. "I hate it when you get so opaquely philosophical with me, Pius. Speak plainly. It would be called something else? What then?"

"I think so," Pius said. "To answer your question, I don't know.

Likewise, a person who denies Gaia because he hasn't experienced it may be closer to Gaia than someone who *believes* in Gaia, but has never experienced it. The absence of belief can be—in this limited way—a form of purification."

"You know," Auger said, "for a believer in religion, you sound weird. At least, every now and then, you reveal the oddities of your eccentric thought processes."

"Ordinarily, I'm more circumspect," Pius said. "Till now, this application of my thought process hasn't gotten me into too much trouble. Hopefully, in the foreseeable future, it won't get me too much into trouble. I guess I was trying to give you something deeper."

"Oh, you haven't converted me," Auger said. "You think you had! You'll get no consolation, or whatever you want to replace that word with, from me."

"Hoped not!" Pius said laughing. "That'd be boring. The day I get you to admit you believe in Gaia is the day I know I'm in trouble. That's no consolation! My ancient predecessors in the Obsidian Order used to pull that stunt a thousand years ago. I bet you didn't know that. 'Food-for-belief' is what they called it. More specifically: 'Food-for-belief *conversion.*' A brutal practice? A bargain? A stain on the history of the Obsidian Order? Yes. Two out of three. They'd pull that stunt, to convert some poor slob half way up his tree, to the true religion. 'Come down, do the right gestures, here's food.' They'd coax the poor wretch down from his perch with an offer of food. That's what they'd say to him. How much of this world had been converted that way?"

"You talk so glibly about the failings of your religion," Auger said. "Ordinarily, you have a scriptural-like reverence for all the sayings of The BLESSINGS OF GAIA DOCUMENT. Don't you get into trouble with your religious brethren...."

"You can't serve truth if you forget the falsehoods from the past. Remember the true stories of what the wronged ones had endured. You have to remember. Enduring remembrance. If you value your own views, it's dangerous being a mourner, my friend."

"Con...So...La...Tion!" Auger enunciated, pronouncing each syllable slowly. He wiggled his finger at Pius. "You once said that only a person of deep faith can afford the luxury of skepticism. Most of the people who believe in Gaia are scared to death."

Pius did not reply.

"No?" Auger asked.

Before Pius said goodbye, he said, "I'll visit you once more. Wait for me. Wait." Then he departed.

It took the occasion of the death of Rornar for Auger to be reminded that Pius could be oddly cosmopolitan about his otherwise staid, conservative views. It was a side of Pius that he rarely displayed in public. It would have been a self-indulgent showing off that Pius would have detested, and would have been seriously frowned upon by his Obsidian Order. Did Pius want in some way to undercut the fact that he had been two steps away from being offered the post: "Chair Intellectual Supreme of the Obsidian Order?"

Before he died, Andromenus had nominated him himself. It would have made Pius the youngest Chair Intellectual Supreme in 1,500 years and would have made Pius an intellectual in theology *and in history*, as well. In the annals of the Obsidian Order, that would have been a combination never before experienced. But, in the end, they gave the Chair to an older man named Xanus. Xanus despised the study of history, *especially ancient history.*

"Theology is timeless, close to immortal, what need of history?" Xanus was often quoted as saying. The Obsidian Order establishment feared Pius might look at theology differently from the reliable Xanus. Xanus hated Pius. He was contemptuous of Pius with a vehemence that was exceptional for the day and age. And Xanus represented the majority view of the Obsidian Order in this regard. In the eyes of Auger, Pius was a conservative. But not in the eyes of Pius's religious brethren.

It was given to Auger alone to share Pius's private thoughts, never to be aired in public. Auger understood, as Pius put it: "this sacred boundary." Auger would have gone to his death before he betrayed an oath given to Pius.

For Auger, the evening was far from over. As it wore on, a piece of news was hand-delivered to him. (In Eccles, medical services and health services were considered to be on a par with the near sacrosanct, so for these messages, the authorities didn't rely on hand-held electronic contrivances, or boxes. They used what had been called in most of the human communities of the Inner World, 'human voices.' The sacred could not be mediated by the box.

In this case, a 16-year-old boy, wearing a sharp uniform and matching cap, arrived at the door and announced in a cheerful and respectful voice: "Your daughter's fine. All is going as planned. She's still a bit underweight. Therefore, the nurses say they want to chubby her up. You're alone. You're a widower. We understand your situation. You'll be able to bring your daughter home soon. Possibly as early as in two weeks' time. Soon, she'll be making wonderful cooing sounds. Progress is certain."

Auger tipped the boy generously. The gesture was gratuitous, in light of the fact that the boy was actually performing a coveted job, and by the standards of his age group an extremely well-paid one. Such were the values of the city of Eccles. Auger was grateful.

The news of his daughter's progress cheered Auger up. In fact, it made him happy in the midst of his sorrow.

'The public ceremony' was to commence in six days. This was the closest thing to a funeral in the world of Eccles, a ritual popular with believers, non-believers, and unbelievers alike. Its origins seem to have gone all the way back to the time of Gaia's famous children Iona and Kull in pre-history, where mourners would gather in a circle and recite: 'Give Sorrow Its Words,' or, 'Let Us Bear Down All Sorrows,' or 'Give Sorrow Its Due,'. Something became starkly clear to Auger. The old religion pulled Auger when he thought of that singular aspect of its old shadow, the remembrance of sorrow.

Auger loved Rornar. He revered the memory of her. He could not imagine any circumstance where he could possibly reconsider remarrying. He had become firmly resolved on this point. That was one of the outcomes of the tragedy. The other outcome was that it made Auger even more committed to the historian's calling, and to the passion that he had invested in his project. That was a hard thing to do, with everything he had to consider.

As he'd promised, Pius visited Auger again at the beginning of the twelfth day of mourning. He said to Auger: "Think of your daughter. Think of your project."

"What? Those two?"

"Yes. Those two."

"Only those two?"

"Yes. Only those two. Those should be your most profound and immediate touchstones. Zoia, your daughter. Your project, your writing history. Those two."

"Very well," Auger replied. "I'll take your advice. But which of the two is the most important?"

Zoia was delivered to his home twelve days later. She weighed six pounds and she was a fully healthy baby. Auger was filled with delight. He felt as if he had been blessed. He cuddled his daughter in his arms. Already he could see the tell-tale signs in the features of her face—the eyes, the chin (with the deep dominating cleft), the ears—where Zoia so much resembled her mother. Auger realized he would always see his wife in the face of his child.

The university had already made a special arrangement for Auger, so he could work at home for the foreseeable future. That way, unimpeded, Auger could take care of his baby at the same time.

Also, the university made an arrangement in advance that would allow Auger to bring his daughter with him to his office once Zoia had grown older, should he choose to. The times, in so many different ways, were changing.

As a father, and as an academic, Auger was to become a different sort.

Chapter Three

NAGART AND MIMNAC were husband and wife. They lived with their two daughters, Odey and Nimesis. Together they inhabited a hardscrabble survivalist family ranch. The ranch was located in the corner of what had been defined by a Gaia archeologist as The Greater Colorado, Utah, Arizona, New Mexico Quadrant.

Why use a name from the distant past? Because of the religious implications of it being "holy," from the "Origins-Of-Gaia" time. The name was taken from a heavily damaged and discolored map that had been lodged in the Gatetar Museum. The original was at least 2,650 years old, a map that had been printed (yes, it was a laminated reprint of an original paper copy found in the ruins of a Manhattan Gaia-Dome), dating back to at least 15 years earlier than Iona-In-The-Cave time, maybe even as early as September Snow's Defection-From-The-Gaia-Domes time.

In physical terms, the ranch was 321 kilometers east of where the seasonally dry Little Colorado flowed west and met the swift and powerful Colorado, in what had once been described as an extensive dry grassland. After the World-Wide Great Climate Collapse in 2052 A.D., climate change denuded the region into a retrogressive desert; then, later, into a semi-desert. But after 2,000 years, it had miraculously turned back into its original state. There were only a few places where this had happened. In most parts of the Outer

World the places were still "in the darkness." The area south of Albu was part of the world in recovery. All parts of the tropics, and most parts of the semi-tropics, had not recovered, ditto most portions of southern Asia, the wastelands of Siberia, much of Africa, and much of the southern portions of the Americas. They were thousands of years away from recovery.

In fact, virtually all of the Inner World—representing almost 25 percent of the global land mass, had recovered, but only a little of the Outer World had.

The ranchette was located 200 meters from the Escavada Wash, 21 kilometers east of the ancient ruins of what had once been known as Chaco. The location of Nagart's ranchette was just barely within the boundary of the Inner World, pinioned in by the Inner World city of Albu, located just 12 kilometers south of the original ancient human settlement of Albuquerque.

Albu was situated along the Rio Grande River. The city of Eccles had sponsored Albu for its entry into the Inner World. But if Nagart's ranch had been located just 15 kilometers farther south, or 200 kilometers west, it would have been beyond the border of Albu. So the ranch existed in a sort of twilight zone, between the borders of the Inner and Outer Worlds. Nagart's family was considered part of the outer people of the Inner World.

Eccles was one of the 10 major power centers in the world. The Inner World comprised a string of mega-cities—42 larger cities, 28 satellite medium size cities, 80 smaller ones (like Albu). Almost all of them were situated on the coasts of oceans, on the banks of major rivers or their tributaries, or on the lakeshores of major lakes around the world. There were no countries or nations. There were no fixed geographical entities except cities and their environs which could stretch a measly 20 square kilometers or as many as 2,000 square kilometers. And then, of course, there was the Outer World. The population was more or less evenly distributed and balanced between the Inner Worlds and the Outer Worlds, 750 million people in each zone.

Four months after Rornar gave birth and died, Nagart's wife, Mimnac, gave birth to a son. The parents named him Rathman. There were no doctors or midwives close enough to the ranchette to provide assistance.

Nagart did what was necessary to aid in the birthing process. His two daughters, Odey and Nimesis, helped too, mainly by heating water and providing wraps.

Fortunately, the birthing process had been easy. Immediately after the baby arrived Nagart cut the umbilical cord with a knife, then placed the child in the mother's arms. Mimnac held him to her bosom. Mother and baby both seemed vital, healthy, and fine.

The new baby needed no encouragement to suck. He was an animated child, opening on Nagart his bright unfocused eyes, waving his starfish hands, butting his head against his mother's breasts, the small open mouth ravenously seeking the nipple. It seemed near miraculous to Nagart that anything so new could be so vigorous and energized. The baby sucked and then slept.

Nagart lay down beside his wife and placed an arm around her. He felt the damp softness of his wife's hair against his cheek. The three of them lay on a crumpled linen sheet that smelled of sweat, but Nagart had never known such peace, never realized such joy. The birth of a son! They lay half-dozing in a wordless calm and it seemed to Nagart that there rose from the child's warm flesh the agreeable aroma of the newborn, wet and pungent, like newly cut hay.

Later, awaking from a state of semi-sleep, Mimnac, as she had done previously after the birth of her daughters, recited something from the oral tradition. It was a riff that had been passed down through her family over many generations. Because of losses and forgetfulness over time, all that was left of what had been a much longer version were a few scattered words: "Love and affection passed down from the lost tribe of the Judic (sic); you are the product of the loins of Pallas and the womb of Telia. Telia is the head. Telia, Pallas, Aura, Teanna, Vivianna, and Pontus. The six. Of The Pallinate."

The first part of the saying was spoken in modern vernacular.

However, the six ancestral names were no longer in general use, and the words around them were in a little known tongue. Pallinate was the one word that stood out. It was the name of the alphabet. According to historians, the Pallinate was presumed to have been established by the Obsidian Order, sometime between the years 550 and 600 A.G.

Logic dictated there had been more to the sayings but this was all that was left after centuries of oral transmission. Since the word "Pallinate" was included, it was surmised the saying's origin could have been no earlier than 550 A.G., 2,000 years ago.

All Mimnac was doing was reciting what her mother had recited to her. She had no idea of the meaning.

She had been told by her mother and grandmother to recite it after the birth of a child, recite it again on the fourth birthday, recite it again on the eighth birthday, and once again on the 15th birthday.

It was the closest thing Mimnac had to a family "bible."

After the birth of the child, once the household had been made secure, Nagart stepped outside his hovel. He walked far enough so that he could no longer see the glare from the single oil-lamp glowing inside one of the windows. There was no electricity where Nagart and his family lived halfway up the arroyo leading to the mesa. Indeed, there was no running water, unlike in the cities. In the Outland the night skies, assuming there was no cloud cover, could be viewed in all their unobstructed brilliance.

Rathman's father wandered slowly over a gentle hillcrest and ended up hunkering down in a small hollow. He crouched down and lay on his back, placing his arms under his head as a pillow. He looked up at the stars. Even though he was a man of little imagination, the stars looked utterly impenetrable to him, but also oddly beguiling.

Taking account of himself, Nagart realized there was not much he would be able to bequeath to his two young daughters and infant son as an inheritance. There was the large herd of goats who remained vigorous even in the worst of dry seasons. There was the

much smaller herd of sheep that had been doing reasonably well for
five years running (the second best run in Nagart's lifetime, the sixth
best run if you also included his father's stretch of luck). Then there
was the greatest mainstay, their strong, reliable, unstoppable family
horse. In an unusually wet year, when the Escavada wash overflowed
and some of the water could be captured, the family was able to
grow fields of hay. Sometimes they were even able to plant a few
small patches of barley. And fed from the waters of their intermittently usable well, there was the family garden. Sometimes, in the
fat years, they were able to sell excess produce in town. Mainly veg-
etables, but also goat milk, goat cheese, goat meat. Sometimes, in
the lean years they had just barely enough meat for themselves, or,
in the leanest years, not enough meat at all.

The sheep and their wool were always "the gravy," "the bumper
crop." Once or twice a decade for the meat, once every two or three
years for the wool. Chiefly because of that, and sometimes from the
produce of the goats, they were able to buy cheap trade goods and
articles. Otherwise, homespun and hand-crafted clothes and articles
were what they made do with.

Chapter Four

GUNTER GATETAR was the richest man in history. He was also the most powerful man in the tech world, a colossus, having amassed more power than the next 250 persons in the tech world combined. He was what was called in business circles "The Untouchable." Starting in sophisticated boat-building in his father's backyard at the age of 16, he branched out to where he owned more shares of stock than the rest of the planet's inhabitants combined. Boat-building had little to do with it, except for providing the initial capital. He then became a pioneer in the production of silica and code. He brought the first computer into existence. Three decades later, he was pretty much the sole designer of boxes, little boxes, BIG BOXES.

When he was young, he made his tech debut as an early designer of a pre-transistor. The patent was allegedly stolen from him, but he made sure that *those kind of shenanigans didn't happen to him again. And according to his reckoning, they never did.*

His inventions combined to make him Number One Oligarch among the four. He outstripped Number Four, who commanded old-communication production, money orders, wire transfers, street-level sub-lending, newsprint, and magazines (with the exception of academia, now all but gone) in 2646. He outstripped Number Three, who owned gas and oil production, in 2657. He outstripped Number Two, the food production oligarch, in 2659. Change was headed in one direction. Data!

As Gunter Gatetar was fond of saying, "Why buy titles when you can purchase land? Why buy high officials when you can purchase machinery? Why buy data when you own it?"

The only thing that was bigger than Gunter Gatetar's electronic empire was the Inner World electric power grid and its related plants. These were, according to Gaian law, designated "near sacrosanct." That is to say, publicly owned. This program, as large as it was, was only slightly larger than the medical program, which was also designated "near sacrosanct" and publicly owned. The educational system, had up until recently been designated "near sacrosanct," but no longer. It was still, for the most part, publicly owned.

According to Gaian law, you could *not* buy, sell, or own land unless it was located directly under your private domicile, or it was located where your business and factories were. But you could buy and sell land and ocean water surface on the open market in the *Outer World*. That became law by means of the second heaviest lobbying effort in the history of the legislature, in 2620 A.G. The law was passed by the general assembly by a narrow vote of four. It stayed in effect for 42 years. During this time, G. G. bought large swathes of land and surface water. Gatetar actually *owned* islands and portions of continents!

For example, Gunter successfully bought thirty percent of the landmass of Australia and forty-five percent of the archipelago of eastern Indonesia and checkerboard parts of Papua-New Guinea.

This purchasing of land and surface water had become an obsession with Gunter, but with the birth of his son Juggernaut, the obsession turned into an out-and-out fetish.

Just now turning 14, Jug, (everyone called him Jug, no one dared refer to him—at least, not to his face—by his real name, except for his father) was Gunter Gatetar's sole heir, his only son. He did not see purchasing large amounts of surface water as *his* obsession. But upon his father's death, Jug was destined to inherit all the family's wealth, all the family's businesses, all the family's assets, all the family's land, and all the family's ocean surface water. At the age of 85, Gunter was intermittently ill; he was slowly dying of cancer.

Gunter was known to rarely let an opportunity slip. At Jug's birthday party, attended only by the two of them, Gunter said: "The name Gatetar has been synonymous with electronics for 50 years. We pioneered the pre-transistor prototype, though we were told we were beaten by someone else. We were one of two who introduced silica. Tenestra released their body computer two years before us. Their operating system was *much cleaner and much better than ours*, but it didn't matter. In eight years we had completely outflanked them thanks to our vastly superior marketing. BIG BOX is just a later and newer incarnation. New BIG BOX is smaller and more affordable than its most recent predecessor, old BIG BOX. But that just means, in the imagination of the consumer, it's a better product. If, as a business, you're not growing and expanding, you die. All the fruits of your labor will expire in time. Even if it takes 50 years, that's inevitable. If vigilance is not stimulated and strictly enforced, when the time comes, and it's coming soon, I will *not* give you this vast empire unless you swear an oath you'll continue to follow the family tradition. That means you'll continue to enable Gatetar Industries to grow, to expand, to become more successful. Through diversification and expansion there is growth. But there is something more important. Singularity is growth too."

"Understood," Jug said. He had grown accustomed to hearing his father's speechifying even when it was spoken at an event that was supposed to be carefree and un-business-like, like his birthday party.

"Gatetar Industries made Eccles more or less what it is today," Gunter said with a note of satisfaction. He laughed. "Oh, I almost forgot to mention our most important totem: 'Computer in the sky,' which will become almighty, and with the evolution of this very same computer in conjunction with the evolution of the universe, will become, and although I think it's impossible this will happen during my lifetime, I think it's quite possible it might happen during your lifetime, or during your children's lifetime: omniscient, all-powerful, all-knowing—this computer will be loved by all, and it will in return love all of us very much."

"Understood," Jug said. He nodded. "I'll work on it. You need not have any doubts along those lines. It's a wager you can freely make. Your family fortune will be in good hands at the time upon which you should leave us."

Jug thought: Why should a product have to be created so that it needed to feel love? The old man thinks he's doing something more than just making money. On the part of my father, the curse of our times? Hope? Loneliness?

"I'm ill," Gunter said. "They've given me a few more years to live. Sure. Can they give me more?"

"You'll receive more," Jug said.

At the age of 14, Jug was technically a kid. But, like his father at about the same age, he was showing signs of being fearless, and becoming ever more fearless. Gunter hoped he'd taught his son how to stand on his own two feet. Why else had he given him such an outlandishly, absurdly powerful name? Juggernaut? His very young and beautiful wife, forty-six years Gunter's junior, had fiercely objected to the name, but Gunter, as in almost all family matters, had called the shots.

Father and son settled down to their accustomed glass of wine, one thimble-sized glass for Jug of course, considering his age. Gunter sometimes refilled his own larger glass, once or twice, from a decanter. They sat under a deeply blue-hued glass awning, overlooking magnificent fields of early harvested wheat, rice, and corn, and a sun-dappled lawn, a short, brisk walk away from the oligarch's six-storied mansion, adjacent to modern imitations of Roman imitations of Greek wood nymphs and variations of Athena/Sophia/Venus/Diana/Gaia womanly types and satyr-looking, lute-playing Pans—alternating with trees along an ascending circular driveway. An underground parking garage for a bevy of cars stood to the far left, not one, two, three, but four helioplane-launching pads lay to the right, and further on was the mini-Safari Park—lions, tigers, bears, etc.

What kind of party was this going to be? Jug thought to himself. Where were the guests? Were there any guests invited at all? Of course not.

In the mean time, two doves alighted on the right-hand banister of the adjacent veranda. The birds were accustomed to being in the presence of humans. You could stand six or seven feet away from them and they would scarcely stir. Jug had seen the birds land there in all seasons. His tutor Jason had taught him that doves, unlike so many other species of birds, typically bonded for life. The female was sleek, fastidious, alert, and trim. In contrast, the male was withdrawn, dumpy-looking, a bit overweight, his movements erratic and ill-coordinated. Jug imagined that the female looked disappointed with her mate selection, like she was forever lamenting: Look at him. Must have been drooling or nodding off in my sleep when I first hooked up with him. Look at him. What was I thinking! What a catch!

Jug adored observing and studying all kinds of birds in all kinds of weather. His mother, having observed him while he was observing birds, approved of the practice as well.

"One thing I hate," Gunter said, finding himself in a more relaxed mood after his second glass of wine, "In spite of my philanthropy, I've given more than all the other private philanthropies combined—journalists still insist on calling me The Oligarch. A radical journalist gutter-sniped me with that sobriquet 55 years ago. Fifty-five years ago! It stuck. I resent it very *much*. That's the one thing I hate. I'm not an oligarch! I'm a pioneer. I'm an inventor. I'm a master scientist. I'm a friend to humankind."

It was a set, formulaic speech. Jug had heard variations of it many times before.

Along with his green pantaloons and matching suspenders, Gunter sported a flamboyant goatee. It had been streaked salt and pepper before Jug was born, but now it was alabaster white. Gunter had gray eyes. They flashed fire in rare instances—but otherwise his eyes revealed nothing. Ordinarily, his face was a perfect mask.

Jug had come to know by heart pretty much all of his father's

eccentricities and obsessions. But Jug remained, as always, judicious-
ly silent. He wanted to say: 'if you're such a great pioneer, a great inventor, a great scientist, as you say you are—unless you've morphed
into an entirely different species, Mr. Power-Driven Business Man!—
at some point, you'd have thought to give more back to the people.
There could be social change, but only you have the power to define
it. You sure as hell didn't have to wait until you were 85 to think that
one through, and even share a thought or two about it with your
son.'

"If you're not a subversive by the age of 20, what will you be
by the age of 30?" Jug's tutor, Jason, asked that in the lull of a very
boring history lesson. *"Of course! Your father! Even before he turned
35. He'd been deeply embittered. Having completely dropped the ball
on his patent, he blamed others for his mistake. For the rest of his life, he
blamed the world for his mistake."*

Once Jug had made the unwise choice of mouthing a very crude
wisecrack about that, in reply Gunter demanded to know if Jug
wanted to inherit *anything of value at all.* Neither his tutor or his
mother were going to be able to bail him out after such impetuous
speech. Lesson drawn and concluded.

At first, on the elitist playground, (it was hard being the equal of
others, even when they too were from ridiculously wealthy families),
then, in the larger world, life had taught him the efficacy of silence.

"Not always easy growing up the richest man in the world's
son," Jug complained to Jason on one occasion.

"Not always easy being the richest man's son's tutor," Jason
retorted. Jug's hand went atremble, as if he were a thief nabbed.
Jason was an excellent tutor. Humane. Great teacher. Gunter had
bestowed upon him full discretionary power.

By now, Gunter was sipping his third glass of wine and was feeling very pleased with himself. Jug gazed at him and thought (yes—
partially with the critical impetus of his tutor, Jug had grown into
being what his mother had referred to him as, 'a really, chilly, too-
big-for-his-britches, thirteen-year-old smart-ass'), and Jug thought,

now having turned fourteen, doing his best impersonation of a
"fourteen-year-old smart-ass": 'Yes, when you were young, father,
you were a pioneer. But over the years, like turning on a spigot, all
you've done was convert electricity into money. You didn't invent it.
Nope. Electricity man invented it, and died, in the end, in a state of
great poverty. That was more than 120 years ago. Kimmel was his
name. And we know now he didn't really invent it, just reinvented
it. Sort of disappeared when humankind went seriously wacked, then
after wrecking the environment, the Gaia-Domes sprouted up. Soon
thereafter pretty much everyone was forced to live in caves. Then
there was a gap time, at the end of which, kablooey, electricity was
knocked down again. Humanity was frog-marched back into the
caves. This time the darkness lasted not 400 years, but 1500 years.
Then electricity made a strong comeback. But electricity, in all its
glory, existed 2,800 years ago! Tesla is my hero. Died impoverished.
Like Kimmel. My lost hero, decrying against cronyism. Yes father.
Of course I can think with two minds, two different kinds of mental
processes stored in the same brainpan at the same time. Can I not be
a rebellious trickster and the largest business player in the world at the
same time? Your being rich and alone makes life even harder, so much
more... I am not indolent. I'm considerate. Your obedient son?'

But instead he said nothing. He kept his peace.

Yes, yes, yes, the old man thought, patience always. Gunter
planted the tutor—*deliberately planted*—the tutor—as a subversive,
according to the philosophy that sharing a road to subversion was
better than being blindsided, ending up being on one's own, falling
into the abyss of subversion unawares. That's how old man Gunter
played his son. You had to let the new leader rebel against the old
leader, if only for ritual's sake, because how else can he become a
leader. But, wisdom-finger-wagging aside, keep it within borders.
Limits. Let the patient have an inoculation. He might get a little
sick, but then he'll get better. Certainly, at 14, spare the rod, give
the boy another seven or eight years of freedom, and then put the
hammer down.

Clearing a path didn't always ensure Juggernaut would choose the right path. Even for an experienced manipulator like Gunter Gatetar—contingency didn't always translate. Moral of the story is you can't control everything, including your own son. When the time came, if worse came to worst, maybe Gunter would just get someone else to run the company for him, and all his fretting would have been for no reason at all. On the other hand, a person like Gunter was someone who didn't let go. Why wait 50 years, then decide to have a kid at the age of seventy-two? To say he had no interest in his legacy would have been absurd. He had a clear picture of what he expected his son to turn into.

Chapter Five

J AIME AND RAINE stood atop Mount Eta. There was an inch
of snow lying on the ground, remnant of a recent overnight
snow dusting. The snowy mountaintop looked out upon Eccles
and points north. To the right there was the bay, to the left a valley
extending northward, 45 kilometers out, as a piece of land, stream-
lining itself into a peninsula. This valley and peninsula lay 4,200 feet
below the mountain. Jaime and Raine gazed out. The city looking
almost magical in the distance.

Beyond the valley floor, curving west, then northwest, the valley
itself and the lower section of the peninsula had been ground zero
for the place that had once been called—in mythological, Pre-Gaia
times—five decades before, and up to four decades after *the birth of
September Snow in 2022:* 'California's Silicon Valley.'

Milton, and what had been San Francisco, and had become the
San Francisco Game Reserve, had been fur-trading outposts 900
years before. Farming communities Newfield, Job, and Blake sprang
up later. Then all four settlements flourished, especially with the
growth in trade. In four hundred years, the four cities combined had
become the single largest settlement on the West Coast of America.

The ancient city of San Francisco was, of course, never rebuilt,
instead it had become a "wildness reserve," after an effort at refores-
tation. Black and grizzly bears, bison, mountain lions, wolves, a few
hyenas (transplants), a tiny number of genetically spliced Tasmanian

Devils (transplants), and no fewer than 11 large, sprite-like groups of coyotes, roamed the area.

Before it had been a mythical place. And as Jaime and Raine looked down on the valley, and the beginning of the peninsula, they wondered about it. Silicon Valley had developed before The-Dark-Age-End-Culmination California that began around 2062 A.D. Forty years before that catastrophic period of time, the most populous sub-state of an even larger nation-state was seen as the undisputed powerhouse of the post-industrial world and the capital of the first half of the 21st century. With its worldly, wealthy techies, their well-heeled upper-managers, their sturdy lieutenants, their graceful and beautifully nerdy, yet often—too often—docile, assistants and underlings: the valley was the Foremost Seminal High Technology Mecca Of The World.

Or so the jetsam and flotsam, the dribs and drabs, of mythology, had so implied.

In the year of 2662 A.G., Jaime Flores, age 22, was an astronomer and chief telescope tech. His boss, Raine Huston, age 75, was a renowned yet retiring and withdrawn astrophysicist. They were two of nine full-time employees, along with five part-time employees and six volunteers, at the small Love Observatory atop Mount Eta.

"It agitates me when people talk about the secrets of the universe," Raine said. "It irritates me. The universe doesn't have secrets. It reveals itself to us...."

"Will there not continue to be questions about the unresolved and unexplained?" Jaime asked. "Will there not always be questions about the unresolved and the unexplainable?"

"Plug it, Jaime," Raine said. "Button it."

"Of course, what are we?"

"Plug it, Jaime. Give it a rest. Save it for the library. Don't you ever wake up in the morning and just feel sunshine?"

"Math *is* the world," Jaime said. "Math is what keeps chaos at bay. That's what I think."

"Why you insist on doing that? *Going dark. Going negative.* I have work to do."

"Now for the light side," Jaime said, smiling. "Question is, may I conduct a study—of asteroids—stretching out over the skies, between the inner and the outer planets. Between Mars and Jupiter. I'm asking you again."

"*That whole ball of wax again?*" Raine replied. He looked tired and weary. "For what purpose?" He asked the question even though he knew in advance what Jaime's reply was going to be.

"For purposes of asteroid collision research."

"Oh. Asteroid collision research! You mean, banging into each other? Bumping? What? Out there... From here, rocks look close. If there are millions of them in orbit around the sun, our previous studies have tracked about 25 percent of them. How many more do you want to study? Hundreds? Thousands? Tens of thousands?"

Raine's mind raced through the gamut of Jaime's previous penchants for absurdities, oddities, eccentricities, and how these peculiarities had been legion ever since Jaime was orphaned and rendered a refugee. Raine remembered when Jaime showed up at his doorstep, frail-looking, undernourished, clutching a beggar bowl, a crutch under his left arm, with a handmade sign stitched to his breast pocket: Save Gaia. In the meantime...feed me?

Maybe it was the forlorn, pitiful look in Jaime's eyes. Maybe it was just the day. A nexus of the personal and the practical ruling over random events. Raine was known to be a sap, an easy mark. In the past, he'd taken in anybody. He took Jaime in.

When he figured out that Jaime was neither openly psychotic nor vicious, Raine let him stay *indefinitely*. During the first two years, Raine was not attentive to the details of Jaime's case. He only saw glimpses of Jaime when he was doing kitchen chores, taking out the slops, or working in the garden. Raine had no idea of the boy's potential. On a dare, proposed by an assistant, he gave Jaime a mathematical problem to solve.

"Come on, Raine," his assistant said, "just because the urchin comes from the Outer World doesn't mean he's brainless. Look beyond."

Raine said okay. And when he took Jaime aside, he said, "Look, you don't have to. If you do, and you can't solve it, it's okay. Take your time. Take it with you."

Jaime looked at the problem for a brief instant. "Take it with me?"

"Yes."

"Why? That won't be necessary."

Jaime solved the problem in two minutes. Then and there, he sat at a table, jotting down figures on a piece of paper. Having made some calculations, he handed the paper back to Raine.

Raine's mind was blown by Jaime's precisely arrived at correct answer.

Raine gave Jaime a more difficult problem.

Over a period of four years, Jaime solved increasingly difficult mathematical problems. At last Jaime accomplished the *piece de resistance*. He found proof the equation a3 + b3 = c3 had no solution for nonvanishing integers. The most renowned mathematicians unanimously agreed the "finding" was not trivial, causing Jaime to be mentioned in two small annals, that were dedicated to the recognition of mathematical geniuses.

Jaime wasn't just a potentially competent academic in the making, he was the future of the observatory.

Over six years, Jaime completed what should have been a ten-year study, so he became an astronomer, taking the place of an early-retiring assistant.

Jaime was seen as having a strong vocation for mathematics, a secondary knack for astrophysics, and a broad and impassioned curiosity about the Earth sciences. He was also a loner, a brilliant intellect, an extreme obsessive, and way too frequently, a depressive.

"No, I mean an asteroid colliding with Earth," Jaime at last added.

Raine looked at his assistant in a gentle and affectionate way.

"That's a jump. Just looking at rocks in the belt? Don't you think your odds are better for finding a cure for Darkness Depression? Of course there's Rutherford's study. In the Andes. Asteroid orbital displacement hypothetical. Sure, there's always something plowing into Jupiter. With the behemoth's extraordinary gravitational pull, that's new? We have only 30 percent of Mount Taylor's telescope capacity. We can't hold a candle to Mount Granon's radio capacity. Want to do it here?"

"Yes," Jaime exclaimed with delight. "Yes. Exactly. But different. I'll act differently."

"Of course you'll act differently!" Raine said. He looked like he was ready to explode, but somehow he calmed himself. He paused, sighing. He took his handkerchief out and ceremoniously mopped his brow. "When have you NOT acted differently? This may come as a surprise to you, young man, but we can't fund it. Not in a big way, not in a small way, not in any way. Have to scrimp, borrow, toady, bend at the waist, prostrate myself, to get a pittance that is delivered reluctantly, that is, EXTREMELY BEGRUDGINGLY, by an officious, coldhearted board. You've no idea. You'll have to do everything on your own, Jaime. Everything. After hours. How many asteroids are you planning on studying?"

"I'll start with the big ones," Jaime said. The litany of limitations did not deflect his enthusiasm nor dampen his eagerness.

"All right," Raine said. He sighed heavily. He smiled. "Only provisionally granted. Rule number One: No stealing volunteers without my approval."

"Wouldn't dream of poaching," Jaime replied quickly.

"You will share...that is, if you actually find something. You'll share? Won't you? One of those rocks comes near Earth? Say, within 75,000 kilometers? Say, within 50,000 kilometers? You'll be sure to give us advance notice? A heads-up? So we'll have plenty of time to do whatever's necessary?"

"Of course!" Jaime exclaimed. "That's my mission! I've taken an oath!"

Raine looked skeptical. "Yes, of course. But one of significant size? Hasn't happened in a long time. Something, say, one-twentieth the size of Mount Eta? Yeah, right. Twenty meters wide more likely. Near collision? Doesn't count. Bouncing, grazing, fragmenting? Doesn't count. Burning up on its own? Doesn't count. A big light show, impressive, accompanied by thousands of broken windows, frightened animals, startled people. Who cares if *that* happens? For every hit, there are thousands, tens of thousands, near misses. Now an out-and-out collision, of course, that's different."

"It's been three million years. Actually, a little less than that. Manson. A rock two and a half kilometers across." Jaime started ticking off the information. "Manson made a hole five kilometers deep and more than 30 kilometers across. Within hundreds of kilometers of the impact point, it vaporized life. But what about one 300 times smaller? Say, one as big as a large building? Destroy a city. Two, TWO! collisions have been documented. One that crashed in Siberia. It had a 300-kilometer-long path and it was believed to have weighed 280 million pounds, traveling at 53,913 kilometers per hour, disintegrating four-and-a-half kilometers up in the sky, setting off an explosion. The other plowed into Arizona. This one weighed only 500 tons, driven into the ground, 150 meters down—burning itself up at the point of impact. But look what damage it did."

Raine feigned boredom, but his interest was piqued. "With a population of only one and a half billion people on Earth, some pin-point collision isn't going to make a difference in the mind of anybody. Yes. Your vows. You and your vows. You're still a member?"

"Of the Forandi Order?" Jaime asked. "Renewed vows, three months ago."

"Strange order, ancient order," Raine murmured, shaking his head. "I know I've asked you before. To put it mildly, you're the only one on our team who is at all *religious*. Don't you find the contradiction between science and religion a problem, notwithstanding the Secularization Act, a piece of legislation that constitutes our *protection from you know what*, don't you find it a little perplexing, or at least, a little puzzling?"

"No."

"Well, as long as you limit yourself to mathematics, you'll do fine. Keep it that way. I warned you about those *persons* in U. Presbyr, in the Rhetoric Department. Like they'd emerged from hell. Get too close to them, you'll smell their sulfur."

"I'm a science man," Jaime said. "I don't suffer. *I stay away from that.*"

"Keep it that way," Raine said. "That way you won't get in trouble. The scientific community has enough trouble as it is. The disorderly conduct of demonstrators! Those lotus-eating revelers. Where are their leaders? Nowhere! Of course not. Must be anarchists! Lotus-eating anarchists!"

Jaime looked the other way.

"They perform antics in places designated as sacred, as if they need to make things worse. Cavorting! In the portico of the shrine to Iona! In Iona's portico! Can you imagine? Did you see that? Deranged, semi-nude, writhing bodies. Quoting Tom Novak like he's the end-all of the Gaia religion: "All history is philosophy, all philosophy is religion, all religion is literature, all literature is art, all art is music, painting, dancing, and all music, painting, dancing are the heart, brain, hand of man and woman, through time." Well, they do know how to dance! Participants were forced to apologize for that one, but, no less, spewing vituperation, constantly spewing vituperation. My word..."

"I'm a science man," Jaime said. He thought the anarchist riffraff of the Rhetoric Department were pranksters or, at worst, supercilious imps, rather than existential threats to the public order. Why did Raine have an obsession with these people?

"Science man," Raine nodded. "Steady. Keep it that way. You know it's good you're a member of the Forandi Order. Proving science and religion can go hand in hand. Do you still do your prayers while walking?"

"Only when I choose to," Jaime replied.

"We're such a small operation," Raine said. "Kull's Crop on St. Helena, Beak's Bay, in Australia, are the only ones smaller than us. I guess nobody will notice or even care about what we do. If we keep it off the books."

"Over the next 65 years, the study might save a piece, a small piece, of the Earth."

"Yes," Raine said smiling. "Yes." He looked condescendingly, yet good-naturedly, at Jaime. "Maybe a small piece. I'm 75. Not in my lifetime. You're 22. Maybe in your lifetime." Raine was thinking about the project. How long would Jaime's passion be sustained before fatigue settled in? How long would it take before he grew weary of his mission? What would happen if he discovered it wasn't at all likely he'd find any sort of threatening rock at all, 20 years from now, 40 years from now, 60 years from now?

"Could there be worse ways, or, for that matter, better ways, for me to serve out my sentence of existence on this planet?" Jaime asked solemnly, as if he were sensing Raine's doubts and reservations. As Jaime spoke there was a steely look in his eyes, indicating that beneath his exterior lurked the equivalent of a religiously inspired devotion.

Oh, the religiously zealous! Raine thought.

"Isn't it I, the old one, who gets to play?" Raine asked grumpily. "Why do you get to have all the fun." Raine pretended to pout. Then he smiled. "Too old. Too late for me. Okay. But not too late for you. Let's give it a try."

"Thank you, Raine," Jaime said.

The story seemed as fresh as the day it was related to Raine by a Forandi monk three months after Jaime had settled in at Love Observatory. Raine remembered the details, how the Forandi Order saved Jaime, how they brought him out for resettlement. He remembered when the monk explained with horror what the boy went through when he was nine, how his entire family had been destroyed, he being the lone survivor of an entire village. Lone survivor. The Forandi brother held his hands out pitifully in front of himself as he explained, Jaime's seven older brothers were lined up in front of him, starting with the oldest, slowly tortured, limbs hacked off, ears, nose, lips, split open, then, one by one, executed. When it came to Jaime's turn, at last, a counterattack occurred. Within minutes, there were bodies strewn everywhere, bodies next to each other, and on top of each other, peppered with shell splinters, above, pieces of bodies impaled on branches. Jaime had been left in the rubble, miraculously alive. It was 24 hours before four Forandi brothers arrived. They dug him out.

It was they who nursed him back, if not to normality, then at least, to sanity.

It took Jaime nine months before he managed to stop himself from quaking.

Six months after that, he improved. Six months after that, he improved even more. Two years after Jaime emerged from his village's ruins he improved to such an extent that he could function in life, as if he were a normal human being.

There were also moral certitudes and norms of behavior that contributed to Jaime's calm.

Jaime believed in Gaia. Most importantly, he believed in Point One of the Forandi Credo: "When you save the least, the weakest among you, you save the whole of humanity."

Jaime believed the Forandi was the key to everything. After all, the code stressed the main goal of the Gaia Religion: preventing human mismanagement of the physical environment, and making sacred the biosphere of the Earth. *But there was more.*

Forandi Point One was the very thing the Forandi Brothers were adhering to, when they brought Jaime out.

Forandi Point One was taken from 'The Blessing of Gaia Notes,' an underground screed penned by a Forandi theoretician named Matthew, written to supplement THE BLESSINGS OF GAIA DOCUMENT.

Jaime had explained to Raine that though not a founder, Matthew had been deeply influential and powerful in the Forandi Order in the early years. The Blessings of Gaia Notes had been posthumously published in 732 A.G.,150 years after the author's death, just before a cultural darkness came descending again.

In 'The Blessings of Gaia Notes,' Matthew explained that: *"When you save the least, the weakest among you, you save the whole of humanity,"* echoed an injunction issued in a tale sparked by a Moslem wing of the three, a part of antecedent "Abrahamic" religions, all of which—a 1000 years earlier—2000 years earlier—had largely disappeared from the face of the Earth. The original Islamic injunction had been: "When you save a single human being, you save all of humanity."

Raine had asked Jaime why the Forandi Order meant so much to him.

"Brotherhood!" Jaime answered. "That's what makes the Forandi different—and so vastly superior—to all the other religious orders combined. Brotherhood!"

Raine knew that the Forandi Order of the Gaia religion had given Jaime something that had become a necessary part of his life, but what was it? Raine didn't know exactly, but he also knew he wasn't the best judge. *Raine was a humanistic secularist, who only before, semi-openly, but now, because of the quickening pace of change that allowed for more freedom of thought—more openly—like others in his profession, and a powerfully growing number of people in society in general, was completely and absolutely a non-believer in the Gaia religion.*

Raine thought that Jaime's Asteroid Collision Research project was lively, engaging, albeit possibly—rather, more probably—impractical. But statistics weren't everything. They never told the whole story. The one thing Raine knew after being an astrophysicist for fifty years was that sometimes things can be revealed that were of greater value than numbers bear out."

Chapter Six

IN SPITE OF THE SPREAD of Gunter's cancer, with the doctors oftentimes using the most recently created and refined drug regimens and treatments, they managed to keep him alive for another 10 years. The drugs worked in such a way that Gunter remained conscious and lucid right up until the last year of his life, out of pain and reasonably comfortable.

Barely lasting up to eleven days short of his 95th birthday, Gunter managed to hang on. More than anything else, he wanted a world-class funeral, in fact he wanted the greatest funeral ever.

"I've arranged everything in advance," Jug reminded his father. "There won't be a hitch."

"You'll make sure the flowers are really fresh, won't you?" Gunter asked.

"There is no more pressing issue that I can think of among my goals," Jug said. "Those flowers will be fresh beyond imagination."

"And you need to guide the team in their work. And don't let Jason interfere. I hired him to be your teacher, not your secret master."

"I'll guide all. Jason will not interfere. Not in any measurable way. He's actually very philosophical about these things related to this. But even though he is no longer actively my tutor, I've insisted he continue as my advisor. You'd be surprised at the things he can see, when he's standing apart and not being actively engaged. There's a role in that."

"All right," Gunter said. "That's yours.... You're not disappointing me Juggernaut. So far. I can assure you of that."

The way Gunter died surprised everybody. Somehow he had gotten himself out of bed and into his shower, under his own power. In his condition it must have taken a sudden, miraculous rebirth of energy, which no one could have anticipated.

It happened at a time when Gunter was normally asleep, and the least monitored, between three and four. On his own, in the shower, he collapsed. He was found with water cascading on his crumpled body, scalding him. His wife, Jug's mother, had been estranged from her husband for 10 years, so as the end was drawing nearer Gunter had been placed increasingly in the care of strangers.

Jug and his mother had arranged the funeral in advance, just from the point of view of expectations, that had been a prudent decision. They took great care with the details. Dignitaries, business tycoons, extended family, politicians, community leaders, the three other oligarchs of the vast regions of the Inner World, and many other notables from around the world, would attend.

Poet Gaia shamans from the Outer World were asked to come and recite their poetry. Gunter had absolutely no interest in the Poet Gaia shamans or their poetry, and that had been the case during the entire length of his lifetime. But at the last minute he thought their presence would add dignity and class to the proceedings, so he instructed that they'd be invited. The poet Gaia shamans were known to provide entertaining performances. There was always some who were hungry and attracted to travel, even if that meant they had to ingratiate themselves with worldly Inner World dignitaries so they could get—at least for the shorter term voyages—into the most advantageous postings and venues. Coming from the darkest places in the world, because of that experience, that was the reason why they were considered such good poets.

A representative of the Obsidian Order attended of course, but the leaders of the Forandi Order politely declined. Yet they sent flowers. It seemed as if everybody in the Inner World sent flowers, so it was no wonder that the Forandi did not want to be perceived as the odd group out.

Both Jug and his mother knew this was meant to be a giant of a production and they intended to pull out all the stops.

Following Gunter's explicit instructions, the family fleet of 40 state-of-the-art helioplanes had been dispersed to the far corners of the Earth. They were dispersed to gather flowers, some of them plain, simple, regional, others difficult-to-find exotics, from the many lands and the many islands that Gunter owned. The world had never seen such a large assemblage of so many flowers in one place before.

Jug's comment to his advisor Jason: "Not as good as a giant pyramid or a massive mausoleum, to be sure, but flowers will do. They die, too. Isn't that the point?"

"Did he get a bit religious at the end?" Jason asked. "You know, sometimes, even with the really tough and steely ones, that's been known to happen."

"You should never count on something like that happening, certainly not in my father's case," Jug said. "You knew him almost as well as I do."

Whatever love Jug felt toward his father, it was, at best, a strange and complicated love.

So at age 24, Jug inherited Gunter Gatetar's entire business empire and his vast fortune.

Chapter Seven

O N HIS NIGHTS OFF, Jaime had been devoting himself to his asteroid hunt mission. After just six months of
seeking but not finding anything favorable, instead, just
comets streaking by like they'd done for millions, if not billions, of
years, asteroids monotonously going through their routine orbits,
the uneventful findings of bits of space dust, debris, rubble, icy rock,
space junk...*nothing*.

As there were great distances between objects in the asteroid
belt, a slight gravitational bump from a rogue agent could trigger
a "directional change." But that didn't happen often, and when it
happened it usually didn't amount to anything.

Jaime kept his spirits up by doing detailed relief mapping. He
eventually spotted more than 750 large S-type asteroids which
had sizable quantities of nickel, cobalt, and platinum, as well as a
25-percent chance of containing at least some deposits of gold.

Jaime hit a cul-de-sac. He couldn't deny the truth any longer:
extreme amount of space to cover, very little "action."

He realized he had to narrow, not broaden, the scope of his
inquiry. The key was the planet Jupiter. Jupiter was the answer to
everything.

What Jaime realized he needed to do was look for maverick
objects in the asteroid belt that had been thrown off their orbits,
and subsequently, captured by the extremely powerful gravitational

pull of Jupiter. The pull would *either* fling the object farther out into space or bring it into the planet's orbit, thus making it one of the Jovan moons, almost 115 of which had been counted thus far. Every once in a while, Jaime knew that the gravitational pull would sometimes cause a tiny object to be "consumed" by the massive gaseous planet, but if he was counting on that happening, it was likely to be more than just "a long wait." More importantly, the object who managed to escape that fate and was gravity assisted into a new trajectory was the one for him to watch more carefully. Seven years after beginning his search Jaime found what he was looking for. What he found alarmed him greatly.

Almost three years earlier, a " gravitational bump" sent an asteroid in the asteroid belt around Jupiter—altering its course. Now it was headed on a new course, and *if* Jaime's calculations were correct, this course was going to bring it very close—perilously close—to the orbit of Earth.

This 6.5-kilometer-wide asteroid was the anomaly Jaime was looking for.

Jaime calculated that the new trajectory of the asteroid would take it very close to Earth, coming within 15,000 to 75,000 kilometers. When it passed, in about three months' time, it would be brighter than Haley's comet by a factor of four. Then it would continue on its journey around the sun, out to Jupiter again, thus completing it's *first* new orbit.

Each subsequent orbit would take a little more than five years to complete. And each time, mathematically, it could be coming closer to Earth.

Jaime thought to himself: What a rarity. If it came within 15,000 kilometers, *potentially*, it would be considered a once-in-a-three-million-years asteroid. If it hit Earth it would be a once-in-a-30-million-years asteroid. Jupiter ordinarily acted like an asteroid magnet, protecting the planets, the Earth's Moon, and larger asteroids. But this time it was bringing danger right to Earth's doorstep. An asteroid several times smaller than this struck the Earth three million years before. One twice the size hit 65+ million years before, wiping out the dinosaurs and fueling the ascent of mammals and humankind. Each time, Jupiter played an indispensable role in the process.

Jaime brought his findings to Raine. He diligently explained to him the first part of his study: "Look, I spent three years monitoring the asteroid's movements, just in case I was wrong. But so far my calculations have held up. On its first pass it won't hit. If I'm correct, the second pass will bring it closer. The third pass will be truly dangerous. Lethal? Well, not for the planet, but for us sojourners on this rock, that is to say, humanity? Yes. as you know, Raine, if it comes within 15,000 kilometers of the Earth the gravitational pull will warp its orbit, even if by just a fraction. On the third pass it will be relentlessly pulled in, or at least there's a strong chance it would be. We'll know better after the first pass. Better still, after the second. Then we will be able to make more precise calculations. With all these caveats, I believe there is a chance the asteroid will strike Earth, on the third pass."

"How can you be sure about the effects?" Raine asked. "Some would say that's too pessimistic. Maybe a few humans, small groups of humans, would survive."

"Well, we can let it collide. Then we can find out."

"On the third pass? Not before? That's the danger?"

"Yes."

"About eleven years from now?"

"Eleven years, two months, 22 days, four hours, 27 minutes from now, if nothing else changes. But unlike other potentially dangerous asteroids, we will have time to study this one. Maybe that's the only good thing about this potential tragedy."

"Is that calculation based on 15,000 kilometers or 75,000 kilometers?"

"15,000 kilometers. Let's just call it a one-fifth chance. This being its first new orbit there is inevitable uncertainty. Of course, that could change in the next three months, so I hesitate..."

"So it isn't eleven years, two months, 22 days et cetera, Jaime. You can get away with that fuzzy way of thinking with me, but you can't get away with that with the board. You have to tell them it's a one-fifth chance. You're insisting on what? *That's not accuracy. That's guesswork.*"

"The rock is big. That's what makes it different. It's 6.5-kilometers wide. Once it comes closer than 8,000 kilometers, pulled in it will be. Our estimations become less guesswork. Past a certain point, gravity is inevitably going to pull it in."

"And what if the asteroid misses by more than 15,000 but less than 75,000 kilometers?"

"Calculations could be wrong, but if this asteroid comes within 8,000 kilometers on the third pass, it'll be pulled," Jaime said. "That being said, this has the makings of a one-of-a-kind."

"Time for caution?" Raine muttered to himself. Jaime's words impressed Raine deeply. He stood motionless for a while. Jaime didn't dare break the silence. Raine seemed to be gazing at some distant point. He was visibly struggling with something. "As you know, we could be blindsided by an asteroid without any warning time. Or, in the case of a larger object, we could know about it's possible impact, but only six months in advance, therefore not enough time to do anything about it. But with your asteroid we may have time to do something about it."

"Is it a matter of bad luck or beginner's curse?" Jaime asked. "Indeed, the better way to define it is to say it's a random fluke. A random fluke I discovered. Everything about this asteroid creeps me out. As I said, this asteroid is one-half the size of the one that killed the dinosaurs. And it may be harder, denser, than the big one. Even an asteroid one-tenth that size would do incredible damage. At its present size it's larger than a quarter of Jupiter's moons. Now this is where I'm getting even more speculative, I know, but this is where my calculations lead me. There are three places on Earth where the asteroid is likely to intersect, assuming everything happens the way I expect it to happen: first, the South Atlantic Ocean, a bit northeast of the tip of South America; second Antarctica; third just south of the eastern edge of Australia. I think it will be Antarctica. I only mention the other two points because something could happen when the asteroid hits the atmosphere. But I think it will hit Antarctica. That's hitting land! We should send a scientific team, or at least a couple of guys, down there right away, to study the terrain."

"Wait a minute," Raine said. "Hold on. Slow down. You're getting ahead of me. And you're getting ahead of yourself. Get the scientific community to send a team down there now? Why?"

"If they were predisposed to sending a team down there for other purposes, why not add another purpose on top? *Get them thinking. Get them started. Give them something to do so they'll be more predisposed to seeing the threat.* Hitting open ocean, flat ice, solid mountains, makes a difference. Throwing up dust rather than a mixture of dust and water vapor, both would be devastating, but the outcome could be different. And even if we have to recalibrate where this asteroid is likely to hit, data about the impact area will be valuable to us. It sets a baseline. In fact, wherever it lands, this data will be valuable. We might be able to figure out which is more likely: the extinction of all of humanity, or something short of that."

"I can just imagine the objections," Raine said. "You realize how stupendously random this event is."

"Yes."

"Do the calculations again."

"Of course I will. I've done them over and over. I've done them in my sleep."

"Have someone... Not just peer review. Randomize it. See what comes up."

"Okay, excellent, right away. Would three sets of calculations suffice?"

"Send them out to four. Hartman for sure. The board thinks he's as close to infallible as any scientist could be. It's going to be hard to convince the authorities with just your numbers. His numbers, arrived at independently, would be interpreted as more impressive."

"I shall. Not too hard to convince our colleagues to participate when you consider what's at stake."

"If you get unanimous confirmation from three out of four, I'll start working on getting the scientific community to look into sending a team down to the mountains of Antarctica. But I warn you, we may have to wait until after the first pass before I can hit pay dirt on that."

"Takes time. That's right. That's why I want to get started now. One more thing that may increase your chances at persuasion."

"Yes?"

"The asteroid is large enough to punch it. At the other end of the Earth there will be volcanoes, other things squirting out. There will be a condition of seismic super-hyperactivity. If the rock is harder than the one that did in the dinosaurs, it could be more devastating. Dirt and debris floating around the Earth for years and years. It'll get cold. There'll be a big die out. Not as big as the one 65+ million years ago that destroyed 70 percent of life, but big enough. We can't delay this."

"If we can get scientists," Raine said, "even just a small party of them down to Antarctica anytime soon..."

"Make it happen," Jaime said. "Sooner is better. Get them to at least understand that this asteroid is not like others we've studied in the past. If we can publicize it then everyone will sit up and take notice."

Raine came back to Jaime four weeks later with an answer.

"The arguments didn't work," Raine said in a dejected voice. "I'm not surprised. The authorities aren't biting. They aren't convinced this represents an emergency. Not yet. To them, this isn't urgent enough. After all, if it swings out, say, 45,000 kilometers it's impossible for it to hit the Earth on the third or the 3,000th pass. Study the phenomenon, sure. They're on board for that."

"But you showed them that all the mathematicians came up

with something related to what I'm saying," Jaime retorted. "Hartman. Hartman said he wasn't as clear on the numbers as I was but he said of all the things to be frightened of this is it. The other three mathematicians were even more uncertain of the numbers, but they all agreed that going out tens of thousands of years there was nothing more ominous and dangerous than this asteroid. You showed them, didn't you? This isn't just me."

Raine smiled grimly. "They just said: 'Come back with better numbers, then we'll look at it. This is 11 years away, or it could be 400,000 years away, or it may never happen. Anything can happen to that rock between now and then. We need more information. I told you this might happen. And why the location? Antarctica? Hartman and the other mathematicians helped us but not enough."

"This is unfair," Jaime said. "I did my work."

Jaime looked perturbed. He not only looked disappointed, but his sense of disappointment was turning into something gloomier.

"But I got them to agree that if the number on the first pass is 15,000 kilometers or less, they'll allocate resources," Raine said. "A 15,000 kilometer pass means an Antarctica crash-point is possible on the third pass—that's assuming all the rest happens as you say it will. Then they'll agree to the Antarctic expedition. Getting the first number right lends credibility to all subsequent numbers. And you're right, they want to get the ball rolling on this. A two-man helioplane mission is going down to Antarctica in five months time. The board is now willing to call this the most stupendous discovery in modern times. Well, that's real progress. So if your numbers on the 15,000 kilometers pass is correct, we're in."

"So what did you do?" Jaime asked. "How did you manage it?"

"I thought it through," Raine said. "Changed my tactics. Came up with a completely different argument. I remembered what you said about risk insurance."

Raine smiled. "I realized that what was the most important thing to them was to lower the level of fear. If they falsely dubbed my initial presentation as an alarmist scare tactic, I had to alter my approach. Fortunately, because of my age, and because I had never made such a request before, they allowed me a second chance. So I came back a second time and said, 'make this your first-of-its-kind cosmic fire drill. Doesn't matter how likely the event is or not. You never expect the building you work in to catch fire and to be trapped inside, right? But don't you still have fire drills anyway? That's what this is. That's the analogy. It's a fire drill.' And the argument seemed to carry the day. Of course, having this research piggyback on an existing expedition cut the cost and I'm sure that was a factor in their decision, too."

"Risk insurance!" Jaime exclaimed.

"That's science," Raine said with a huge grin. "Or, at least, that's how you get around the moats they dig, the walls they throw up, just to keep us out. It's a beginning. They're going to call it 'The Worldwide Asteroid Warning System.' That's the name. It's a start. Technically, you started it. But we let them take credit. Let them name it. Define it. That way they move. Always let them name the project. Rule number one in grant seeking. So if in eight weeks the asteroid does its first pass at 15,000 kilometers, this will help vindicate your numbers going all the way out to the third pass. *This has not established its orbit yet, except in your head.* We'll learn even more on the second pass."

"You're a genius," Jaime said. "I like the name. Worldwide Asteroid Warning System."

A week before the pass, after the luxury of being able to conduct more precise computer simulations, Jaime was able to predict: "At least a 42 percent chance it will be 1000 kilometers less than 15,500 kilometers. Well at least the percentages are better."

Then it happened. The pass occurred. And, as Jaime predicted, the asteroid came within less than 15,000 kilometers.

The night sky showed the powerful light of the asteroid while it did its swing toward the Sun. People were in awe of the passing phenomenon.

"We need to get all the space agencies informed," Jaime said.

"Worst case scenario, we've only got eleven years."

"Listen to the general," Raine said. "Listen to Jaime. Listen to the man. He has all the answers."

"No, just a Forandi brother," Jaime replied. "That's all. No more than that. With that base, however, with that foundation, everything is..."

Chapter Eight

2673 A.G., four months later.

I T WAS THE LAST DAY of the last week of the last month of summer, the high point of Antarctic warmth.

"It looks like the surface of the moon down there," the co-pilot of the helioplane said as they crossed the southern tip of Marie Byrd Land Island.

"Wait till you see Antarctica," the pilot said. "I know this is your first trip to the Southland. I've flown over this continent a dozen times over the last 30 years."

Twenty minutes later they were crossing the blue-green sheen of the waters of the hugely enlarged and elongated Ross Sea. Two thousand five hundred years before, the Ross Sea and Ross Ice Sheet were just barely 400 miles long, 300 miles wide. Now, the Ross Sea completely separated Antarctica from the old Peninsula, Thurston Island, Ellsworth Island, and Marie Byrd Island. There were 2,414 kilometers of navigable ocean, conjoining the Ross Sea with the old (melted) former Ronne Ice Shelf in the north, leaving Antarctica without a land-bridge of ice to the outer islands.

The pilot and co-pilot could see the Trans Antarctic Mountain Chain in the distance.

"Thank Gaia we don't have to land on that *monstrosity*," the co-pilot said, scanning the towering mountains ahead.

"Well, we might have to. We might have to land somewhere in between those peaks," the pilot replied.

"Only if we pick up a signal. And you've never picked up a signal yet, right captain?"

"Right. But you never know. Forty years ago, they picked up a signal in the Himalayas. One hundred years ago they picked up a signal in the Sahara, and 50 years after that, in the Andes. Two hundred years ago, they picked up two signals in the Gobi desert. All five of those signals were old. And what did they highlight? Remnants of old stone buildings, sometimes just the remnants of foundation stones. Five signals. What did they tell us about the past or the present? A faint pulse from the past. The Gobi desert sites had some high-value tech memory apparatus stored carefully underground there, a string of eighteen mini-computers, fine acquisitions for our tech museums, but we weren't able to access any of the information *inside* the mothballed computers. Codes too old. Or corrupted. What's the point? The Himalayas site was more limited. Ancient religious relics. Rich in ancient religious relics. But no technology, no science, therefore, *no information*."

This type of interest in the record of ancient history was of a serious concern to the pilot, but to the co-pilot, the interest—not to mention the concern—was nil.

But the co-pilot decided to humor his boss nonetheless. "Yes, as in, *you never know*... I don't understand your fascination with these ghost signals, captain."

The pilot shrugged. "We're explorers. Signals were placed by ancients in extremely remote places in the world. The Gobi Desert, the Andes, the Sahara Desert, the Himalayas."

Thomson the co-pilot showed his indifference and his skepticism. "But think of all the ice down here. You said so yourself. For that reason alone, Antarctica would not be a good site. Where are the guarantees of protection, of permanency? You don't want to place anything on ice. It just turns into water. Placing a signal in Antarctica? Why here?"

"Why not? They placed signals elsewhere," the pilot said.

"In deep secure valleys, in protected valleys, of the Andes and

Himalayas Mountains," the co-pilot countered. "Does such a comparative advantage exist here?"

"Fair point."

"They've never gotten a signal because there is no signal. Dream on, captain."

"I will dream on," the captain said. "I will."

"Explain again, why do we have to cross the dry valleys?" the co-pilot asked.

"I don't know. They just added this on to our a primary mission—something to do with space. Let's do our job. That's what we're paid to do. I've had two occasions were I was authorized to fly over dry valleys. In the first instance, all our instruments were down, because of an impending storm. In the second, we had to travel at maximum speed. This time it will be at one tenth maximum speed. We're going to stroll along. We'll be able to actually see concrete things down there. Take temperature readings. Reconfirm topology. I'm excited. Let's do what we're paid to do."

It was when they were crossing Taylor Valley that something extraordinary happened. On the pilot's audio-visual signal screen, there was a blip. At first he thought he had just imagined it. Then there was another. Then another. The pilot slowed the helioplane more, down to 55 kilometers per hour.

"The screen's just acting up," the co-pilot said.

"Maybe," the pilot said. "Let's get closer."

As they followed the tracer blips, the blips became more frequent.

"What is this, this is strange," the pilot said. He dropped the helioplane down to 25 meters and slowed the air speed to 30 kilometers per hour.

"Look at the screen!" the pilot said. At first, the blips were coming in at intervals of every 15 seconds, then every eight seconds, then every four seconds. They were getting closer.

When the frequency of the blips occurred every two seconds, the co-pilot was able to spot the site. What's that? Is there something there? *What's that?* It stands out. When they got closer the co-pilot could make out something that resembled a badly faded red stripe. Down there?"

"Where?"

"Down there, captain. Look. Don't you see it?"

"Yes. I think we found something. There's something there. In a dry valley, Thomson!"

"Dry valley? What does that mean, captain?"

"No snow has fallen here for thousands of years, Thomson. That's what it means. It means nothing has changed here over thousands of years. The dry valleys of Antarctica are unique in the world. Here's how it works. Any snow that falls here sublimates, going directly from ice to vapor without passing through a liquid state. The same happens to the ice in any of the glacial tongues that try to invade. As a result, glaciers come to an abrupt end without a melt stream runoff. The valleys are kept dry by katabatic winds. These high-velocity winds are cold and extremely dry. They make the valleys some of the driest places on Earth."

"Bare earth, dryness," the co-pilot said.

"Oh, if you can't see how thrilling this is," the pilot said. "There's something down there. Can you make it out, Thomson? What's that? *What's that?*"

"It's hard to make out, captain. Looks like a large lump."

They'd gotten so close the pilot was ready to land the helioplane, just hovering seven meters above the site. "I think it's a body. A mummy? Think of it, Thomson! Preserved? If my eyes aren't deceiving me. For the love of Gaia, this is exciting!"

They landed the helioplane ten meters away.

Chapter Nine

I T TOOK SEEMINGLY FOREVER to penetrate the frozen earth. They broke the tip off one of their shovels. Eventually the pilot and co-pilot rigged up a pneumatic drill from the helioplane itself. It worked. Less than two feet down, they hit metal. All the time they were working there was the mummy's face, staring at them. The grin was bizarre and hideous-looking.

"Look at that ugly man's mug, captain," Thomson said. "Look at him. The lines on his face... Look at the creases. What has he been doing all this time? He's ancient."

The pilot laughed. "What kind of man would deliberately leave his body exposed here."

"Deliberately?"

"I mean that's assuming he did this on purpose. I mean why is it that this body happens to be here? Did he know in advance, in all this coldness and dryness, his body would be preserved? Why would he do such a thing?"

"An eccentric?" the co-pilot suggested in a tentative voice. He shrugged his shoulders.

"Oh yeah, right," the pilot nodded. "An eccentric. That explains everything."

"Maybe there was nobody around to bury him? Maybe that's why he's here?"

"That makes sense."

When they cleared away the dirt, they realized they had uncovered a 20 foot by 3 foot conical metal capsule. They found the door to open it. They rigged up a blowtorch to expand and make the hinges more pliable. Then it was easy to open.

"I'm hoping for the mother lode," the co-pilot said in anticipation. They opened the door to the capsule. They searched inside. It took them about half an hour to sift through all the materials. "No gold!" the co-pilot said at last in a dejected voice. "No precious stones! No emeralds! No rubies! No diamonds! No lucre! No silver!" He threw his hands in the air. "Ancient writing materials! Worthless. You're killing me!" He looked at the mummified body lying sideways just a meter away. "Is that what you've been protecting all this time? Words! From the past!"

Inside there had been a mass of material carefully arranged: picture books, hand-written scriptures, printed pages, stacks of computer disks, scaled down micro-maps, cylinders of music, altogether five different codices of information.

The pilot and co-pilot carried all the materials up the ladder portion by portion and deposited them in the helioplane.

"They've never found anything like this before," the pilot said. "Those disks, I've seen in tech museums. They contain data. But without a computer to read them, they're useless. The maps are good though. And I bet you they can do something with the music cylinders. The picture books, the hand-written scriptures, the printed pages, they're priceless. *We can digest them. We can interpret them*. This could be the greatest find of all."

The co-pilot mumbled dejectedly, "No gold."

Chapter Ten

Four months later.

"YOU'RE NOT GOING TO BELIEVE THIS," Auger said. "They found a whole new cache of documents. From the ancients! Oh, this is incredible. We could have been waiting forever for something like this to happen. We *have* been waiting forever. You really don't understand what the hell I'm talking about, do you?"

"Slow down," Pius pleaded

"I'm not kidding Pius..."

"Documents you said?"

"Documents."

"Okay. What does that mean?"

"Documents found in a time capsule buried more than 2,500 years ago, actually, to be more precise, 2663 years ago. Printed pages, hand-written scriptures, picture books, computer files, maps, music cylinders. Some of the computer data is of course useless to us. Junk. But the rest of it is a treasure trove of information."

"Found where?" Pius asked.

"In Antarctica!"

"Wha...?" Pius asked. "What are you talking about? Don't do this to me. If this is one of your ideas of a joke, Auger, I'm not in the mood."

Pius did the math on 2,663 years. His eyes lit up. "I get it. You mean....events *after* 2051 A.D.! Just at the beginnings of the great

worldwide collapse? If that is so, this is unheard of." In a soft voice
Pius added, "This is a revolutionary find."

"No kidding!" Auger said. "And a breakthrough for us!"

"Jeez," Pius said. "This could cover the first 12 years of the loa,"
he said, laughing nervously. "I mean when did this happen?"

"It was in the news. These astronomers were studying a potential impact...."

"An impact?"

"An asteroid impact. Doesn't matter. They find these amazing documents that are 2,663 years old! It's in old calendar. But
the dates are there! It was easy for them to make the calculations.
They're delivering all of it to us tomorrow morning!"

"Tomorrow?"

"Tomorrow. 10 a.m. Without restrictions. No religious restrictions whatsoever. We have complete freedom to codify. It's because
of our books covering events leading up to the loa that they chose
us for this great privilege. The authorities think we're perfect for the
job. We have the exclusive rights. They're going to let us pore over
the papers to our heart's content."

"You're kidding."

"You keep repeating that. All to ourselves. The best research
project in 2,700 years, falling into our laps."

"You say there will be no restrictions?" Pius asked. "This may be
true, but it may not last."

"From a historian's point of view," Auger said, "this is bigger
than the partially burned diaries buried in old Montreal, Canada,
2111 A.D. (60 A.G.)—all locked up, which we have not been
allowed to study. Bigger than the memory sticks found in the old
ruins of Singapore, 2236 A.D. (185 A.G.)—all locked up, which
we have not been allowed to study. Bigger than the old books, 200
of them, found among the Vorungi around 1300 A.G. in central
Europe."

"Give me specifics again about how these scientists chanced
upon these?" Pius asked.

"It reads part Odyssey-like adventure, part dumb luck science. Part of the area these pilots in the helioplane were called upon to analyze and chart took them into a dry valley in Antarctica. They picked up a signal. The signal emanated from a beaming device that had been placed in Taylor Valley in 2063 A.D. Or year Gaia 12, new age Gaia. The scientists have speculated that the conditions of this valley is exactly the same as it was 2,700 years ago, thus why they buried the documents there. As to why they buried them in such a remote place, the scientists have speculated that the buriers didn't want the documents to be discovered until way into the future, this they confirmed when they learned that the beaming signal had not been activated until 2,400 years after it was set, and was only emitted once every three years for 261 years, from 2,400 to the present. This is the wildest, most bizarre part of this discovery: In a very shallow indenture, a 20 foot by three foot conical shell, of a fifty-kilogram nuclear warhead, was found, buried just beneath the surface. This conical shell, supposedly originally built to house a nuclear weapon, had been turned into a storage unit to house a home for a library-for-the-future, time capsule. September Snow, who had fought against the Gaia-Domes is sending us brand-new information unfiltered or censored by the records of the Gaia-Domes. Do you see what information we've dug up? We are two lucky historians. I may have to change the title of my book after studying these documents. Who knows what truths we may uncover?"

Pius was amazed. Like Auger, he was beside himself.

Auger continued. "I'm telling you. Well, here's the part that's truly amazing. They also found a dried-out mummy, lying for eons right next to the capsule. Preliminary evidence suggests the corpse is the same age as the capsule itself. They're calling the mummy, Capsule Man. Strange, isn't it? Well, it appears this scribe left some hand-written papers in the time-capsule that had only been penned just before the documents were buried. Apparently, he was a poet. They represent the only direct records we have from the first three months of 2063 A.D. I intend on spending a lot of time studying them."

"It is amazing," Pius said.

Twelve months later, Zoia burst into the room. The twelve-year-old daughter of Auger was being her typically free-spirited self. Auger and Pius had been working on their new time-capsule material in a frenzy, albeit with an academic's devotion to not making mistakes.

Zoia was not just an inconvenience, a 'thing' deposited in the corner, nor was this arrangement just an alternative to employing a baby-sitter or nanny. Auger's academic office was Zoia's domain. She ruled it like it was her roost. Auger loved his daughter. Spoiled her? Well, of course.

Zoia had become such a mascot in the department of World History, and had become so popular among the students and the professors in the department, that the administrators decided to ignore the rules making her case the one and only exception to the no-child restriction.

Like a hurricane, like a tornado, like an indomitable force of nature, between the ages of three to nine years old, Zoia had raced around the office with complete abandon. Or she sat in the corner, reading from her father's large collection of books.

But when Zoia turned twelve she decided she had become more mature.

There was a brief knock on the door. And without even waiting for a response from Auger, Pius entered the room. He gave Zoia a semi-indulgent, semi-approving nod.

"Uncle Pius!" Zoia said. "The man who always comes."

"Zoia," Pius murmured, nodding slightly. "I'm just down the hall."

Seated at his desk, at last, Auger looked up from his work.

"Yes, Pius, I do let Zoia do exactly as she wants. And I approve. I don't worry about it. She will become a well-formed adult human being, I'm sure of it."

"She runs this place, you don't," Pius observed. As he made this comment he smiled warmly at Zoia.

Zoia was doing her best *not* to appear to be her younger self, something she had especially been trying to shake off during the previous year. In just one year, at least mentally, she had grown into a person with the knowledge and memory of an adult.

"She reads voraciously," Auger said. "So don't be put off by her antics or occasional wildness. She's kind of settled down too. The range of her reading has grown by leaps and bounds."

"Yes," Pius said, "if she chooses to, she will become a scholar like her father some day." He smiled again approvingly. "Oh, I almost forgot the purpose of my visit. For the time being, the authorities are going to keep the ban on releasing information to the public dealing with events between 2051 A.D. and 2063 A.D. in the documents."

"All of them?"

"No, not all of them. Only a few of them."

"Did the Obsidian Order have a hand in this?" Auger asked angrily.

"Of course. They cited some archaic law about protection of morals and public decency. You know the drill. But it goes deeper than that. The secular authorities want to go slow on this too, Auger. They're not frightened about the information as such. They're willing to release 95 percent of the documents. All of the materials dealing with the events prior to 2051 A.D. They're just leery about how believers in the Gaia faith will take the later, more controversial parts."

"Have they cited reasons for this?"

"I can name a few. According to the documents, the Gaia-Domes were in full attack mode to enact a genocidal policy toward all opposition, and their euthanasia policy toward all those over the age of sixty. Everything in the documents suggest that September Snow is not a Goddess at all. In fact, they suggest she was a warrior against the Gaia-Domes. There is an even greater problem. The

documents make it abundantly clear that not just the top leadership of the Gaia-Domes were guilty of 'excesses,' as our own THE
BLESSINGS OF GAIA DOCUMENT so firmly stipulates. It seems
responsibility and culpability ran deep, ran all the way down through
the Gaia-Dome top-down organization, ran through the security
services, through the ranks of Suits, Upper-Minds, Middle-middles,
down to the bottom, all the way to the level of slaves. In many of the
relevant documents, the security services were seen as being responsible for unspeakable acts. This is serious business, Auger! Then you
pour oil on the fire."

"I don't pour oil on fire."

"You do. Or you will. If you advocate for immediate release of
all documents before we've had a chance to properly vet them."

"Well, that's just full disclosure. It's being a responsible scholar.
And a responsible citizen, I might add."

"You insist on making the claim that the cursive handwriting
on the pages of those of the Capsule Man—or as you call him, the
Curmudgeon, are from the hand of Tom Novak. In other words,
Capsule Man and Tom Novak are the same person. With what proof
do you make such a claim? The documents associated with Capsule
Man are not to be shown to anyone, anyhow. Do you realize there
are places in his pages where he repeatedly makes fun of the Gaia
religion!"

"The thoughts of the Curmudgeon run closely parallel," Auger
said, "so closely parallel, to the thoughts of Tom Novak. What other
conclusion can I come to?"

"According to what?" Pius asked in exasperation. "According to
THE BLESSINGS OF GAIA DOCUMENT? We don't know!"

"Well, if we had independent documents that included events
after 2063 A.D., we'd find out what happened to Tom afterwards,
wouldn't we?" Auger said. "We have only what we have to work
with. But I will defer to your judgment. We will bracket off for now
the question that the Capsule Man and Tom Novak are the same
person. But I'm going to explore the possibility. And I believe the

authorities will lift the ban on the release, eventually."

"Oh, they've come out with the finding."

"What finding?"

"You didn't hear it? Course not. Too busy pouring over the Capsule Man's cursive scrawl. There's been talk..."

"What?"

"Just a notification," Pius said. "There may be a possibility of an asteroid impact on the horizon."

"Oh, percentages, percentages. It's just them doing their fear-mongering again."

"Fear-mongering? Scientists are fearing the worse. Too premature to come to an absolute conclusion yet, it's too soon...but."

"But what? Would you please get to the point."

"This asteroid could cause human extinction."

"Out of here! You jest."

"I don't. The asteroid's pass in 2578 will confirm or not confirm our worst fears. But already they're making preparations. They're gearing up to make a rocket program so they can make an intervention. They're planning for the worst."

"So it's not confirmed?"

"Exact science isn't...well...always...entirely *exact*," Pius said. "Right after the second pass they'll know better. In less than five years. They're preparing for the worst now though."

"Right."

There was long pause. Auger started tapping his fingers nervously on his desk.

"Well, that's all peachy-keen great, isn't it now, isn't it. Now can I get back to my work?"

"I'm sure that's what a lot of people are saying. Something along those lines."

Zoia looked out from behind a book rack with a grin on her face. "Are you trying to scare me? Suggesting the world is coming to an end?" she asked.

"Of course not," Auger said. "Pius didn't mean that at all!"

Auger gave Pius a withering look. "Isn't that right?"

Pius nodded his head.

"World's not going to end, Zoia," Pius said. "I was just speaking, well. You should get back to your reading. You shouldn't be eavesdropping on us. Not the proper way..."

"See?" Auger interrupted. "Pius, look what you've started. Look at the can of worms you've opened up. That's what all this alarmist talk can lead to. Zoia is too smart to be frightened, but others younger than her could be frightened. Asteroids attacking humans. Of course we know it's more complicated than that, but imagine, a child's imagination. You want to talk about censorship in the interest of maintaining public order, why would the public be so concerned about something that happened more than 2,600 years ago? When you talk about the extinction of humanity, who cares what these good-for-nothing Gaia-Dome people were up to back then! Why can't we just do our work? How is that going to matter about what is happening in the present?"

"It does matter what happened more than 2,600 years ago," Pius said in a deeply earnest voice. "It does matter. There's something very large at stake here. For the Obsidian Order? Yes, naturally so. You'd expect that. But for all the believers in the Goddess September Snow and the saintly Iona as well. What do you know about that? And for all the believers in the Gaia faith, you know, garden variety general believers. Yes, even if you don't think so, it'll affect them. Now, don't object. I know what you're thinking. Even for people living in the present who have no *apparent* belief in Gaia, who think that what happened in ancient times could be of no concern to them, who are so sophisticated and so modern and who take pride in their sophistication and modernity, this is going to be big, Auger. Because it involves truth, ancient truth, modern truth, either way. Truth is put to the test. It's bigger than you realize."

"Yes, well..." Auger began.

"What is truth?" Pius interrupted. "Can we know what it is? Is truth merely *relative*? That's a very modern idea. It's also very dangerous. Once we've allowed the public discussion to erode the fundamentals of the absolutism of truth, we knock away the ground, the soil, the land, upon which we stand. What is truth? If we end up saying we cannot know what that thing is, what is then left?"

"The drama queen of truth," Auger said. "Yeah, yeah, yeah. You give people too little credit. You make it sound so stark and final and 'yea or nay' existential. Can we not trust people with the truth? Isn't that the point of the Enlightenment Project? After all, you coined the term. Let's let truth find its own way."

"Let the chips fall where they may?" Pius asked. "I get it. You understand people better than I do. I admit it. You do. That's your strength. But I understand belief, especially—the nature and onto-logical base of belief in its relationship to provisional, contingent, and universal faith; and in its relationship to the simplest forms of faith too, better than you do. We'll see. Perhaps I'm wrong. Or I'll be proven wrong in the future. As long as they won't let us release our findings, it's still an open question."

"I know there's something philosophically wrong with what you're saying," Auger said, scratching his head. "But, for the moment, I'll suspend judgment. However, I do maintain that we should trust people to figure out things for themselves. No authority, certainly not yours or mine, should take freedom away from people. I guess that's why I simply cannot be religious in the way that you are."

Zoia stepped forward. Standing between Pius and Auger, she turned and addressed Pius, "Should people be kept in the dark, as if they were children?"

Pius replied, "People, your ancestors, going back more than 100 generations, stayed in the dark, living in caves. That was Gaia. That was the origins of our religion. That was *their* religion, not *ours*. I suppose there probably wasn't a lot of talk and debate back then about the notion of truth, as they were too busy trying to keep the spark of humanity alive for the future."

Zoia gave Pius a small smile. "It's pleasant when I'm able to get a rise out of you."

"There you go again," Auger said. "You evade the issue, Pius. Always exiting through the backdoor. Always ducking out. Always justifying repression. The time of sacrifice! Like those benefits of Gaia cancel everything out, all the bad stuff. Even when you're addressing my 12-year-old daughter, you sanctify the corruptions of the establishment today with the dubious sanctity of thousands of years ago. Capsule Man, the Curmudgeon, he was sort of dismissive of Gaia religion. Apparently, he even on occasion laughed at it! Saw it—at least sometimes—as an alien force in the world. But even he had *some* ideas that ran parallel to Gaia doctrine."

"Boys, why don't I get the chance to see you fighting more often?" Zoia asked, placing her body between them, as if her sarcasm was going to prevent them from verbally jousting. "Won't the two of you ever let up? Like a mangy old married couple, eternally squabbling, endlessly needling each other, but devoted to one another."

With love and laughter, Auger, seeing the justice in his own castigation, beamed happily at Zoia. "Look at her! Modernity strikes again. Okay, it's not me. Don't hang this one on me, Pius. You've created The Monster. It's you, Doctor Frankenstein. All I get is an assist."

Zoia grinned with delight at all the attention that was being bestowed upon her. Even with her youth, she was brilliant. Her fondest memory was of her father reading aloud to her Mary Shelley's *Frankenstein* over the course of 24 straight evenings when she was ten-years-old. Those many evenings had opened the door to her, to investigate, and to take great pride, in her studies. "J. S. Mill studied Greek when he was three," Zoia said. "He coined the term dystopia in 1868, creating an antonym for More's *Utopia*. 'One who is too enamored with the siren calls of utopia, even if drawn to them for the best and most noble of reasons, typically ends up becoming a thug, if not an evil-inclined, degenerate fanatic!' Quote attributable to who? Dad? If you please?"

"Yeah, yeah, yeah."

"Quote attributed to pre-Gaia writer, Orsen Pipes," Zoia

answered for her father. Orsen had been one of Zoia's dad's favorite authors from the distant past. Other fiction authors were Franz Kafka and Kurt Vonnegut, their works also among the Antarctica documents. Auger loved their work so much he was successful in placing some of their stuff in the otherwise closed 'Great Gaia Canon of Literature.'

Auger and Pius loved how explosively Zoia dug into the documents found in Antarctica. But Mary Shelley's *Frankenstein* (and some of Kafka) had been part of an earlier Gaia tradition, from earlier sources.

"If I had my way I'd have all the documents released today," Auger declared with finality.

Chapter Eleven

RATHMAN TURNED TWELVE years old. Most of his duties on the ranch were repetitive, but not always boring. Rathman's father taught him special skills that had been passed down for many generations. Most of these lessons involved learning how to survive on his own in the desert for days, with no water, no food, and the barest of clothing.

Rathman enjoyed this more than his father had expected him to. Rathman heartedly embraced the challenge. He gave no indication he was frightened. He just put his head down and went at it. And he succeeded. In the desert, he managed to stay two extra days beyond the allotted time, living off the land.

When his father asked why he had done so, Rathman replied that he wanted to prove his stamina and enthusiasm. "Six days is good," Rathman said. "But eight days is better. I want to live long. I want to know how to survive. There is no other knowledge in this world that is more important than this, I believe."

Nagart was proud of his son. Even at the age of nine, Rathman had already learned the rudiments of good ranching. Or, as his father joked, used the lingo of the Inner World to describe their family's pursuit of a livelihood: "land management."

"What's the meaning of land management?" Nagart asked Rathman. "It sure isn't what the food corporations say it is. It means getting out of the way of the land, molding yourself around the land, doing the land's bidding, not doing what the land was never intended to do. It entails being the silent partner, being the steward. That's what it's all about, yes, being the steward. You don't *own* it. You don't *control* it. You don't *shape* it. And certainly you don't try to shape it to your will. You leave it the way you found it so it will go on the way it went before, for those who follow you. Whatever you take from it, be sure to leave something in return."

Three years later Rathman's father, mother, and two sisters all died. It happened while Rathman had been in the mountains gathering firewood. When Rathman returned home he found them seated at the kitchen table, all slumped over, the food half-eaten on their plates. Oatmeal and barley cakes. He just stared at the bodies, in a state of complete and total incomprehension.

There had been problems with some of the neighbors, boundary disputes over straying animals. But none of these had led to fistfights, much less to threats of death. Water rights had always been a much larger issue. Water was more important than life itself—since life depended on water, but there had been no issues about water for more than 20 years. There had been a drought that had lasted three years, but still it did not cause conflict among the neighboring ranchers.

At that time the girls were three and four. Rathman was not yet a toddler.

Rathman suspected poisoning. He saw the crusts of saliva around the lips of his sisters, his father's hands and arms were extended in a state of extreme rigidity. Rathman's mother looked like she might have been the first to succumb, for she was the one where it looked liked there had been signs of struggle. Her hands were semi-clasped around her throat. But there was no sign of panic among the others. Perhaps they had been poisoned earlier and the bodies arranged around the table after they died. Then Rathman saw a clue to the mystery. The daughters never ate oatmeal with small spoons. Mimnac, Rathman's mother, used to make fun of them because they used spoons that were so large they could barely fit in their mouths when they were small. The way the buttons on Mimnac's dress were fastened at the neck didn't look right either. She had been left-handed, the buttons looked like they had been buttoned—or re-buttoned—by someone who was different. Rathman realized that maybe he was reading too much into the picture but there was something about the setup that just didn't seem right.

All of their sheep and some of their goats had been poisoned several months before. It had happened at other ranches as well, some as near as 40 kilometers away, some as far as 200 kilometers away. In fact there had been an epidemic of poisoning, but to the best of Rathman's knowledge, up until then, no humans had even been poisoned. There had been one person poisoned up in Crail, outside Margo, much farther to the north, but in that case it had been a mentally deficient aunt who was suspect. It was a small world, but where there was experience, everybody came to know about it, that was what life was like on the edge of the desert. What had happened was clear even though the motives were more elusive and murkier.

The ranch was so close to the boundary of the Outer World, Rathman considered the possibility that someone could have come over the boundary. No. Rathman knew that this was something that could only happen in the Inner World. Even over something much smaller than murder, culprits from the Outer World were hunted down and the penalties inflicted against them were swift and draconian. Rathman didn't think it could have been their immediate neighbors either, disputes or not, none of this fit at all.

Now if somebody wanted to make it *look* like it had come from the Outer World then everything did make sense. There was one troubling occurrence. Weapons, clothes, and tools, associated with the Polinic tribe had been found near the ranch, and they suggested a border crossing. With them were iconic totems of the Gaia religion. Wooden figurines of the Goddess September Snow, were also found near by. These sacred objects had been associated exclusively with the so-called primitive Polinic.

But Nagart's family had never had any problems, much less disputes, with the Polinic. And the Polinic were never known to travel this far north, unless for purposes of attending one of their religious festivals. And those only happened once every decade or so.

Rathman used the buckboard to bring a doctor to do an autopsy.

The doctor concluded that Rathman's family had all been poisoned, but he thought the bodies had very likely been moved after they had been poisoned.

The sheriff brought in to investigate the case dismissed concerns about the case out of hand. "There is not enough evidence of anything. I doubt the implication of the Polinic. They are just too unwarlike and docile to do something like this. But we'll keep an eye out to see if something else comes up."

Solving crimes among the outer groups of the Inner World had always had a very low priority from the point of view of law enforcement. In the past, there had been plenty of unsolved crimes. Rathman's family just didn't count for much.

But later, a wicked outsider tried to do the same thing, some 80 kilometers away. But this time he was caught red-handed planting Polinic artifacts before he was able to poison his target, another hardscrabble, survivalist family. But this family had been much better off than Nagart's family had been. Their possessions were a fairly sizable herd of cattle. By virtue of that fact, they had a much larger influence with the law enforcement community and the case was solved.

That was just the way things were done in that part of the world.

All of this didn't matter to Rathman because by the time the culprit had been caught and executed, it was too late. The malicious outsider was tried and executed. Before his sentencing, he even confessed to his crime. He had coveted the Polinic's land. If the Polinic had been charged with the crime of poisoning Rathman's family, and convicted, their lands, all of them, would have been forfeited to the Albu state and then eventually put up for auction. These types of unfair, antiquated laws were still on the books. Pursuant to one of these antiquated laws Nagart's land was confiscated by the Albu state, thus depriving the underage Rathman his inheritance.

Rathman was placed in an orphanage 450 kilometers away. And by the time he had been moved, the legal papers dealing with the case had been, perhaps too conveniently, "lost."

Chapter Twelve

RATHMAN HATED the orphanage at first, but he eventually got used to the place.

He was housed in a large dormitory that took the form of a long, low-ceiling rectangular room. Pinewood bunk beds were arranged three feet apart, in two long rows, 100 beds in all. It was called Dorm Room A, also known as "The Bunk House." It accommodated orphan boys between the ages of 10 and 17. It was located near a dirt path leading to Dorm Room B, also known as "The Rabbit Hutches," accommodating orphan girls in the same age group.

Four hundred meters away there were two other dormitories segregated by gender, accommodating boys and girls between the ages of five and 9. And a kilometer farther there were two more dormitories, actually more nurseries than dorms, for orphans aged two, three, and four.

The eatery, where the orphans took their communal meals, was called—with a *very, very* dark sense of humor, "The Restaurant." The meals were bland and ranged from the very bad—barely edible—to the mediocre. When the orphans were lucky the food was semi-nutritious, but even then, always leaning heavily on the starch. The mess hall was a long, low-ceiling building with six rows of tables and matching benches. It was used for meals, roll call, and breviary. The children took their meals at different intervals, but regardless of the time, the benches were always kept rigorously segregated by gender.

In the orphanage the state of existence for Rathman became simple and simply defined: regimentation, lousy food, close quarters, rigorous discipline, and absence of privacy.

Getting over the initial adjustments, Rathman fit in fairly well. He discovered he was good at adapting—though he wasn't entirely sure if that was a good or a bad thing. Did adjusting to poor conditions mean he'd also be adept at adjusting to better conditions? Probably. In the future.

As his avuncular counselor observed, "It's a lot more effortless and painless going from Hell to Heaven, than it is going from Heaven to Hell."

Rathman was very good at his chores. He attended to them with respect and dignity. His before-school and after-school duties and responsibilities involved mainly the tending of smaller animals: partridges, chickens, pygmy goats, potbellied pigs. Brought up on a ranch, he had already been well trained in animal husbandry. Soon he was put in charge of herding cattle. Though he had to do it on foot, he quickly became very proficient at that too. He was able to walk great distances, even in extreme heat, without suffering from fatigue. In this job he tagged-teamed with five other 15-year-old and 16-year-old orphans, who replaced four 12-year-old deaf-mutes who had been taken in from the Outer World—liberated or captured, depending on one's point of view. They had herded a large herd of cattle from sunup to sundown, seven days a week, without break. All of them fell ill within a few weeks and died.

The nickname "Rathman the Barefoot Herder" stuck to him even after he'd been given a pair of shoes. To him, the moniker was a valuable reminder that his fate could have been worse if he had been born in one of the more benighted parts of the Outer World.

In contrast to virtually all of the other orphans, Rathman excelled at school. Book-learning in general agreed with him and he took to books with a passion. He also learned quickly that the only way to get away from the orphanage, and have any sort of opportunity, as slender as that opportunity might be, was to become educated. He knew he could never return to his father's ranch, so unless they changed the law, which was never going to happen, he would have to prepare to live in the Inner World.

The second year he applied himself even more to his studies, and more than caught up with the other pupils, (only a tiny minority of whom applied themselves to their studies). Two hours a day of schooling began at age eight, raised to four hours at age 15. Rathman's teachers soon realized that they had never encountered a student quite the high caliber of Rathman.

Rathman's reading and writing skills were his strongest suit. It took him merely nine months to learn how to read proficiently, and shortly thereafter he taught himself, in a sort of autodidactic way, how to write. His teachers helped him along too, of course, but largely he propelled himself. In the history of the orphanage, in accomplishing this feat, he was also unique. And in less than three years time, a writer he had become.

What he liked most was reading. The counselor happily loaned Rathman copies of his books and Rathman read them voraciously.

Chapter Thirteen

2678 A.G.

THE SECOND PASS of the asteroid came five years after the first pass. The space agencies had been gearing up with a plan to send an unmanned probe, to be followed by a two-person manned spaceship to intercept the asteroid two months before the third pass—which would probably not be a pass, but a hit. The ship would send explosive charges, proton bombs, designed to slow the asteroid down and send it in a different direction, away from Earth. Some had proposed the alternative of destruction of the rock itself, but that was dismissed absolutely because it would have involved a much larger charge, and therefore, a much larger ship and crew. That would push back the launch date as well. Moreover, disintegrating the asteroid would actually produce many pieces, the debris dispersing in random directions, which would not alleviate the risk to the Earth.

Jug, an early proponent of the project, having been at the helm of Gatetar Industries for five years, had been one of the first to promise an outright gift of a large amount of money, plus free use of Gatetar's space-related facilities. This precipitated a range of donations and grants-in-kind flowing in from the business community around the world.

Jug had been in agreement with the conventional wisdom that the smaller the ship, and the smaller the payload, the better.

He also coined a phrase, (with an assist from his speechwriter, advisor, and former tutor, Jason): "An attack on the asteroid is the closest thing to the moral equivalent of war." Nothing like this crisis has happened since the climate-change, global-warming phenomenon that struck the world millennia ago.

It was not difficult to convince people that they should be profoundly concerned. There were, of course, still doubters among the public. And even among scientists. But now there was no problem getting virtually all of the most influential and prestigious people of the planet—the movers, the shakers—behind the goals of the project, the stakes being so overwhelming clear.

In the Outer World, inhabited by people supposedly more inclined toward primitiveness and superstition, seeing a large asteroid streak by was all well and good, but for those who could not see it directly, Jug deployed the Gatetar Empire's worldwide information machine: magazines, papers, Wallscreen, Internet, radio, et cetera. Word was sent out. A broad net was cast.

Jaime at his observatory had been deeply chagrined by one calculation. It was determined that there was no way of knowing exactly where the asteroid might impact or collide with Earth if it were not successfully intercepted. The most likely place was the Pacific Ocean. That would have meant that Eccles, on the coast, would be destroyed early. Jaime's prediction that it was going to be Antarctica had subsequently been mostly ruled out. Some unknown, faraway object may have exerted just the tiniest gravitational pull, causing the asteroid's path to change just a tiny bit. Even the most precise science wasn't always absolutely precise.

On the first pass Eccles was in the wrong position on the planet during the brightest, closest point of the asteroid's passing. The sun's rays prevented observation. People on the southern tip of South America, parts of Africa, and western Asia, had been able to get glimpses of it. But the second time, on this pass, Eccles' inhabitants could see the asteroid in all its radiant glory between 11:00 p.m. and 4:00 a.m. It was like an explosion streaking across the sky, incredibly bright and getting brighter, then fading, as the Earth revolved. Heading into the sun's glare, at last it was gone from sight.

Zoia, like any other Eccle's inhabitant jaded by materialism and the absence of want, asked herself the question, "If it's going to be absolute annihilation, what was there, now to believe in at all?"

Zoia had enough sense not to ask her father, this penetrating existential question, as she knew she would have received a snappy, if not entirely satisfactory reply, something like: "Life is what you believe in, no matter what else."

At the age of 15, like so many others, Zoia had come to reason that maybe that was enough.

2678 A.G., two weeks after the asteroid's second pass.

Jaime visited Raine at the retirement facility that he had joined upon reaching the age of 89. Raine's health had been deteriorating for several years and he had turned over the management of the Love Observatory to his chief lieutenant seven years before. Jaime had already been placed in charge of the Astronomical Research Team.

Jaime followed a routine of visiting Raine once every two weeks, but this was the first time he had visited him since the news of the second pass of the asteroid had had a chance to circulate.

Propped up with pillows in his bed, Raine said in a plucky way, "You were right about the asteroid, but you were wrong about it crashing into Antarctica. That's why we always make sure we have more than one person to look at things. That's science."

"Yes," Jaime said. "I was wrong. But it got the authorities to take the first baby steps, didn't it? That's what mattered more than being right."

"I'm amazed how far you've gotten."

"Just following my mission."

"Your mission?" Raine asked in a low voice. "I'm glad I'm going to miss the train wreck."

"There won't be a train wreck. The asteroid will not collide with Earth. There is science, technology, human will, focused and directed Promethean effort. All of us working together. Most importantly, working together. This will be out finest hour. We can do this because we know what we're doing. We can do this."

"Too late for me," Raine said in an affectionate voice.

"Oh, you don't know when you're going to die, Raine, so don't assume anything. They are going to send two unmanned runs two years from now. As you know, we sent a ship to a comet 20 years ago. A probe was sent down from the ship and landed. Of course, it landed at a bad angle and fell over. Couldn't conduct many of the tests we wanted to. But it did land. That was quite a feat."

"That target, that comet, was many times bigger than our target asteroid. And it was an unmanned space flight we sent."

"They don't have to land on the asteroid. They just have to hit it. First they're going to send out unmanned spacecraft. They will have to go farther out, the interception point must be farther out in space. Take pictures. Hopefully bring back some rock sample. So we can determine what explosives we'll need. All in preparation for the main event. A manned spacecraft mission. Cost a fortune. A fifth of the worth of the gross collective product of the Inner World for 24 months running. Yes, yes, yes, we have everyone behind this!"

"I'm glad they opted to send unmanned space missions first."

"Yes, you're right. But a manned spacecraft mission has advantages, seeing as cost is no problem. Crew can fix things on the spot if the need should occur."

"You seemed to have everything worked out."

"They are barreling along. They barely keep me in the loop."

"Sixteen years ago, I could have told you not to study it. I could have forbidden your research. I didn't. What did you call it?"

"For purposes of asteroid collision research. And I would have done it anyway if I hadn't received your consent. I would have done it anyway."

"That's right. For purposes of asteroid collision research. How old were you then?"

"Young."

"If you had asked me then I would have guessed you wouldn't have lasted eight years. I would have given you, at most, seven years."

"I would have lasted a thousand. You forget, I'm a Forandi brother."

"Religion!!! *Your religion.* That baffling mystery."

"And I love you too, Raine."

"You know, the amazing thing...." Raine's voice trailed off.

"What's the amazing thing?"

"What's that quote? The Matthew thing? The Forandi thing?"

"When you save the least, the weakest among you, you save the whole of humanity," Jaime said.

"I'm sure that Matthew, whoever he was, only meant it as a figure of speech." Raine said, laughing. "Maybe we know something more than he did."

"Spoken like a true nonbeliever," Jaime said. He reached over and pinched Raine's right cheek. "You know it was so many years ago when you took me in. In more ways than one, you saved my life, Raine."

Eight weeks later, Raine died. The funeral was a small affair, attended by only 80 guests. Everyone took their turns meeting on the apron of the 120-inch telescope platform for the rededication of the Love Observatory. Then there was Raine's service itself, and, in the end, the spreading of Raine's ashes on the precipice overlooking the valley. They were all looking north by west, a spectacular view of Eccles. The 216 story Gatetar Tower could just barely be seen with the naked eye, 70 kilometers away. Jaime gave a speech. It was short. "He was an astrophysicist. He was a scientist. He devoted himself to the study of the stars. He was, by his own admission, a secular man. He was a friend of Man. He was a friend to me. Raine."

It was entirely to the point and it was something that Jaime knew Raine would have liked.

Jug had become very good at running his inherited tech empire. He expanded some of the operations throughout the Inner World, and he became very proficient at cutting his losses whenever that became necessary. He learned it was just as important to know when to stop a particular line of betting and pull one's losses as it was to know when to start afresh and enter into a different round of risk-taking. He was better at volume than product line, but what he was radiantly brilliant at was delegation. He picked his lieutenants well, and these lieutenants picked their subordinates well, too. Jason, his advisor, said: "Just get people to buy our goods and services."

Jug nodded. He knew that Jason would appreciate the gesture, so he cited his father's most famous quote: "Be three steps ahead, and be ruthless."

"I don't know if that's always the wisest piece of advice to take," Jason said. "In that game, there's a winner, to be sure, but there's also a lot of losers. Sometimes it's better just to have a lot of winners."

"I agree," Jug said. "It was tiresome of my father to talk to me like that: Be three steps ahead, and be ruthless. He said that on every one of my birthdays, from age seven to 24. The exception being when I turned 15. He was so pissed off at me for smashing a helio-plane into a wall when I was misbehaving, he didn't acknowledge my birthday. Since then I've learned I don't know how to fly a helio-plane. But it was my favorite birthday. Otherwise, he was consistent. And I did react to it."

"Don't listen," Jason said. "Don't care. Be an heir. Remember what I told you? You can be anybody you like."

"I'm not sure that's true, but I like your advice."

Chapter Fourteen

Nine months later.

'D AD,' WAS A NAME Zoia still liked calling her father. She didn't want to make the thing too formal.

"Look, we can put this off," Auger said, "but at some point we're going to have to address it."

"I could have anticipated this," Zoia said. "Choice of School? Right? Well, that's obvious. The answer is U. Presbyr. Choice of department? Well, that question is more problematic. But don't you want to hear something that I've drummed up in the meantime. The title of my dissertation."

"Yes," Auger said.

Self-mockingly, Zoia curtsied. "Before the Darkness, before the Fall, 2051 A.D., Humanistic Secularism as a failed philosophy. That was the past. It's a good subject. After all, if you take away progress from history, what's left? Two millennium, seven hundred years of darkness."

"Oh, boy," Auger murmured, wishing he could change the subject. "This again."

"Philosophers have always debated the questions of objectivity, rationality, and empiricism, that will be a part of the narrative, of course," Zoia said. "But what I'm more acutely interested in are the beliefs of these people, and even more importantly, the underlying beliefs that the believers believed in, without them being entirely aware of their beliefs. Were they beliefs at all?"

"Okay," Auger said. "Give me a thumbnail sketch. But remember you have the advantage of knowing the results, thousands of years later. You can't blame them for not knowing the future; how everything was going to turn out."

"Agreed," Zoia said, exuding self-confidence. "To be sure, the thumbnail is the humanistic secularist urge where they tried to replace a notion of a deity, whether a limited-power deity or an omniscient, omnipotent deity, with an abstraction called human progress. The whole ideological meta-platform was a replacement of man's 'afterlife' with—tick, tick, tick, in historical time—progress—the default safety net provided by something as frail as—again *default*—not a choice, after all, what's there to replace a religious axiom, here it comes, *the best lessons of the world's greatest literature?* Homer, Dante, Pipes, Kafka, Vonnegut... A poor place to capture all of those of the hitherto, having been obligated to be corralled into a religious crib for too long, to be sure, but most humanistic secularists, for the most part, were proud they were able to rid themselves of *all* faith. But were they able to do that? Human beings must learn to survive and endure without religious consolation. I have no problem with that, that's what you taught me, does it matter if others have a problem with that? To act for the good of a religion, or to act for the good of a society; OR, to act according to the good of Gaia, or to act according to the good of humanity: these are radically different beliefs, but are they not conjoined together by an expression and experience of faith? Or do they have that much in common? It is in this delimiting instance that I define humanistic secularism as having an aspect that is religious in nature, *a hidden one, as it were.* A theology without Gaia, perhaps... Or, as it was in the olden days, a theology without God?"

"Okay," Auger said. "I'm listening."

"Look." Zoia broke into a wide smile. "Why all the fuss? Look, I know, but I mean to go from 9 billion people to 125 million in less than 400 years—then to go down to maybe as few as 40 million people, 1,000 years later? I know, that's a long time, I mean, therefore nobody "seeing" through those many generations what it was: NOT THE BEST TIME IN THE HISTORY OF HUMANITY! It's an eschatological question, recast and reclaimed from the past. By the end of 1000 A.G., they could see where this was leading. What kept them going?"

"In the first instance, you're dealing with the time of the loa, Forbidden Time. Then—in the later case—the second darkness time, that came later, right?"

"Are you rebuking me?" Zoia asked. "I hate it when I can't tell if you're approving or disapproving of me, Father."

"The day it doesn't matter whether I approve or disapprove of you is the day you'll make real progress. A teacher succeeds only when the student exceeds him or her."

Zoia smiled. "Well, that's my default idea of a dissertation. Just spit-balling here."

"I like it. Don't be upset. Look, I thought it over. I know... I know... You don't belong in the World History Department...."

"Now wait, Dad!" Zoi exclaimed.

"No, now listen to me," Auger said. "How about Philosophy?" Auger suddenly looked very pleased with himself. "Wait. Scrap that. Bad idea. Wait. Go directly to it! Why didn't I think of it in the first place? To hold the notion that one can change *anything* by one's participation in a place like U. Presbyr, that would truly be illusionary! The Rhetoric Department! That's the ticket for you. They think they can change everything! Or at least, sneer at everything! Or both at the same time. The place will delight you. And you'll shine there as if you were a magnificently pulsating star!"

Zoia did not resist. She was taking it all in. She temporized. "Wouldn't dream of being in your World History Department, Father, after all, that would be incestuous. That can't happen of course. Screams of nepotism! Shouts of exercise of a corrupt practice of family privilege! It wouldn't look right. You want me close to you, but not too close. But I wish I could be. I understand that privilege must be denied to me. If I could have been in the World History

Department I would have comported myself with grace, dignity, good behavior. But if it's a choice between Philosophy or Rhetoric, I choose the latter. Besides, the Rhetoric instructors and professors let you study anything you like. And everything is so open-ended."

"Done." Auger looked content that what might have turned into a disagreeable task had been concluded so well.

"You spoil me terribly," Zoia said. "You know you do. And you decided it so quickly."

"I did," Auger said. "I wish I could give you your first choice. Not just World History, but it's subset, Ancient World History. But you know I can't do that."

"I'll study my first choice in my spare time. Ancient World History is my home, it always will be."

"Maybe we can make you the mistress of your own department some day."

"Stop it, skip it," Zoia said. "Maybe I can contribute. You're embarrassing me. And you're embarrassing yourself. Let me be like any other ordinary student. That's my fate. Being the daughter of my father."

"You're not like any ordinary student, Zoia," Auger said. "If you haven't figured that out yet, well, you're really in trouble."

"Let's pretend I have to grow up. Here's my idea of how to begin the dissertation. Here goes: 'We live at the end of a fruitful yet slowly dying epoch, where, when looking to the possibility of any type of utopian solution, we turn inevitably to the now empty promises of a once explosive technology. Dangerous to think it? Or dangerous not to think it?'"

"That does sound like 2051 A.D.! The anti-technology thesis? Or, at least, the anti-Utopia-thru-technology thesis? Of all people, I didn't expect you to be infected by that backward-looking virus. Game One, climate change and global warming with the help of mass slaughter in wartime, the Eleven-Years-War, verses humankind, and its technology, the losers. Long, long time ago. Game two, if we defeat the threat of the asteroid through the application of space

technology, technology wins. Thus allowing, in the future, a Game
Three. The oscillations of technology between good and bad, Mary
Shelley and Regis Snow's darker versions verses a more optimistic
version, September Snow's version, Iona's version."

"A rubber match," Zoia said. "You remember the quote you
found in the Antarctica Papers that must have come down through
September Snow, about her late husband. Of course he was the guy
who set up the nuclear-powered, climate-changing wind machines
and was in charge of the entire project for the Gaia-Domes. This is
what he said: Science as a value is in the same metaphysical realm
as the Promethean madness that leads to men striving to become
gods. Perhaps the only ultimate value of human life is to be found in
this Promethean madness. I once believed that *nonsense*. I was once
quoted as having said that. In all its delusional, bombastic overreach.
Seeing the results of my experiment, I know how stupid and false
that was. If we try to command or control nature, on a planetary
scale, we may destroy ourselves." Zoia took a deep breath. "You
can't say that technology, no matter how much lipstick you slap on
the lips of that pig, is going to make that pig look beautiful. Small
wonder the world went agog over Gaia, which is, Father, *ultimately*
a very backward-looking religion."

"It *is* a backward-looking religion," Auger agreed. "Regis Snow,
who was, by the way, never mentioned in THE BLESSINGS OF
GAIA DOCUMENT, sacrificed his life in the attempt to destroy
his own creation, the wind machines. Modern Prometheus and the
Faust legend mixed in one. What if September Snow really did finish
the job for him? What if she destroyed the machines? They didn't
just disappear or self-destruct on their own. You know you have
to do something pretty spectacular to become a Goddess, whether
it's 2130 A.D., or 2679 A.G. I wish we had more comprehensive
records of world events after 2063 A.D.—the aftermath, 40 years
later, 80 years later, something to fill in the gap. What did September Snow do, what was her ultimate gift to humanity, before she
levitated up to heaven? And we learned something that was never

given to us by way of THE BLESSINGS OF GAIA DOCUMENT. Regis Snow smuggled out the detailed plans and diagrams of the wind machines, their points of vulnerability, from the Gaia-dome platform in the diapers of a three-year-old Iona. Daughter and notes smuggled out to the mother, September Snow, by way of pirates. I learned all this from the Antarctica Documents! Stuff of a powerful passion play? What? They didn't know? Or they just cut this large piece of history out of the final version of THE BLESSINGS OF GAIA DOCUMENT because there wasn't enough room for it? A fascinating question. Quit being so negative and gloomy, daughter. Your obsession with Mary Shelley may turn out to be worse than a distraction. You're young."

"Mary Shelley was 19 when she wrote *Frankenstein, A Modern Prometheus,* Father," Zoia countered. "Without the approval of her father or her husband I might add. And because she was a girl, they wouldn't allow her to put her name on the first printing. Author? Anonymous. The rationale? You know this all happened at the time Lord Byron wrote his poem, "Darkness," about a volcanic explosion that caused a Year Without A Summer in the Northern hemisphere. But nobody could admit that Mary Shelley could have written a novel like *Frankenstein.* Do you think they were right in thinking that?"

Chapter Fifteen

Three months later.

"I'M YOUR COUNSELOR, father, mother, best boyfriend, best girlfriend, Ancient World psychologist, Ancient World priest, confidant," the counselor said. "I attest to it. Unprecedented. I can't believe it. Chewed through it like a hungry mouse. Tore through it like a desperate ferret. Ground through it like a deranged badger. Drank the ocean-size syllabus dry like only a child of the desert could. Cruised through the puzzle-games like they were easy as candy, like a buzz saw. What are you? Ward of Eccles? Resident of an orphanage? Long as I've been here, never seen anything like it."

Rathman was uncharacteristically silent.

"Well, that's an accomplishment," the counselor said.

"Thanks counselor."

He shrugged. "They come along with a one time application for a scholarship. First one for U. Presbyr. Reaching to you. To the forgotten. To the downtrodden. You aced it. Beat everyone. First scholarship awarded by U. Presbyr to an orphan from anywhere in the Inner World. I suppose you should be thankful to Albu for allowing you the opportunity to apply for such a one-time prestigious award."

Rathman looked at the counselor with a pained expression.

"No, that was stupid of me," the counselor said. "I take it back. What do you want to study?"

"The Dark Time."

"The *what?*" the counselor asked. "Did I hear you right?"

"Yes. The Dark Time. Beginning with...well...through the prism of Ulm's poetry."

The counselor said in a loud voice, "Ulm's *what?* Lord have mercy! Lost yourself? You think I worked so hard for that. To waste your efforts? To waste all your Gaia-given talents?"

Rathman just shrugged. "I want to study the Dark Time. What's so bad about that? If I can't get there through Ulm's poetry, then, whichever way I can."

The counselor looked unhappy. "Oh, I knew you were strange. But I assumed you were going to study something practical, something with a utility value. A trade. Shoe repair! Makes more sense than studying...what?"

"Ulm's poetry is the only thing we have written, passed down to us, from that time," Rathman said. "Short of the oral traditions, that's all we have left."

"Well, there's a reason for that, because there's nothing there!" The counselor tried to calm himself. "So where do you seek to apply this...*work?* World History Department I imagine?"

"Rhetoric."

The counselor closed his eyes. This was the last straw. "Those... misfits. Disrupters. First poor orphan's scholarship ever. And the money's going to be for...studying Rhetoric? You're not even going to have enough money to live in that place! Eccles is...well...I can't think of a word to describe it. Do you know how much it costs just to eat there?"

"Nobody in their right mind studies the Dark Time," Rathman said. "I understand that. And if they did, they sure wouldn't be studying it by way of Ulm's poetry. Maybe by way of Imaar's theory of *Primitive Man in Darkness.* Or through a SOC study. Anyway, unlike all the other departments, Rhetoric will leave me alone to do the work I wish to do."

"You won't have any competition," the counselor said. "Yeah, I can see that. Your journey. Your choice."

"I can't say I'm going to miss this place much," Rathman added.

"I'll miss you though."

A moment passed. The counselor studied his hands carefully. "I was the first person ever in this orphanage to complete a full education. Ever! That was thirty years ago. All that fine education... guess where I end up? At the same orphanage where I started. You want to study darkness? I'll tell you what darkness is. It's coming to this place when you're three. My mother whose face I only pretend I can remember, was shipped back to the Outer World. She disappeared into an inferno, a real meat grinder, somewhere west of Delos, somewhere east of despair, hell, and misfortune."

"Yes, counselor," Rathman said. "We've talked about this before. At least I'm not going to have to rub shoulders with cowpokes and be forced to fend off some aggressive big fellow who wants to swap spit with me in the shower. And that's a matter I'm obliged to deal with from time to time. Or get eaten up by crazy predators on the range. I don't hear any of the other students saying they had to deal with that one. Unless they confronted a mountain lion in the San Francisco Game Reserve. I don't foresee any of that happening while I'm busy doing my studies at U. Presbyr. In the darkness of the Rhetoric Department."

"So what are you going to do with this education? After you've tasted the delights of Eccles? Want to come back to this place? This orphanage? As a janitor? Replace me as counselor? Or better still, shoe repair."

"This scholarship may open up new opportunities. Maybe I'll be able to stay in Eccles."

"No," the counselor said. "You won't! Apply yourself to leather—either when it's still on the hoof, or when it's treated, tanned, and needs to be applied to footwear. Leather. Eccles is going to eat you alive. It's going to chew you up—bone, gristle, flesh, blood, fingernails, toenails, then spit you out."

"In that event, may I come back and spread my loose bits here and there. Over a garden?" Rathman said. "Fertilize it. And then I won't have to think about things like shoe repair."

Chapter Sixteen

THEY'D BEEN DIGGING all the way up to the Sixth Zone and all the way down from the Twelfth Ward, two parallel lines converging, when they slammed into an underground hole. The cut was an extension of a new subway line on Manhattan island, hoping it's diagonal, north-south pitch would clear up some of the worst traffic congestion that'd been accumulating over the previous fifty years—caused by insane, rapid, massive, vertical development.

What the construction workers and sappers found in their diggings were two large clay jars. They were as old as the hills. All construction had to be immediately halted until a team of trained archaeologists had an opportunity to snoop around, use their brushes, picks, pincers, whiskbrooms to pull out all the valuable stuff, so that the real heroes could bring the dead back to life again in their labs by doing their painstaking restoration.

The two cylinders that they found were half a meter wide in diameter by one meter long, buried in heavily compacted soil, two meters down. One was broken, crushed, and the materials that had been inside had turned to sawdust and gray debris. But the other jar was completely intact, and the hermetic seal had not been breached. What they found made headlines. The contents of the jar came to be known as, "Lloyd's Diaries, a Special Magister's Record of the Earliest Era of the Gaia-Domes, 2051 to 2133 A.D."

Some of the sensationalist press referred to it as: "The greatest find since Tutankhamun," albeit minus gold, precious gems, mummy of the physical presence of the God-man. Just words. It was being celebrated as potentially more important than the Capsule Man's Antarctica Treasure, that had been discovered seven years earlier.

The archeologists finally figured out that Clay Jar One, the damaged one, contained the records of the period of pre-2051 A.D. They learned this from the dates and title recordings stamped on a broken shard. If one of the jars had to be lost, it was extremely lucky that it was this one. Because the other jar contained material from the period of 2051 to 2133, the most important period of history that had not been studied before.

Just like the arrangement seven years previously, the Manhattan subway find was given to the historians Pius and Auger to study exclusively.

After three months of study Pius observed to Auger: "You ought to think the Antarctica Papers had the potential for being subversive, but this stuff goes much, much farther than that. Now we know that Tom was a consort of September Snow. Goddesses are not suppose to be intimate with mere mortals. Even worse, a mortal who was un-Gaia in so many ways, and clearly not a believer."

"Restrain yourself," Auger said. "Sure, Tom was a pre-Gaia thinker. Like Virgil was a pre-Christian thinker. Consider the historical analogy. Why do you think the Christians preserved Virgil's writings? Because in spite of his otherwise condemning paganism, Virgil was seen as being virtuous and wise, in other words, saintly. He was also seen as being a model pre-Christian. Consider that Dante's guide into hell was Virgil? You're making too much of a fuss."

"For a secularist like you I'm making too much of a fuss?" Pius asked. "This is a challenge, a direct challenge, to our faith."

"But, it's a great historical find," Auger said.

"Yes it's a great historical find," Pius replied. "But it radically changes our understanding of that historical period. We find that Tom became a surrogate father for Iona and they hid in the desert, and he raised Iona from the age of five to 13! Just in terms of concrete details, we now know the route September Snow's helioplane took to the hiding place where Iona was raised. Lloyd himself didn't know where they were until he entered negotiations on behalf of the Gaia-Domes with Iona, when she was leader of the rebels on the Colorado plateau, and that was forty years later. We learn everything from Lloyd. But in spite of his honesty and sincerity, he was still a creature of the Gaia-Domes. Also, the rebels under Iona called themselves The Unseeing Watchfulness of Gaia. I can't imagine they could have known how prescient that was going to be, especially in light of the coming of the Dark Time. Oh, last but not least, at one point Lloyd expresses a hope that Iona would turn into a Goddess, especially after September had been such a great saint and all. Now you see how potentially dangerous that is for the Gaia religion. He reversed their status roles."

"He was just being metaphorical," Auger said. This was unusual for Auger. Auger was actually making an argument that favored the integrity of the Gaia religion. "There is nothing literal in that, Pius, he was speaking informally."

"Everything's metaphorical!" Pius erupted in a burst of frustration. "You could suggest that!"

"So, let the truth take us to where the truth wants to take us," Auger said. "And stop worrying about it."

"I thought it was a mistake releasing the controversial bits from the Antarctica Papers. You pushed it so hard. And you won."

"People adapt. It's going to be okay."

"People adapt? Did you know people burnt copies of THE BLESSINGS OF GAIA DOCUMENT when they were told that our new histories of the time contradicted the official record?"

"People actually cared about our study of history? How many of them were there?"

"Three hundred known cases we're aware of. The devoted..."

"Well, that will be a passing phase," Auger interrupted. "People move on to the next fad, year after year. Did it happen in the Outer World?"

"No! They don't care about history there. They care about eternity!"

"See. That's my point."

"But what's at stake here is material that is much more controversial. Lloyd's documents drive brass tacks into the coffin of huge sections of THE BLESSINGS OF GAIA DOCUMENT. The people who were just sort of bad, or a little bad, were really bad!"

"Cheer up!" Auger said. "Look at the bright side. These materials prove that Tom could not have been the Curmudgeon, a.k.a., the Capsule Man. The two knew each other during their lifetimes, the Capsule Man and Tom, but the Capsule Man had to have been several decades older than Tom. So obviously they were not the same person. You insisted that I was mistaken about inferring that. But now you have the Capsule Man's hand-written stuff along with the stuff going all the way up to 2133! Seventy more years of information. Just past the last dates of the loa. You've put me on the right track interpreting the Capsule Man's papers. Feel jolly good about that. You corrected me. You're always my conscience, Pius. You're always my sounding board."

"Xanus, Permanent Chair Intellectual Supreme of the Obsidian Order, hates me," Pius said, changing the subject. "He despises me. Vilifies me in public. Can't restrain himself from humiliating me in public. Most of the elders of the Obsidian Order distrust me. Many of them go further. They synchronize their abject loathing of me. Particularly after the release of the Antarctica Papers. Why they hold me responsible I don't know. Only the young novices, some reformers, some maverick oldsters, are like me. All of them together comprise a minority."

"Long march through the institutions," Auger said, smiling. "Right? Maybe these novices you speak of will become a new generation of leaders, a change generation. Given enough time. Maybe in 25 years? Then, in retrospect, you could be looked up to as their flaming sword of reform, their modern day version of Andromenus. Leading the charge. Channeling their energies."

"You know I think sometimes you have no respect for me at all," Pius said. "Gaia knows why I haven't given up on you. Your ideas are insipid: *We can't do that. We move together collectively. We act with discipline. We respect our elders. They hold positions of authority because there are reasons that they do so.*"

"Maybe you should act," Auger said. "Why not? Take command. Be bold."

"Can't," Pius said.

"Can't? Why not? Because you don't have power? Why should that stop you?"

Chapter Seventeen

THE FIRST THING Rathman discovered when he first entered Eccles was that when he walked by machines, they made strange, flute-like tooting sounds, or sometimes yipping sounds. In the latter case, Rathman was reminded of the noises coyotes made in response to a perceived threat. When Rathman walked within 150 feet (he actually measured the distance with steps)—of a gargantuan forty-foot-long limo he saw, the car emitted dominance establishing barking sounds.

The gold- or silver-tinted vehicles that were shorter made gentler barking sounds, the size of vehicle apparently determining the volume of sound.

Then Rathman saw something else, a fairly large truck with gold lettering spelling the word "infinity" on its side doors. Rathman thought, sardonically: If I got into the truck, will it take me to infinity? Or was infinity just the name of a company, an organization, or an *idea?*

A block away, the next truck he spotted spelled out on its sides in bold, block letters: Experience Virtual Reality Here. Beneath the words was a logo of a stick man running out—a black and white box, suggesting a way to make an escape from the drabness of a black and white world, hinting at the pathway to enter the realm of a multi-colored, multi-dimensional world.

The third truck Rathman spotted reminded him of home

however. The advertisement on the side appealed to him. The truck also played a recording of a craggy voice crooning: "Adam and Eve's Rib Truck. Sandwiches and Meats Galore."

Advertisements like these were seen by Rathman as not too offensive or not too intimidating. Rathman hadn't attached filters yet. Maybe it was only because everything was so brand-new and "yea-yea!" that Rathman was temporarily thunder-struck by Eccles' sights, it's peculiar sounds, but within a month the 'on wheels novelty vistas' wore thin, then became part of a weave of a completely filtered-out reality, or rather, unreality. A trick of the eye, no less.

Rathman was trying to follow one of the counselor's maps. He must have gotten confused and taken a wrong turn. Five blocks in, before he knew it, he was in the middle of something that was more foreign than anything he had ever seen before, he didn't know what to make of it. An unconscious man was sprawled out faced down on the sidewalk while another man knelt to rifle through his pockets. People of different ages, some young, some middle-aged, a few who were elderly, were milling about, some seemingly confused, some unhinged, some clearly mentally challenged. Garbage was in the street, not just lining the gutters. Filth was everywhere. People were openly taking drugs, sticking needles in their arms, right on the street. People were lined up like cords of wood, sleeping on the sidewalks, in soiled blankets, four in a row, eight in a row. It was a pandemonium of pavement dwellers, plastic and aluminum can pickers, and panhandling beggars.

A young prostitute, very short, wearing a fake blue wig, swirls of rouge on her cheeks, with gaudy red fingernail paint, caught Rathman's eye for a split second, and the next thing he knew she had followed him for four blocks staying a dozen paces back.

He changed directions, crossed to the other side of the street, turned a corner, once even reversed his direction, but when he looked back, sure enough she was there.

Finally, he turned to look back once more and she had disappeared. Rathman turned one last street corner and realized why the prostitute had dropped him. Further on there was a metal barricade near a long wall, constructed in an attempt to restrict camping there. It didn't work. In the two to three foot gap between the metal barricade and the wall sat a long makeshift mini-shantytown with a web of tarps and cardboard. It wasn't clear whether anybody was inside until a rabbit on a leash emerged, and a hand yanked the creature back. There was a massive group of street people, sleeping in bags and blankets, forming a huge circular mass, covering both of the sidewalks and the street. Rathman had to step gingerly between the disorderly tangle of sleeping bodies, just in order to not disturb them, to get through the mass, to the other side.

So, by accident, Rathman discovered the city had at least one tightly compacted slum. Evidently, he had traversed the radius of it.

Only a few kilometers farther on, Rathman came across a mixed gender group at a place called "Chess-playing Park." Seated at tables, these young people were engaged in their favorite game.

Rathman watched some of the chess action for a few minutes, started to get a little bored, then decided to set off again.

Of course, coming from the edge of the Outer World, Rathman owned no gadgets. So when he left the general terminal, located across the street from Pleasure Park, that led on to a wheel of subway spurs, he noticed near the entrance a long row of coin-operated public-access telephones. They were something he had never seen before. Apparently these telephones had been placed throughout the city of Eccles, in and around parks, libraries, recreational facilities, in the anterooms of public safety stations, but most abundantly, at transit hubs and transient crawl-ups.

Rathman learned later that these devices had been created explicitly for the use of the indigent, the marginal, the homeless, or people on the lower end of the income scale, in other words, people like Rathman.

Rathman examined one of the phones. There was a pogo, but the squibs were baffling.

Press *10 Bank of Gaia

Press *12 Receive Gaia's Blessings. Get Your Daily Prayer

Press *13 Resource Servicing? Curb Debt Slavery

Press *14 Need Cash Now? Quick, Easy Terms

Press *15 Need Help Finding a Job

Press *16 Need Help Finding a Home

Press *17 First Step? Easy Credit

Press *18 Eccles' Four Seasons Bank

Times had not been prosperous for *everybody*, Rathman surmised. Pushing loans and...simultaneously decrying debt bondage? What was that? In confronting this paradox, he needed the gifts of a *street-hipster* combined with the steel-trap mind of an *urban anthropologist*. He was trying to be so non "yea-yea," and he feared he was failing at it!

Rathman felt everything in Eccles. The *extreme* looks, *extreme* sounds, *particular* textures—which were distinct and dissimilar from what he had been accustomed to. Also, there was the tech web itself. With time he'd become sort of familiar with that too.

Finding U. Presbyr, however, was simple. It was located seven kilometers from the famous Gatetar Tower, and five kilometers from the equally famous Pleasure Park.

In anticipation of Rathman's potential situation, in advance, the counselor had armed him with letters of introduction, travel instructions, directions, guiding dos and don'ts.

Rathman enrolled and matriculated. The college assistant to the assistant administrator said, handing him a little box, "You don't have one? You're a scholarship student? Compliments of Gatetar Industries. Welcome to Rhetoric." And a few days later Rathman landed in the reading room in the Rhetoric Department. In six weeks time, having the look of an alien coming from the edge of the Outer World, he had acquired a nickname.

Rathman was slumped over a reading table, his long, ungainly legs drawn beneath him. He was trying to get his electronic gadget to work and after the second try, in frustration, he tossed it across the table. Then foolishly, seemingly against his will, as he watched the device spin, he retrieved it. But instead of playing with it or pushing a button, he stuffed it in his pocket and looked at the book he'd been reading. The gadget, donated by Gatetar Industries, was something new and oddly other-worldly. 'Get-you-hooked' gadgets they were called. Years before, it'd never occurred to Rathman's parents to consider purchasing a luxury object on the exchange. Maybe they could afford a box but could they afford two? No. Out of the question. And with one gadget, living on the edge of the Outer World, what would have been the point? Without another box, to communicate with whom? For the Outer World people, there were no boxes for communication to the Outer World, just for communication to the Inner World, which was THE GREAT SUBJECT of many parts of Outer World literature.

There had been boxes at the orphanage, of course. The counselor had one. But they were not issued to individual residents until they reached the age of 18. Rathman had just turned 18.

Rathman first entry into his diary was: "I enter this world of associates and friends-to-be, dripping with an intellectual atmosphere marked by carefree assurance (if not devil-may-care exuberance), marked also by optimism, and a sensual *joie de vivre*. A world combining elements of the louche, the decadent, the cynical. I intend to keep my distance. That's why I've received the duel sobriquets: 'alien' and 'Cowboy.' The first, I'm sure, with time, will fade. The second, I fear, will last forever. Wait. What lasts forever? Nothing. Correction. Lasts awhile. Maybe I want it to last forever."

Rathman became so embarrassed by the last word he'd written—it seemed so pretentious—that he wasn't sure he should continue to write entries in his diary at all. Was optimism even warranted? From the past, what would there be to surrender?

Zoia threw open the doors to the reading room, both doors, making a grand entrance, and as there was no one else in the room, she introduced herself to Rathman, as if that was the only reason why she was there.

She sauntered over, pacing languorously, as if she were scouting the place, and at the same time, sussing the stranger out.

"I'm Zoia."

"You're not THE Zoia?" Rathman asked, looking up nervously. "Who hasn't heard of you? I've heard of you. I'm a... I'm a...poor..."

"I know who you are," Zoia said. "What's that? What's that you're reading?"

"Nothing," Rathman said. He tried to hide the pages, although that was impossible to do. "Small something. From the deep past. *The Time Repairer. Darkness.*"

"Ulm?"

Rathman looked up amazed. "You're familiar with Ulm's poetry?"

"Course," Zoia said. "Father read it to me when I was a child. Could have taken it in with my mother's milk, but I didn't have any mother's milk to begin with. But Ulm is considered to be out of fashion. His poetry is seen as too depressing."

"Depressing, yes," Rathman said, agreeing. "I have an idea, a theory, or a guess, if you will: why people during the Dark Time seemed to appreciate Ulm's poetry so much. It's conjecture, of course. I need to think it through more carefully before I share it in public." For an instant, Rathman had an almost panicked look in his eyes. "You know, I'm new here. I'm a beginner. I'm just fumbling along."

"That's what reading rooms are for," Zoia said. "Fumbling along. So let's do it. Fumble along. We're able to talk, no? Those people that you're referring to could talk. In the dark?"

"Yes," Rathman said. "Want to go there, explore that? Sure you want to? It was a place where stones cried and a face in the clouds could not be seen but could be imagined. Where madness posed as the sublime, and the sublime posed as mental lethargy and cerebral instability..."

"Yes, I want to hear more about this theory of yours," Zoia said.

With a flicker of shyness still in his eyes, Rathman said, "The theory meshes on more than one level. The theory says, *Time*

Repairer. Darkness, fed these people's negative vision of the past, the old—what they considered to be—a Techno-Utopia. You know, in ancient-history, the time Before the Fall, there had to be something that was different from what they were living in, right? The oral tradition, the story telling, involved one living person transmitting experience of life to another in a vital exchange. The personality of the storyteller was important, but the story was forefront. The passing of the oral tradition translated into a form of collective memory. History was transmitted in the form of an oral tradition, say, from the time of the earliest uses of electricity in 1880 A.D., all the way to the catastrophic blow-out in 2051 A. D. That's 170 years. That's the subject matter. Didn't matter if it had turned into a fairy-tale because this was 500 years later, 1,000 years later, 2,000 years later. The Earth is in terrible shape. These people are primitives, what do they know? And just thinking stories were true might have given these poor souls solace in their moments of hopelessness... agonizing, terrifying hopelessness."

"Hopelessness?"

"Hopelessness. I've been moving toward that interpretation. That *is*, of course, from the point of view of the wretches who were living all their lives in the darkness. In the caves. And what did they know? And what do we know that they knew? Only what we can glean from Ulm's poetry. Darkness, a period which lasted thousands of years, was there ever a streak of light? On the horizon? And if there was, the perception thereof, was that how they were saved?"

"Two thousand years out of 2,650 years is a fair chunk, as my father would say," Zoia said, smiling.

"I know who your father is. Everyone does. Therefore, everyone knows who you are."

"And you're the Cowboy?"

Rathman looked down at his horny, rough-hewn hands. He thought of covering them up. There was a nasty inch-long, yellow-purplish fingernail spike, souvenir of a mishap in blacksmithing, and an ultramarine-cinnabar-colored fingernail spike, result of a messy roping mishap. Hide the damage? Why bother? Rathman was carrying the portrait of his past, in minuscule, on his split, discolored fingernails, for all to see.

Zoia noticed the damaged fingernails, but did not comment because she could sense Rathman's sense of self-consciousness about them.

"Aaaaah, such a weird pet name," Rathman said. "They're respecting me... I guess. Maybe making fun of me too. A bit of fun. Thus, the nickname is ambiguous. Look, where I come from, the rural orphanage, even though it's 450 kilometers north, it was close to the border of the Outer World. I was given a nickname there. It means more to me than this name does. It was the Barefoot Herder. Why don't you call me that?"

"No, you're the Cowboy. Don't try to change things. Give me another example of what led you to contemplate the thoughts of these troubled people in the darkness."

"I'll do better," Rathman said. "I'll tell you something that happened to me that got me started. When I was living in the orphanage they sent me on a mission to visit a 95-year-old lady. A 95-year-old *blind* lady. Believe me, this was a plum. A reward for doing so well at school. Better than slopping pigs, cleaning latrines, administering cattle dips, mending fences. I was instructed to bring a book along to read to her. From the orphanage library I brought Jay Zehennie's *Gold Across The Horizon,* a classic. Jay was born with sight but became blind when she was 15. Between then and her death at the age 35, she wrote *Gold.* Such vivid descriptions. Even descriptions of Planet Xs. But more importantly, the breathtakingly brilliant descriptions of scenes in and around Earth's Arctic Region. As I read the author, the old woman taught me much. When you interact with someone, typically, you have the benefit of sight and sound. Not just one sense. Both. But what if the person is blind? Why not replace sight with another sense? Smell? No. Taste? No. How about touch? I held her hand while I was reading to her, watching her eye movements beneath her pallid closed eyelids, reading from the book those descriptions of high color resolutions of gold and blue on the horizon of planet Earth, or just gold, on Planet X. Her heart racing as she listened. So instead of sight and sound, we had *touch and sound*. Enhanced the experience. Did they do that in the darkness? So many questions. It's so complicated!"

"Not the same thing," Zoia said. "She was blind. It's not the same thing as having your vision *impaired to the point of mutation*, which is what happened to the people of the Dark Time. That's why your study is so daunting. Why you can't see what you're trying to see. Enter the cul-de-sac. Have you heard this before? *This* message... Don't kill the messenger."

"You *know* so much...," Rathman murmured. "You're famous for knowing so much about the earlier period of modernity, with our 2,700-year-gap. How do you know so much? When did this happen?"

"2007 A.D. to 2022 A.D.? Zoia replied. "It went on longer than that but the last year was the birth-year of September Snow, so 2022 sticks. You said you knew who my father was, right? The historian?"

Rathman was overwhelmed. She was way over his head, in another galaxy. "Look. I just started. Want to hear the rest?"

"Sorry. Please continue."

"The blind lady couldn't read with her eyes but she could listen with her ears. Also, she talked. I encouraged her to tell me her story. Remember, she's living not far from the edge of the Outer World, and it's more than 85 years in the past—the story she's relating to me. When she was a young girl her family had been living on a farm in the east. The family loaded up a wagon and headed back to their original home, having failed at their new homestead. Drought. Repeated droughts. Crop failure. Repeated crop failures. An old story. But just as they were departing, giving it up, something strange happened. It had been raining solid for two weeks. Nonstop rain. The river they had to cross was not just overflowing, its rising waters were way over the river's banks. The river was raging. They had four horses to pull the family wagon. The blind woman was a child on the large cart. The father hooked up a pregnant mare to the front on the right. You understand? The lead horse. He figured the mare would fight to the death to keep her baby alive, and that would be the safest way to make it across the swollen river. And they did."

Zoia thought of her own mother. Her death in birthing her.

"Is that why the blind woman's story is so important to you?" Zoia asked searchingly. "You remember this, so it must be important."

The words sprang out of Rathman's mouth. "Well, you read my mind. I want to study the Dark Time."

"You seem to have an interest in history," Zoia said. "Why didn't you enroll in the World History Department?"

"I could ask you the same question."

"My father's department? Imagine the embarrassment and awkwardness of that."

"I am not a sophisticate," Rathman said. "I don't pretend. I don't claim..."

"Your nickname?" Zoia asked, harkening back. "Ah, yes. Cowboy? Some of the other students made that up. Not I. I don't think it works. I don't think it fits. You're not really a rustic. But you're stuck with it, aren't you? You're the Cowboy. After all, they could have called you Holy Fool, Backward-Looking Contrarian, or Irredeemable Caveman. But I like your story. And I see you appreciate the utility of the oral tradition. You know how to seek drama."

Zoia was the unreachable goddess of the Metaphysics and Moral Philosophy sub-section of the Rhetoric Department. And in 15 minutes time Rathman had done something his male peers rarely succeeded in doing. He'd piqued Zoia's curiosity.

"Hope is the greatest when it confronts the greatest adversity," Rathman said, speaking with such solemnity it almost sounded like a speech. "Doesn't mean it always wins," he added. He smiled. Showing a certain worldliness, he hoped he'd salvaged something from his clumsy start.

"So, you're a little religious."

"A little."

"Gaia?"

"Gaia pantheism. Sort of works for me. That's why I'm here. To learn."

"I'm researching the first Post-Period of the *Westernized* Trope of the Upanishads," Zoia said. "Subject? End-Time Theology Plus Possession of Nukes—as in thermonuclear weapons. Theocracy gone mad? Or, alternate title, Prometheus Stealing Powers from the Sun With Intent To Spring Forth Chaos. Sound tantalizing? Aren't you the least bit interested?"

Rhetoric students were always known to strive to impress, and even though Zoia was many times brighter than any of the other students, so did she.

"Cautionary tale?" Rathman asked. "Warfare?" His words were jumbled. Now that he was completely out of his depth—talking about a subject he didn't know anything about—he figured he might have been looking again as if he were an object of ridicule. He figured he should have kept his mouth shut. Oh, he realized he had so much to learn.

"What?" Zoia asked. "No. Splitting atoms. When there were still functioning states. State actors. Nuclear exchanges occurred at the end of the Eleven-Years-War. Luck more than good management had more to do with these nuclear exchanges NOT escalating into a massive 3,000-unit worldwide thermonuclear exchange, concluding with a Nuclear Winter. That's the scary version. The version according to my father. PSSST! DRAMA! DON'T TRUST! Pius has a different version. Who is Pius? Another historian like my father. Danger wasn't that close to happening in his view. How much Pius loves to differ with my dad. In any case, by the skin of our teeth, Auger, or not by the skin of our teeth, Pius—we dodged it. Why even bother with this might-have-been of ancient history. They were always dodging bullets. They were dodging hot lead more often than we eat gorgeous olives, from the best olive trees grown in south

Eccles. You know they say that eating Mediterranean Climate olives is good for you."

Zoia plucked an olive from her pocket and dangled it over her mouth. Then, when she was sure she'd gotten Rathman's attention, dropped it in. Rathman fixed on Zoia's lips moving. She chewed and swallowed. It was like Zoia was saying the subject was just an olive away. Rathman realized Zoia was beautiful. She took another olive from her pocket and, commanding Rathman to open his mouth, dropped it in. Rathman obeyed. He chewed and swallowed.

"That would be during the time of light before the time of Darkness," Rathman said. "Then again, in light of what you're saying, why should we wonder at the improbability of most people back then, Before the Fall, embracing Gaia? Could they have resembled us? How could we know? Either way, not my brief. I'll stick to my specialty."

"If a group existed," Zoia said, "they might have called themselves by a different name. And if they did devote themselves to the force, or power, or fury, of Gaia, it could have been a different one. It's such a continuously baffling mystery. Different times. I'll give you one more chance. Tell me what you think it was? Way back?"

"The religion of Gaia represented the last and final chapter of the collapse of modernity," Rathman said. "I mean the old modernity. Not our modernity. We think we're so much superior—than anything that could have happened in the past. That's our crime. But the religion of Gaia is the default myth in the absence of an alternative, plausible myth. Why not study the Dark Time? Via Negativa. The heart of the Dark Time is the soul of humanity."

"Wow," Zoia whispered. She wanted to shout, "It's a cul-de-sac, dummy!" But she didn't. "Ambitious," she muttered instead. "In putting yourself in harm's way. Of a gravitational pull? With a potential nudge? Toward the suicidal? Forgive me Rathman, Daddy can't get enough of these wooly astronomical metaphors: '*Gravitational pull of this phenomenon, gravitational tug of that power.*' It's the killer asteroid, cluttering up our otherwise reasonable verbiage. Father would love you for what you just said. He'd adore it."

Rathman was thrilled by Zoia's knowledge and intellect. Also, by her charm.

"The religion of Gaia represented the last and final chapter of the collapse of the old modernity," Rathman said. "In the worst of times, most human beings, back then, out of choice, or out of necessity, didn't care a bean about what happened to the human species. Does anybody think a religion can plug a hole that big and mighty in a greater human consciousness? Not on your life. Gaia was a lost cause redoubt, it's a default myth."

"Made it up?" Zoia said. "Right? Made it up? Didn't you?" Zoia laughed joyously. She clapped her hands. She thought that in spite of Rathman being a bit of a rube, he was able to stumble onto an original penetrating insight. Maybe because of, not in spite of, but because of, his unrefined manners, he could see things differently than a typical Rhetoric student was able to see.

"Yes, I rest my claim," Rathman said. "Expressed with originality." He wanted to add, "I don't know if I'm cut out for this," but he hesitated, having not the courage to admit he had so little of it. The newness of Eccles was weighing heavily on him, intimidating him. He was so "yea-yea."

"You know, I like to take walks, just to loosen up," Rathman said. "It loosens my thoughts. Occasionally, I jaunt through the Favela Shantytown East. I see it."

"See it?" Zoia asked. "See what?"

"Graffiti. For example, 'if it's money art, call Guterman.' That's my favorite." Rathman sighed. "Graffiti is all over the place. If it's money art, call Guterman. Or Pinksy. Or Drago. Or Streetman. Lots of Dragos and Streetmans. Favela Shantytown East, it's 49 blocks. It's a mystery to me. I've seen it at different locations, in obscure places—*presumably* a hiding place—under a flowerpot, or a trash bin, scratched with a penknife on a bench, or on a fire hydrant, marked on the front of a dumpster, tattooed on the top brick of a well. I've

seen it scribbled on official signs. Days later the message is erased
and something just as cryptic replaces it. What does it mean? I know
art can't replace religion. Can art replace commerce?"

"Contraband products, illicit services," Zoia said, bursting out
laughing. "It's like advertisements! For crime! It's not about giving
money for art, Rathman."

"They're allowed to do that?"

"'Course not dummy. Code. If there's a demand there's a
supply. You close up one flow of commerce, it will flow in and out in
some other way."

Rathman did not understand what Zoia was saying, but she
knew that eventually he would.

"Not typically, not atypically, people murder people over this,
so use caution," Zoia said. "But you can keep yourself free from all
that. Become a well-heeled inhabitant of Eccles. Become an urban
crow. Hop around on your feet, rarely fly, and eat your meals from
dumpsters."

Rathman looked at Zoia warmly. He was filled with a strange
tenderness.

"I have to run," Zoia said. But she yearned to linger with
Rathman. "I'd say, Welcome to the Rhetoric Department, but
you're going to be hit by a storm of every type of rhetorical device
in existence, so be forewarned. Rhetoric—whether it's cool as water
or it's hot as fire—is as useful for the worst as it is for the best.
The humanities, *unfortunately and fortunately*, belong, alas, to
humanity. Though I think you have the guts and moxie to harbor
and cultivate good instincts. And one should never deny or downplay
the importance of good instincts."

Zoia wanted to add: 'Yet I think you're wasting your time on the
Dark time.' Hadn't she hammered that point already? But after all,
she'd just met him. She didn't want to scare him off.

Little over a month passed before a development occurred that
would allow them to have an opportunity to converse with each
other again.

Chapter Eighteen

JUG TRIED TO CONTACT the historian Pius, subsequently realizing what a mistake he had made. He sent him a letter. Pius did not reply. Jug sent another. Again Pius did not reply. Jug was accustomed to receiving prompt replies. After Jug sent Pius a third letter, a weary and defiant Pius at last replied: "I've no interest in your endeavors. Do not make further inquiries. I'm not impressed by your manners. I'm just a teacher, a historian, a scholar—in your eyes, a fool. So if you seek special favors, like everyone else in this world, go through proper channels. You'll receive no preferential treatment from me. Not today or tomorrow. Good day to you, sir."

Jug realized he needed a change in tactics. He assigned an assistant to do the necessary research. "Find out everything you can about the other guy."

"The other guy?"

"The other historian. Auger. The usual background. His likes and dislikes. Stuff I can use."

The assistant did as she was told. Returning a day later, she reported, "What he loves to study is the time after the *Westernized* Version of the Upanishads, the last peak of modernity before our own modernity. Auger's wife died many years ago and he has a daughter. Her name is Zoia."

"Research *her*. A daughter can be the weakest link. What's the daughter's name again?"

"Zoia."

"Delve into it. Give me a full narrative."

The assistant came back with a 50-page report. "Zoia is her name. She's 18. She has a passion for Mary Shelley and, more, a passion for Mary Shelley's mother, Mary Wollstonecraft. Above all, she has a passion for *Frankenstein*. The writing of it. The meaning of it. She also has a passion for what she calls, The Modern Prometheus. She's a rebel and she's obstinate about it."

"Who in the hell is Mary Shelley?" Jug asked. "Who in the hell is Mary Wollstonecraft? I don't know any of these names. Modern Prometheus! Wait, modern Prometheus? Don't I have a video game or a digital game or an action doll named after that?"

"She also stole a chocolate bar when she was eight," the assistant continued. "Charges were dropped on account of Zoia ate the chocolate bar and the wrapper in front of the police before they had time to start their paper work. So they lacked material evidence. Again, when she was nine, she let her fellow students cheat, using her answers during exams. No one in her class flunked that year. Zoia's father Auger refused to sign up her daughter for the dopamine project or the x-drugs that were all the rage back then, so rebelling is in her blood. Gatetar would have no problem with the petty thievery, after all, she was eight at the time and there were never again charges issued. However, she'd never be hired by Gatetar for allowing her fellow students to cheat off her. Even at that age, it suggests a genetic *warp*, a serious character *foible*, you wanted to know everything I could find on her, so that's why I'm going into detail. She attended a protest when she was 14, but it was Eccles-sanctioned. She also attended protests when she was 15 and 16, and others when she was 17, but none of them achieved a level five. We have some face visages on file from some of the street demos, 1000 or so, but they only reveal...*what?* We can still do electros. *We...can... look*. We can do extra mining, some data..."

"Stop it," Jug said.

The researcher smiled. She particularly loved the cases where

someone was obsessed with the ancients, though they were extremely
infrequent. "Her heroes were ancient British luminaries. Rabble-
rousing rascals posing as political radicals. Unremembered treatise-
writers. Poets and artists. Bohemians and semi-bohemians, some
scruffy, some more genteel, a small clique of artists and pamphleteers,
altogether from 1790 to 1827 A.D. The group represented 37 years
of precocious modernity. Name of a work of art, as well: The British
Luminaries. I'll write you another report, Sir, if you want to know
more."

"Think it's worth it?"

"You decide, Sir," the assistant replied. "By the way, they love
Zoia in the Rhetoric Department. She's a fixture there. Her father's
in Ancient History, not Rhetoric, be doubly clear on that."

"Thank you," Jug said. "I got that. I'll let you know if I need
more help."

That was the key, Jug had already determined. He would send
a letter to Auger, but the wording would be different from the Pius
letter. This time the request would include no magisterial imposition
or authority. Instead Jug would write it from the point-of-view of
soft power. Implicit in his request would be what the money could do
at U. Presbyr in the fields of Archeology, Ancient History, SOC, *even*
Modern History. Jug would include more details about the purpose
of the inquiry, indicating his idea of the approach. He would include
supplicating humor. Where Jug lacked imagination for that, Jason
would supply it. Jason knew academic literary decorum.

Jug enclosed a self-addressed envelope to make the replier's job
easier, a compliment Jug had rarely extended to anyone.

Auger's reaction was the exact opposite of Pius's. He didn't
demand that Jug go through "proper channels," whatever that
meant. His response was positive. He was speedy and cheerful. He
showed enthusiasm.

"Of course I'm interested," Auger shot back in a missive within a
week. "I think your proposed project has great merit. In fact, I think
the parameters are delightful. It is my opinion that your proposed

archeological dig will push forward and outward the boundaries of our knowledge in a most redemptive way. All the information of the decade Before the Fall, that we can glean, is of critical import. I must confess to you how much I, as a historian, love studying that period of ancient human history, I'm actively going through that treasure trove of materials from the main body of the Antarctica papers with a colleague and a team of assistants right now. Parts of it are actually sitting on my desk at this moment. I am giving it my number-one priority to see if we can find what you're looking for. I have a hunch we will, but I have a hunch it will be in a miniaturized form. In essence, what you're asking for are precise maps. Fortunately you're asking for locations that fall within the boundaries of Eccles and I think the Gaia followers of September Snow may have included these in the materials we have. Of course, I would need to get authorization before I can divulge the information you request, but I see no problem in this regard, especially as there are no religious implications or spiritual dimensions. If I'm able to secure them, I propose we meet straightaway."

A research aide found what Jug was seeking 84 hours after Auger posted the letter. It was titled "Antiquities: Location of Bay Area Technology Firms, 2022 A.D."

The documents were sandwiched between other heritage site maps: Saint Petersburg, Athens, Rome, a bevy of pyramids in Egypt, Susa, Fernsworth, Babylon, Varanasi, Machu Picchu, and 55 others in a file called, significant Archeological Sites—2020 B.C. to 2020 A.D.

Once the documents were found and amplified by a sufficient factor, Auger invited Jug to his house for supper so he could view them.

Jug promptly sent a letter accepting the invitation.

Jug descended on Auger's modest home without his usual entourage of underlings and chauffeur. He drove himself in a company vehicle, not a forty-foot-long stretch limo, but a regular, plebian coup.

It was a four-door black and tan sedan, electric with lithium-ion batteries, the vehicle that the assistant to the assistant to the secretary, a part-time gofer/part-time understudy, used to ferry food and drink to office parties and company picnics. There was a large wine stain in the trunk, beginning to smell of vinegar. Jug, not in his role of the biggest business player in the world, but rather, as a secret, rebellious trickster, *loved* everything that this car represented.

Jug dressed as casually as decorum would permit: charcoal gray slacks, white canvas shoes, plain white shirt open at the neck, no gloves, and no tie, no shoulder frills, hat, or tails—much of which he was loath to wear anyway.

Auger met the 32-year-old commercial titan at the door.

Jug had brought a small gift, wrapped with a bow. He handed it to Auger.

Auger laughed and threw his hands up in the air in protest. "You'd be surprised, but U. Presbyr are sticklers when it comes to staff accepting gratuities, even small ones. There's a code we have to sign. Provost Kite is adamant about it."

"Well, it can be given to a family member, perhaps."

"You mean my daughter?"

"Sure. Look at the gift yourself and decide."

Auger opened the box and discovered a black velvet bag. Inside the bag was a clear container with a matching pen and pencil set—black, elegant, and monogrammed in white with Auger's initials. Well, that was something, Auger thought.

Auger smiled. "Zoia would enjoy this. She loves the practice of cursive writing. For things that are really important, she even performs the art of calligraphy, a long-lost art if there ever was one. My colleague Pius taught her that skill when she was quite young. You don't make physical pens and pencils do you? I'm referring to your business, Mr. Gatetar?"

"No. We only make software and hardware, electronic hardware.

No old-fashioned items like these. But I think writing instruments are valuable in their own right. In the act of giving at least. Amongst friends, I go by the name of Jug."

"Thank you, Jug. I won't say it's a gift from you."

Auger invited Jug inside and showed him papers and maps.

"These are the sites you're looking for. Apple, Google, Facebook, plus the other three sites. Why those? Why the obscure ones?"

"HP garage, Yahoo, Mark Zuckerberg's house, you mean?"

"Yeah. Kind of funny, don't you think? I guess with the tech history references it makes sense."

"Well, only my father would have been interested in the HP garage, so I'm including it as an homage to his memory. I thought I might show it to my mother. She'd like it too. Yahoo, I just threw that in as an extra. Zuckerberg's house, I'm only interested in as it regards to a wager I've made with my advisor."

"We have maps of all sorts of electronics farms back then. You'll only be able to do partial excavations of the Ring. The underwater sites—Facebook, Google, Yahoo—will be easier to access."

After Auger folded up the copies of the maps and gave them to Jug, he escorted him into the dining room where dinner was being served.

Zoia was bringing out a soup tureen from the kitchen when she caught the eye of Jug.

Jug thought she was unusual...and unusually beautiful. Her eyes, set wide apart, were coal black. Her skin was like porcelain, except for the faint smudge of light freckles on the sides of her cheekbones, that suggested wholesomeness, earthiness, healthiness. Auger introduced them.

"It's my night to prepare dinner," Zoia said. "My father and I alternate nights."

There was something about Zoia...Jug realized. She may have been young, but she was also clearly the matron of the house.

Fish. Fish soup. Potatoes. Peas. Tea. Asparagus.

Zoia said, "Mom, thanks for the lovely dinner!"

"Mom, thanks for the lovely dinner!" Auger echoed.

Jug looked confused as he attempted to spear an asparagus tip.

Zoia turned to her father and said, "I guess I should explain it to our guest. It's an oral tradition," Zoia said, addressing Jug. "Before each meal, we say that as a way of remembering my mother."

"I see."

Once the soup had been completed and they dug into the main fish course, the presence of Zoia had turned Jug into stone. He was so besotted with her, he was embarrassed to look at her for any length of time.

Zoia finally broke the silence by commenting on Jug's apparel.

"I call this plebian and hip," Jug said.

"What?" Zoia asked. "You can call it whatever you like but plebian hipsters are not hip because they're plebian. Plebians have some skills, but too often no money, or little of it. People are not hip because they've no money. Your clothes suggest to me someone going to some lengths to look like someone who doesn't have huge, fantastic amounts of money. As if, you're trying to pretend to be somebody you aren't. Am I mistaken?"

Jug felt a huge wave of chagrin come over him. "That's what my advisor said."

"You need an advisor to tell you what you yourself should already know? Are you part of that group—the what?—techno-grandees, who attend rich parties in rich people's houses where there's a lot of drug-taking and licentious sex going on?"

"No," Jug said. "I have to be very sensitive to appearances. I'm very exposed and vulnerable in that department. I have nothing to do with—socially—ahem, the louche *technorati*."

"Louche *Technorati!*" Zoia exclaimed. "Is that what you call them? I think it'd be more fitting to call them the creepy and the neurotic. The techno-creepy. The techno-neurotic." Zoia proceeded to pile titillating vignette upon sensationalizing anecdote, all spoken with humility, joy, irony, and barely disguised paradox and ambiguity. Zoia was being her usual incorrigible self, and Jug wasn't used to receiving this kind of treatment.

Jug squirmed. "No," he said. "I don't mingle with that...kind. You know what you're talking about, I should think."

From that point forward, during the entire dinner, Zoia led virtually all of the conversations.

At the end, Jug jumped up, and without asking, started clearing the table, trying to make up for his miscues by conducting himself as if he were a servant or a member of the family.

He said, "Thanks Mom, thanks for clearing the plates!"

Both Auger and Zoia laughed at that. Making separate trips, Jug carried the dishes, platters, and cutlery into the kitchen. After all the cookery and crockery had been cleared, he gave the table a vigorous wet wipe, followed by a thorough dry wipe. He moved his shoulders with a powerful circular motion, energetically, expertly, as if he had been clearing tables all his life.

After completing the task, he sat back down at the table.... glumly.

"I almost forgot," Auger said. He gave Zoia the pen and pencil set Jug had brought.

Zoia smiled in a non-committal way. "How interesting. Why are the cylinders so fat? Thin ones fit so dexterously in a slender hand. Like mine. My father's hands are beefy and fat."

Jug said, "I'll take them back. Change the initials. Bring thin ones. I should tell you now, I inherited a business, and I...."

"Look, you clearly did research on me," Zoia said, her face held tight as a clam.

"Yes, I'm guilty of that." At this point Jug felt terrible. Nothing was going right. "But I did it on your dad too. That wasn't as hard to do. He's famous."

"And you didn't ask for my permission first?" Zoia asked.

"No."

"An invasion of privacy?"

In Jug's conversations with people who were outside the company, he was willing to go to extreme lengths, greatest extremes, if it meant he could skirt the philosophical issues of violating a person's *privacy*. Over the years, he'd gotten pretty good at that, just blame the *system*, like a meteorologist blamed the weather, like an astrophysicist blamed an asteroid.

Auger looked down and stared at his hands. He wished he could become invisible. He was not intentionally a rude man but he had raised his daughter to question authority and make her own decisions.

Although Jug was a new acquaintance, Auger felt oddly drawn to him.

After all, for a historian living in the isolation of an academic department, finding someone in the real world, a mover and a shaker at that, who shared an apparent interest in the ancient times, was gratifying. Archeology, even when done by an amateur, was only a hop, step, and a jump from studying history.

"I know you're going to kill me for saying this," Jug said, turning to Zoia. "Well, I did the research. You love history. But especially you're drawn to studying Mary Shelley."

"Where did that come from," Zoia murmured.

Having already been caught interfering with her privacy, Jug decided to pull out all the stops and double down. "Well, let me finish. Put those thoughts aside for the moment. You love her. Part of the reason you love her is because her mother, Mary Wollstonecraft, died ten days after giving birth to Mary, and your mother, Rornar, died while giving birth to you. You and Mary have a link. You both feel that you killed your mothers. Aren't you the least bit flattered by my knowing this?"

"Needn't bother about the pen and pencil set," Zoia said in a flat voice. But while her anger subsided, she thought: How many students in the Rhetoric Department had even *heard* of Mary Shelley, someone who had lived and died almost 3,000 years before?

One? Two? Three? How could Zoia not be impressed, considering the lengths the guy had gone to to learn about her favorite heroine. Dad had already been seduced by this celebrity, she could read his reactions. Being the richest man in the world, and from an economic point of view the most powerful, he struck Zoia as having a low-grade star quality, even if he took undo advantage of it.

However, was she not driven by curiosity to find out what made him tick, to see revealed what hitherto had not been revealed, to discover what lay beneath the surface? Who was he?

"No bother," Jug said. "Besides, according to the rules of U. Presbyr, not permitted. As a gift to your father, not right. I admire your father's adherence to principle. With his permission I'd like to give you something more suitable."

"All right," Zoia relented. "Another pen and pencil set? But let's call it a gift in the name of calligraphy. A gift in celebration of pen and paper."

"A gift in the name of calligraphy. Pen and paper. What nobler cause?"

"And quit the bullshit about being a plebian hipster. Okay?"

Jug nodded his head. "In the future I'll conduct myself as I am. Not a monster. Yes, I'm hated. Yes, I'm eccentric. Yes, I'm the richest man in the world. Yes, I'm into the future and technology. But there's more to me than that."

Auger smiled inwardly. Considering how audaciously Zoia had confronted him, Jug was more or less holding his own. When first meeting someone Zoia was often testy, if not abrasive. Later on, she softened up, if she deemed the person worthy.

"Just about everybody thinks they're eccentric," Zoia said. "If we meet again, it will be in a cemetery. If you can brave the graveyard, you can brave me."

After a long silence, Auger said, "Zoia is her mother's daughter. In more ways than one." He thought of Rornar, who after all the years was still fresh in his mind.

"If you're willing to extend the favor of your company," Jug said, "I'll meet with you anywhere. In a graveyard, in the streets, in the forest, on a mountain, in the desert, on the ocean, in the sky, on the top floor of the Gatetar Tower. Anywhere you choose."

"All right," Zoia said. "Do you think he's too old for me, Father?"

Auger did not give his daughter the victory of a punishing look. Instead he gave Jug a mock-disapproving look with just a brace of laughter in his eyes, as if to say, 'I hope you know what you're getting yourself into.'

Auger knew full well that Zoia knew how to take care of herself.

Before Jug departed, Auger took him aside. It took Auger a moment to gather up the nerve to say what he thought he was required to say. "Don't worry about Zoia. The way she behaved toward you, she's like that with everyone, or nearly so. Like her mom. Her mom was the same. My daughter Zoia is an appealing, independent-minded young woman who doesn't yield, unless she really, really wants to. So you have been notified."

When Jug left the house, he realized that in the report on Zoia, her interest in calligraphy had not been included. Jug thought of reprimanding his researcher for not digging deep enough, but he changed his mind. He decided that he shouldn't come down on his assistants just because they hadn't provided him with everything there was to know. As his advisor Jason had often repeated, "Insist on being the dictator, but don't be the chump. If you don't like what they do, especially that which was not work-related, but personal, do it yourself."

After all, Jug's instincts had been right about the gift, he just had the wrong recipient in mind. Yet ironically, this worked to his advantage. Now he had an excuse to meet with Zoia again. He always believed there were women who were intelligent enough to understand what he was saying. He was always looking for women who were intelligent enough to have opinions that were worth listening to as well. The mind of a 32-year-old in the woman of 18. Or maybe the mind of a 42-year-old, or a 52-year-old, or a 62-year-old, in the woman of 18. A woman of wisdom. A woman with a sharp tongue. Jug was beside himself. He was completely smitten.

Jug knew he couldn't impress Zoia by downplaying his wealth. He also knew he couldn't impress her by flaunting it. It was a conundrum. It was also a challenge.

Chapter Nineteen

JASON HAD TRIED to explain to Jug that he had made a mistake. "Just be yourself. You're trying too hard. You're too much of a control freak. This younger generation, some of them are different."

"I'm embarrassed about being myself," Jug said. "Well, my mother ... you know ... It's not like she was the best preparation for me." Jug left the rest of the sentence unsaid.

"Well, just do what I say," Jason said. "It was a mistake when you looked up all that information on Zoia behind her back. Nobody likes that. Would you like it? I wouldn't."

"I decided to act like an idiot because I thought she'd find some sort of grace lying beneath the mask...of the idiot and all."

"Well, think again, idiot," Jason said. "There is nothing beneath the mask. Take my advice. You're awkward? So be awkward. Sometimes there's grace in awkwardness. Sometimes that's the best way *you* show grace. You don't have to knock women dead."

Jason studied the lines on his young boss's face carefully.

"They want a truce."

"Truce?"

"Well, that's why they're asking for a repeat convention," Jason said. Only then Jug realized Jason had changed the subject. "Read the leaves. Maybe not a truce. An armistice? I know how keen you are..."

"Oh, that repeat convention," Jug said. "About planetary-wide energy use."

"How do you maintain order in a lawless world? You hold a convention. Then another convention. Invite everyone. Let everybody show up. Of the five Gatetar departments formed by your reorganization, three voted against, two voted for. The ones who voted against were firmly opposed, the ones who voted for, well, wishy-washy. Second-guessing you, I would guess. What do *you* think you should do? You run things."

"If Gatetar doesn't attend, the convention will be a bust. Few are going to take it seriously."

"You'll have the high ground. Your potential competitors are all vulnerable. You really *want* an armistice?"

"Yes, I think I am going to go against the wishes of those three departments who voted against me," Jug said. "I think we'll commit."

Jason nodded his head. "Okay. I've studied it. Don't let the electric power boys push you around. The convention will be good for society. It'll be good for the public interest. Bend humanity toward the arc of freedom. Not toward chaos, not toward the *absence* of freedom. Toward the generation of light, and for many generations to come. Of course this is all about the Inner World."

"Oh." Jug smiled. "Bending humanity toward the arc of freedom? Rather than bending humanity in the opposite direction? This is all about an energy policy that I hope not just to benefit from, but to capitalize on. Jason, how do you do it? You straddle the chasm between self-interest and idealism with the dexterity of a mountain goat. When I need rhetoric, you provide it. When I need a piece of heart-pounding polemic, something that really pops, applying just the right turn of phrase, you're the bomb." Jug abruptly changed the subject. "I've got maps. Contact the archeologists and their assistants. Get them on line. I want to move swiftly. I want to find and show something new, something that will truly impress Zoia."

"Zoia?" Jason asked. " The academic's daughter?"

"Yes, I keep bringing her up."

"Okay, okay, okay, so you want to impress her," Jason said. "You're not going to win her over, until after you've completed the war you've been conducting within yourself for over a year."

"War? Which war?"

"You know which one," Jason said. "You know a year ago you were saying: The only thing that matters is the future. I don't even know why we study history. It's entertaining maybe, 25,000-year-old Pleistocene Man, Industrial Revolution, Civilization's Collapse, Dark Time, Recovery. You went on to say, "What already happened doesn't matter. You don't need to know that, you just need to build on all that has happened. In technology, all that matters is tomorrow.""

"That's old, that was a year ago," Jug said. "I've replaced that with something new. Now I've discovered archeology. I've discovered the joys of unearthing ancient antiquities. Frankly, I love it. I dream of it. But that's the half of it. At least I'm halfway there. Jason, I'm beginning to think I'm actually going to enjoy looking afresh at history. So one side has won *that* war."

"The Bureau...they're not going to give up."

"Let them burrow in. Why are you always trying to change the subject?"

"You're doing it again," Jason said. "You promised. You said you'd drop the practice. In '73. In '76. In '77. In '79. In '80 A.G. All you do is hide it. Hide it. You lie about it. You still lie about it. People from other companies send people in to be hired, give you their best candidates. You have your underlings reject them. They don't do it on the basis of reading the applicant, which is still the fair and correct criteria of hiring for most companies. But no, your grunts snub them on the basis of outside *information*, there's an oxymoronic word for you, not information. You were caught driving a car in a state of intoxication, you got in a fight with someone, or you didn't get caught driving a car in a state of intoxication, or you didn't get caught fighting with someone, false information, which you can't challenge because you don't know it exists, and that is your unspoken and unwritten hiring practice? For what purpose? For maintaining the purity of the Gatetar culture? Uniformity of workforce?"

"Make it a law to prevent me from doing this practice I'm denying I'm doing," Jug said, "and I'll follow the law!"

"I'm not worried about legislators," Jason said. "I'm worried about the wannabes who will abuse the info."

"I don't want to talk about this now!" Jug said. "You always overreact! You *worry* too much."

"Bet's still on about the Zuckerberg house question?" Jason asked breezily, knowing when to change the subject. He knew deeply when an issue, especially a delicate one, shouldn't be brought up because of the impediment of bad timing.

"Yeah," Jug said. "Bet's still on. If we find it, you're going to lose."

"Stupid bet. Foundation of company buildings, easy. Foundation of house, difficult."

"Well that's what I'm betting on, isn't it?" Jug said. "Who's the better archeologist? You? Me? Finding it."

Jug had not dated in a year, and in the previous four years, it had not gone well. The years had not been kind to him. He had been working too hard, putting in too many late nights, too many long hours. One of Jug's father's persistent fears turned out to have been baseless. Jug, once he'd gotten used to the demands of work, was great at plunging in and following through. He had acquired both the art and the science of leadership, if success is to be considered a reliable measuring stick. He liked work and it smiled on him.

It had been too long. Last time dating Jug had made a complete thrash of it, he was 24. The year his father died. Just before he departed, Jug had put someone else in charge. Jug took 12 months off. Coming back, he noticed the wheels had not come off the industrial cart, so he took another 12 months off. Then another 12. Three years. He traveled all over the globe. Now Jug was looking for something different. Fun. Or diversion. But, unlike the last time, he was also looking for something more, something meaningful. Just thinking about that phrase, 'meaningful,' caused Jug to stir. He was 32. He wasn't as young as before. He instantly thought of the image of Zoia's bright youthfulness, her roving eyes, the deceptive skin of porcelain and the strange but beguiling freckles on her face. "She's supposed to be a prodigy," Jug said to Jason. "I believe it. Even though she just started, she's worshipped in the Rhetoric Department. *They worship her like a Goddess!"*

Jason was noncommittal in his reaction. He had seen this kind of weirdness in Jug before, but he hadn't seen it in such abundance.

"So intelligent," Jug continued. "Zoia. Mary Shelley's Frankenstein's doppelganger. In a graveyard."

"Don't get cute," Jason said cuttingly. He realized that Jug had grown obsessed with this young woman. "You have a bad habit of doing that. Because she's 18. I've seen her. *You are what the files say you are, even if you're not.* She'll cut you to ribbons if you don't show respect. Don't be mistaken. I'll be rooting for her. Loyally at her side. All the time," Jason said.

"You're supposed to be my advisor. You're suppose to me on my side. You're suppose to be helping me."

"I am."

Chapter Twenty

THEY MET SIX HOURS after sundown, the "gathering" the custom of Gaians (whether they believed in Gaia or not), for visiting the dead. Old customs, particularly regarding the dead, died hard. The first date, therefore, took place at the graveyard, on a bit of ground sloping up toward the surrounding hills, where the oaks gave way to the redwoods.

Jug arrived first. He was early. He stood around, waiting for almost 50 minutes. It was cold. He dug his hands deeply into his front pockets, took them out and hugged his ribs, stamped his feet now and then, trying to keep warm. He wished he had brought a coat, perhaps a scarf and a hat too. It was very dark. But when the moon broke out from behind a cloud, Jug felt like he was gazing upon a moonlit ruin.

Cemeteries in Eccles where like unkempt, overgrown gardens. The graves were covered with grass and there were luxurious green vines running up and down, covering the twelve-foot-high stone walls that formed a sort of sharp, demarcated boundary. The smallest tombstones were lost in the greenery. Peace reigned.

Zoia finally arrived, with an excuse.

"There was a man who jumped—or fell—onto the rails in the underground. They had to shut down the line for half an hour. Sorry. That's why I'm late."

"Why would someone do that?"

"Do what?"

"Jump."

Zoia did not reply immediately. "Maybe he fell."

Jug, holding a lamp and directing its light to the stone, said, "I've never seen a tombstone like this before."

The tombstone, a gray slab of stone, had only a singular name carved on it: RORNAR.

"There are no dates, no last names, nothing else," Zoia said. "As Rornar insisted. She and my father always lived on—what they called—Babylon time. Did you know what my father said she used to call it when she looked at the present with jaundiced eyes? The Gatetar Tower?"

"No," Jug said. "What?"

"The Tower of Babel."

Jug laughed.

"So you see, no dates, no last names, no nothing on her tombstone, no babbling," Zoia said. "Ironic, don't you think? Especially in light of the fact that my father as a historian is obsessed with dates, dating systems, historical dating processes. He has overcompensated for his alleged lack of skills in math by obsessing over numbers. That's as close to immortality as my mother thought she'd get: no dates on her stone. I call this *my* Saint Pancreas churchyard."

"Isn't this place called the Rainbow?" Jug asked. Before Jug thought a cemetery was a hideous, despicable dump, a pit formed of detritus, grit, bones, stones, rot. Especially rotting plants. Now that Zoia had brought him here, in the dead of night, he'd already altered his vision, changed his opinion radically. Now he marveled at the cemetery's greenery and its feeling of peace and tranquility.

Jug had no idea what the phrase Saint Pancreas churchyard meant. All he vaguely knew was it was a reference to something 3,000 years old, and was somehow related to Mary Shelley.

"Would you make love to me on my mother's grave?" Zoia asked.

"What?" Jug gasped. He almost choked. He looked at Zoia quizzically.

"Okay, these are my conditions," Zoia said, switching her tune. "We meet 18 times, one time each week, to signify my 18 birthdays. What do you say?" She laughed and smiled gaily. "You know, you don't have to be so glum, just because we're meeting in a cemetery. Rornar would have liked it if we laughed."

"Oh, do you really mean that?"

"Of course not. I'm only joking. Does anyone know how many times Wollstonecraft-Godwin made Percy Shelley visit her at her mother's gravestone before she agreed to become Mrs. Shelley? Shelley was expelled from Oxford University at the age of 18 for advocating the virtues of atheism. I know my mother, Rornar, who loved the idea of Babylon, would have enjoyed that. She thought Babylonian numerology was fun, albeit a joke. London, 1797, Mary Shelley's birth-year. Eccles, 2662, my birth-year. All of them radicals... No saints."

Jug looked at Zoia like she was crazy. Next he thought she might talk about Algonquin chieftains' graves, shaman mounts in Siberia, skull piles on abandoned ghost ships in the Bering Sea, Pharaohs' crypts, the original Tower of Babel, *all* places of death. Jug had determined that these young urbanites were corrupt, jaded beyond redemption. And the Rhetoric Department breed of hooligans and misfits—of which Zoia was apparently a bona fide, paid-up, card-carrying member—were particularly bizarre.

"Okay, I've already decided to lower the bar, but this is still a test," Zoia said. "Visits to my mother's grave, four times, one a week. Four visits over four weeks. Agreed?"

"How about four times but within the space of two and a half weeks?"

"You haggle with me as if we are in the marketplace," Zoia said. "The answer is no."

Jug felt embarrassed. But not embarrassed enough to not persist. "How about, as you said, four times, but over three-and-a-half weeks?"

"You haggle with me still? What is this? A shakedown?"

"I guess being a businessman is natural to me."

"I'm the boss here," Zoia said. "Quit haggling! All right. I'll punish you. I'm going to up the ante. I increase the number of visits to five. Over the length of five weeks. Agreed? If you haggle with me yet again, I'll add another week. Do you want to push your luck?"

"No. Agreed. Done. Five weeks."

Jug then thought to pose a question on a subject that he thought would be important to Zoia, relating to an ancient epoch.

"Name the one thing that's different."

"Different?" Zoia asked.

"In the old modernity as compared to our modernity?"

"We care more for our past generations. We pay more attention to our ancestors."

"For better or for worse?" Jug asked.

"Neither."

"Then the difference doesn't matter?"

"I favor the notion of our time being better. It's in the contract, specifically spelled out, as a responsibility for being the daughter of a historian," Zoia said laughing. "I'm kidding! I'm not being serious!"

There was a long painful and awkward silence. Jug realized Zoia was just incredibly good with thought.

"Now what do we do?" Jug asked.

"Jug!" Zoia suddenly exclaimed in a joyous, happy voice. "Who are you?"

"Well, I'm a member of the Homo sapiens. I guess that sounds too general. Plain speaking? Well, I'm a guy. I'm, well, just a man. I'm just one. One of many."

"I didn't ask you *what* you were. I asked you *who* you were."

"I could ask you the same thing."

"Yes, you could. And I'm sure you will. Shall we begin?"

"How do you answer a question like that when, like many, if not most people, you don't know who you are."

"Well, that's a start."

"I am a man who was born fabulously rich. I had Ebola at four years and mumps at six. I fell out of a tree when I was 10. I have a jagged scar on my knee to prove it. I'm not as smart as I pretend to be. Now my father was ruthless and smart, not only toward others, I inherited a great deal of that intra-family animosity, too."

"Oh, so you choose to start with such self-revealing candor and honesty?" Zoia asked. "Do you still love your father?"

"My father's dead."

"I mean...when he was alive."

Jug wanted to evade the question. "Some questions are best left unasked. Some secrets are best left secret. I love my mother. Does that help? Can you love someone who spent his life trying to make sure his son would never emerge from his shadow? Do you realize my father was 71 years old when I was born? And he lived another 24 years. No matter how many garlands of exotic flowers you placed around his neck they could not hide his stone-cold, manipulating, intimidating stare. *He was a jerk.*"

"But you loved him? When he was alive?"

"Don't you ever get tired of it? Doesn't it ever get old?"

"Old? Tired? Tired of what?"

"Aren't you tired of beating me up. Busting my balls? I care about you. I mean it. And I won't get cute with you. I'd sleep with you on your mother's grave, but only if I can get your father's permission first. I'm a decent and honorable man. And I'm 14 years older than you. I guess I'm an idiot for reminding you of that embarrassing fact."

"You're trying awfully hard. You're sweet. And I'm cold," Zoia said. "Shall we get a drink?"

Things went smoother after that.

They went to an all-night lounge/bistro that was only a kilometer away from the Rainbow, after ordering drinks and bringing them to the table, Jug said, "You know we could.....travel."

"Only after the fifth visit to my mother's grave," Zoia said. "Only then. How?"

"By helioplane."

"Helioplane?"

"At top speed they go 1,660 miles per hour. At least ours do. We could be in East Indonesia or Australia in less than six hours. There's a more or less uncharted island near there I'd like you to see. There are creatures there that don't exist anywhere else in the world. How they survived the big die off, the one 2,500 years ago and the one 55 million years ago, is beyond me. It's a complete mystery to me. Also some very exotic flowers that have been around for 30 million years. You know, so much of the Outer World is veiled in darkness. Not this place..."

"You know now why we must make five more visits here to the cemetery first, don't you?"

"No. But I'm sure you're going to explain it to me."

"Maybe afterwards."

Jug wasn't sure whether "afterwards" meant after the fifth visit to the graveyard, or after their trip to the East, but he was too intimidated by Zoia to ask for a clarification. He knew his cards were better played if he took it slowly. Also, Zoia had won Jug over to her way of thinking. Jug was now convinced it was important they got to know each other better.

They dated, and each of the dates took place at the cemetery, though by the second date they were spending much more time in the all-night lounge/bistro than they were spending at Zoia's mother's gravesite.

On the third date, Jug brought it up. They had been sitting for more than three hours at the lounge/bistro, and it had gone past three in the morning.

"I know there's just the three of you. Your father, of course. I've met him. And a historian I've never met. But the other historian is close to your family, right? His name is Pius?"

"What about us?"

"The three of you have this one thing in common. You have this fascination with events of an epoch—an epoch that virtually everybody else in the world couldn't care less about—that happened so *incredibly* long ago."

"Before the Darkness. Before the Fall, you mean?"

"Yes, though I don't know in detail what that means. I know archeology. I don't know the history part—the rich, alluring story— the eschatological part that underpins *my* archeological pursuits."

Zoia liked it. Jug was getting better at talking about these things. "Well, THE BLESSINGS OF GAIA DOCUMENT could give you a glimpse, if you're interested in the eschatological."

"I'm not interested in that. I'm not interested in myths."

"Is history a myth? That's one of my father's favorite counter-tropes when he's in his cups and browbeating someone in a motor-mouth fashion—badmouthing poor Pius, say—over some very old, cherished yet unprovable idea."

"Yeah. But why are they so concerned about this utterly inaccessible stuff?" Jug asked in exasperation. "Two grown men arguing over stuff nobody cares about?"

Zoia thought for a moment. "We want to find out—how to put it—what went wrong. *What really went wrong 2,700 years ago.* It's that simple. If you don't understand that, I fear you never will."

By the end of the fourth date, before the final one, Jug received the initial findings of the archeologists.

Chapter Twenty-One

The Ring, the Cloud, the Basement, and the
Greek, Italian, and Spanish Monasteries.

THE CHIEF ARCHEOLOGIST and his sidekick, the chief Antiquities' Science Officer, met Jug at his office. After shaking hands and exchanging salutations, they thanked Jug for the use of the maps.

"Without them, none of this could have been possible," the archeologist said. "The maps were pretty good, but they weren't always accurate. We couldn't find Yahoo. The site had been underwater for more than 2,000 years, but the real problem was that we found a huge bomb crater there. It may have had something to do with the Eleven-Years-War, or it may not have. Subsequent events in history can obliterate a site, and without any more information we assume that's what happened."

"Did you find the Hewlett-Packard garage?" Jug asked. "My father Gunter had had a soft spot for that. Always tried to imagine what it might have looked like. And if you found *anything*, even if just a tiny splinter of wood, it would make a splendid gift to my mother, who is so deeply bound to the H/P Mystical Cult of the Ancient Rites of Technorati. H/P is the one cult my father could tolerate. One of the reasons why he married her I think was because she wasn't tempted by any of the more goofy ones."

"No," the chief Antiquities Science Officer said, "we didn't find anything. And I'm not surprised. Wood breaks up in soil easily. Although the fact that the site was a little more than 250 meters inland means it would have been a land excavation. Tiny rectangular building, too small to pinpoint. And there's a 50-story-tall building that may be covering it. It's a heavily built up area."

"That piece of wood would have made my mother happy," Jug said with a note of regret. "I guess I could substitute another piece of wood, but you don't want to do that, you don't want to fool your mother over something that's quasi-spiritual. What about the House of Zuckerberg?"

"Worse than daunting. Difficult or impossible. The bay has extended three kilometers inland in 2,700 years. It's six feet under. There's no creek-side *there* to serve as a point of reference. All that's there is a barely detectable indentation of what might—or might not have been—a submerged underwater trough, the remnants of a creek. That was the closest thing to a guide post."

"I lost my bet," Jug said with a note of dejection. "Jason's going to be happy about that."

"The only one that was on dry land was the Apple Ring. We gave pet names to each of them. The Cloud, the Basement, the Mediterranean-style Monasteries were the underwater sites. The Ring itself was the only one that was still on dry land, not counting the H/P site. We had to employ scuba divers and use underwater excavation equipment for the first three." The chief Antiquities Science Officer was going to say something, but Jug rudely interrupted her.

"But you found the Ring?"

"Ahhhh! Yes. The Ring. To be more accurate, we investigated the debris field." The archeologist then explained to Jug that the second most productive part of the search was the Apple Site, *because* it was above water.

"Of course there's no Ring there now. But we found remnants. We were able to excavate in a small park, also at a construction site. The rest is mostly covered by some very tall buildings. Some metals, pulverized glass, tiny taffy-like remnants of asphalt from surrounding parking lots, chemical compounds, probably from remnants of paint, fragments of concrete. We found three, three! steel girders driven deep into the ground. I don't know what else you could have been looking for. That's all we found. But we could tell it was quite an architectural feat, the building of that structure. It was a ring all right. We made a dozen boreholes, so we were able to establish the shape."

"The Facebook?"

"Monasteries. That's what we dubbed them. Twenty-two to 24 feet under water. So named because the structures apparently were built to resemble a cluster of Mediterranean-style monastic dwellings. Best foundations we were able to find, with one exception."

"One exception?"

"Yes. Clouds. There were two of them. That's what we dubbed them: The two cloud buildings. In their heyday they were magnificent. We have facsimiles and one good illustration of them picked up from the early Gaia-Dome era, which was confirmed by a picture that we found in the Antarctica papers. Splendid architecture, especially the roofs that vaguely give the impression of clouds. They were on the east side of what had been Gaia Creek, before it was submerged by the rising waters of the bay."

"What can you report about the site?"

"*The cloud, in the clouds...* Can't contact anybody inside it," the archeologist said. "Cloud, without a long-faced, white-bearded god, sitting lotus-style, on top of a ball of mist. *In the clouds. They wrote with light.* At least those words sound religious, don't they? Electronics equals light. Not more than that. *Poof! Gone!*"

"What did you find then?"

"You mean the real stuff?"

"Well, yeah, " Jug said in a slightly irritated and impatient voice. "Let's get back...to the archeology."

"We found the basement."

"The Basement?"

"Another foundation of a building, but not a Google building. Not on any of our maps. And it's the biggest find of all. Because we found a basement, intact, with documents inside. In all the underwater sites, in all of them, it's the only place where we found such a thing. This was an institution located where it was not supposed to be located, at least according to the maps."

"But what was it?"

"The basement sort of acted like a sealed vault, because there were huge slabs of concrete we had to break through. It took a long time. And our guess is that it was a large parking garage built on top of an old basement. There was a sealed vault inside the basement itself, and it managed to keep the water out and preserved the documents. From these papers we were able to determine that it was a five-building mini-campus of Microsoft. This mini-campus was bound by Google buildings, at least on one-and-a-half sides, and what was then Steven's Creek. In present times, it would be what we call Gaia Creek. The Microsoft buildings were torn down in January 2018, according to the records. They were replaced by newer buildings. It's amazing the records we found. Gatetar tower is located close to the intersection of the ancient cities of Mountain View, Los Altos, and Palo Alto, about 50 meters from where there was something called a Tower Records *something or other* ... At the intersection of San Antonio Road and El Camino Real, *whatever that means* ...."

"But we found something that is even more important. A document. A document written on paper. Not in light. Not in the cloud. *The Time Repairer. Darkness.*"

"What?"

The chief Antiquities Science Officer couldn't believe Jug's ignorance, but she realized she was being unfair, it was a fairly arcane subject, from the point of view of the general public.

"*The Time Repairer. Darkness,*" she said. "It was a story, fiction or non-fiction, that was passed down through the Dark Time to us, through the oral traditions, then captured like a butterfly in the poetry of Ulm. Ulm sort of looked at the previous world of electronics with horror, disgust, ill-humor, anger, so I warn you we're not even sure about the numbers. It could have been written 500 years after, there's at least a 350-year-long gap between the document and

Ulm's script. Maybe it wasn't even his. Maybe it was just an add-on.
Added to the original script. We know there was an oral tradition
of the Time Repairer. Some handwriting experts believe it was written in a different hand than Ulm's. But Ulm's hand changed, wavy,
straight, then wavy again. There's no way of knowing for sure."

"Who's Ulm?"

"A great poet, the greatest poet, the only poet we know from the
early Dark Time. *The Time Repairer. Darkness* as a piece of poetry, is
considered a profound masterwork, a sublime piece, a great work of
antiquity. Though it's true, not many people know anything about it."

"Can I have it?"

"Finders keepers? Is that the principle that is operating here?
Well, you paid for the excavation, didn't you? It's a great treasure.
Something for the public archive, if you ask me. I'm sure the Antiquities Bureau will want to have a say in its final disposition. As the
chief Antiquities Science Officer I'm duty bound to remind you that
there are laws on the books about this, Mr. Gatetar, difficult-to-
enforce laws, but laws no less."

"I have no intention of breaking the law. But we can keep it a
secret ... for now. Just for now. Can't we?"

"For a short while. I must inform you that there are risks
involved."

"It's from 2,700 years ago? Correct?"

"Yes."

"I know what we can do with it. I know who to show it to.
She'll know what to do with it. And if she doesn't know what to do
with it, her father would. We can talk to the Antiquities Bureau in a
few months. Let's keep our special find under wraps for now. Who's
going to miss three months in the context of 2,700 years?"

"Who's going to challenge you, you mean," the chief Antiquities Science Officer said, "that's the more important question. It's a
scribbling of Ulm."

"A pre-scribbling of Ulm."

"Yes! Now you're getting it."

Chapter Twenty-Two

S O, ON THEIR LAST VISIT, the sixth visit to Rornar's grave, Jug presented to Zoia the *Time Repairer. Darkness.* It was wrapped in a protective cover, replacing the original vellum that had been damaged. The document itself was four pages long, but each page was four and a half feet wide by two and a half feet long, and the print covered most of the page. And though there were wide margins between the pages, the print was very small. Basically you got twelve pages for one. Thus 48 pages of script.

"This is it?" Zoia asked. "This is all you got?"

"Yes, we weren't looking for it. But yes, this is it. Well, the chief Antiquities Science Officer said it was an extreme rarity. How did she put it? Priceless. Just thought with your fascination for ancient times and all."

Zoia was amazed. "I'm joking. This is marvelous. Fantastic... Why the small type? Saving space? Why four pages? My father and Pius will get enormous pleasure from reading this. But I have somebody else in mind."

"Who?"

"Rathman."

"Who?"

"He's a nobody. Student. Rhetoric Department. Poor. Broke. He's the genuine article. Show him these scraps of paper, from 2,700 years ago, and he's going to be impressed, he's going to go ape crazy, he's going to bark like a raving, mad dog."

"Who is he?"

"I told you. Nobody."

"Why him, then?"

"Met him once. My father should have first dibs on this, but he's too busy. Can't manage it. Nor can Pius. Pius is on retreat. The Iona Festival, an event that happens once a year. The Obsidian Order sticks its prominent members in a cave for five days with only water to consume. Then they take them out, feed them, rest them up for a couple of weeks, and stake them to the ground, facing up at the sun for eight hours straight every day over eight days. For what? I don't know! Crazy! Too bad. Pius would love this."

"But we have only three months and Dad's deadline with the *Eccles' Literary Gazette* is 24 days from now. They're expecting an essay from him on: Ancient History and Modernity, Clash or Coincidence? He's written bits of it but he's way behind schedule. Way behind. Then, on the heels of this project, *Eccles' Review of Books,* three weeks further out, they're expecting an essay on: Asteroid attack? Fear of the unknown? Eschatological orientation? Scientifically-orientated? Both? My dad's already mapped it out in a baggy sort of way—but so far—treading with difficulty. So his default position is to treat it like a survey. Surveys are good, as far as that goes, but that's not going very far. So, unless Dad pulls a rabbit out of his hat, harsh yet reasonable and fair critics will relegate the essay to being a puff piece. If my harebrain scheme works, he'll switch the first essay of course, and if Rathman does a stellar job, maybe the second one too. *Eccles' Literary Gazette* will print dad's essay in a later issue. *Eccles' Review of Books,* maybe they'll allow it, too. For Rathman, especially if both happens, luck. Auger will have more time to complete his work, after all he loves to procrastinate in the winter. For an 18-year-old hayseed from the sticks to be published in one of the two most prestigious intellectual journals, luck, if two out of two, incredible luck! All because of this manuscript. Oh, Pius, you're going to hate me for letting down the Antiquities' Bureau, forgive me Pius, I'm being out of character. But how often does this happen? You don't have to be a Prussian, wear gaudy military ornaments and tinsel, be 91 years old, to do scholarship, as my father used to say. And I don't know why, but Pius, had always agreed with him on that point."

Jug had no idea what Zoia was talking about. He did not understand the first part, the middle part, or the latter part. Although Jug was happy that Zoia was grateful for the gift, he couldn't summon up any interest beyond—the archeology, and the archeological aspects, which he had a fond and genuine feeling towards. He didn't care too much about people who died a long time ago.

"And now you'll let me take you to that tiny island in the east end of East Indonesia?" Jug asked. He summoned up the courage, popped the question, sensing something in Zoia... "I've been faithful. I've been kind. I love being faithful. Next week will be six weeks since we met. Five weeks now, not a miss on our visits to the graveyard. I've kept my part of the bargain."

"Been counting the weeks, haven't you?" Zoia said, smiling radiantly, then displaying a look of disappointment. "I need to be back in six weeks. Mid-terms. And I need to talk to Rathman. When he sees what I have to offer him he's going to pee in his pants. Rathman's deserving. And you're going to be a good boy."

"And being a good boy means you're going to give this precious art-treasure to the Antiquities' Bureau! But not yet. Of course you're going to be convicted and sentenced to death for corrupting me when this is over, but I'm sure that's minor compared to the stuff you're used to dealing with. You can handle it. I know you can handle the Antiquities Bureau."

"Yes?"

"I know you don't know what this is." Zoia pointed to the *Time Repairer. Darkness.* "How important it is. Gaia. We're co-conspirators. Among the teensy-weensy number of brave historians in the world, this is hot copy. I met him. Rathman was reading *The Time Repairer, Darkness.* Not this version. Ulm's version. This is an earlier version from before the Dark, before the Fall. Get it?"

"No."

"Well Rathman will," Zoia exclaimed. "It's fascinating. But it's also scholarship. It was meant for him. And I'm not just being superstitious here. He was reading this, or rather Ulm's version, in the Reading Room at the very moment I first met him. Call it a coincidence? I don't. You don't know what you're giving me, even if you are just lending it to me for a short while."

"I'm glad I'm able to give you something," Jug said, "that just luckily, fell into my hands. I am, in this small way, contributing."

'Okay, he won't leave me alone,' Zoia said to herself. 'Was it worth a six hour flight to East Indonesia?' She did the calculations. 'In a helioplane, 1660 miles per hour, and the—should-have-been-extinct—animal viewing. And the exotic flowers that shouldn't have been around for the last 30 million years. Your father raised you to be too lax. How often do you get a chance to have a look-see into the land on the other side of the looking glass? This Jug guy can charm you and creep you out, at the same time. But you're tough. Where's the harm? And his advisor, Jason, the one who's reliable, and who is truly likeable, he's going to be there at the beginning and the end of the journey. As I've insisted.'

"Pius, please forgive me," she thought. "I'm going to loan *The Time Repairer. Darkness.* to Rathman. Not turn it over to the Antiquities Bureau immediately. Like you would have insisted. Father raised me to be like my mother, Rornar! Titans clashing! You want to blame somebody, blame him."

Chapter Twenty-Three

FROM THE DIRECTORY on the Rhetoric Department bulletin board, Zoia knew how to find Rathman.

She found him where he was temporarily residing. He was sleeping above a closet.

His little nest was located in a small wing of a very old manor house, a sprawling building surrounded by granite stone walls, and an entangle of trees and bushes. On all four sides loomed buildings multiple stories higher than the old house.

One of the better-off students rented a partitioned annex of the former servants' quarters of the 155-year-old house. The first occupiers of the home lived at a time when the house was three kilometers outside the Blake city limits. It had been a country home, surrounded by apricot, cherry, and pear orchards, with an extensive zucchini garden and a small pasture. As was the mode of architecture at the time, the residence had gabled archways and very high ceilings.

The servant quarters were commodious by the standards of the time, almost spacious. The student occupied only a third of the original servants' area. Above the closet was a space, four-and-one-half feet high, accessible using a ladder. Rathman occupied this crawl-space which was large enough only for a mattress. He kept his clothes in a bundle, having no chest of drawers to store them in.

Unlike the students, Rathman had no family, friends, or relatives in Eccles to fall back on, to cushion him from whatever blows might rain down on him.

Even though Rathman had been promised a 50 percent reduction in his tuition in the next academic year, his scholarship wasn't sufficient to cover everything, not with the rise in the cost of housing. By 2680, rents in Eccles soared, making it the costliest city in the world to live in.

Also, as an orphan, from the edge of the Outer World, Rathman's stipend was only half the usual amount. No one had expected him to submit his application to U. Presbyr. But Rathman was young, he was tough, and he was ready to play the game.

What kind of work would an 18-year-old be able to find in Eccles?

Right away, upon arriving in Eccles, Rathman took a job as a 'pot-and-pan-man,' a washer and dryer of cookery in the students' commissary kitchen. One free meal a day was thrown in helping to compensate for the low pay. On weekends, he took a secondary job in a kitchen in the basement of the Gatetar tower. He was required to work erratic shifts; sometimes they began at 2 a.m. and ended at noon, sometimes they began at 9 p.m. and didn't end until 5 a.m. As the number-two pot-and-pan cleaner, he was at the lowest rung in the kitchen hierarchy. He didn't mind. However, the people he was required to work with were very strange indeed. None of them had papers. They were all Outer World "non-registered," and, with the exception of Rathman, most had come as refugees from the farther out regions of the Outer World.

These people were what were called in Eccles non-people. They lived underground. Many of them lived in conditions that were worse than Rathman's. And unlike Rathman, they could be caste out from the Inner World in an instant, they were the targets of informers but also of bounty hunters, paid to collect "heads." Upon capture, the refugees would be barred forever from returning to Eccles, no appeal possible.

When Rathman told his co-workers the course of study he was engaged in at U. Presbyr, they thought it absurd. Indeed, they thought it was the most preposterous and hilarious thing they'd ever heard of.

"So you're studying darkness?" they'd ask. "*Darkness?* They pay you to study absence of light? We've been running away from *that* all our lives. And you embrace it?"

But in spite of the seeming foolery of his business, they liked him. They trusted him. And they were moved by his orphanage stories. Hearing that he had lost his entire family, in one fell swoop, they felt just a twinge of sorrow for him. But he wasn't hunted. He had papers. They were hunted, and thus they had to have different places to hide, sometimes switching locales overnight, rarely staying in one place too long, living a life perennially on the run. Everyone had a rabbit hole they could pop into in case things got rough: a hobo's hovel, an attic, a basement, an outdoor shed, the sewer, the always open underground tube stations, the buses on certain, select routes.

When Zoia was escorted to Rathman's digs, though it was midmorning, Rathman was on his mat sleeping. He had ridden a bicycle home before 5:30 a.m., so he'd managed to get some sleep, but only a few hours.

Zoia shouted at him from below. "Come on. Get up! Get up. Rise and shine!"

Awaking, Rathman shouted out in a confused voice, "Who's there!" He then crawled to the edge of the closet and peered out over the ledge, only his eyes, forehead, and scruff of hair showing.

Having let herself in without even knocking, what was this young woman doing staring up at him? Then he recognized her.

"What a move on her part," Rathman whispered to himself. He wasn't sure his words had been heard and he hoped that they hadn't.

But Rathman was delighted to see Zoia. He was overjoyed. Though it'd been a little over a month since they'd briefly met, he had not forgotten her. He had thought about her every day. He wanted to say: "Come on up and sit beside me and let me look at you."

But he didn't have the nerve.

"Bad timing for Rathman," Rathman finally blurted out. "You want to check out the hole I'm living in? I've discovered early on that people in Eccles need the skills of a pots-and-pans washer more than they need the skills of a herder. Minor wages received. Major hassles, too. I've just worked through the entire night."

"The orphan of insecurity and geographical vagabondage," Zoia said. Then she gave him her best enigmatic grin. She wanted to raise him up, lift up his spirits.

"The utterance of these words rouse me above my benighted condition," Rathman pronounced. He was quoting, line for line, a local actress who had played an orphan in a recently released, highly successful play. Zoia also recognized the quote. She thought of saying something, but she didn't. Rathman erupted into a smile, making the words sound even more yielding. Sauntering into a private place uninvited, was this a practice that was common in Eccles? Rathman wondered. Of course it wasn't. But Rathman wondered all the same. He was such a "yea-yea." Zoia had taken a shocking liberty.

"You don't take offense?" Zoia asked. "I've practically ambushed you."

"Should I?" Rathman asked. "I could get used to you. I could even get used to your ways. So now, what's this about?"

"Okay, your luck has changed. Your ship has come in. Good time for Rathman. I have something special for you. That's why I'm here."

"Special? Something special?"

"You're NOT going to believe what I have for you," Zoia said, shouting upwards. "Hurry up. Come on! Shake a leg, Rathman! Let's go!" She waited for him to descend.

Rathman didn't button his shirt, but while he was stepping backwards down the ladder he at least hastily stuffed his shirttails into his pants.

Zoia showed Rathman the manuscript. She unfolded it, with delicacy and painstaking patience, and laid it out on the floor. That was the only place they could put it. The space was filled with Rathman's roommate's genteel clutter, calligraphy scrolls on the walls (Zoia liked that), rosewood furniture, and lots of sheet music and hand-written compositions, even in the kitchenette and the tiny bathroom, there were rolls of sheet music and hand-written compositions lying on small tables and pasted to the walls.

"Your roommate's an artist I presume?" Zoia asked.

"He's *not* my roommate," Rathman said. "This is his room. I'm here only by *his* sufferance. He's a modest and beautiful musician. He's also a composer, in an *avocation-that-doesn't-put-food-on-the-table* sort of way."

They both got down on their hands and knees, so they could examine the document more closely. Rathman admired the flow of the writing, the flow of the calligraphy. The quality of the artwork wasn't just competent, it was beautiful, even gorgeous.

It took a while for Rathman to read the first page, which was the equivalent of eight book pages hinged together. There were three more broadsheets beneath it.

Rathman was astounded at what he read. "This is not *The Time Repairer. Darkness.* This version includes other things which are not found in Ulm's version. Look at this here!" Rathman exclaimed. He pointed to a particular passage. "Where in Gaia's name did you find this? Do you know what this is?"

"Your ticket to some sort of recognition and success, I'd imagine," Zoia replied. "And you're only 18! Don't show this to anyone. No one. Until you're ready. WAIT UNTIL YOU'RE READY. Write it up, you have to work quickly. Work stealthily. You have three weeks. Then you can show it to the world. Later, I have to give it back."

"I'm confused," Rathman said. "Three weeks to do what?"

"To complete a study and to write it up. I'll explain later."

"Don't abandon me," Rathman said. "Work with me. Share the

glory with me. Let's make it a collaboration. I'm scared to death of dealing with this all by myself."

"You have nothing to fear. *It's meant for you.* I'm going away for six weeks. Read it. Right now. Read it tonight! Sleep on it. Start writing. Put it aside. Take it up again. Read again. Sleep on it. Start your narrative. Put it aside. Revise it. Dream on it. Give it a dab. Give it one last thorough romp. Then when you're ready, submit it. Submit it no later than 21 days from now. BUT NO LATER. Trust me. Time's important. 'The document will embolden your commentary, while simultaneously your commentary will illuminate the document.' That's exactly what you will tell my father. Those very words."

"Shouldn't I submit it to one of our Rhetoric scholars?" Rathman asked. "Professor Golden? Professor Leisterwhile?"

"Whatever you do, don't do that!" Zoia said. "Are you crazy? Neither of them will know what to do with it. They'd think they'd know what to do with it, but they don't. They're teachers of Rhetoric. They'll sit on it forever. Then some muckity-muck will take it up, re-imagine it, then submit it as his own work. I know how these academics work. Submit it to my father."

"Should I mention you?"

"Of course you mention me! Absolutely. That's your entree. That'll help grease the skids."

"Where are you going?"

"Doesn't matter. East Indonesia. And other points." Zoia looked around, examining the room carefully, a second time, and the closet. The room was cluttered, but the space above the closet looked pretty ridiculous.

Because the ceiling was so high, the musician had improvised something that was very clever at the opposite side of the room from the closet. With jibs, hooks, and boards, he had clothes, entire batches of wash, drying. The clothes were hanging like flags.

"Boy, I like your digs." Zoia said.

"Cowboy?" Rathman asked. "You were going to start calling me the cowboy? Admit it. Weren't you?"

"Well yes," Zoia said. "But no. If you do a great job, a splendid job... Prepare to surprise the hell out of me. I'll start calling you the Barefoot Herder. That's what you wanted, wasn't it?"

Rathman smiled. She remembered! Rathman pointed to the top of the closet, an embarrassingly droopy bit of wrinkled bedding hung over the side. Just below, there was a violin on a stand. It was located in a place that was so central to the room, it was as if it were on display.

"I was told the trees" Rathman said, "of the wood were planted a century before my roommate's violin was constructed. The wood-working guild planted trees so their grandchildren would have the right kind of wood to harvest. Then the wood was cured. That took another 20 years. Such wood. This violin was composed of that! Therefore, there it is, a venerable instrument, made of the finest wood. I'm married to a music nut."

"Is it yours?"

"What? So glad you're listening to me. You think I can afford something like that?"

"When you're being preachy I don't listen to you. Is it yours?"

"*That?*" Rathman asked "No. Like I said. This place belongs to the musician. It's his. *His.* His father works—has high station, lordly status, recently received a high promotion—at Gatetar. At the age of 14, his son won the Eccles' Young Musician of the Year Competition, but after that, awards have been sparse. Son is in competition for a chair in the violin section at one of our orchestras. This has been a life-long ambition of his. I don't know exactly which seat it is. Sometimes, when he's more confident, he's aiming at the third, or when he's all wound up, the second. Don't know what any of that means. Violinist. Prides himself also on being a composer. Has a gramophone and a collection of long-playing velco passed down to him from, now get this, his father's lover, but he still has plenty of modern gadgets, too. His family's old and well-placed. The violin's been in his family for 150 years. Almost as long as the age of this house."

"And those?" Zoia asked, pointing to a fine golden-edged collection of books: fiction and literature of the most famous authors and writers of the Outer World.

"Nope. His again. Now separate me from this grandiosity," Rathman said. He pointed to the top of the closet. "Imagine that. Impressed by my estate? My father would have commented, 'Worse than a decrepit, rotting corn crib, or a shit-dripping hayloft, but a crawl-space so small you can't stand upright in? That'll cramp your love life.'"

"Yeah," Zoia said. "Charming."

Bad move on his part, Rathman thought. He decided to change the topic of conversation. But what should be his next move? He decided to go philosophical. "Stuff that passes for what? Value? Perhaps the old age of Gaia is an illusion, an annihilating white vapor expansion of emptiness. What if modernity, as its replacement, is nothing more than an illusion?"

"But we're living in a new age," Zoia said.

"Are we?"

"We're able to entertain possibilities of looking at things from as many perspectives as we like. As many ways as we choose to. A product of the newfound freedoms."

"How many ways do we need to see the heartlessness at the heart of humanity, in spite of all of this *so-called* newfound freedom?" Rathman asked. "What's to hold humanity together then? Does anybody in Eccles think you have to hold *anything* together?"

"Impressive. Another time. You have work to do. Impress me later. But don't get so preachy. I don't like it when you get so preachy." Zoia smiled. "Sometimes it doesn't sharpen the edge, it has the opposite effect, it dulls the edge. If you want to survive in Eccles you need an edge. Work on *The Time Repairer. Darkness.* That'll be your edge."

"You came to my digs, didn't you?" Rathman asked "I didn't invite you. You came to see me. I've heard you like to talk."

Rathman wasn't accustomed with being so assertive, so border- line aggressive. He wondered where this newfound confidence had come from. Just being with Zoia, if even for such a brief bit of time, made Rathman feel confident. At least outwardly he tried to curb his enthusiasm, but the feeling was exhilarating.

Zoia smiled. "Keep your eye on *this*. Think about *it*. Put *all* else aside. Can you write your own ticket on this? You can. YOU CAN DO IT. You'll never have an opportunity like this again. Think of this in terms of generations. 2,700 years of generations, divide by 21 years, 130 generations then. By that calculation we're the 131st generation. This isn't about Ulm. This isn't about the Dark Age, which is supposedly your topic. It's about you. Why did you come here, barefoot herder? Orphan of modernity. Orphaned to modernity. Step out. Step into another world. Step into the Time Repairer. See what's there."

"You're generous."

"Well, Jug, in his own way, was generous too."

"Who's Jug?"

"Another time. Get to work, herder."

Chapter Twenty-Four

THE DOCUMENT WAS DATED January, 2018 A.D. In its beautiful calligraphy Rathman read all the pages. It meant so much to him to have the privilege to read something that had not been read in 2,700 years. He read it through. Waited 12 hours. Read it again. This time he was determined to spend whole days on it. He re-read it slowly. He devoted himself to it. He devoured it.

His roommate came in. "What's all this crap? Studying a play?"

"Not a play."

"Studying a novel?"

"Not a novel. It's a poem. Not much of a plot."

His roommate scratched on his violin's strings for a few hours, Rathman found the music peaceful and soothing. His roommate left, returned hours later, scratched on the violin for another three hours. Then he huddled at his study table and composed a short piano sonata.

When playing, the violinist looked thoughtful, serious, and intense. When composing, however, he often had a glum look of disenchantment followed by a grim look of uncertainty.

But whatever the value of his roommate's work—and Rathman was certain it had value—he admired his roommate's discipline and stick-to-it-ness. He marveled at his roommate's powers of concentration.

After his roommate left, having been given permission in advance, Rathman played one of the velco's from his roommate's father's lover's gramophone collection. He pulled the needle up from the velco and turned the device off. He read through the manuscript Zoia had given him, for the sixth time. He had now acquired a much greater familiarity with the work, along with its sudden lurches from promise to sterility.

Rathman was going to read it again, give it a seventh shot, but before he took it up again, he changed his mind. He decided to shift gears. He decided it would make more sense to study the later document, the work of Ulm, coming down from the Dark Ages—and by doing this—he could contrast and compare the January, 2018 document with the later 359 A.G. document.

Rathman started in on Ulm's poem. Ulm's introduction to his poem was written when he had been 17-years-old, a little over 2,300 years in the past. "As far back as I can remember," it began, "I have lived in caves. In darkness. I have known no other place, no other time, no other life. An aged man, a complete stranger to us, came one day to visit our small clan. He claimed he'd seen a great deal of the world, having crossed the Western and Eastern Seas, having been as far south as Satroovee, having seen the ruins of the Great Empties, and the two ranges of the Big Mountains. The stranger spent three years with me. In the darkness. He told me about the sights and sounds of the world he traveled. I am not entirely sure why he chose me to be his interlocutor and sole audience but my elders told him I was the 'youngest of the pre-men' and that I was also one of the laziest of the clan and that I was afflicted with a supercilious and useless imagination.

"In any event, some of the stories he told me were edifying. That is to say, they revealed that life wasn't just an unbroken string of beastliness, hellishness, and nastiness, cut short by death. There were interludes (brief) between episodes of horror. These interludes included well-being, contentment, and dare I say it, happiness. That was the genius of the stranger. The stories made you feel that it was not so bad that you had to live all your life in caves.

"One day the stranger departed from our caves. Disappeared. He didn't even say good-bye. Three days later I had a dream inspired by his talks. I dreamt of a desert so vast it was as if it were an ocean. I then dreamt of an ocean that was so desolate it was as if it were a desert. There were no fish. No people. Very few animals. Very few birds. Precious few plants. Sterile places. But when I awoke from this dream I decided to write about a world that didn't exist, but could exist. I knew that these words had no application, no purpose... But I also knew that I had to write them nevertheless.

"One day later, I discovered among my possessions a stack of 450 clear and clean unbound blank pages—a large inkwell filled with ink, and two wine-sack-like containers of ink, and six new squib pens. These must have been sacred instruments taken from an old Gaia-Dome. I have often speculated and wondered how the stranger acquired these esoteric items in the first place. There also was planted among my possessions a grammar; a small, well-thumbed dictionary; and the first 29 pages of something called *Robinson Crusoe*.

"At the top of the sheaf of blank pages the stranger had written: 'Why begin?' But I knew these words had not been written for me. The stranger must have gotten cold feet, changed his mind, but he kept the blank pages, ink, squib pens. The words he wrote to himself were perhaps a reminder of his decision not to proceed. How did I know this? Well, that's easy. After all, he never crossed out the words nor did he write another word. It was like it was a signpost commanding him to stop. I myself never crossed the words out either.

"So, at last, it is under these strange and peculiar circumstances of living forever in caves, I write my poem. After all, I cannot help but think that the greatest power of a text is in its profound resistance to amnesia. For humanity, the worst thing that can happen is forgetting. So, at last, here I begin. For a time now, we live in a world where nature and human economy are working together in health and harmony. I dedicate this poem to our time. As for the future, I am an optimist."

Were the people of Eccles now as optimistic as Ulm was then? Rathman wondered. With an asteroid threatening? he wondered. He read on.

Skipping to the very end of the poem there was supposedly a 'tacked-on' section of *The Time Repairer.* Was it even written in Ulm's hand? That had never been proven with certainty. Was it appended in a later age? Even though it was from an earlier age, was it deposited at a later age, perhaps 500 years later?

Then Rathman switched gears and took the other document, the original document of *The Time Repairer*, dated January 2018 A.D., written by the Microsoft building basement's author. It began with a quotation: "And for us this is the end of all the stories, and we can most truly say they all lived happily ever after. But for them it was only the beginnings of the real story. All their life in this world and all their adventures in Narnia had only been the cover and the title which no one on earth has read: which goes on forever: in which every chapter is better than the one before."— C. S. Lewis.

And so Rathman studied everything he could find about this supposed author, C. S. Lewis. But the record was spotty. Yes, there was a record of Lewis' name and the title of his principal work, but no lines of the book had apparently been preserved. Except for the lines above.

So Rathman looked into all the data bases to see if he could find anything about this author. And there apparently was nothing more. Rathman was ready to give up. Several days went by. And then when he looked where he should have been looking from the beginning, in the most recently published works in Eccles, he finally found something in a work written by Pius, the historian, Zoia and Auger's friend.

Pius's article was based on something found in the documents discovered among the Antarctica papers. Pius wrote that Lewis was considered, in his time, which was called then 'the mid-20th Century,' to be the atheists' favorite "Christian" thinker (whatever that meant). Pius had discovered from the documents that Lewis had also written a book, a non-fiction book, called *The Abolition of Man*. The book had been lost over time but Pius had been able to read a synopsis. Lewis had prefaced his remarks by saying that forward-looking thinkers who wanted to reshape society, and eventually the human species itself, had no way of determining what progress meant. For many it meant increasing human power and using it to make Nature (Pius had translated "Nature" to mean "Gaia,"). But the power of humanity over Gaia meant in practice the power of some human beings over others. If the societal order was planned so as to maximize power over Gaia, other human values would have to be disregarded. *'Boy, looking at the historical record, that sounded all so familiar...the Gaia-Domes...'* Rathman thought.

The endgame of humankind remaking Gaia had the potential of remaking humankind itself. As Lewis wrote, the one direct quote Pius was able to find in the documents pulled out of the Antarctica papers, "Human's final conquest could prove to be the extinction of humanity itself."

And so that's what *The Time Repairer*, the original *Time Repairer*, was about? Rathman scratched his head. This was an enigma. This was, above all, confusing. Maybe the Microsoft building basement's author was just quoting at the time an important literary flasher, C. S. Lewis, to buttress his absurdly half-baked work of dubiously fashioned fiction. That was a possibility. Rathman hoped he had the acuity to unravel the mystery—if there was a mystery—of *The Time Repairer*.

Chapter Twenty-Five

S O, RATHMAN PROCEEDED with the theory that *The Time Repairer* was originally a work of fiction! Then Ulm, 369 years later, or someone else who assumed that name tacked on the orally transmitted *Time Repairer*. Therefore, Ulm didn't know whether *The Time Repairer*, originally, had been intended to be read as fiction, or truth, or moralistic fable, or just reportage.

Rathman read the story again. He had more insight now. But it was such a simple story. And, in some ways, a stupid, crude, and incredible story. Or was it?

The Microsoft building basement author began: *"I buried this here for a reason. For the deep future. Because nobody's going to understand this now. In the future, time will come unstuck. This problem will be amplified because there will be a cyber war in the future, a mysterious cyber war, because no one will recognize it for what it is until it's too late. It will escalate beyond anyone's imagination, even those who set off the cyber war itself would see it moving in strange and unanticipated directions, thus becoming A Sorcerer's Apprentice devolution of a cyber war.*

The war will start with people having to reset their passwords, their pins, not just once a year, or once every six months, or once a week, but once a day. Finally, the cyber war will get so complicated that people will be forced to change their password two times during the day, but at the same time: 3:00 a.m., and 3:00 p.m., with only 13 seconds either way allowed for the reset.

Which is no problem if you had a very accurate time piece at your disposal. But if you didn't?

Until there is an electricity blackout that hit, bringing down the entire electrical grid. This lasts for two days. Yes, this is the ultimate in cyber warfare, you have no access because you have no pin, you have no password. You have the physical world but you do not have access to the cyber world. You can't access your bank account. You can't get to work. You can't communicate. For the most part, you can't obtain food, gas, water, or guns. Cooking food over wood-burning fires becomes necessary. Equestrians and bicyclists suddenly have the only advantage over walkers, and walkers have to walk everywhere. That lack of communication and mobility increases the feeling of vulnerability, exposure, and in extreme cases, a dizzying anxiety and trauma.

Then just after the power comes back on and everything comes back up, there is another shutdown. Another powerful blackout. Everyone is told that this attack in the cyber world is far worse than the first one. It infects the entire electrical grid in some deep way. The authorities are predicting that it will take four or five weeks minimum, perhaps longer, before they can bring the system back up.

A company may have a backup data center and redundancy, but there are often no workable plans in place for when the entire electrical grid comes down.

Facing this problem there are two categories of people. Those who can live for four weeks or longer without access to the cyber world, and those who can not.

The ones who are most dependent on their gadgets and devices, have jobs or stations in life that force them to be dependent, even if it is against their will. All those who completely rely on availability, speed, and correctness of data streams are the ones most in jeopardy. In some instances, cyber contact is the only way they can keep their businesses afloat. Here is an example that the author of the Time Repairer quotes: "I've always responded to messages as soon as I get them. I don't wait. If I get up in the middle of the night, I check messages. First thing in the morning, I check messages. And then during the day, I check it many times and reply to messages. But I can't now. And it's not just annoy-ing, it is completely upending my life.

And these people have very few "analog age" time pieces at their disposal. Why preserve those antiquated ways of time counting? They can't use the clocks on their devices, THERE IS NO ELECTRICITY! They have a choice. They can wait it out, or they can get back up and running using an old-fashioned time piece. And then they can, alas, reset their passwords, their pins, at 3:00 a.m. and 3:00 p.m.

Suddenly accurate mechanical or battery-operated time pieces be-come extremely valuable, and very much in demand.

People hunt their drawers, (poke shotguns into their surprised neighbors' faces to force them to turn their time pieces over,) look for old family heirlooms—a late father's or mother's watch, for example—an old wall clock no longer chiming in the attic. But in most cases, these ancient clocks and watches don't work.

So they have to go to the most derelict, seediest, poorest parts of town, the places that are at the opposite end of the urban tech centers. These neighborhoods are called Jude's No-Man's-Land, or Old Man's Croak. They need to find the old man, the man who can save them, the jeweler. The Time Repairer! Typically he resides in a tiny hovel, looking up from his workbench and blinking beneath his eyeshade. Suddenly his otherwise lowly status has been elevated. His services are—in great demand. The public comes. They plead with him to repair their watches or to dig up a time piece that can serve the same purpose. He is the watch man.

They throw money at him. They try to cajole him. They give him anything short of their first born. So they won't have to wait four weeks or longer to access their cyber accounts."

But this was the part that Rathman realized was the scariest part of the story.

The Microsoft building basement's author concluded the story by writing, *"In the future, there will be a similar collapse. What form it will take I know not. But it's coming. And those who can wait it out, rely on the plenitude of the normal, physical "regular" world, long after this particular crisis is over will bear children who will bear children*

who will inherit instincts, habits, modes of thought, routines, sensibili-
ties from their forebears that will allow them to have a better chance of
surviving than the children of the children of those who can not wait out
the collapse. Survival is in the DNA, not in the truth.

And that is the message of the watch repairer: The Time Repairer.
Darkness is coming!

Rathman paused. He knew there were things—something was wrong with the "story." On multiple levels the plot was maddeningly coarse. Also, maddeningly obscure in meaning. So he wrote down his objections:

"*The Time Repairer* may have been read in 2018 A.D. as a complete joke, or an incomplete fragment of a story, or an appealing failure of a would-be story. In some instances, the story doesn't even hold water. Why wouldn't the authorities have set up an emergency center, run by generators? And if they didn't do that, why would someone need access to their account if the networks were down? And if they had their pin, just to access their own computer system they'd have to operate with an off-the-grid generator or perhaps with auxiliary batteries. Rathman was getting into the weeds. As a story, for its time, it was nonsense, and carried no significance or relevance. But to the people—only to them—who lived in the darkness, it meant something, and that's why the story had "legs" and had been passed down through multiple generations through the oral tradition."

Rathman wrote in conclusion, "So it means nothing to us, in our modernity, as it meant nothing to them, in their old modernity. So in the light, it has no meaning. In the darkness, it has meaning. *The Time Repairer* is talking to us from the "place" of the non-regenerative light in the basement, the basement that was underwater. So, if we were to speculate, the Microsoft building basement author could have been in the context of his or her time a madman, or madwoman, or simply a very lousy science fiction writer. But not in the darkness of 2,300 years ago. Except for the addendum at the end which was different and at least was graced with logic and reason.

That section had a special ring to it. And Rathman knew he was going to quote *The Time Repairer's Credo* in total in his paper. In fact he was going to make the passage the centerpiece of his paper.

THE TIME REPAIRER'S CREDO

1. *Tech can't solve everything.*
2. *Tech isn't a meritocracy.*
3. *Tech isn't always progressive, sometimes it's retro, reactionary, and even devo.*
4. *Efficiency isn't always inherently good, and when efficiency is good, and often it is, it's not always caused by profit-sharing, profit-making, growth, lack of regulation. Sometimes it comes from elsewhere. Even from a cave.*

I am not advocating living in caves, in darkness, but if we embrace the seeds of Techno-Utopianism, and allow these seeds to come to full growth, to full maturation, that's where we're likely to end up, at least those of us in the bottom and middle percentiles of the world's population.

And with climate change unchecked you won't have to wait 100 years to see most of that actually happening. And let us not talk about the unborn over the next thousands and thousands of years... We cannot speak for them. People think I'm crazy. I am perhaps. January, 2018."

Wow, Rathman thought. Someone spewing this forth in lonesome solitude.

And I can say it at last, Rathman thought, whatever it means.

"The darkness carried this deformed light to us. Our future lies in memory. In memory our future lies. Memory is all."

Rathman acknowledged that there were a multitude of unanswered questions implicit in the document.

The first thing that came to Rathman's mind was that the people in the darkness—centuries after the document had been written—would have thought that the story was true, if only that it would have been too weird of a story to have been made up.

Rathman thought he had figured it out, more or less. No wonder the people living in the darkness of the caves loved this story so much. They had no way of knowing whether the story was based on what had actually happened or whether it was just made up! But to them it didn't matter, either way. No wonder it was passed down through the oral tradition. Other stories, inferior ones, stories irrelevant for the times, that did not have the intensity of a moral lesson, or did not ring true, falling by the wayside even if they were true. This one survived because it continued to provide purpose, reason, a ringing truth, continuing to provide the two things they had so little of in the caves. Like the one, for example, Ulm inhabited. Meaningfulness and succor. 'Look at those people before the Fall! They didn't have it so good, did they! We are brave! We will prevail! Those in the past are our inferiors!'

Rathman would take this piece of writing and shape it into something, turning it into something better. And that would be the article to be submitted to the historian Auger, Zoia's father. As soon as possible. Rathman worked like a demon, skipping meals, skimping on his sleep, to the point he felt like he was working almost in a drug-induced, feverish state. He completed the piece in just under 19 days. And then he went to meet with Auger.

Chapter Twenty-Six

RATHMAN FOLLOWED Zoia's instructions. Using Zoia's exact words in requesting the meeting, he was able to draw Auger's attention and set up a time. The meeting was to take place two days later, at Auger and Zoia's home, that being the earliest time convenient for Auger.

Auger answered the door. He invited Rathman in. "Looks like spring, doesn't it?" Auger said in a casual voice. "Can't hardly wait. Not a lot left of winter, I hope. I want to start digging a garden. Zoia's been cavorting around the world. Drops me a line now and then. Flew over New York. Some darkness in between. Flew over Europe. Lost of darkness in between. Headed for Alexandria, then they'll cross the desert, then the Zagros Mountains, then they're headed for the Himalayas. Lots and lots of darkness in between. Rathman, is it? You're a fellow student of Zoia's, no? In the Rhetoric Department?"

"Yes, that's correct, sir. I met your daughter only a few months ago."

Auger looked Rathman over carefully. He didn't look like Jug, who had a paleness about him. Rathman was thin, wiry, solid, but in a stringy way. His hair and skin were dark, suggesting he had spent a good deal of time in the sun. He had the unsettling look of the unfamiliar and the alien about him, but the look did not strike Auger as a negative.

"In the Rhetoric Department?"

"Yes."

"Neaaah," Auger sniggered. "So, what's this about?" he asked. "Over the phone you were vague. Something to do with a manuscript? If you hadn't mentioned my daughter's name, and given proof you knew her, I'd have hung up on you."

"I was vague on the phone, I admit it. No, Sir. No. I was... I was nervous. I was very nervous. Here it is."

His hand shaking, Rathman handed Auger the manuscript. Then, reluctantly, almost as if it were an afterthought, he handed Auger the article he had written.

"*The Time Repairer. Darkness*?" Auger asked, looking up, examining both pieces. "The narrative at the end of Ulm's poem, right?"

"No, this is the original story on which Ulm based his poem," Rathman said. "Or so it seems."

"We're talking about the Dark Age," Auger asked frowning. "Wasting my time on the Dark Age! As my daughter would have told you, I spend very little time on that. So what is this? You didn't explain this part over the phone...young man."

"Wrong. It's from before the Fall."

"Wha...?" Auger asked. "Before the Fall? Well now. This can not be."

"I know. But it is."

In detail, Rathman explained the circumstances of the find: the excavations and the discovery of the manuscript. He explained how in ways the manuscript was similar to Ulm's version of *The Time Repairer. Darkness*, but in other ways, different. He explained how the archeologist who had accidentally found the piece had given the document to Jug, who passed it on to Zoia, who passed it on to him.

"To you? Placed in your hands. Zoia thinks that highly of you?"

"No."

"No? Why did she give it to you then?"

Rathman smiled. "She told me you'd ask me that. Well, she told me to tell you, I was reading Ulm's *The Time Repairer. Darkness* at the moment we first met, in the reading room at the Rhetoric Department. Merely a coincidence. That's what it meant to me. But she seemed to place more importance on it."

Auger thought for a minute, struggling with something weighing heavily on his mind. It looked as if he were making an assessment. "Oh, my daughter and intuition... You sit down. I am going to make some tea for you. Have you any plans for the evening? Yes? No? No, right? No?"

"No," Rathman confirmed. "I have no plans for the evening."

"Good. Relax. You make yourself at home. Make yourself quite at home. I'm going to take this into my study and read it now. With your permission, your piece as well, of course."

"Fine. But you don't have to read my piece. Nobody else has even looked at it!"

"Of course I will. If Zoia tells me to do this, I'm going to do it."

Rathman did not know what to say to that.

Rathman went to a place on the couch, sat down, unlaced his shoes, pushed back, lazily placed his hands behind his head, and whispering in a relaxed voice, said, "Take your time."

Ten minutes later, like a good host, Auger brought the tea in for Rathman. And since there was nothing else to do, after finishing his tea, right there on Auger's couch, Rathman took a nap that morphed into a profound sleep. Regardless of what would come next, Rathman felt as if a huge weight had been lifted from his shoulders. He told himself not to presume to have any expectations or anticipations.

Two hours later, Auger returned to the living room. "Took longer than I'd expected. This is fabulous. I propose we get this published in the Eccles Review of Books, then, immediately after that, in the Eccles Literary Gazette. With my lobbying, it's likely they'll both accept. After all, this is new—utterly new—material, not the usual rehash."

"You mean this early version of *The Time Repairer. Darkness?*"

"No. Can't do that. Parts are what? Boring? It's way too long. No, I meant your article, silly."

"Really?" Rathman asked. "My essay!" He was flabbergasted. "It's that good?"

"We may have to cut it down some, because we have to include selected parts of the original manuscript, but that's okay. Especially for the Literary Gazette, they may only want half of it. Even if we do that, the heart of the piece won't change. I do propose, however, most earnestly, that we change the title: *Avatar of The Time Repairer, before the Darkness, before the Fall,*" Auger intoned. "A garish title, don't you think? It's *only* 2,700 years old. It's only Post-Westernized Trope of the Upanishads, so let's be cautious. Let's not create a *mythical* aspect, when there's nothing of the kind there. I propose we change the title to. *Document of a portion of Ulm's Poem: Time Repairer, written prior to the darkness, 2018 A.D., as found in the basement of an underwater Eccles' ruin.*"

Except for the last bit, Rathman thought Auger's title was flat and unimaginative. But accurate and modest. He instantly agreed to the change.

Auger sensed that Rathman had too much of the cavalier in him to be a steady-handed academic, but he had grown fond of the boy all the same. He thought Rathman's style resembled Zoia's own sense of flair, her own bent toward sensationalism. Whatever he changed in the paper, Auger would keep it in Rathman's name alone, which was only right.

"You know it's a miracle this dropped into your lap, Rathman," Auger said. "May I call you Rathman? This is going to make you an instant star at the university. Do you know that?"

"I didn't do it for that reason."

"You didn't?" Auger asked. "Well no. Of course not. And the darkness carried this deformed light to us. What a phrase! Sharp! Sounds like what I do. That's what I've been doing all my life, as a historian, bringing to the modern age deep, deep time. And the

Abolition of Man philosophical puzzle via Pius... Oh my, Pius is going to appreciate that. And be entertained!"

"I'm not sure I should even take credit for this," Rathman said modestly. "The words just came to me."

"Let me quote the final paragraph of your work," Auger said. He took a page out, put on his reading glasses, cleared his throat, and said, "This is good." He read: "How much living memory is there in 131 generations? If we're living in the darkness, is there living memory going back 1,310 generations? That's right, let's add a zero to the number. That would take us to the Pleistocene. But let's go farther back, 200,000 or 300,000 years farther back, when humans may have gone into a vicious population tailspin, down to 40,000, or perhaps just 10,000 or 20,000. More dire, more existential, in terms of the possibility of extinction, than be reduced to a population of 40 million—which happened about 1,000 years ago. And what if we had—a virtually imponderable hypothesis, but what if we had—some other species, well, not humans obviously—looking at us. If humans were wiped out from our epoch 10 million years from now, what would remain? Residues of plastic—a seamless hybrid with stone-rock? Flecks of pink, luminous green blotches, milky-blue spots, fibrous orange twists, black and silver streaks, alloyed with the rock *au natural*, that is to say, human made part-plastic, part-rock. What else would be left of us after 10 million years? Nothing, perhaps. Facing the asteroid we must ponder these imponderables, thinking about those people, our ancestors, living in the darkness.'"

Tears welled up in Auger's eyes.

"Lovely," Auger said. "Tender. A true homage to our ancestors."

"Yes," Rathman replied hesitantly. "I understand the paradox. Maybe some lessons can be learned about light from the time of darkness, better even than from the time of light. But making fun of people of the light can only get you so far. That, of course, is the limit of finding a purpose and meaning in *The Time Repairer. Darkness.*"

Rathman was silent. He thought he might have overstepped.

"Well," Auger said. "Let's shoehorn that into your work somehow! At the beginning? No. At the end. Nearer to the end. I'll help you write it if you like. Name your poison, young man."

"I don't drink alcohol. I don't like it. Tap water will be fine. Simple water."

"Okay, but if you won't drink with me, you'll dine with me. You might as well join me. Do you like Francis Bacon? He's an ancient. How about Carl Jung? I hope not Sigmund Freud."

"I'm not Zoia, Sir. I'm Rathman. I study only the darkness."

"A yea-yea?" Auger asked, slapping Rathman's leg. Auger exploded with laughter. "Zoia will remedy that. If you let her. Do you really love the darkness? Like some ancient Upanishad medieval scholar would?"

"I'm not a scholar, Sir, I'm a kid," Rathman said. "From dawn to dusk, I scarcely know what I'm doing. But I do know this, *The Time Repairer* came to us *through* the darkness, that much I know for sure."

"Well, it's well written," Auger said. "Not the half-baked stuff that constitutes the story itself. *The Time Repairer!* Make no mistake, it's ascetic and decrepit. But your paper? Fun. It's fun. And engaging. The paper changes the document for the better, making it mean something. By virtue of that fact, your interpretation improves it. Now I'll have more time to devote to my own writing: because... for the journals, no longer burdened by dreadful deadlines, which makes for a win-win-win situation. I win. You win. The journals win. I'm pleased to have met you, young man. And make no mistake about it, I truly wish to help you."

Chapter Twenty-Seven

19 days earlier.

JUG SAID, "YOU HAVE A CHOICE, Zoia. We can go to East Indonesia, as had been our first plan. Or we can follow the 2,700-year-old circuitous nearly-around-the-world route September Snow and Tom Novak took from New York to Mexico. The long way. What do you say?"

Zoia asked, "Are you changing the plan?"

Jug smiled and looked very relaxed. "He was hesitant at first, but I actually got your father to agree. They have to keep a clamp-down on all that so-called super-sensitive material relating to the Gaia religion from the finds in the subway tunnel in New York. You know, 'Lloyd the Special Magister's Papers?' The papers found in an urn contained a commentary on the events from 2052 A.D. to 2133 A.D., the *loa*. I got a dispensation, a 'limited', 'non-sensitive-material' dispensation for a very small portion of Lloyd's papers. Authorization made by your dad himself. Also confirmed by Pius. All I was given was the route of the voyage, and some points, not all, where September Snow and Tom Novak may have landed and disembarked. All those years ago, they traveled by helioplane. That's what Lloyd's papers told us. There were only two of them on the trip, most of the way. September Snow flew the helioplane herself. She was reputed to have been a brilliant pilot. This was 2063 A.D. Your father told me everything about the record of Lloyd. Lloyd knew something about what happened in the Himalayas, and something to do with a character named Curmudgeon, apparently an old friend of Tom's, who lived for a short time on Heard Island. But the most important part was when they picked up September's daughter, Iona, in Bolivia. Above all, it's second-hand news. Lloyd's interpretation. But I got the route. You want us to be the second ever to go on it?"

"You're making this up," Zoia said. "I don't believe you."

"I haven't made it up. Why would I do that? You can interrogate your dad, double check with him, if you think I'm lying. They knew some of the things, from the other documents, the bare-bones information, but not what happened after Antarctica. Well, they know now."

"Take the route of a goddess? Or a trip to East Indonesia? That's the choice?"

"Your choice. Jason could join us in New York. For the first leg. I promised you he would accompany us at the beginning and the end of the trip, whichever trip we take."

"You're serious?"

"'Course I am! Upon our return, I'm going to add to the second floor at my father's Gatetar Technology and Science Museum, a new Helioplane Wing, which will include an entire section on September Snow and Tom's trip. What should I call it?"

"Call it September Snow's vehicle of love," Zoia said distractedly. "Call it the trip to Mars and back. I don't care what you call it."

"The religious fanatics wouldn't mind?" Jug asked laughing.

"They take this stuff in earnest. They won't take kindly to the most important world religious figure's defamation and slander. Ask my dad. Don't get me started. Give me the layout of the East Indonesia trip."

"The East Indonesia trip. Here it is. We fly west. We fly to the island of Masagua. I'll show you. It's a lost island of flowers and the should-have-been-extinct land creatures in the East Indonesia archipelago. That trip will take only two weeks."

"Let's leave them alone. Sounds like they don't want to be

disturbed, even if it is high-end aristocrat tourism. Do they really need their privacy interfered with by the richest man in history?"

"I was just suggesting. Then there's the September Snow trip. We will go to New York. Then we'll fly to Europe, to Alexandria, cross the Zagros Mountains, to the Himalayas, to the southern end of the Indian Ocean, to Antarctica, to the southern spine of the Andes Mountains in Southland, to Bolivia, then to northern Mexico. It will be an around-the-world whirlwind, an out-and-out extravaganza."

"Fine. But you must make two promises. First, get me back in six weeks' time. Second, promise me you'll postpone the creation of the Helioplane Wing in your museum, or at least the part about September Snow and Tom's trip, until later. I don't want you doing something that might embarrass my father, or put Pius in danger. Let the historians decide what gets released, and when."

"Absolutely," Jug said. "You have it. I'll do it exactly as you say."

"Then it's the trip of the goddess?"

"It's the trip of the goddess."

Chapter Twenty-Eight

EVERYTHING for the September Snow trip started auspiciously enough. In spite of it being near the end of winter, the weather turned out to as good as they could have hoped. And the winds were either still, or blowing in the right direction. From Eccles, including take off and landing, the first leg of the trip took just over three and a half hours. They landed in New York and picked up Jason, who was there doing business for Jug.

Exiting a limousine at the skyjack tarmac, Jason ran up the steps leading to Jug and Zoia's helioplane and upon entering he smiled and clasped both of Zoia's hands in his. "The bright one!" he exclaimed. "The formidably bright one!" Jason brought Zoia's right hand up and kissed it in a manner that was semi-joking but also semi-respectful. "I've read one of your father's books. I'd forgotten to mention it to you when I first met you. Well, I skimmed it at least. Years ago. What was it called? *Age of Involuntary, whuh, Movement?*"

"No," Zoia said. She corrected him. *"Age of Involuntary Revolution.* My father's first book. Took him eight years to write it. I read it when I was nine. And 11. And 13. And 16. Give me a quiz on it. I'll pass it."

"Ancient history, right? Bad reading. No, I don't mean it was a *bad reading,*" Jason said, looking flustered. "I mean, from the point of view of humanity, *bad ending.*"

That brought a broad smile to Zoia's face. Jason seemed to like irony and wit, Zoia realized, and she was charmed by his endeavor to attempt both, in such a self-deprecating way. Jug had been preoccupied, not deigning to pay any attention to their conversation.

"Look, I'll make no bones about it," Jason said. "I've got just a layman's knowledge of, what do they call it, Post-*Westernized* Upanishad?"

"You're not in enemy territory," Zoia said. "My father used to put a gun to my head and forced me to learn it."

"What?" Jason asked, expressing slight alarm.

"Gaia," Zoia said. "Nobody knows when I'm joking. I'm joking. But I love Ancient World History."

The three of them ate their dinner together more or less in silence. Jug seemed completely withdrawn, lost in his thoughts. The fare was simple but excellent.

During the course of the meal, Jason wondered why the two were being so reticent. Before dessert came, Jason broke the silence. "I wasn't going to bring it up, but we don't have much time. A serious obstacle has arisen. Do you want to hear about it now, Jug? The contract? Can it wait for the office? Do you want me to talk about it here?"

"I intend on keeping nothing from Zoia," Jug said in a mild voice. He smiled in her general direction. "You can say anything you want in front of her."

"Deal's off."

"What?"

"There was a big, ah, call it whatever you want. Protest. People from the community. They knew about the terms. Nothing was hidden from them, mind you, everything was on the up and up. But they went crazy. I didn't anticipate this development, Sir. I'm sorry to have to be the bearer of this news."

"They need to get their act together," Jug said in a mild voice. "I'm being blindsided. As far as I knew, it was a done deal."

Jason nodded his head. "There are some unexpected new actors in the game. I didn't see it coming. They came... Unrate-payers. Residents. They're stubborn. They wanted to reopen negotiations."

"No," Jug said in a mild voice. "A deal's a deal. The bow on top of the package had already been tied, as far as I'm concerned. If they don't want it, fine. If they've discovered they have cold feet, fine. If they want to pull out, fine. Even at the last minute, fine. That's perfectly all right with me. We'll just put it somewhere else. End of negotiations."

"It's 50,000 jobs, Jug. I put a lot of groundwork into this."

"And the 50,000 jobs will go somewhere else," Jug said in an agreeable voice. "It's their decision. I'm not over-reacting. It's a normal response, don't you think? Put the jobs somewhere else. As long as the transportation and communication infrastructure is still intact, that is."

"All right."

So fluid, so formal, so impressive, a decision so confidently and resolutely made.

Zoia was honored that Jug was willing to talk about business so candidly in front of her, especially with his most trusted advisor. But she kept thinking: "Juggernaut. The richest man on the planet. What am I doing here? I want to go home." She began to feel a sense of unease.

This would not be the first time in the course of the trip that she would feel this sense of unease.

Was this what it was like to be on the other side of the looking-glass? Zoia wondered. Was this trip turning into something more than she had bargained for?

Jug turned to her and said, "Jason will be going with us on this leg of the trip to Europe, then he will leave our company. He must attend to business there. But he will pick up with us again in five weeks' time, in northern Mexico. Right, Jason?"

Jason nodded.

"Will that be all right with you?"

"Yes," Zoia said. "Of course."

Jug said in a perfunctory way, "Come on, come on, we'll be in Europe before we know it. Let's be merry. I'm really sorry our festivities had to be interrupted by work, Zoia. I'm truly sorry about that. For the rest of the trip, I'm going to do everything within my power to avoid that. I promise."

Jason just smiled. "I have to sleep. I haven't slept... I can barely keep my eyes open. You must be willing to tell me all about the sights you see when we meet again. I very much look forward to that. You were right about making this trip. This is better than the one to East Indonesia."

Jug excused himself and went forward to ask the pilot about the flight path and if there had been any adjustments because of winds or weather.

The pilot confirmed these incidentals and talked again about their list of destinations. By the way the two spoke to each other, it was clear they had made many trips together. "No matter how late you stay up, Sir," the pilot said, "we will be in Europe before dawn."

While Jug was in the cockpit, Zoia said to Jason, "He works a lot, doesn't he?"

"Sometimes he needs to pull himself away. He needs someone to keep him from going crazy. But it's not you. Just watching your body language during dinner, Zoia, I see that. This is something you and I know, but he doesn't. It's not just physical, he's *mystically* smitten by you. I think he's been looking for someone like you all his life. But he'll never find out the truth through you or me."

"I'm really, really, really—I don't know what the right word is— embarrassed?" Zoia said.

"Embarrassed?"

"What I'm awkwardly saying is: I am not his ride to the light, I have my own life to live."

This was followed by a portentous silence.

"Is the trip going to get better?" Zoia finally asked. "By the way, does Jug actually own any of these islands we were supposed to visit?"

"All of them," Jason said. "It's part of his inheritance. Unlike his father, he takes a strictly hands-off approach toward all of his island possessions, especially the ones in East Indonesia. He's paternalistic in the best sense of the term. Is it on the itinerary you're going to the Himalayas?"

"Yes."

"Not to the snowboard country at 14,000 feet?"

"No. But it's supposed to be at a high elevation. Something to do with September Snow? I think it's a different part of the Himalayas."

There was something Jason didn't say. But what he did say was, "Good."

"How in the hell am I supposed to get to know this man— astride the world—at the top?"

Jason laughed. "He's extremely able. At many things. He's capable of being incredibly generous. There are local men in the Himalayas who guide the rich snowboarders. The season's short, they work for barely two months, but they manage to earn enough to support their large families for the rest of the year. Jug refuses to buy *their* land. He's not a monster, Zoia. He just has no game, what do you call it, no talent, for certain types of social interaction. After all, he comes from the world—the race—of Tech Engineers!"

"You are his true friend, aren't you," Zoia said.

"I'm his best friend," Jason said. "That should be a huge clue to you right there."

Chapter Twenty-Nine

JUG DID MANAGE to close his mind to all business matters, as he promised. He relaxed and began to give Zoia his undivided attention.

After England they took a detour and stayed for a week in Paris, even though they knew Tom and September never visited the place.

The flight over Alexandria was one of the most gorgeous parts of the trip. Zoia thought this was a good time to show off. "If you had to attend one of Pius's lectures, you'd have learned that during the earliest time of the *Westernized* Upanishad, Alexandria flourished as the most cosmopolitan city in the Mediterranean. It was a crossroads that, in its day, would have rivaled Eccles. It was the shining star of Hellenistic, Egyptian, Roman, and Jewish art and living, home to what was then the world's largest library and the greatest university."

"Oh," Jug said, listening attentively. "You don't say."

"I do say," Zoia added. "Mistress of Egypt, queen of the Nile delta."

"Makes U. Presbyr seem puny in comparison, don't you think?" Jug asked. "A Johnny-come-lately, no?"

"Not a ruin, a reproduction," Zoia replied in disappointment as she looked down on the scene beneath her.

Over the artificially built Pharos Island, with its new lighthouse, Jug and Zoia looked down at a famously reconstructed Eunostos harbor.

"Dad was very proud of this," Jug said. "We rebuilt the Pharos lighthouse, but we had to rebuild the island first. We had to move lots and lots of sand to do it. I know it's just a reproduction. I know it's drenched in artificiality and bogus authenticity, but what difference does it make? Gatetar Industries considers this to be one of its greatest accomplishments. A gift to the world. A lighthouse. You see the metaphor? Would you like to visit it?"

"It's a theme park," Zoia said. "No, I'd prefer just sand."

"All right" Jug said. Secretly, Jug was glad Zoia didn't want to visit the site. He didn't want to visit it either. The site had been one of his mother's favorites, which had been the only reason Jug's father had spent a fortune building and maintaining it. Jug's mother had been enthralled by this tourist spot, to the chagrin and embarrassment of her more sophisticated son.

Jug went forward and gave the pilot his orders. Soon, at speeds exceeding 1,100 miles per hour, the helioplane roared across the desert and headed east to the Zagros mountains.

"Do you wish to stop here?" Jug asked Zoia.

"Did Tom and September stop there?" Zoia asked.

Jug said, "Lloyd is silent on this. We don't know. Probably not."

"Well then, let's keep going. This is supposed to be *September Snow and Tom's* trip, right?" Zoia said.

The pilot gave up the controls to the copilot and came back to explain that they were going to land before they arrived at the Himalaya Mountains. "Give the helioplane a rest. I could use a rest."

Jug smiled. "Fine."

"It's a place of—what the locals call—a place of darkness," the pilot said. "Everything looks horrible out there... I don't even want to look. I suggest you remain inside the helioplane."

"We can rest here," Jug said. He turned from the pilot to Zoia. "Does that sound reasonable to you, Zoia?"

"Yes," Zoia replied.

So, after the pilot's brief rest, they proceeded on to the Himalayas. Jug asked the pilot to whisk them up to the site where the PLOP-SOBAS monastery was supposed to have been located in a high mountain valley, at an elevation of 13,800 feet. The valley that had sheltered the colony 2,600 years in the past was about five miles wide, with three small rivers running through it. The high Himalayas dominated the northern horizon, even from a distance of 35 kilometers. The former monastery was mostly just a pile of rocks, ruins with a couple of semi-dilapidated spires still protruding. Lloyd apparently had been thorough in explaining the details that Tom and September had visited this place. Jug had wanted to provide something on the trip that would be viewed as extra special by Zoia.

For that purpose Jug had 10 tents shipped up from below on the backs of donkeys. A support group of 30 villagers who lived in the valley below had been recruited for purposes of attending to Jug and Zoia's needs while they were staying in the upper valley. Should Jug and Zoia have decided to explore the surroundings they were provided with horses for that purpose.

Jug planned for them to stay a week.

"That's all I know," Jug said. "They went there. Anything else about Tom and September on this leg of the journey was completely redacted from the information given to me, but the location was pinpointed pretty accurately. If you want to be in a comfy place in the Outer World, then it's the Himalayas."

Zoia thoroughly enjoyed the visit to the place, riding a horse almost every day. The meals they were served were tasty, hearty, varied, and nourishing. Locals said that the place was haunted, well, the sound of the wind which was brisk during the day and late at night literally howled—only increased the eerie sensation of the place. The single problem was that Zoia wished she was visiting it with somebody other than Jug. She felt guilty about that fact—after all she was enjoying her stay, but she discovered to her chagrin that whatever had been appealing about Jug since she had come to know him was diminishing everyday. It wasn't something exactly that she could put her finger on. It was just him. As time went on Zoia could not fool herself into thinking that she wasn't feeling increasingly estranged from him.

At the end of their stay when everything had been packed up and they were escorted down the valley by the villagers to the helio-plane pad, she almost thought of asking Jug to cut short the trip and return to Eccles. Knowing how crestfallen Jug would have been had she done so, she changed her mind at the last minute. She still held out hope that things—their relationship in general—might improve.

Next they flew over the length of the Asian subcontinent. Their next stop was supposed to have been Heard Island, but there had been so many blotches of darkness (places where the effects of climate change had been so devastating), to cross over along the way, and the weather turned very nasty at the end, so they decided to go directly to Antarctica, to Taylor valley. Jug wanted to keep the journey as authentic as possible, within the limits of the huge blotches of darkness, but in this case they knew the exact spot. It was the end of the summer in Antarctica, the most clement time for the South Pole, so they stayed for ten days.

The trip did have a sort of lunacy and absurdity about it, having to fly through so many vast expanses, some of which were covered by large blotches of darkness.

They went on to Tierra del Fuego. There were some incredibly beautiful falls there. They stayed there for five days even though Tom and September never stopped there. (Patagonia, in spite of being part of the Outer World, in the year 2680 A.G. was a nice place to be in terms of climate.) Then they flew up the spine of the Andes, to Bolivia, to a two mile high plateau. Lloyd had noted that it was: "at the base of the Guallatiri mountain, in the Andes range, near the intersecting borders of Bolivia, Chile, and Peru, three ancient nation-states. Here is where Tom and September picked up five-year-old Iona. She had accompanied them on the rest of the trip." What did it take to follow the path of a goddess? A fleet of helioplanes, pilots to fly them, and a staff of four (cook, server, maid, janitor) to take care of the two passengers and the crew.

They decided that they needed to stop for a few days, here just below the equator.

So here they were in Bolivia, 12,500 feet above sea level, in the Andean altiplano desert. There was nothing there. It was just a place. A shrine to September Snow, Iona, and Tom? A Three-In-One religious site phenomenon? Zoia scoffed and thought snidely: "Think of the real-estate value, a Gaia Holy Trinity site." But it was only because of the information contained in the documents they possessed that they knew the three people were there at that time, in 12 A.G. So, naturally, there was no shrine, no markers, no nothing. It was sixty kilometers to the nearest building. It was cold at this elevation, 28 degrees Fahrenheit. But when the winds kicked up, the temperature dropped another 10 or 15 degrees.

Then they got into a fight. All the pressure building up during the course of the trip exploded. Zoia wanted to blame herself, but she also wanted to not blame herself. This ambiguity unsettled her as their voices grew in intensity, pitch, and agitation.

The arguments tacked back and forth, like a drunken, careening nightmare.

"We're not right for each other," Zoia shouted. "This is wasted time. We're not suited for each other. It's over. Better to get this out in the open now than to suffer from the consequences of a misunderstanding later."

Where did this come from? And where was there to go? The freezing cold 12,500 foot high desert was the only place to go. And now the winds were really whipping up.

Jug looked like he was going to burst into tears. Angry and dejected, he felt betrayed.

"It must have been hard taking over the business from your father," Zoia said, desperately trying to find another subject to replace the clamor. But it was clear from Jug's reaction that it was too late for that. Zoia had already crossed a boundary.

Jug still looked like he was on the verge of crying, but instead he didn't even pout.

"My advisor once told me that famous people don't have the privilege to pick and choose *what* they are going to be famous for. My father was famous for what he did—what he created. I'm famous for having inherited that creation. *That's all I am.*"

"So, it wasn't hard," Zoia said. She didn't want to be hurtful but she couldn't help it. "You can't talk to me without being intimate, Jug. So, needing to be so self-protective, that came with your inheritance?"

To say that Jug at this point was caught in a cauldron of emotional tension, hence wasn't thinking straight, would have been a gross understatement.

"I will offer this to you now," Jug said. He felt a profound sense of desperation. "I'm not joking, I'm serious. What if I gave you D2,000,000,000? No, I'm not trying to buy you. You could do whatever you want with it. No strings attached. You could set up a charity. Or a philanthropy. Or a trust fund, for purposes of aiding in medical research, in the sciences, in the arts, in Gaia, in floral design, in the study of folklore, in the study of *history.* You and you alone would choose how the money was to be spent. For example, you could help the neediest in the Outer World. You could build agronomists' outposts for research in world food production. I've done that. It accomplished good results. You could build instruments for promoting peace, social justice, democracy. You'd be able to choose how that project would be administered and how it'd be carried out. You could hire people to do whatever you want. I wouldn't interfere in any way. This'd be your project. You'd make all the decisions. You'd do whatever you wished."

"Now, this is curious," Zoia began to say, a feeling of dread overtaking her. Independent of the merits of Jug's offer, the presentation had been an exercise in very bad timing and represented breathtakingly bad judgment.

"You talked about my inheritance," Jug said. "Let's double what I offered you. A substantial piece of my inheritance. The sky's the limit."

"This is a very generous offer indeed," Zoia said. "But in the end, it's an indecent and improper proposal. This offer is confirming all the feelings I have. I don't have to deal with you anymore."

Zoia grabbed her coat and got out of the helioplane.

"What are you doing?" Jug shouted. "Where are you going? All right, I take it back. I take it back. There's nothing out there, Zoia! It's freezing."

Zoia ran. She ran, stopped to rest a bit, then ran some more. In a straight line, *away, from the helioplane,* she ran.

Jug grabbed his coat. Then he paused and looked outside and when he saw the cold wind kicking up dust he took more time to put on a pair of gloves, a pair of special felt boots, and a hat with ear-coverings. Then he had to go to the cockpit to give the pilot instructions on what to do. The pilot, when Jug told him what to do, looked at him in a state of alarm.

The pilot shouted at Jug: "You think you're going to impress her by doing this? By running after her? This situation, which is hazardous enough as it is, could turn dangerous quickly. That's how fast the weather's been known to change."

That made Jug more angry, more certain, as to the righteousness of his course of action.

As Zoia had slid the door open and jumped to the ground, Jug did the same. Then he followed Zoia. It had taken him so long to get suited up that she had already outdistanced him by 250 meters or more. Jug was astonished at how strong Zoia seemed to be, how healthy she was, running in the cruel elements, how tough she was.

Amazingly, as fast as Jug was running, and he was a strong runner, he couldn't seem to gain on her. When she stopped, having tired, he, having tired as much or even more, was forced to stop too. So he never closed the distance. In running-style, stamina, and strength, they were more or less equals. Over the course of an hour Jug lost a little distance on Zoia before he finally gained some. Jug finally outlasted Zoia, largely because of his protective clothing. By the end of eight kilometers, Zoia collapsed.

Jug came up slowly. She was lying in a small drift of snow.

Jug screamed so loud that in the high-desert's frozen air it seared his lungs.

"I'm clumsy. So clumsy. I'm a fool. I'm clumsy. I'll do anything for you, even never see you again, if it'll make you happy."

Twenty minutes later, as the pilot had been instructed, the helioplane came up from behind, waiting at a distance of a few hundred feet.

Zoia turned on her side and looked up at the hovering helioplane, then, in the foreground, she looked up at Jug's face. He'd taken off his hat and gloves. Zoia could see his face clearly. She could see he had been crying, or maybe that was just because his eyes were running from the bitter cold. Zoia's eyes were moist too, her immobile state more the result of the fatigue that had overtaken her than a decision to abandon the charade of escape.

Jug felt extremely embarrassed. He looked concerned, as if he wished to seek atonement. He was trying to be utterly contrite. "I'll do anything to make amends. I promise you that. I do not wish to ever do anything—ever—to make you feel frightened of me."

The expression on Zoia's face did not soften.

"Imagine people, Zoia, living on the edge of a cliff," Jug said. Everything in Jug's mind was screaming at him not to discuss this matter, certainly not now, but in light of Zoia always accusing him of holding his cards too close to his chest, Jug couldn't resist a full, untimely disclosure. "And the cliff represents madness," he continued. "Total collapse. Insanity. Most people live their lives many kilometers away from the edge, so far away that during their entire lifetimes, they may never even know the cliff exists. And a much smaller group lives maybe 50 meters away from the edge, but unless something horrible—truly terrible—happens, they also don't know the edge exists. The truly, hopelessly deranged and insane live at the very edge of the cliff, right on its precipice, barely an inch away, most of their lives, or all of their lives. Most of the time, I pitch my tent fifteen feet away from the edge. In those circumstances, I'm fine.

But I better not go wandering in the darkness, waking up, out of my tent, discovering I'm a foot away from the precipice. Like I am now. In those instances, all you have to do is give me a shove, a gentle push. I'll topple over. That's where I am right now. In my 32 years, there are very few people I've confessed this to. My mental instability. Mother, Jason, a girl I thought I was deeply, hopelessly, madly in love with a dozen years ago, you remind me of that girl. Now you can include yourself in that group."

Zoia was adamant. "I want to go home now. *I don't need to know this stuff about you.* You are trying so hard, you are breaking my heart. You made a promise to me less than a minute ago. Do you understand? We're not meant for each other."

Whether running out on Jug was a rational or an irrational act on Zoia's part, she had reversed the power relationship that had existed between the two of them. Maybe not permanently, but as they stared at each other, she had reversed it.

As they returned to the ship, Jug awkwardly put his arm around Zoia's shoulder. Whatever Jug meant by the gesture, Zoia gently rebuffed it. As they mounted the steps and closed the sliding doors of the helioplane, the last bitter blade of cold slid in with them. After they had had an opportunity to warm up, they assessed the situation. "Jason is in Mexico," Jug said. "He's already waiting for us."

"How do you even know whether the Goddess September Snow was there?" Zoia asked. "All these maps, charts, measurements, conjectures. Some of the maps are pinpoint accurate, some of them are not."

"Well, in the case of Mexico, we don't know, do we?" Jug replied. "We know by what Lloyd's record has told us that they were in the high Mexican desert, just below a mountain range called the Sierra Madre Occidental. We still have five days before you have to be back in Eccles. There will be the three of us, Jason, you, and I.

We will be chaperoned."

"No," Zoia said insistently. "I want to go home now."

So Jug honored Zoia's wishes by ordering the pilot to set a course directly for Zoia's father's home.

Zoia thought ruefully, "So this is what it's like to take the first Gaia's Holy Land Guided Tour. If all you feel is sorry, well, you feel sorry. None of this would have happened if Jug hadn't met my father, and I, like him, hadn't loved ancient history." Zoia knew Jug deserved to be told that to his face, out loud, but she thought that it would be better to postpone that event to a more suitable time.

Zoia told Jug how desperately sorry she was. He had put himself through so much strain, trouble, care, and expense. "You're generous, Jug. You are. Jason said you were. You are."

Chapter Thirty

RATHMAN AND JUG MET at the front entrance to the Gatetar tower. Above them, doves and pigeons nested in the nooks and crannies of the tall building, which meant that on occasion hawks also frequented the area. The upper 107 floors of the spire were sleek with stainless steel and glass. The bottom 107 floors were gothic, heavy, ponderous, with gargoyles, statues, gnomic elves, and also caricatures of historical figures dressed and draped in effigy. This made for a distinctly eccentric architectural hybrid. The old man Gatetar had been the boss, about all things related to his myriad business interests, but also about decisions concerning what became known as "the generic Gatetar corporate architecture."

Rathman returned the *Time Repairer. Darkness.* manuscript to Jug.

"It's not yours to dispose of, Jug," Rathman said laughing. "You have to give it back to the people." Rathman had never met Jug in person before. But Zoia had spoken about him. And on one occasion she spoke about him in such detail that Rathman felt like—after acquiring this knowledge—he knew him.

Jug smiled. Rathman smiled.

"Of course, Auger made copies of it," Rathman said. "Didn't ask your opinion about it. It's being distributed to literary groups and it's also being circulated in academic circles. Zoia told me you know Auger. If you know him you understand why he took the action he did. He's all about freedom, freedom of information, freedom of distribution of information. But if you'll allow me, there's something else of a more personal matter I need to address."

Rathman took Jug gently by the arm and guided him to a spot two blocks from the tower, a secluded spot, surrounded by tables, benches, and a rich concentration of greenery and trees. Rathman guided Jug to a corner and whispered into his ear, "I come here as routinely as an animal to a salt lick. I work in the basement."

"What?" Jug shrugged his shoulders.

"In the Gatetar building. Your building."

"What for?"

"A story for another time. But there are people I've inadvertently come in contact with who don't have papers. I worry about them. I don't want to give any more specifics about them than that."

"What's your concern? Police in general don't mess with Gatetar."

Rathman gave Jug a wary look.

"I mean over matters that are within reason," Jug said. "About reasonable things."

"They're okay then? They're okay?"

Jug couldn't put his finger on where this was going. "I have little influence over this. There are bounty hunters. Can't do anything about that. I look at it from the point of view of benign neglect. Are any of these...people, relatives of yours?"

Rathman looked very relieved. But also concerned. Rathman gasped. "Relatives? You kidding! I'm a mystery to them. They think I'm nuts! They think I'm an idiot. They think my studies at U. Presbyr are buffoonish, a fool's errand. They just look at life from a different angle."

"So they're not your relations, but you still care about them? In spite of that?"

Rathman gave Jug a nasty and angry look.

Jug placed his hand reverently over his heart. "I'd bend over backwards not to be harmful to them. I swear."

Rathman tilted his head curtly, implying just a little skepticism.

"What!" Jug said. "Just because I'm a rich man I can't be a cosmopolitan? I'm the one who is supposed to put on airs. You're among the ones who always act like you have all the knowledge. You don't have a lock on..."

"Okay," Rathman interrupted. "I'll tell you a story. Once my mother said, 'When something you don't understand pushes in at you, Rathman, you can't always push the push back out.' Understand?"

Jug didn't, strange wordplay, odd syntax, and peculiar phrasing. He thought, just another strange one coming from the outer edge of the Inner World.

"But I thought you grew up in an orphanage?" Jug asked. "Zoia told me..."

"No," Rathman said. "Just between the ages of 15 and 18. Before I came here."

"I'm sorry," Jug said, "I didn't mean to..."

"Why sorry? I'm not ashamed of the truth. I should be sorry, that I have no more interesting story to speak of. My family wasn't talkative you know. But... As my father was fond of saying, 'Don't let the priest who owns the granary tell you what to do!' My father had a hard, irreverent way of talking about religion. But he respected businessmen. If he were alive today I'm sure he'd have been mightily impressed by you. Though I'm young, I have a different way of looking at things. To be honest, I'm not impressed by you at all. But that's just me. Maybe it's the Rhetoric Department rubbing off on me. Or maybe not. I say this to you now so you understand where I'm coming from."

"You talk direct," Jug said. "I like it. As you'd promised Zoia, thank you for delivering the manuscript. I'll now try to smooth the feathers of the Antiquities Bureau, at least to the extent that they don't go totally berserk on me. I'm sure, as you think, the people will take care of themselves. How long have you known Zoia?"

"Long enough to know what I think of her."

"By the way, I saw the articles you wrote in the two journals. Plain speaking. Impressive. You may go far."

"There's nothing in it," Rathman said. "Like all things, it'll pass. From the home where I come from, we'd call it, 'an old goat farting in a desert windstorm.' I don't know why all the fuss. As far as I'm concerned, I don't understand any of this. Without Zoia and Auger, none of this would have happened to me. Without you, too, I suppose. I don't understand why any of this has happened to me. Except that there's nothing to gain from the study of the Darkness, except to discover that which comes to us from before. Writing the article was my way of fooling myself into thinking I do understand. But I don't. I don't at all."

"Love your honesty," Jug said. He was going to say something lovely, something about Zoia, but then he decided not to. When it came to rivalry, Jug had always been skeptical about the efficacy of first impressions, but he really liked the first impression Rathman was giving him.

Jug suspected that Zoia liked Rathman, and vice versa. And Jug could see the reason why. Rathman had resources, innocence, charm, something *else* too. Jug also knew that if he had taken one thing away from the disastrous trip, it was that there was nothing he could do about Zoia liking *him*.

"Yeah, well, don't feel so bad," Jug said to Rathman. "There's nothing really impressive about me. I'm terrible at women. I'm a complete idiot at it, especially with regards to timing. I'm terrible at talk. I'm terrible at timing. But I can talk to you."

Rathman thought of saying, 'That's because you're not in love with me.' But he realized to say that would have been censorious, undignified, unkind, and perhaps even undeserved. Zoia was Zoia. Jug was Jug.

"Oh, if you're wondering why I'm speaking this way," Rathman said ruefully, as if something else was preoccupying him while Jug was speaking, "I don't have to impress people who are rich, but I do have to impress people who are academics."

"Getting tired of it?"

"Not really. Just thinking about it. I can only stretch my intellectual legs so often, before I want to throw a leg over a saddle. I didn't think it possible, but, consider this, Jug, I'm getting homesick. Restless and homesick. Six months ago when I got here, I'd have thought that impossible. Now I'm beginning to think differently. Home is everything. It's the point of origin from which we set our bearings. Without our bearings, there's no way to navigate the unknown. Without our bearings, we're lost."

"Has Eccles left any sort of impression on you?"

"A lot of people here seem to get bored easily?" Rathman stated. It was a question, not a statement. "Other than that, I don't know."

Chapter Thirty-One

RATHMAN WAS EAGER to meet with Zoia anywhere. Meet at the cemetery? Sure. Why not? She had always been an oddity. Separately, but from different directions, they arrived at the designated spot, almost exactly at the same time.

Rathman wanted to say, "Mary Wollstonecraft's daughter, Mary Wollstonecraft's daughter, Mary Wollstonecraft's daughter." Or, "Did you see the sunset? Did you see the sunset? Did you see the sunset?"

But instead, he said, shyly, "Oh, since you always need to be impressed, now can I say the stuff that's supposed to impress?"

"Sure," Zoia said, as if he were joking. But Rathman wasn't joking. He'd come prepared.

"I did my research. Mary Shelley and her mother. The two of them, are mentors to you, right?"

Zoia nodded.

"Okay. *Frankenstein, The Modern Prometheus* is really Mary Shelley's satire skewering her father, William Godwin, and his lonely cry for improvement, for secular humanism, for progress."

At first Zoia didn't say anything. Then she burst out laughing. She nodded her head, wanting to congratulate Rathman, but she wasn't sure what she would be congratulating him for.

"Godwin," Rathman said, "was utopian. He thought that human nature was perfectible. He believed that society could be ordered in such a way that the need for any person to work might be reduced to an hour or two a day. Did anybody then believe in that? Does anybody now believe in that kind of utopia? Wasn't it Pius who said that *after* the Great War, the First World War, the very idea of utopia should have been forever banned?"

"For the longest time you've held out," Zoia murmured at last. "Arise, my Frankenstein. Arise, my smart-ass. You're worse. Worse than the worst. Nobody in the Rhetoric Department can touch you. Since when you're talking about Mary Shelley, you're actually talking about me, and when you're talking about Godwin, you're actually talking about my dad. Remember, Godwin believed in an archetypal spirituality that united all of humankind in some common purpose, united through some common thread."

"Oh, crap!" Rathman sputtered. A different idea entered his mind. And in that brief moment the thought of comparing the two fathers and the two daughters went completely out of his head. "Oh, shut me up, Zoia! Sorry! Dope! Gatetar tower! He's already heard it. Not that stuff. I mean *my* stuff. Your father. I told him. When I saw him. You know you can get addicted to this kind of historical sleuthing, if you let it go to your head, Zoia."

Unlike Jug who bored because he was predictable, Rathman rarely bored because he could be so very unpredictable.

"Maybe we should move on."

"Where did that come from?" Zoia asked. "That's vague. Move away? You mean, move away from here?"

"Well, we could stay in Eccles," Rathman said. "But what I had in mind was moving out of the Rhetoric Department. There's something about the place, it's creepy, it's..." Rathman wasn't able to finish his sentence.

"My blood is that which is mixed in with the mortar and cement which mortared and cemented these stones, bricks, rocks of this hallowed institution," Zoia said. "U. Presbyr?"

"What? The Rhetoric Department! You've got to be kidding me!"

"No, I mean, the World History Department," Zoia said. "That's were my blood has been cemented."

"Oh well, World History stuff is it?" Rathman asked laughing. "It isn't going anywhere, is it? Nailed down, isn't it? Not likely to slide down a hill. Or fly off the surface of the planet. Nor is your father. It was a thought."

"Wait a second," Zoia said. "You're a star, even if that status isn't going to last long. You published in two of the most highly regarded literary journals, haven't you? My father had to wait five years after he'd got his Ph. D. before he published in just one of the journals."

"My gut tells me I shouldn't be here," Rathman said. He suddenly looked remote and pale.

"Where did that come from?" Zoia asked. "Are you beaming out from beyond the stratosphere? Earth to Rathman? Hello, come in, Rathman. Rathman, please return to Earth."

"Of course, as long as you're in Eccles, I'm here too. If it's a matter of timing, you're going to decide all of the 'ifs' and 'whens.' However, I do consider it my duty to telescope my thoughts to you on this matter in advance."

"Oh Gaia! You're driving my crazy. Stop it. In a month you'll be telling me something different. The problem with Jug is that he is never serious enough. But you're too serious."

"No," Rathman said. "Not this time. I won't. My mind's pretty made up." In the semi-darkness there was the light of a three-quarters moon. It peeked out from behind a scudding cloud. As the moon poked free from its cover, Rathman stared at Rornar's tombstone. With his fingers, he reached out and felt the chiseled edge of the lettering. "I like it. I like the name Rornar. But you know you could add something else to your mother's tombstone."

"Why would I want to do that?" Zoia asked. "Okay, what?"

"Rornar did not die."

"But she did."

"No," Rathman said. "You don't understand. So when you or

someone else comes up to show their respects, they can read the words."

"But she's dead."

"By saying the words, you don't preserve her. You preserve her memory. Memory. It's her memory that did not die. You wake up one morning and you think of something, some small thing, some little thing, something from your childhood, something of greenery and finery, something very small, from 40 years before. And when you do that, you're doing what people have been doing forever."

"You and I are soon to be 19 years old. We have no thoughts going back 40 years."

"Yes, but we will, decades from now. When we're together. When we think back to this occasion, this moment, when we revisit this site."

"So you do believe in the importance of ancestors?" Zoia asked.

"Yes, yes I do!" Rathman exclaimed. He felt the conversation taking a good turn, turning a corner. "Yes! You study history. I don't. I dream of ancestors. That's what I do. And I told your father that, too. Subliminally, that's what I was thinking about, before I wrote the article. I was thinking about that. I think that's what originally had drawn me to the Darkness in the first place. Now that I understand that, I don't need to study it anymore."

"Are you sure?"

"No."

Zoia smiled.

You follow instinct, Zoia thought, you follow yours guts, you follow intuition, OR, you follow elders, authority, society. But then she thought, don't let the sirens of conformity lure you off course. She felt that she was ready—she could, would—jump off the edge of the world with Rathman, no matter where that took them.

"Are you really good at washing pots and pans, Rathman?" Zoia asked.

Rathman didn't feel offended, but he did feel like he was being unfairly tested. "I don't think I'm worthy of making an assessment. But in five months time, I've gone from being the number two washer of pots and pans to being the number *one* washer of pots and pans. Now that's a Godwin-like progress you can believe in."

Zoia smiled. "There's so many people on the make in this town, you're the most trustworthy person I've met." Zoia smiled. "Insider or outsider." Zoia laughed. "The most. The *most* trustworthy." She gushed. She laughed. She was embarrassed. "The most adorable, too."

"These mighty steps we take," Rathman whispered. "I'm only flesh and blood. And I am in love with you."

They kissed. The moon stared down. The tombstone stared at them, too. As if rediscovering their modesty they recoiled back, but then they turned their backs on Zoia's mother's tombstone, and they kissed again.

Chapter Thirty-Two

AND SO Zoia and Rathman fell in love.

They were taking one of their long, scenic walks. "Look, I have to do something," Zoia said.

"What?" Rathman replied.

"We have to invite Jug."

"Invite him?"

"To an event. To show him our respects. If it wasn't for him—his lending me the Microsoft building basement author's papers, *The Time Repairer. Darkness.*—we may never had gotten together. Without him, you wouldn't have met my father."

"You would have invited me," Rathman said, "to meet your dad eventually."

"Yes, but events happened the way they did. We have to do something."

"Okay."

"There's a concert coming up. It'll be perfect. Even better, they're going to hold it in the plaza in front of the Gatetar tower. A crowd of 30,000 is expected to show up."

"Who's performing?"

"Sallow singing. Sallow talking. Sallow dancing. Thousands of years ago, they called this phenomenon *punk-rock au feminine*. Dirty down, like looking past the stars, like looking at hell."

"Huh?" Rathman asked. "Okay, not too familiar with that.

Anyone I know?"

"*Savage Future.*" Zoia said.

"What?"

"The opening act. Not bad, huh?"

"And the main? The main performance? *Savage* isn't the only group who's going to perform, are they?"

"No, of course not. *Opium and Raw Pork.*"

"Oh!" Rathman exclaimed. His eyes widened. "Haven't they gotten wildly, suddenly, quite famous? Even the out-of-bounds stew-masters in the Outer World have pushed them to acclaim. It was reported that they nearly caused a riot in Delos."

"Indeed," Zoia said. "The group is radical, defiant, innovative, visionary. They've also been described as subversive and unladylike. Delos is where they hail from. They can sing those songs there, but they can't sing here. If they performed them here, they might risk ending up in jail. With their first velco, they've become an overnight success. I had a little hand in it. A small hand. I met the group just as they were forming. I used to hang out in the Favela Shantytown East, south of Pleasure Park, and they steamboated directly into the Rhetoric fringe. They call me their History Daughter. And as their adopted History Daughter, their name was my idea. I taught them Mary Shelley worldview, Mary Shelley thought, Mary Shelley legend, now, through them, through their Sallow talking, it's broadcasted out, it's an Oral. She is sung about town. We're not the only ones who know all about Mary Shelley now, Rathman. But Mary's been placed in the wrong millennium, a millennium closer to the ancient Greeks. The ancients have never been treated so badly when it comes to accuracy, and she stands alone, worm-holed out of context, into the wrong section of the Upanishad, as my father would say. But what difference does that make? By the way, I also supplied the names for the groups *Flee The Angry Strangers* and *Luna Cognita*. Didn't make the cut. Some reviewers say they may go into ascendency later, others say no. So, without unanimous concord, left out. Agreed?"

"What am I agreeing to?" Rathman asked.

"To attend."

"Sure," Rathman said. "Gatetar. Convenient. Close to my work. So I'll just be coming out of the basement and off the shift, hands still dripping with water. I'll wipe my hands on your hair. Or on Jug's coat."

"Jug's coat please...of course," Zoia said. "That I came up with the group's name helped in my securing free tickets."

"Ooooh," Rathman said, licking his lips. "Got it. Got to hear more about that."

They entered the concert area. A very large crowd had formed and was surging forward. The previous concert's organization had turned out to have been a bust. For some people it took two hours to enter the concert area, and the concert started an hour late. But this one had been—apparently—excellently organized.

Jug told Zoia and Rathman he was delighted they had invited him. He said he'd join them, but it would have to be at some time after the concert had started. Jug promised that as soon as he could get himself free he would meet them at the designated spot.

When Zoia and Rathman asked him if he might have trouble finding them in the crowd, he replied, "I'll find you. My father and my mother had been taking me to the Gatetar before I was able to walk. It's like a home away from home for me. It's a building with my family's name on it!"

At the opening, *Savage Future* warmed the crowd up. It was an eight-woman set. They performed *Addict*. Then *Critic*. Finally *Vanity*. This was not your typical Eccles' sallow singing group. They had biting talent and the crowd responded with enthusiasm.

When they left the stage the crowd immediately demanded their return, wanting an encore. Reemerging, the group performed a work-in-progress, *Skating Away (From Extinction)*.

The song was still sketchy, but they managed it.

There was a small gap between the acts. A young man dressed like a giant white rabbit bounded up on the stage. He had fake light purple hair in the form of rabbit ears, fake pink eyes, fake nose, and fake paws. On all fours he hopped across the stage, supposedly representing *spring pastoral, time of universal-birth, creation time.*

The main act finally emerged. *Opium and Raw Pork,* the three Sallow singing women were all dressed in black. As was their wont, they took their time setting up and plugging in. But everything went well. By the completion of the first song, everything was going smooth. They even thought to include four love songs, and an 18-minute-long instrumental anomaly that left the audience stunned, hanging, pulverized, panting, and waiting for more.

Suddenly the group just walked off the stage. This was unexpected, (but they often did the unexpected.) An announcer extemporaneously rushed onto the stage and said into the microphone: "*Opium and Raw Pork.* With *Back to Nature.*" Upon hearing the title of what they were hoping would be the next song, the crowd erupted with delight.

"Back in 10," the announcer added. "Or 20."

Just off stage, the lead singer extended her arms. She pushed her shoulders out menacingly and shoved the other two performers, simultaneously, giving them a mighty push. "You're busting my balls. You can't... You can't... You can't... No golly-wagging. I'm busting it. Don't wait for me. After the first riff. After the second. Come in! You want to bust up *Back to Nature?* You want a callback? Or do you want to crawl back and hide in Delos, waiting to be gunned down?"

During the break, Rathman commented to Zoia, "You know my roommate has reservations about Sallow singing. Calls it background music for the process of skinning live cats. To him, abomination. He looks backward to Rafky, Kilea, Jansci, and Barking, titans of the last century, only second to Beethoven, Mozart, Bach, and Brahms. Looks forward to the future with horror. Little music came to us from the Dark time. The little that did is, as he explained it to me, hopelessly repetitive, atonal, and unmelodic. Not even remotely like G-Chants

from the early *Westernized* Upanishads, with their otherworldly seren-
ity. 'This is culture,'" my roommate says, as if he were guardian and
grand vizier of correct musical tastes. Have to hand it to him though.
I never knew this kind of stuff existed before I met him. Taught me a
taste for classical music. By the way, where's Jug?"

"Jug's a very busy man," Zoia said. "He'll be here."

Rathman wanted to wait until Jug arrived before he asked, but
he changed his mind. "Come on! I'm on tender hooks. I'm wondering. Where does it come from? The name? *Opium and Raw Pork?*"

"It's indirectly derived from the name of a painting by Henry
Fuseli, a painting completed in 1781A.D. Fuseli was Mary Wollstonecraft's first love you see."

"Oh," Rathman said.

"After Fuseli ditched Mary," Zoia said, "she attempted her first,
fortunately half-hearted, suicide. So don't get any ideas. I'm strong."

"Mary Shelley again," Rathman said. "And her mother . . .
Mary Wollstonecraft! Mary Shelley and you. Mary W. and your mom
Rornar. So you got a copy of Fuseli's painting from your father, who
got it from documents found in Antarctica? You have such unique
privileges."

"Exactly," Zoia said. "Of course."

Rathman beamed. "Your father is very indulgent towards you.
What does it mean?"

"What does *what* mean, Rathman?" Zoia asked. "You're always
asking me what something means! Is that what's going to happen to
us for the rest of our lives, you asking, *what does it mean?*"

"*Opium and Raw Pork.*"

"Ah, the name! Of the Sallow singers!" Zoia said laughing.
"Fuseli. Before picking up his paintbrush, he scarfed down opium
and ingested raw pork to power up — in his words — his imagination. To paint what turned out to be his best of his very lucky best:
The Nightmare. So you've never seen it?"

"Oh, yeah, sure," Rathman said in a dejected voice. "As if I can
afford to buy a pricey velco from the proceeds of my washing gig.

Oh! There's the outside chance my roommate purchased it! Why not? He has money to burn, to buy tons of culture! Considering how much he loves Sallow singing and all."

"So you haven't then!" Zoia exclaimed. She fished into her handbag. "Wait a second. I have it somewhere." Retracting from her bag, she handed a print to Rathman. "There."

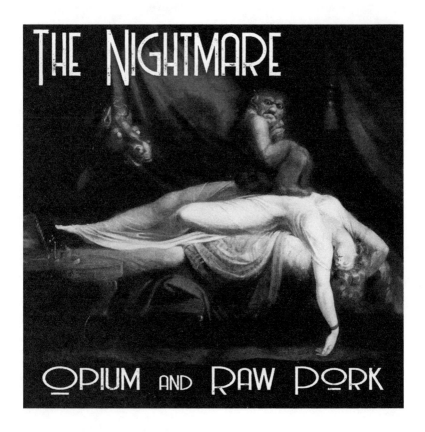

"Oh. Sounds like an almost kill after an almost kill of a more clay man than a man man," Rathman said.

Nearby six drunken, maybe seven, drunken and sweaty young men, and four valiant young women, careening, wandering, recited a self-composed ditty, "Two years plus change. Will we still be alive? No way. Whether we go. Whether we come. Whether we hide.

Whether we disappear."

"Listen to them," Rathman said, "28 months to go. People can't get enough of it. Astronomers say that's when the asteroid's going to clip. Now they're saying there's a 65- to 80-percent chance of a bore descent and thus a collision. It'll come at us from the west. Will the anxiety heat up as we get closer to the collision? Ah! No worries. We have *Opium and Raw Pork* to guide us in the mean time."

"Or at least entertain us," Zoia said.

Twenty minutes later the group returned. When they finally got started again the crowd responded with a roar. Their full-throttled cheer grew into something near deafening. The group performed *Behavior*. Then they performed their biggest hit, *Back To Nature*.

The performance of the former was excellent, the performance of the latter was perfect. That was followed by a silence that was creepy and strange.

Two ragged young men careened into Zoia, shouting, "The end is so near!" into her ear.

They were twelve sheets to the wind and in a state of self-inflicted head-banging, having drunk a "whole lit," a tamer Inner World version of an Outer World's potent brew of moonshine.

The young men wanted to sing another refrain, but they were too falling down drunk to do so.

After the song, the lead singer awkwardly tried to thrust her shoulder into the microphone. And then she wailed. That was nothing new, but the effect had something that was visually noteworthy.

The Sallow singer's mouth was plastered against the microphone and the building of Gatetar was behind her, with its Gothic exterior, the physical incarnation of the all life consuming, all life devouring, Moloch God of Tech. She commanded the stage crew to reposition the speakers so her voice would bounce off the tower, assuming they could get the acoustics right.

The Sallow singer turned her back on the crowd. Alone on the stage she faced the tower. She said "Tower of Gatetar." She repeated it, this time in a girlish voice, morphing into a snarl. "Tower of Gatetar."

Fully bending at the waist, she made a mocking gesture of worshipfulness.

It was a lovingly administered mockery. And the crowd, of course, adored her for it.

Unexpectedly she hit the ground. She quickly rolled over and formed herself into a tight ball. The members of the crowd in the back could not tell if she had disappeared. She seemed to have tried to make herself as small as possible.

The other band members were distressed. They stared at each other in a state of confusion and consternation. This had not been planned. One of them wanted to go over just to make sure the lead singer was not hurt. For a minute, the Sallow singer huddled. Sneering veneer, fear-induced confusion, hurt, rage, she closed her eyes.

Then she rose like a bird. With a warbling, semi-robotic-sounding voice, she waved her body like she was a cross between a Kali goddess and a wavering Coochie-Coo doll.

She cried out: "Tower of Babel! Make us your slaves, savage breathe, savage beating heart, savage mind-devouring, heart-eating god, we worship you. A slave stays a slave, or dies. A slave cannot be freed. One can only free oneself."

After this, there was an electrified cornucopia of clamor. The point of "Tower of Babel" was to suggest that the experience was in some sense indecipherable.

The sound-scape lasted for a moment.

People in the audience instinctively plugged their ears in reaction to the feedback. The cacophonous sound was very shrill, and it literally hurt their eardrums.

"It's okay, it's all right," the Sallow singer said in a gentle, comforting voice, attempting to un-ruffle the ruffled feathers caused by the horrible, detestable noise. She quickly directed the crew to adjust and turn the speakers back around. Scurrying about, they did so. The singer turned to face the audience. She waved, commanding the crowd to submit, to quiet down. "Stop being slaves," she said.

The Sallow singer smoothed her hair, one side, then the other, in one sweeping gesture. The crowd could not be repressed. As if it were a single entity, it was clearly responding with pleasure. She adjusted the microphone. As clear as possible, she stated, in a surprisingly mild and pleasant voice, "Tower of Babel. Back to Babel. Back to Eccles. Back to Nature. Back to *what?*"

"That's a first," Zoia said, even she a little in awe.

"You're the conduit!" Rathman shouted out energetically. "Zoia! You're The Nightmare! The conduit! Zoia! Bringing the ghost back. Nightmare. Henry Fuseli's Nightmare. Oh, History Daughter! You're the best History Daughter there ever was! Non-rationality driven Dionysian, romantic, emotional . . . modernity. Fuseli's Nightmare is both the epically imbued icon and the iconic symbol of all modernity."

'*Opium and Raw Pork*' continued to bang marvelously on their guitars, and the singer sang. Entreated by the crowd, the group performed their latest hit, *Back to Nature*.

How did the concert end? Straps of her guitar hanging from her neck, a loose cigarette dangling from her lips, in the midst of the harmonic progression in the middle of the song, the singer slapped the beat with alternating sweaty palms on the rose-colored body of her pedal guitar. She kept the beat. Sweat dripped. They all rose for the occasion—crowd and musicians alike—in unison, having splendid fun.

Dropping her cigarette, the Sallow singer blared out one last bit of lyric. "It's not the electricity alone, no, no, it's not the electricity alone, we're only fooling ourselves..."

At the completion of the set, energetic hoots, warm-hearted howls, and oodles of yodels came from the adoring crowd.

"Maybe I should get my roommate to listen to this!" Rathman said at last. "He's already part of the way there. After all, he loves— *adores*—literature from the Outer World, some of which is—by Inner World standards—very strong, very subversive. He collects the stuff diligently. Or maybe I can get him to review the group as a worthy-of-consideration curiosity."

"Just trying it on for size wouldn't destroy your roommate," Zoia said, speaking in a temperate voice.

It wasn't until half of the crowd had dispersed that Jug finally showed up.

He apologized profusely, saying he had been unavoidably held up.

"No matter," Zoia said. "Tickets were free."

The three of them walked to a cafe.

Jug clearly understood the change in Zoia and Rathman's relationship, so no one had to spell it out.

Jug behaved like a perfect gentleman. Zoia was surprised, yet happy. What surprised Zoia even more was that Rathman and Jug seemed to, more or less, hit it off. Jug clearly liked Rathman and focused most of his attention on him. Zoia was agnostic as to whether Rathman actually liked Jug or not, but he definitely accepted him for what he was.

And there was something in that acceptance that deeply gratified Jug. It was as if the two of them were brothers. Seemingly unexpected as that was, as they broke up to leave, all promising to meet again, it was as if the two were...brothers.

Zoia was so proud and glad she made the call she did.

Who would have guessed the two would have been so accepting of each other?

"What did you think of the concert?" Jug asked Rathman.

"Liked it. Well... But it was a performance. A performance."

"Rathman sometimes has trouble enjoying," Zoia interjected. "Enjoying the moment of life? Remind you of somebody. Remind you of...anybody, Jug?"

"That's a start..." Jug said. In mid-sentence, in mid-thought, awkwardly, he stopped himself. "Music is beautiful. It doesn't have to have a reason to be wonderful."

Gathering up all of their belongings as they stood up to leave, Zoia said, "How did things go at the Antiquities Bureau, Jug? *The Time Repairer. Darkness.* document? Throw you in jail?"

"Oh that," Jug said smiling. He seemed to return to a happier place in his mind. "Whatever else you can say, they're snooty. Thirty years ago, Gatetar Industries loaned them an 11th century A.D. copy of the *SHAH-NAMA*, a calendar poem that covered the history of the ancient Persian kings. I don't know what it was valued at then, when we first loaned it to them, but today, conservatively, it's worth maybe D20,000,000. I formally transferred the deed of ownership to them, making it an outright gift. You'd be amazed at how that had the desired effect of calming them down. They will not forget long this superb piece of generosity from their old buddy, good old Gatetar."

Chapter Thirty-Three

AND SO Rathman and Zoia returned to their studies, their classes, their thoughts.

Three months later, Rathman had an encounter with the Mythmaker. The Mythmaker, as he was called, though merely a student, was a mover and shaker in the Rhetoric Department. He had been studying in the department for more than six years, so he had become a sort of informal historian of the place.

The Mythmaker caught Rathman in the hallway. "I've been trying to coax you into seeing this fascinating thing, but you rebuff me. You rebuff me, Rathman. Being an outsider, being the Cowboy, you'd be the best to judge this unorthodox group. They formed themselves from three previous graduating classes. You've got to see them."

"But they didn't graduate?"

"No."

"So they're dropouts from the Rhetoric Department?" Rathman asked.

"Correct."

"If I promise to visit them will you leave me alone on this matter?" Rathman asked.

"Yes," the Mythmaker replied happily. "I promise. Yes I will. Yes. Then you can make your own assessment, *which is what we are all anxiously waiting to hear, of course.*"

Rathman realized he would have no peace of mind, if he didn't submit. And he had to admit to himself that he had become increasingly intrigued by the group and their increasingly bizarre and ludicrous gestures. They at one time visited a secluded portion of Pleasure Park in the dead of night and pretended to strangle wild coyotes they had previously captured in the San Francisco Game Reserve. Two of the members were badly bitten while capturing the creatures, and four others were bitten and scratched while *pretending* to strangle them. (This performance piece achieved no notoriety.) One of them had even tried to capture a full-grown hyena, and was lucky not to lose a hand. The point? The strangling coyotes were supposed to make the sound that fat limousines frequently emitted when approached by a potential violator of the parked property. But that point was so obscure that no one outside the group could figure out what it was. Once they even poured blood on files and papers of Gatetar-techusers in a public ceremony, the point being lost to most people. But the act did get them—for a brief period of time—noticed.

Rathman had been told by Zoia that the members of the group were all very well off, or at least their parents and grandparents were. "They are at the top of the list of shiftless deadbeats, the most notorious and outrageous group of dropouts on this side of the Pacific Ocean, or on the eastern side of the far reaches of Albu," she said. "They are a phenomenon. They have even tried to set up chapters."

Not a month went by without someone in the Rhetoric Department mentioning this group or one of their most recent exploits. They had given themselves an equally bizarre name: "The 4th of July Anti-Application of Subversion of Technology Commune."

So Rathman set out to visit this outgrowth of the Rhetoric Department, one of the most bizarre examples in the odd category of "Fringe Groups of Eccles."

They rarely came out of their lair to give interviews, so it wasn't that easy to get to them. And they were all semi-serious about keeping away from the law.

So this required Rathman to visit them at their den, in the equally bizarre Franz Kafka House. (This was an expensive place to live.)

The Mythmaker was so keen on getting Rathman to do this that he had made arrangements in advance so Rathman didn't have to do anything but show up.

But he had his instructions. He had to leave both of his Eccles identity cards, his student card and his residency card, with the concierge. She would then give him a key that would enable him to enter the premises. The building was opulent, large and square, four-stories high, built a little like a fortress, with an ample parking garage beneath the ground floor and a lovely stone water fountain at the front entrance. Within a short walk were a food market, clothing stores, a shoe store, hairdressers, dry-cleaning services, medical and dental facilities, a pharmacy, and numerous restaurants to suit a variety of tastes.

The concierge did the exchange, taking his two IDs, and gave Rathman the key which he needed to get into the next room and then to an outside walkway that led to the main building itself. The key did not work on the lock at the last door directly between the office and the main building. "You have to use the other door, go outside, go around the building to get to the main building to use the key." This confused Rathman but he finally figured it out. Rathman had to use the key a second time to open the front door, then a third time to enter the elevator, and a fourth time to access the third floor. The unit number he was trying to find was #3216, but to Rathman's chagrin it was NOT located on the third floor as he had assumed from the number "3," but rather on the second floor since the numbers on the third floor began with "4." So he had to retrace his steps, re-enter the elevator, (using the key a fifth time), then go back down to the second floor (using the key a sixth time). Of course the unit was located at the opposite end of the building, and the path to it was winding, indirect, and complicated.

Along the way, there were lovely glassed-in enclaves with displays of bamboo trees, as well as six aquariums with fish swimming inside: catfish, carp, mud-flippers, cuddlefish, octopuses, and some *very* creepy-looking eels. On the second floor there was a bust of

September Snow, and just down the corridor from it, two large velvet portraits of Tesla and Kimmel. These portraits faced each other like titans, set off by beautiful lighting—gods or diviners of electricity! No matter which direction Rathman chose to go, at each intersection there were exit signs, radiating out, at one intersection radiating out in the direction of four different hallways. At this intersection he saw 24 little green signs, six located in each hallway. But the exit he knew, at least the one he was aware of, was located in the direction he came from, at the winding end of the hallway he had just traveled, but were there three other directions that provided exits?

Were the signs intentionally deceptive, or were they just part of the layout which said no matter which way you went, it led to an exit? Rathman felt as if he had entered a reverse labyrinth.

No wonder the 4th of July Anti-Application of the Subversion of Technology Commune called the building the Franz Kafka.

When Rathman got to the door he knocked.

The leader of the commune answered the door. He had multiple scratches on his face, still unhealed, presumably from an attack by a wild coyote. He had a dead look in his eyes which alternated with a disconcertingly riveting gaze.

Already Rathman was having second thoughts about all this.

"From the Mythmaker himself you've come, I presume?" the leader of the commune asked. "Why he hasn't dropped out of the Rhetoric Department yet, I don't know. Why study rhetoric? You won't be able to breed with a woman if you don't succeed in life. Is that the message?"

Rathman nodded his head.

"Enter."

The room was filled with people. Their ghostly look took him quite aback.

The leader noted his reaction. "They've been starving themselves," he said. "No, I'm just kidding. Of course not. We've been engaged in long prayers. Prayers to Gaia. An ancient religion, filled with submersions, subversions, superstitions, all of it coming up, welling up, from a deep and murky past. That's what a watch on the asteroid collision will do to your head. Reconsider."

"Reconsider what?" Rathman asked.

"I'm just kidding. This is not a prayer group. We're all just tired. Very tired. We've just come back from a long mission!"

In the corner of the room Rathman noticed an in-house shrine. In the center was a glowing goddess, missing arms and legs, consisting of only a head, neck, and torso, flaked gold in color. There were what looked like offerings: bouquets of flowers, sheaths of wheat, apples, pears, grapefruit, kale, green spike-like plants, and smooth, worn, beautiful pieces of wood.

"We've dedicated this to Franz Kafka," the leader said. "Patron saint of Literary Existentialism, patron saint of inaccessible castles and never-ending trials, *the* Franz Kafka, patron saint of fighters aligned against unyielding bureaucracies."

Rathman looked puzzled. He scratched his head. For more than eight years Franz Kafka had been *de rigueur* in the Rhetoric Department. If there was anything relevant and germane from the old time that Rhetoric was eager to take and call its own, Kafka was it.

"It's a joke," the leader said. He was visibly upset that Rathman hadn't gotten his humor. The leader's voice was marinating in a syrup of disappointment. "We do it as a joke. Life is a joke. Do you want to join us?"

'No,' Rathman thought. 'These crazies! Put a Buddha in a shrine, put a Christ in a shrine, put a Mohammad in a shrine, put a September Snow in a shrine, but a Franz Kafka in a shine, that's devo.'

So then Rathman settled in to hear what the group's general complaint was.

Being good hosts, before starting out, they first served Rathman a meal which consisted of sweet and sour rolls, a bowl of succotash, and a cup of some very brown-looking tea.

"For dessert, would you like an apple? Or a pear? Or a grape-fruit?"

"An apple," Rathman said. "No, no, excuse me, a pear."

"Okay," the leader said. He snapped his fingers and a young woman went to the kitchen and fetched it.

Musical instruments—a string instrument, a wind instrument, and a tall, beautifully carved drum—were played by three bored-looking instrumentalists as Rathman ate his meal. Rathman had to admit the performance was having a positive effect on his digestion, so there was no reason to complain.

"It's about electricity," the leader finally blurted out as Rathman finished eating his last bit of roll.

"It is?" Rathman asked, burping silently, swigging his last swallow of tea.

"Electricity. We take it too much for granted. In our lives. Ubiquitous. Sometimes I think it turns us into non-reflective people. We know it changes the way we sleep. The presence of electricity. We know it changes the way we think."

Then the leader explained the group's mission. "We want to shut down the entire electrical grid of Eccles..."

"Are you crazy?" Rathman blurted. "They're going to throw you in jail! And, well, they should."

"But only for a brief, limited period of time," the leader added quickly. "We don't want to hurt anybody. We want to shut it down for, say, 30 minutes. Forty-five minutes tops."

"What for?" Rathman asked, shaking his head. "As a...protest?"

"As a reminder of our needs. Our true needs. A wake-up call about what should be our true concerns and our ultimate values."

Could they accomplish such a thing? Rathman wondered. He looked at them and thought, no. After all, they were former Rhetoric students. Then he remembered that some of them were former electrical engineering students. *This changed things.* The leader pointed them out to Rathman, perhaps for no other reason than to buttress the plausibility of their mission. They had their badges and they were wearing them proudly. As introductions were being made, they each rose in turn and bowed to Rathman.

"Three know circuitry, one code," the leader said. "The one who knows code also worked on network security."

"It's simple," the engineer said. "Backdoor it. My particular malware can be set apart from others because I target infrastructure in all its payload components. These are in turn connected to switches and circuit breakers at, for example, an electricity distribution center. The prototype for this was enhanced when my father and I did the theoretical: 14 revisions later, better. Not perfect yet, yes, but I think it's ready to go. The malware also contains features that are designed to enable it to remain under the radar, to ensure the malware's persistence, and to wipe all traces of itself after it has done its job."

It wasn't simple. At least Rathman didn't think so. *But he thought that at least the engineer sounded like—perhaps—he knew what he was talking about. Or didn't.*

"If you do this," Rathman said, "you'll get everybody's attention, but your action will also cause extreme consternation. Look! Assuming you pull it off, it'll cause you to become extremely unpopular. Who are you doing this for? The people of Eccles? The people of the Outer World?"

"For the enlightenment of the people of Eccles," the leader said. "They don't need gadgets. Not all the time. You don't have any gadgets, I've noticed, at least not with you."

Rathman didn't want to step into that river. All in all, he wanted to put as much distance as possible between himself and the commune. He'd give his report to the Mythmaker, and leave it at that. Rathman wondered why so many people were so bored in this town. It was like an ailment. Why use boxes and gadgets in the extreme, then condemn them? What was the point?

Had Rathman forgotten his path back through the building's maze?

Before Rathman passed the bust of September Snow he passed the portraits of Tesla and Kimmel. THE GREAT KIMMEL. The portraits reminded Rathman of a history lesson he took at the orphanage, taught by his beloved counselor himself. Rathman paused. He stopped and reflected. He missed his counselor and his sense of humor.

Both of the inventors, Rathman remembered, Tesla too, but especially in the case of Kimmel, died in a state of poverty. Kimmel quite literally starved to death. Tesla died penniless. He remembered that was one of the most important lessons the counselor wanted to teach Rathman, especially in light of his going to Eccles. On his way back out of the building, he found that the last door to the front office couldn't be opened with the key. As with his first trip he had to go out a side door, walk up the side walkway, and enter the front office from the side street.

"I told you the last door didn't work," the concierge said. "We arranged it that way on purpose. Cautionary. We like to confuse. Helps keep the riffraff out."

Rathman returned the key to the concierge and she returned his identity papers to him.

Chapter Thirty-Four

RATHMAN THOUGHT, Mary Shelley, Mary Wollstonecraft ...sure...acceptable. But not Franz Kafka. He decided then and there he was going to try to persuade Zoia to join him in quitting the Rhetoric Department as soon as possible. But Rathman knew Zoia, and for understandable reasons, would resist his request. He needed to confront Zoia before she left on an extended promotional tour with her father. The purpose of the trip was to guarantee funding for future academic research throughout the district of Eccles. This would be only the second time Zoia had accompanied Auger on such a tour, but her father was vehement about the necessity of the trip and was counting on her participation.

Rathman had been driven into such a funk by his disturbing experience at the Franz Kafka House that he felt compelled to meet with Zoia as soon as possible.

"So what are you worried about?" Zoia asked, after hearing what had happened. "Write them off. Write them off as freaks. With all the atomization of people, it's always one bunch of freaks, or another, who're willing to do anything they can to get even a tiny bit of attention. For themselves, it's all about thrills. Thrill-seeking counteracting boredom, ennui. Put the experience behind you. Look, are they dangerous?"

"You kidding!" Rathman said. "They want to shut down the grid!

Even though everything about them suggests they are incompetent. Or super incompetent. Or catastrophically incompetent."

"Well then," Zoia said. "So they're not dangerous."

Rathman turned his hat around. "They don't even have enough snot in their noggins to blow their brains out, much less shut a grid down."

"So there you are. No worries. By the way, Jug met with me and wants you to do something for him."

"What?" Rathman asked.

"Talk to the students at the Starboard School. Give them a Rathman's rap. You can do it on a day you're not washing pots and pans. The school's located midway between the south entrance of Pleasure Park and the Gatetar tower, a block from the bicycle Strata-Dome, next to the Milk Bar, right across the street from the Children's Science Farm."

"I know where it is," Rathman said. "Why would he want me to do something like that?"

"Tell them their gadgets and boxes are useless. Or tell them anything you want. You're the savage from the edge of the Outer World, remember. You're a token. You're a token freak! He wants you to shake the students up. Jug said he knows as many as a quarter of the executives and their spouses who send their children to the Starboard School. They are special children. Elite of the elite. My guess is Jug wants to use them as guinea pigs. You would be helping him to conduct an experiment. I've never seen him do something so unpredictable before. What do you have to lose? Do it on a dare. I dare you."

While this was happening, Jaime and his chief assistant were looking down on the southern end of Eccles from the vantage point of the Love Observatory.

Jaime said, "Look, it's going to hit. Yes, we may feel lucky now, but I don't want to sit around and lollygag...and stare at the ceiling...

and navel-gaze...and get my lotus drops...until my mind feels numb. And while we're all waiting, well...'let's just see what happens' is on the lips of nearly every citizen in Eccles. This is science. Science is practical. But this particular case also involves the human, all too human. I wish Raine was still around to speak on our behalf. He was so much better at fighting betrayal. He was so much better at being eloquent. There is no more time for debate!"

"They're ramping up," Jaime's assistant said to Jaime in a soothing voice. "Debate's over. You've won the debate. You won it a long time ago."

"They're ramping up, sure!" Jaime said. "Yes. Right. They're ramping up. Okay. It's going to happen."

Since having discovered the asteroid 15 years before, Jaime had grown—changed—as he acquired the burdens of responsibility. Less carefree now, less young now. But that was in spite of the pressure and resistance from parts of the scientific community and the public. But he was more determined than ever. Jaime had become the 'Raine-like' boss of the Love Observatory.

"They're into a two-year countdown," the assistant pointed out. "You think you can scare them any more than you've already scared them? They're taking care of business. Let them do it. You've done your work. *You've won!*"

"Nevertheless...I...wish...Raine...was...here," Jaime said in a halting voice. "I wish he could be our voice. You know we've had a cluster of solar flares going back all the way to the wintertime. It's too early to tell, but we could be in for a big one. Pattern suggests we haven't seen anything like this in over two hundred years, or longer. On the other hand, it could be nothing."

"I'll put some assistants on it. We just got some ominous reports from the Rutherford people on Mount Taylor. We should monitor and cross-reference with them. Remember, Jaime, we've done our work. Now let the people in the space program do theirs."

"Good," Jaime said. "Let's get on with it."

And the project *was* ramping up. The connectivity among science, technology, and the private sector was excellent. Fuel, velocity, payload factors were all being worked out with mathematical precision. A spaceship already in existence was being revamped and a brand-new spaceship was being built, (which, if they finished it on time, would be the one they'd use.) Cooperation worked in Eccles. It was a two-way street, three-way street, four-way street, and no less so than in the case of space exploration, and it's exotic step-sister, the 'space war,' that was being waged against a hurtling inanimate object. It wasn't the same as delivering somebody onto the surface of a celestial object. They'd done that before. Fifty years before. Mission accomplished. Also 2800 years before. But something much more momentous was at stake. They were preparing to deflect a *planet-maiming* event (that pseudo-Gaia religious talk crept into the science new-speak everywhere). In the eyes of the Outer World, this was about religion, plain and simple: follow September's example and commandment, be stewards of the Earth. In the eyes of the Inner World, a brain trust was in charge of a mammoth scientific and technological endeavor. That's what the modern world was all about. This was for the rock of ages...

When asked what resources were being applied, the reply was always, "We don't have a budget. We have an imperative." For a politician that was the one line that always drew a standing ovation. The political goal was to achieve or at least create momentum toward, a *climate* of public calm.

The politicians were confronted by anxiety-ridden, fretful, frightened citizens, facing the looming peril of extinction. It was a sentiment growing by the day, spreading like a virus through the population, just beneath the surface. Growing impolite. Growing disruptive. Growing aggressive.

"Money is no matter. Cost is no concern. Promises were given and those promises will be kept."

The space project wasn't about lost time, creaks and grunts in the engines of industry, purchasing orders delayed, cost overruns, *'whatever it is, we're getting it fixed'* talk, these were just incidentals, mere particulars, in the global endeavor to make the space mission successful.

"Do whatever's necessary." The entire world was metaphorically shouting it out loud in unison, and it had become the universal mantra of the day.

Chapter Thirty-Five

"YOU KNOW I HEARD somebody in the locker room, or maybe it was in the showers, say that there was this guy 2,700 years ago who put a car in a space rocket and launched it," Johnny said.

"Heard that one," Frankie said. "On an astronaut and space trivia game show."

"Why? What for?"

"Why what? Johnny, you don't always make yourself clear."

"Into space?"

"Put an automobile into space? Why are you asking? I don't know."

"Weird then, weird now," Johnny opined. "Or the gasman making *that* decision must have been smoking some really potent Outer World cannabis at the time. You're suppose to know all about astronautics and history, Frankie."

"Yeah, right," Frankie said. Her smile was forced. "I'm just the pilot, Johnny."

Johnny frowned. "You're more than that. You're the thinker. *Something I rarely am!*"

The astronaut selection process was still fresh in Frankie's mind. "I knew I was going to receive the call. But I didn't expect to see you here. Not this late in the game."

"They called Eddie first," Johnny said. "But they couldn't reach him. There was a reason for that. He's dead. Victim of a boating accident. Like a day after they give him the call, the boat comes back empty. At least they found the body. How strange is that? So they call Montaigne and just for good measure, they bring in a back-up. Who could that be? Striker! They both end up in the morgue after a freaky electrical malfunctioning during a stupid and totally unnecessary capsule reentry simulation. Phlat! You'd think they'd keep the two apart, but it was a simulation! You'd think! Eddie and Montaigne were the very best electrical engineers in the program. Nobody could touch Striker at nerves of steel and quickness of innovation. I think Eddie, Montaigne, and I were considered the best mechanics. The 'mechanics' mechanics.' So I was the next in line."

"Congratulations," Frankie said.

"They had no choice. They had to give me the call. Eddie's third replacement. Four's a charm."

"Congratulations," Frankie said.

"Frankie, there's a *huge* difference between being an electrician and an electrical engineer. I'm literally the scrapings at the bottom of the pot."

From the early years, Frankie had been a star pupil, star pilot, star navigator, and in the more theoretical realm, an ace, one-of-a-kind physicist. (And no emotions. That's what they were always looking for in a pilot.)

Johnny started out as a superb mechanic—a natural—and an extremely competent engineer. And over the years following the old-fashioned principle of 'practice-makes-perfect,' he semi-successfully honed his skills in what he called, 'the dark carnival arts of electrical engineering.'

Between 2673 and 2676, Frankie and Johnny were star-crossed lovers, head over heels, inseparable and, by all accounts, happy. Frankie especially loved Johnny's peculiar sense of humor, which had different variations. One time he took his shirt off in the middle of a marketplace and ran around with bright red circles painted all over his stomach, chest, and shoulders. Why? For no reason. *He was wild.*

After four years they were, according to their own definition: "ex-lovers." Immediately after their breakup, they had been conveniently assigned to opposite ends of the continent, Frankie to a highly prestigious West Coast program, Johnny to a subordinate East Coast backwater sideshow. Frankie's assignment was absolutely a "career-ladder builder," Johnny's assignment was not. Since then they had not seen each other, and had only spoken a few times on the phone. The first time was when Frankie had to notify Johnny that her father was dying from a rare blood disease. She called Johnny because she wanted him to send a letter of condolence to her mother, (Frankie's mother had a fondness for Johnny and his sense of humor, which in his genius he was able to convey even in his condolence letter.) The final time they talked was after Johnny had picked up a mongrel street dog with the intention of turning it into a pet. He wanted Frankie to give the dog a name. Frankie waffled, then agreed. When she learned the dog was female, she told Johnny to name her Pria or Iona. Johnny named the dog Iona, but called her Pria.

Johnny had become his colleagues' last minute replacement. As a gifted pilot, navigator, and physicist, Frankie had been the first in line for the assignment from the very get go. Her only rival for the job was Struddle, who had graduated from the academy eight years before her. He had been her boss at Wakefield, and now he was her boss again.

The two of them, Frankie and Johnny, were now "first team astronauts" whose sole mission was to attack and neutralize the asteroid. It was to be a two-year long work assignment and there was no getting around it, even if they had wanted to. They had sworn an oath to duty, and the academy had taught them to honor that oath.

"If you hadn't been reassigned to the East Coast, you would have been Striker's equal at math now," Frankie said.

"Is that true or are you just trying to buck me up?" Johnny asked in a muted voice.

"Yes, I'm looking forward to working with you, too," Frankie said, but she was smiling as she said it. "You want a shoulder to cry on, the world is indifferent. You're the best mechanic in the world. You are, Johnny. No one can touch you. Montaigne, and especially Eddie, could design and build a system from scratch. You couldn't. But after they had built it, you could keep it running. Striker in an emergency was the best. When there wasn't an emergency, she wasn't the best. Mackie was as solid as they come. Boring and dependable. But you're still the best mechanic."

Johnny started to say something but Frankie briskly interrupted him.

"You've been chosen and when you're chosen, that's that. We have a job to do. That's all we need to know. You're going to be your own man, Johnny. You're going to do it your way. I know that."

"I was just going to say, where would you drive the car? I mean, in space. I'm sure they checked the air in the tires first, and maybe kicked the tires, and if it was me, I'd make doubly sure the radio was working without static. The gasman! But did they really make certain the turn signals were functioning properly before they put it in the rocket?"

Frankie answered him with an obscure math equation. Striker would have gotten it, but not Johnny.

He had fallen for that trick before, but he didn't fall for it this time. He didn't say anything, for fear of understanding even less. Frankie was as fatalistic as they got.

Chapter Thirty-Six

AFTER NOT GENTLY KNOCKING—rather, banging fiercely—on the space project commander's office door, Frankie's boss asked her to enter.

Without any exchange of salutations, Frankie immediately lit in. "Why did you do this?" she asked.

"I assume you're referring to the selection of your new crew member," Struddle replied. "You want me to put him on the second team? Short him? Give me a reason to do that. I'm not going to do that. Sure, the frontrunners—before they died—were in the top two percent. But Frankie is in the top four percent, and the best in that group. You're stuck with him."

"But you know our history?"

"What?" Struddle asked. "Your *liaison paramour*? That was a long time ago."

"Don't get cute with me," Frankie said. "We're going to be up there for a long time."

"You're too serious. Frankie, you're too serious."

"How can anyone be *too* serious when you consider the importance of this mission?" Frankie asked.

"You're right," Struddle said. "Johnny is extremely motivated. I appreciate you coming to me with your concerns but...."

"But you don't know him the way I do," Frankie said.

"My decision is final."

Frankie shrugged. "You're the boss."

"I am."

"You know what you're doing."

"I do. *You work with the materials you have.* Haven't you learned that yet? Remember Humin? Humin died. He sacrificed himself. Do you think Johnny would ever hesitate to sacrifice himself? We do the drills, but you're going to have to do things under circumstances that you're not going to be able to anticipate. We hope that that doesn't happen. We hope there'll never be an instance where that'll happen. But there's a chance. Johnny is the most competent of the lot...of the available pool."

"Electrical engineering skills...," Frankie said.

Suddenly his temper flared. Struddle was angry. "Don't sacrifice good at the altar of perfect. I know you preferred Striker. Striker's dead. Johnny's going to be good for you. You're a team. You got him, commander. You got him. I don't want to hear any more about this. You're going to come around to seeing things this way eventually."

Chapter Thirty-Seven

RATHMAN CONTACTED Jug two days before the event at the Starboard School to get his instructions and directions to teach at the assembly. Rathman explained to Jug that he had no preparation for such a thing. Indeed, he had never given a lecture before in his life.

"I'm confused," Rathman said.

"Be yourself," Jug said. "Relax. That's all you have to do."

"And what do I do? What do I talk about?"

"Anything you like."

"That sounds crazy," Rathman said. "That sounds stupid. Starboard School? What kind of name is that? How old are they?"

"The students? Thirteen to 17. They're the best and the brightest of the land. Remember you have published two highly praised academic works. For the time being, you're a star at U. Presbyr. The students at Starboard live under a strictly enforced school policy: all gadgets are locked up when they arrive at school in the morning, and they're forbidden to retrieve them until late afternoon. Talk to them about that. Confuse them."

"My job is to confuse them?"

"Why not? You're the mysterious, lonesome wanderer from the edge of the Outer World. To yourself you're not an exotic. To them, you are."

Two days later Rathman set out from his home.

It was a golden morning. The weather was beautiful. Rathman walked along the perimeter of the grounds of the Gatetar Science and Technology Museum, but then he decided to take a more circular, roundabout route through Pleasure Park.

The school was richly colonnaded, gravel for the coach's way, stone for the archway and the walkway. Architecturally it was Gunter Gatetar's wish. At each of the two entrances were mammoth Carrara marble statues staring across at one another, the two statues acting like dueling bookends. And at the opposite end of the quad there was another identical matching set of statues, Kimmel and Tesla, the first in rags, the second wearing late 19th Century trousers and starched white shirt with cufflinks, stars of the AC/DC, potentates of the juice.

Rathman thought that if there was anything that was worshipped at all in Eccles it wasn't money. It was the juice itself, the electricity. *The thing that made the code, the communication, possible.*

The teachers had the classes assembled for Rathman. They appeared a little reluctant. The skeptical looks on their faces suggested that they were wondering, 'Who is this guy?' No one like him had ever been asked to speak, to their knowledge. The students were assembled in stages, five assemblies total, consisting of 55 students each. Three groups were scheduled before lunch, two after.

For Rathman, the first four assemblies served as warm-up sessions for the final one. The students in the first four assemblies were younger. By the time Rathman spoke to the last group, he had more or less gotten his spiel down.

The students entered the hall and took their places in long curved rows of seats, six rows deep, ten chairs wide, wearing their "most" clothes: simple charcoal-colored slacks, long-sleeve shirts, and sweaters, with a "G" for Gatetar stitched on the breast. The sweaters ranged across the entire color spectrum, from yellow to orange to green to mauve to red to blue to purple to black.

Rathman began by introducing himself. Then he sketched his idea of service and responsibility. Why did he even bother, he wondered? "Now let's get down to it," he said. "Technology anxiety. Caused by the absence of technology."

The students were suddenly beside themselves. They looked at each other in a state of bewilderment.

"Technology? Is it an addiction?" Rathman asked. "Or is it a mere convenience? Adapt the technology to you? Or adapt yourself to it? Humans are toolmakers. A tool's a tool. Why do you think the authoritarians lock up your junk for 10 hours a day? Your parents *created* these things. They market them aggressively, as if they were ferocious beasts, the highest level of predators. But they withhold the technology from you. You think they know something you don't? I was told it was within my rights to stir things up here."

"You sound like a preacher," a bold one from the back shouted.

"That's what I like," Rathman said, smiling. "Interaction. You haven't experienced freedom if you haven't taken a break from Eccles technology. Live on the edge of the Outer World. You'll see. I have."

"Your parents love you. They want you to succeed. They want you to live and prosper so they want you to *not* be addicted to certain types of technology, even though addicting others is how they make their living. But it's not technology as such that's the bugbear. It's the effects of the technology. Constant distraction of the captive mind? Confusion?"

Rathman paused. "I'm saying to embrace the inconvenient. Embrace quiet. There's no replacement for hope and loneliness. With hope, anything can be endured. With hope, even loneliness can be endured. Computers can't replace those things. You've not been taught this."

Most of the students' chins dropped. They stared at Rathman as if he were a creature who had arrived from another planet.

"Of course," Rathman said, "I give you a chance to respond. I didn't come here just to deliver monologue. We have time for dialogue."

A student who was wearing a red sweater said, "We're responsible for what we do. Just as you have said. But does it fall upon us to save the weak-minded, the easily manipulated, the lazy, the easily thought-drugged? My father loves to call them the thought-drugged."

Another student in a green sweater chimed in, "Yeah. What if the captured mind—whatever that is—doesn't want to be released? Is it fitting to help those who are captured because they've captured themselves? Their web is of their own making. The predatory spider is themselves. My father warned me of people like you." He whispered something into the ear of the student sitting next to him.

Rathman didn't have anything to say as a rebuttal.

The third student wore a purple sweater. He was different. He, Jonathan, who volunteered his name, and apparently had a much deeper knowledge, a wider understanding of ancient history than the others. "It's kind of like in the times before the Fall and the Darkness when the silk merchants sent their processed opium, lotus drops, from the poppy fields in Afghanistan and India to China to sell. One of those merchants wasn't likely to give those goods to his own children, as if it were candy, to make the journey less arduous for them."

Rathman smiled.

"If the ultimate goal of all strivings and sacrifices of humanity is to optimize shopping, then my father should get the lion's share of the metals and awards," Jonathan added.

"Jonathan barely belongs here, he's a SOC geek," another student said, laughing.

"How long have you lived in Eccles?" another student in a mauve sweater asked Rathman.

"Eight months," Rathman said. "Well, almost nine."

This bit of information seemed to encourage the other students to become even more defensive, if not defiant. A student in a blue sweater said, "No wonder that you talk in the manner that you do. You're an outlander. Have you ever tried to give aid and comfort to those who do not want it? Who resist it? Who defy it? Presto! Shackles off. But when you visit them two weeks later their wrist bracelets and ankle bangles are securely on again, clamped on good and tight."

Finally, a student, three rows back, wearing a white sweater with an extra large "G" monogrammed on it, said, "Regis speaking here. Gadgets, flips, boxes are the black hole. We are Starboard. Starboard 7 to 5. My father reminds me of that. You remind me of his boss, Jason."

Rathman sensed that this student was of a high status, higher than the rest of the students.

He felt awkwardness.

The student said, "If you're wondering why my 'G' is larger than the others, and why my sweater is so white, it's because I have the highest grades in the school. By the way, one person's addiction can just as easily be another person's convenience. And everybody, whether they have an addiction or not, *thinks* it's a convenience. That's why the world functions the way it does."

Rathman had not only been outwitted and outmaneuvered, he had been completely outfoxed.

Regis continued. "Nothing runs better at Starboard than a critique or a protest. Against the weak? Against the world? Against Starboard itself? What are you for? Against? Doesn't matter. Somebody is having a joke at your expense. Is someone pulling your leg? We're sure that something is missing here, like we suspect there're missing pieces to the Eccles puzzle, but we don't know what the pieces are. Sanity, especially among youth, especially among those whose distress is expressed non-psychotically, by common conditions such as anxiety..."

The speaker stumbled. It was as if he lost his train of thought. Then he rebounded. "The privatization of stress is what's behind this outbreak of unhappiness. Affective disorders are forms of captured discontent. I can make counter-arguments that are just as effective, the exact opposite of this. For example. For Gaia? Against Gaia? That's what my mother does for a living. What's her definition of success? The constant promise of a joyous future that's always elusive. Keep the addict's nose pressed up against the candy store window, for an eternity. If THAT isn't a cause for anxiety, one that hasn't yet entered the lexicon of textbook anxieties, I don't know what is. It's Eccles. Missing pieces of the puzzle tantalizingly always missing. As long as you keep them guessing, all is well. As long as you can keep them coming back for more, that's the line."

Rathman thought: grace, civility, well-mannered, filled to the top with rich analytical powers, trained to know when and how to use persuasion to get a job, trained to know when and how to use persuasion to accomplish anything.

Meritocracy without merit, equality without equality.

Rathman started feeling light-headed. In his mind he felt like he had just crawled out of the equivalent of a lotus drop den and he was lost. And with a strange inability to articulate—as if his tongue had been tied to the roof of his mouth—he wanted to bolt from the room. He felt like a fool. He told himself that he would never repeat this experience again.

"I'm sorry," Rathman said. "I apologize for coming so ill-prepared. It must come as a disappointment to you." He looked like he had been defeated. "I'm only a couple of years older than you. So there... Good luck. Best wishes."

Eccles was attractive, Rathman thought. But for Rathman the town carried within itself so many hazardous trapdoors and opportunities for pratfalls. To look stupid.

Chapter Thirty-Eight

The four engineering stars of the 4th of July Anti-Application of Subversion of Technology Commune had done their homework and were ready to put their plan into motion.

They had been waiting for the leaders of the space program to announce the return of the first photos from the space probe that had been sent up months before to study the approaching asteroid and to map its exact size and proportions, down to centimeters. They wanted the photos to be safe and secured before they did their hack.

The first time they did a test run it turned into a fiasco. The coders were able to do their part, but they couldn't coordinate, because the circuitry jockeys weren't up to it. They realized they needed more time to get all their ducks in a row.

So, one week later, they tried it again. An even worse fiasco transpired. One week later, they tried executing again. This time there were fewer glitches, but they still needed to prepare, especially with regards to the electrical grid's backup, fail-safe apparatus. Once they figured that one out, and how to temporarily disable it, they knew they were ready. So a week later they decided it was time to do the real thing.

Stealthily, they entered one of the nodes on the grid at 7:00 a.m. on a Sunday morning, at a time when there was supposed to be less surveillance activity. As they were finishing up the final touches prematurely the whole system crashed.

All of the power in the jurisdiction of Eccles went down completely. The engineers had planned a temporary power outage that would last 30 to 45 minutes.

But what they got was something different. The power went down for 36 hours.

In 95 percent of Eccles, the inhabitants just waited it out, some patiently, some grudgingly, some cursing. Some took it as a lark, an excuse to gather around "the fireplace" together. Once it was dark they took to reveling in the candlelight, singing songs together in ways they hadn't done in many years.

"Where were you when the lights went out?" they imagined themselves asking themselves years in the future—that is, if the asteroid didn't kill everybody. Like the whole thing had been a sanguine—even merciful—break from the mundane. The outage provided a harmless reprieve from the far-too-deeply embedded ruts of the routine. But for five percent of the inhabitants in the poorest and most rundown districts of Eccles the outage proved less benign.

There, the looting and arson began almost immediately. A hundred serious fires broke out, more than 150 shops were looted or set on fire, and 400 people were arrested. Rioters did not touch the more affluent parts of the metropolis, or, for the most part, midtown. They looted and burned the mom-and-pop grocery stores and bodegas, almost exclusively in their own decrepit neighborhoods. Most of those arrested were unemployed or homeless street people, but some were not. It was a frenzy of self-destruction.

As they met a day after it was over, over lunch, Jug said to Zoia cheerily, "The looters were exemplary Eccleans. Their immediate impulse in the crisis was to see to the acquisition of consumable goods. They had no interest in power. Everybody should be happy about that!"

But when Rathman heard these very same words, repeated to him that evening by Zoia, he took it completely differently. None of this comforting "Jug talk" had a positive effect on him.

When Jug heard about Rathman's reaction, he was stirred.

"He's taking this way too personally, Zoia. This is just a fascinating event to study, not something to get all fussy about. It's just a wake-up call that we take our electricity, and our power, way too much for granted, that's all."

Hadn't that been the whole point of the 4th of July Anti-Application of Subversion of Technology Commune exercise in the first place? In Eccles, was Jug the only one who got it?

All Zoia could say was: "All right, Jug. You can have it any way you want. But Rathman is behaving strangely. He hasn't been himself for days. Something's troubling him. I don't know what it is, but this something isn't going away. If anything, it's growing. I wish he had never gone to that Franz Kafka house," Zoia said. "That's where it started. And that obsession he has with *The Time Repairer.* In the entire world, I think he's the only one who actually thinks there's something in it that's *important.* Like it's an oracle. But it isn't. My father surely doesn't think so. It wasn't even that well written. Only Rathman's excellent essay saved the Time Repairer story from its own incoherence and incompetence."

At the Franz Kafka house, everyone in the Anti-Application of Subversion of Technology Commune was completely freaked out. They hadn't bargained for this outcome. In their planning, they did something wrong. There was something that they hadn't factored in. They hadn't even been sure they could bring the entire system down for three minutes, much less 36 hours.

Once the power was back up, first in the city of Eccles itself, later the entire territory of Eccles, they were waiting for their door to be smashed open by units of the Eccles security forces. But nothing happened. The longer nothing happened, the more frightened they became. Their own imaginations were their own worst enemies.

The first thing they did was burn papers and records, not only their plans but also any records that there ever had been a 4th of July

Anti-Application of Subversion of Technology Commune in the first place. They decided by unanimous vote to break up the commune. Some of the members moved back in with their parents. Some moved to the coast, to a cluster of cabins that were so remote you had to hike in 15 kilometers from the road to get to them. Some, the leader and three of the four engineers, moved to a small, out-of-the-way place named Ringwall, a border town 175 kilometers south of Albu, (but with an electronic hook-up so they wouldn't have to endure an extreme state of isolation). They decided to hole up there for a month. Only two or three remained huddled inside the unit at the Franz Kafka house, waiting for the boom to come down.

But the boom didn't descend. Nothing happened. The engineer who had stayed behind figured it out. "We're the luckiest people in the universe. We didn't disable the grid. It was shut down by other means. A solar flare up caused the blackout. It was the largest of its kind since they started studying the phenomena, nine times larger than the one that struck 100 years ago. It happened at exactly the same time we were beginning our hack. Call it a coincidence if you like. The transient. What's a transient? Surge of energy in the core. This transient turned into a *runaway* transient, which is why the shutdown lasted as long as it did. My Gaia, if I could turn back time and cancel all of our actions out, I'd do so in a heartbeat."

Chapter Thirty-Nine

L IKE IN THE CASE of so many others, the outage startled Rathman, but more than that, it traumatized him. Unlike so many others, he completely freaked out. At the precise moment the shutdown hit, he was rereading the story of *The Time Repairer.* Just as the Microsoft building basement author from 2700 years before was describing the time repairer bent over his desk, grasping a delicate instrument that he was using to reset a spring-load gear in the back of an open watch, Rathman's lamp stopped illuminating, the refrigerator shut down, the turntable of the record player stopped, and the clock in the vestibule no longer ticked.

It grew dark. There was not enough natural light to read by. Because of this inconvenience, as if Rathman was dimly aware of what was happening, but a piece of the puzzle was still missing, he shouted out, "What's happening?"

In a state of agitation and nervous irritation, Rathman jumped as quickly as he could into a pair of pants, threw a shirt on, didn't bother with socks, and took the document with him to a park bench so he could finish the reread in the early morning light. With the power shut off Rathman had become frantic, but now he had recovered.

As soon as the power came back up, 36 hours later, Rathman was asked to pull a "10 plus one" in the basement of the restaurant of the Gatetar tower. He couldn't resist the offer. All he had to do was work a "10 plus one" and he would get paid for the entire 36 hours.

Stooped over two deep, vat-like sinks, Rathman worked his hands raw. Now that the hot water had been restored, all he had to do was apply determination and elbow grease.

The steam came up in plumes. After six hours of being hunched over Rathman felt like his shirt was ready to slip from his shoulders and his pants were ready to slip off his hips. But he got into a rhythm, he worked hard, everything was heat and steam, clouding his vision with a thick miasma of soapy wetness. He improvised by cutting the implanted grease with knives and other sharp metal objects. After all, the hardest part of the job was scrubbing the metal bars of fish racks, chicken trays, and beefsteak broiling pans, all made worse because the pots and pans had sat in cold water for a day and a half and the grease had congealed. Small wonder the bosses were willing to pay extra. They didn't want him to bail on them when he saw the mountains of pots and pans.

Thinking of the extra money, Rathman contentedly and happily soldiered on.

On the opposite side of the room there was a raised roof, with a sooty ceiling, that reached up 13 feet. It was in this corner that empty cardboard boxes were stacked. Under normal circumstances these boxes never rose higher than eight feet, but after the shut-down, there was a back-load. The boxes needed to be fetched, stacked, and stored.

The gathering and stacking of these boxes were a minor part of Byron's job, the major part being finding lost or misplaced kitchen items: plates, bowls, glasses, knifes, forks, spoons, and, when called for, special wedding party gear, cake boxes, linen napkins, sometimes even the more unusual anomaly, special expensive china; putting all these items to where they belonged was Byron's specialty. He had a talent for this job, and he had eight years experience (*which in this business was uncharacteristically long.*) Therefore, because of his unique skills he was valued and his immediate bosses gave him a wide berth. The higher bosses completely, totally, positively, absolutely left the 'unfathomable' fellow alone. That was Byron.

From the moment Byron entered the kitchen, Rathman could see that his intake of Outer World cannabis had been exceptionally high. Actually it had been ratcheted up with a few extra doses so that Byron could see himself through the dark time. He had started up again just before he had been called in.

Byron was not just under the influence, he was stoned up to the gills.

There had already been eight-feet-high stacks of cardboard boxes in the corner before the day had begun. But during the course of 10 hours, the stacks had grown to 11 feet. The higher the boxes were placed, the more precarious they were. Just before the end of his 11-hour shift, Rathman had finished scrubbing the last pot and was taking a well-deserved break. Byron entered and threw the last of the retrieved boxes on top of the stacks. As they alighted, three of them landed stably, but one missed the mark by a lot and tipped. It caused all of the stacks to sway.

But instead of reaching out and attempting to steady the uneven stacks to prevent them from falling, Byron just stood back and gawked. They all tumbled. Then, as if coming from a-bottom-of-the-well contemplation, he said, "They all fall down."

And then slowly, in a dull voice, this time with extreme earnestness, he repeated, "And they aaalllllllllll fall down..."

Rathman couldn't control himself. He laughed. The more he tried to stifle himself, the more thunderously the laughter erupted. Staggering over, hiking up his pants, Rathman lunged and grabbed Byron by the lapels and kissed him. Hugging him, Rathman said, "Let's get out of here! Empty cardboard boxes strewn about. That's all we are to the world."

And listening to him, Byron smiled. "The man from the outside world speaks! He actually commands!"

And then Rathman seemed to change his mind, to grow uncertain. "Let's reconsider. Wait a second. Eccles has given me everything. If not in other ways, at least in my great luck in coming to know Zoia. We need to rectify this situation. We can't leave things this way."

Rathman stooped over and began picking up the boxes, stacking them right. He put everything back into order, making neat, even, tall stacks.

Eventually, Byron recovered and began to help too.

Finally, the stacks of empty cardboard boxes, all of them, looked like they were supposed to. It only took the pair of them a few extra minutes to complete the task.

Once they stepped into the street, Byron went his way, Rathman his. All Rathman could think about was the looming darkness that was growing inside him. "What am I doing here? The counselor was right. Eccles has chewed me up and swallowed me, now it's spitting me out. This is not my home."

Rathman thought about returning to his closet, but that state of compressed living now struck him as depressingly predictable and infinitely dreary. Most of the time he could bear it, but sometimes that space made him feel boxed in and claustrophobic. He tried to think of something else, but all he could think about was whether the 4th of July Anti-Application of Subversion of Technology Commune had a hand in the power outage. He did not want to contact them. "Not caused by the perniciousness of Inner World terrorists or Outer World thugs," the authorities' report had said. "Our conclusion is that a massive solar flare caused the disruption. Therefore, the cause was *a natural one*...nature serving itself up to us. We have already learned from our mistakes, and we will handle the next emergency better."

So maybe it hadn't been the commune at the Franz Kafka house that was responsible after all.

Many residents in Eccles had taken the shutdown hard. The system had hitherto been excellent at running itself. The people of Eccles weren't used to having their conveniences disrupted. The economic productivity indices took a slight dip, but other than that there were no other effects. Hospitals and police had been able to run on battery-operated generators; they had planned in advance to have emergency power. Maybe it was just because Rathman was superstitious, but the fact that he was reading *The Time Repairer* at the moment the disruption occurred caused him to descend into a funk. The incidences were too coincidental, Rathman believed. The time repairer story, with its theme of a four-week-long power shutdown, the stunt planned by the commune at the Franz Kafka house, a major solar flare event. There had to be a pattern, a connection, however well hidden or seemingly inexplicable.

Did the study of Dark Time plague Rathman because he was predisposed to a dangerous breed of melancholia? Or was it the context, not the content. Or was it because of negative thoughts about the asteroid? Was that the content? Or the context? Or both? Or was it because of an unlikely string of events that had occurred willy-nilly, the solar storm, the Franz Kafka house, the Starboard school, the "10 plus one" shift at the Gatetar restaurant, the boxes tumbling down? Something about the combination of events seemed to cause Rathman's mind to unravel.

Rathman was seeing too much, that is to say, reading too much into what he was seeing. He saw too many connections. The more Rathman thought about it, the more it caused him to go to a dark place. The funk not only did not diminish, it grew in power and scope and shape.

And then the one person who could have helped him, his lifeline to the light, Zoia, announced that she had to leave with her father earlier than they had planned, and that the two-week trip was now going to be a week longer.

Heading for Auger's seven-stop speaking tour, Albu and points east, father and daughter happened to depart an evening *before* the power outage, so they were in Bankedge by then and missed all the commotion.

Zoia didn't know why she seemed to be the only person who knew how to keep her father's notes and scheduling in order. Auger

claimed he got "the administrative heebie-jeebies," but the claim
was a ruse, an excuse. Zoia figured it was better to go along with
her father than try to fight him. She wasn't allowed to be her own
person in this, but she accepted her fate with poise, passivity, and
resignation.

▶ ▶ ▶ ▶

A week after Auger and Zoia departed for Bankedge, as a stroke
of bad timing, or just bad luck, Rathman's funk deepened, widened,
and careened out of control. He was so depressed he couldn't attend
his classes. He got the shakes at the mere idea of it. He couldn't
wash pots and pans at the restaurant either. Both Byron and Rathman had gotten into trouble, even though they had cleaned up the
mess with the boxes. Management started picking on the two of
them for reasons that remained inscrutable. Rathman had trouble
getting out of bed. In six days' time he looked like a hollowed out
case. He lost his job which he found difficult to lament save for the
fact it had been keeping him afloat financially. The rest of his scholarship money wasn't going to arrive for another two months. He had
no money, and the rent was due.

Rathman was able to scrape together about half the rent, but
that was all. The only solution was to temporarily put himself in the
hands of Jug. And that's when things went from bad to worse, very
quickly.

Chapter Forty

RATHMAN WENT TO JUG in his state of crisis. In his condition he would have been willing to fall on his hands and knees in supplication, to efface himself, to abjectly humble himself. Or so he thought.

"I don't have enough money for rent. Soon, I won't even have enough money for food. Put at my disposal a helioplane. Allow me to go to the toxic waste site."

"You mean Cannibal Land?" Jug asked in a casual voice. "That strange place you've talked about over and over? What a strange request. I thought that was supposed to be a joke."

"It's not a joke."

"There aren't any cannibals there," Jug said. "There used to be, 2,000 years ago. But I've heard that the inhabitants, the descendants of the original cannibals, are very scary indeed. Listen, there are many places you can go to if you need to recharge. Do you want to go back home?"

"No. To the orphanage? Absolutely not. I'll be seen as a complete failure. It would humiliate me..."

"Listen..."

Rathman interrupted Jug. "The story of the Time Repairer, not the one in the book, the original story, from the document—through Zoia—you placed in my hands—through Zoia—is telling me to go."

"To go where? To hell? To the earthly equivalent?"

"To the toxic waste site. Well, the Book of Iona is telling me to go, too."

"You sound confused," Jug said. He had never seen Rathman look so pale and haggard before.

"I'm not confused. This is my way out."

Jug didn't know what to say at this point. He took some time thinking. Then he said: "Well, if the Time Repairer is telling you to go, I guess you should. But there are other places I can send you. I know places in the Outer World that are not so dangerous. Places where we've expanded the limits of the Inner World into the Outer World. Albu, where you come from, is just one example of that expansion."

"No," Rathman said. Then he seemed to changed his mind. In a series of rapid declarations, Rathman expanded on the details of his plans, which were not really plans at all, but in Rathman's mind, they sounded like they were. He intended to be deposited more or less in the place that he had at first requested, only closer to the south bank of the river and farther from the coast. This modest modification was a concession to Jug's concerns.

"You really should think this through more carefully," Jug said after a pause.

Jug agreed to give Rathman money for food. He also agreed to pay Rathman's rent for the next 12 months, and to subsidize Rathman for as long as he needed subsidizing. "Whatever it takes so you can continue your education, I'll give you. I've always been big on education. Do you want to wait until Zoia returns, so you can talk this through with her?"

"No. If I don't go now, I'll never go. The document is telling me to go."

"All right."

Jug agreed to set everything up for Rathman, lending him his safest and most dependable helioplane, and his most reliable and experienced pilot. "Johnson has gotten me out of plenty of scrapes in the past, I can assure you of that," Jug told him. "So trust me, you're in good hands."

"He'll know where to take me?"

"He'll know exactly where to take you. He'll know exactly where to set you down. He'll know exactly where and how to pick you up. I envy you in your new adventure."

But he didn't.

Jug was taking advantage of Rathman's situation And when Jason heard about this ill-conceived trip, he nearly went berserk. "Doubling down on Zoia's absence, aren't you? Unseemly. Coming from a dark, cold, calculating place. Even by your standards. Jug, this is beneath your dignity."

"I'm merely giving a friend a hand."

"No you're not. You're giving yourself over to your desires. You're not sending him on a tourist jaunt, you realize. So, don't pretend that that is what you're doing. It's about Zoia."

"I've been told he's crossed deserts barefoot. He's even done it without any water. His father taught him how to live off the land. By the age of six he'd seen more extraordinary things than I had by the age of 14. This guy's more experienced in the real world than we are. I'll have him picked up at a designated time and place, and that'll be as easy as it gets."

"He's had knowledge and experience of a kind, but not this," Jason cautioned. "He's never been to the jungle before. And you've never seen this toxic jungle wasteland with your own eyes. This is like something from the religious times. Kull's journey to the place of toxic waste? As it was written in the Book of Iona. Kull journeyed across the *Atlantic*—as the ocean was then called—where he landed in Cannibal Land and was set upon by a band of cannibals. I was taught this tale in grammar school, one of the most popular stories from THE BLESSINGS OF GAIA DOCUMENT. I didn't even

know this Rathman fellow *was* religious. From the impression I got
he wasn't. He hung out with that crowd of skeptical, cynical, liber-
tine, anarchists at the Rhetoric Department. I can't imagine what
any of this has to do with anything, except maybe that crazy document, what was it called? The Time Repairer? Who is this guy? Oh,
Rathman. Zoia's boyfriend. Guy's gone crazy, so you want to make
it worse and maybe get him killed. In good conscience, I can't let
you do this. I'll quit."

"Very well, your resignation is accepted."

Jason was left in a state of shock by Jug's reaction. "So, it's *that*
serious?" he said. "Zoia again. You've been lying. Biding your time.
Playing it up with these people like you're all pals, best buddies,
friends. I've known you since you were 10. What an obsessive you've
become."

"Rathman wants to go. He's my friend. I'm not going to stop
him. Zoia has nothing to do with this."

"Yeah right. Keep telling yourself that. Keep lying to yourself.
We've talked about this before. The line separating *reason* from
rationalization. The line you want to cross. I told you before you
can lie to people. You can lie to the public, about whatever you want,
whenever you want. I've watched your father and you do that plenty
of times. But I also said you can't lie when you're talking to your
friends."

Jason turned and walked out.

Chapter Forty-One

ZOIA FOUND RATHMAN in what appeared to be an abandoned lean-to, strewn with broken coconut husks, hitherto used as crockery, and two broken musical instruments, a drum and an *er-banjo*. The latter instrument was just a stick with one string still attached and two other strings broken. There was a worn, ragged, soiled straw mat that many others had slept on in the past.

Upon Zoia's approach, the indigenous people had scattered into the wasteland, the surrounding darkness, making whooping gestures, chortling shouts, and fierce noises as they retreated. As they ran into the darkness, several of the more brazen ones shot ill-aimed arrows over their shoulders in the vague direction of Zoia, as she came barging through the trees, all determination and intrepidness. She had surprised the indigenous people more than frightened them, but disrupted them all the same. The landing of the helioplane, 150 meters away—on what was the nearest improvised landing site—a narrow spit of treeless level land—was the main cause of the indigenous people's concern and fear and reminded them of their desire for reclusion and of their inherent, heartfelt wariness of outsiders. The helioplane's landing and Zoia's stridently bold approach must have reminded them of similar unwelcome incursions from the outside world in the past.

Even with Zoia's limited experience she knew this toxic jungle was about as far off the beaten path, not to mention the tourist trail, especially the elite tourist trail, as could be. To an outsider the jungle looked hopelessly impenetrable, but to these indigenous people it was hospitable. They were nomads. The jungle had toxic properties dating back millennia, so they had to keep on the move.

Six weeks before, there had been nothing in the place where Zoia was standing. In a month's time, the indigenous people would burn their lean-tos and all other non-essentials, pack a few precious belongings, and leave, the jungle swallowing up all trace of them.

Zoia just marched straight into the lean-to (to call it a "one-room hut" would have been an overstatement), unfazed.

Rathman looked up. "I don't feel good. Funny. It happened yesterday. Or maybe it happened the day before. I got lost. I've been in this lean-to all this time. How far are we from the ranch?"

"The ranch?"

"Home."

"You're in an altered state," Zoia said.

"I don't know if I'm awake or asleep," Rathman said after a while. He looked up at Zoia again. She stood in the doorway with the glare of the sun behind her, the light quivering, shimmering. In Rathman's unbalanced imagination, it was as if she had come accompanied by a golden halo.

"Am I awake?" Rathman asked.

"I don't know. Are you? You're in an altered state."

"I'm really confused," Rathman said. "I must be awake. I have a palsy that is compromising my eyes. My sight is blurry. On occasion, I'm blind. Zoia, is that you?"

When the substances had entered Rathman's bloodstream a day and a half before, they had attached themselves to the mu-receptors in his medulla oblongata and the synaptic membranes of the neurons responsible for transmitting pain signals. This made Rathman feel numb and blissful, and caused his blood pressure to drop, his heart to slow, his breathing to become shallow, and his muscles to relax. He experienced such a profound oceanic state he even thanked the indigenous people profusely (at least at first) for administering the potion. He felt better than he had felt before in his life. But 16 hours later, the process reversed itself. The substances tried to leave his system. His pores opened, sweat seeped out of them, soaking his mat. His skin lost its pallor, and his muscles contracted. He felt in turn dizziness, time distortion, physical prostration, hyperventilation. He experienced auditory hallucinations, and scintillating patterns of light exploding across his closed eyelids.

His stomach tried to empty itself, and several times he briefly cried like a child who could feel something had gone horribly wrong with his body, but lacked the vocabulary to explain the sensations.

Several times, briefly, he had gone completely blind. But then his eyesight came back.

In the interim his mind raced and his thoughts became super-active.

Rathman looked at Zoia with an expression of vapidity in his eyes. He hadn't slept in days. Or, alternately, if he had slept, it was a fitful sleep, shallow and non-restorative.

"They laughed at my hair. Then my clothes. Clothed with feathers adorning their hair, otherwise they wear war-hoops and girdles made of plant-stocks and leaves, hanging briefly down from their waists. They gave me something to drink. Then they gave me... yeah...mushrooms, brown, chewy. Or I dreamt they did. Now that I think about it, I think I just dreamt it. I dreamt they put these substances in my food, malformed manioc, puny, pathetic-looking peanuts, deformed kernels of corn...corncobs only six inches long... only 15 or 20 kernels on each cob...yellow, red, and blue in color... as if this wretched cob of corn is an example of the best this contaminated, toxic place can produce. Or I dreamt that too. Oh, my head! It feels like my head's ready to explode! What am I doing here! At first they seemed indifferent to me, then friendly, then like I was something they could toy with."

"Calm," Zoia said. "Lie low. All animals go to ground when hurt or sick." Zoia gave Rathman a confident, comforting look. "This place looks as good as any."

Zoia immediately put her belongings down, a bag containing a flask of water and a large loaf of what that morning had been freshly baked bread, pills, and medical gauze.

After arranging these materials in a corner, she sat with Rathman on the hut's sweat-soaked mat. With the back of her fingernails, so lightly, so tenderly, Zoia stroked Rathman's eyelids. "We'll fix these too," she said.

Then she clasped Rathman and held him in her arms. She rocked him back and forth. "Oh what, oh what, have you done to yourself!" she said.

Unclasping him, Zoia noticed something she hadn't noticed at first. There was a trickle of blood slowly running down the inside of Rathman's arm.

"I tried to resist them," Rathman said in a woozy voice. "Then I stopped. I drank the goop. Then when the manioc, corn, and peanuts were served to me, it smelled funny. I resisted. They stabbed me. Right here! In my arm. Here! Where they stabbed me. They forced me to eat."

Zoia acted fast. She ripped Rathman's shirtsleeve open so that she could bind up the wound. The cut was moderately deep but fortunately not life-threatening, aside from the possibility of infection. Using just a small bit of the water she had brought, she cleaned the wound thoroughly and covered it.

Four uneventful hours passed and during this time Rathman was relatively calm. Zoia took the opportunity to get some sleep herself. Then mercurially, Rathman went from a state of lethargy to a frenzy of rekindled energy.

"No," Zoia said reproachfully. "Calm. We're making progress. You're acting the wrong way. You need to let the substances leech out of you. They will. Imagine it this way. You're on a swing swinging way up. You need for your whole condition to swing down. And you need to eventually level off."

Rathman looked completely confused. Then with a renewed vigor, he spoke. "I have a choice. A or B. But I can't choose others.

A choice."

"A choice?" Zoia asked. "What are you talking about? Calm," she added in a soothing voice. "Calmmmmm..."

"My head's exploding!" Rathman screamed.

"I'm listening to you," Zoia said. "But try. I'm waiting for you. I'm here. I won't abandon you."

"You can hold one view, only one view," Rathman said at last.

Zoia rolled her eyes. What did that mean? What was he jabbering on about, she wondered.

"One. One view. There's no god or god-like thing."

"Oh!" Zoia exclaimed. She rolled her eyes. Sophmoric in nature talk...

"There's only that which I can sense," Rathman continued. "There's no afterlife. For the body, of course. Is there a soul? I don't see... But there's something that the universe can turn into. In other words, evolution. Or us in nature's web of life, there is future, not just past. And at some later point, there is a universe that has become *something else*, something fuller, something grander. And for lack of a better term, that end-point comes only after this evolution, we in nature's web of life...well. What are we? No, we don't know what we are."

Zoia's initial impulse was to ignore what Rathman said. She could see that as long as he was jumping from one extreme to another, he'd be thinking erratically, also perhaps talking crazy.

Flecks of saliva formed in the corners of Rathman's mouth. "Or second choice B," he said. "This one's *dark*. There's nothing. No past, no present. There's no evolution, because there's no future. Nothing. The asteroid. A random act in a non-narrative, non-sequential coincidence of incidence—outside of all sequential actions in a non-linear, non-cosmological world. Because it contradicts even my speaking about it as if it were an 'it.' It doesn't exist, because of the amputation, the annihilation, wiping out the past." Rathman's eyes were blurred but apparently his mind was working. "Destroying all life. Extinction. We know what that means. No nature. No Gaia. No

future. We never existed. If there is not even one single human being
left to have memory, there is no future...but there is also no past. As
long as there's one person left alive who has memory there is hope.
But once that's gone, human extinction has occurred. *Darkness car-*
ried this deformed light to us. Our future lies in memory. In memory
our future lies. Memory is all."

"Let's switch to a scientific way of looking at things," Rathman
continued. "Let's say—hypothetically—a communication, an emission, 125 million years from the past, coming from a far distance
out, a far distant galaxy in the universe—so long ago that it was sent
at a time when we were not apes, nor humans. We're the glimmer of
a prehistoric mind in the evolving bodies of rodent-like mammals,
surviving the last great dinosaur kill off. No, it's even earlier than
that, twice as early as that. Life is on Earth, and the message would
reach Earth, the emission, from a dead species, 125 million years
after we've been rendered extinct ourselves. 125 million years in the
past from the time we are now, 250 million years total. A quarter of
a billion years it took for the transmission to travel. Get it?"

"I get it."

"After it finally arrives. As if we never were here. But if you
go into the darkness, you go into it, when you know not to hope,
there is no emission. No receptors, therefore, no emission. From the
dead, 125 million years in the past, to the dead, 125 million years
in the future. From the un to the un. There never was—there never
will be—an emission, a signpost on a journey that never happened.
That's because it's a human-created invention. A FICTIONAL
INVENTION OF OUR IMAGINATION. This is something that
should be scorned and discouraged because it is something that is
between fairy tale and swindle. Space is devoid of life because it is.
Scientists tell us so. Until proven otherwise. Immigration? Would
life forms that evolved on Earth be able to survive elsewhere? On a
Goldilocks's planet? At an inconceivable distance. Gazillions of kilometers away? Not even close. Not even one-gazillion of one gazillion of .0001 percent of the way! Add a zero. Add two zeros. *Vast*

space! The neighborhood is so far away that it's not within grasp, not within intra-galactic, much less inter-galactic, travel. If we speeded up our HeliosX4 space travel by a factor of 11, or a factor of 115, or a factor of 1150, still wouldn't work. Too many lifetimes. And then what? Even the most degraded environment on Earth, a million times better than life on a foreign object, would be absolutely unable to provide ANY protection for us from the bombardment of high energy radiation, X-rays, and ultraviolet light. Wouldn't that imply that intelligent life on Earth is indeed a one-of-a-kind? What else could it be? An astronomically rare event. Short lived? A wink of an eye. Human consciousness? What is it? A byproduct of the faulty fluke of malevolent *mutation?* Which, for lack of a better term, we call human consciousness. Gone? The dinosaurs lasted 180 to 200 million years. What if we last—if we include the period of time of our nearly human humanoid antecedents as well—four million years? And we are now a few years away from the end of those four million years? Four million out of 250 million. No longer IS. Because there is no WAS. We're freaks..."

"So why even bother prattling on about this stuff?" Zoia asked. "*All this Darkness?* We are alone. My father said that to me. Only on a rare day does one feel the sublime pain of being alone in the universe. Nothing lasts. Everybody dies. To be stoic? To depend on ourselves and the universe. Rathman... Okay. I'm on board. You want to—prematurely—drive another nail into the coffin?"

"You're making fun of me."

"The next nail? Into the coffin? We don't exist already."

"Which one do you chose?" Rathman asked. "Which one?"

"You don't exist already. Some might even argue that this might be the most glorious time to be alive of all!"

Almost 15 seconds lapsed. Rathman wasn't in pain, not at that moment, Zoia was mistaken, all seemed dull to him, except for the sound of the roar of the ocean in his ears, accompanied by a low-level dizziness, and the vision in his eyes fading in and out.

Zoia was in a state of doubt. She had to say—what Auger would have called—'the historically-wise thing.' "If you can't believe in god, whatever that is, if you can't believe in science, whatever that is, if you can't believe in evolution, a subset of science, whatever that is, you can still believe in life. In fact, you don't have to believe in it, it just is. You're on the side of life and you're *not* on the side of the absence of life. How hard is that? Isn't that what Gaia is about? Life? It just is. That still remains."

A moment passed.

Rathman had energy, but it abruptly ebbed. He had lain back next to Zoia, and for more than an hour he felt relief, an approximation of peace. The two of them slept in each other's arms for more than an hour. When Rathman awoke the substances hadn't completely worn off, but they were having a much less negative effect.

But then it started again. Rathman grew agitated and excited.

"I got too much imagination roaring inside me," Rathman said. "Fondane! Onward! Don't know? Wouldn't your dad be happy? Wouldn't he be glad? I'm picking up at least something from the light, from the earlier period of modernism and modernity."

"Yes, he would," Zoia said.

"You know Fondane?"

"No."

"Benjamin F. lets Franz K. win. Even if it's referring to nothing, the meaning of life...still K. *The Sunday of History*, which goes on... Since the beginning of humankind Sunday goes on. Before the Monday of Existentialism has a chance to appear, Sunday goes on. Of course, Monday never comes. We wait for it. But it never comes. Get it?"

Zoia sensed that Rathman was, *perhaps,* out of danger. Waiting for something that doesn't come is better than not existing. She hoped that maybe, soon, he would leave with her, re-board the helioplane. She came to the conclusion that shifting the topic slightly would have the best effect on him.

"Don't let this nonsense bear down on you," Zoia said. "We're freaks. We're super-freaks. We're super-super freaks. Just us four.

Four of us. Pius, Auger, you and me. Super-freaks. That's right, freaks! Hey! Freaks! Four of us... Know this, dope. *Four*. Only four of us *care about this drama!* The four touchstones. Francis Bacon / First World War / Frankenstein / the Time Repairer. Four touchstones. Auger, Pius, Zoia, and *you*. You should hear my father's rap: science, reason, passion, progress, order."

"What are you talking about?" Rathman asked.

"You should hear Pius's rap," Zoia continued, "mechanized slaughter, trench warfare, mutilated bodies, rat-infested, flea-infested mud, barbed wire, poison gas, stalemate, First World War, sneak preview to the bigger one. The Eleven-Years-War. Mine? I go to extremes. But not too extreme. Mary Shelley's *Frankenstein*. But if you want to name the Climate Change and Global Warming thing. 2,700 years ago? It's the subtitle that fits the bill. Prometheus *modern*, stealing fire from the gods, and therefore bound by chains on a rock for an eternity. Extrapolate from that, Mary Shelley's version, then fast forward to what she couldn't see, but she may have intuited. The super-colossal-industrial hyper-explosion, uber-implosion, carbon-revolution-making machine explosion, burning up the planet, Frankenstein-style. The revenge of nature. Not out of nowhere, like a hail of bullets, or an explosion of splattered, splintered meteors, or a single ball of immaculate fire. A world war? Eleven-Years-War? An asteroid? The end of utopia. No. It came at us from a different angle, in an abstruse way, in a difficult-to-understand way. Not from outer space. No astronomers, astronauts, asteroids involved. No. Just our ancestors. I know how much you love *them*. It came from them. Hence, it came back. Causing 2,500 years of darkness, and if scientists are right, causing many more years of darkness in so many parts of the Outer World. Not a minor alteration in humanity's future, don't you think? If we're going to take some lesson out of our collective past, better late than never, wouldn't you agree? We're freaks. Freaks. How many people out of the entire population of Eccles care about this? Remember that it happened? They care about the asteroid! Nothing better concentrates the mind than a pale approximation of extinction. How many people at that concert we attended months ago gave much thought to the lessons of time-honored ancient history? Just us freaks! History is an arduous incubus we struggle to awake from, but for everyone else...well...sleep. Touchstone, Rathman. Touchstones. Frankenstein! Let us leap up! Let's rise up out of this Cannibal Land! Move up!"

"I need to calm you down," Rathman said. "Out of the darkness? Out of the Darkness time?"

"Yeah, pretty baby, out the darkness, out of the Darkness time, yes, time repairing," Zoia said with a beatific expression on her face.

Zoia saying that made Rathman feel happy. "You know, I don't deserve this," he said. "You're making fun of me." He looked flat and dejected.

"Yes... Well... Don't.... Still delirious? The substances, still circulating around in your bloodstream."

In Rathman's eyes there was a glimmer of hope, a slightly edgy look of liveliness.

"I have an appetite," he said.

"What?" Zoia asked. Oh, she was hopeful. *That was something new.* A turning point? "Would you like a drink of water?" she asked. She handed Rathman the flask.

Rathman drank liberally. "Isn't that a sign?" he asked. He hiccupped.

"A sign?" Zoia asked. "A sign of what?"

"Recovery."

"Yes!" Zoia shouted. She whooped with joy. "Yes," she screamed. She beamed. "See! That's my old Rathman talking again. Yes. That's my man. No more foolish talk. Now, are you strong enough to travel?" she asked in a commanding voice. "Give me that strong look again."

Rathman nodded. Dimly, his eyes shone.

Zoia saw no reason to wait for the people in the jungle to return. "You know I've been told that for tens of thousands of years there have been people who just see themselves as being *the people.* And to them, there are no other people but themselves. Their world of humanity doesn't extend beyond the edge of their village, or beyond the edge of a neighboring village. They have no curiosity about the world beyond their immediate range of environment. And why should they? They are incapable of understanding that there is a *universality* of humanity beyond their scope. An asteroid? What does that mean? I'm describing to you these people who just ran away into the jungle. Coming from the outside world, who would want to live in a horrible place like this? That has been the basis of their safety. Make this land valuable and they'll be eliminated."

Rathman smiled at Zoia.

Zoia was suddenly beside herself. "Why do you think these creatures who live here did this incredible thing to you?" she asked. "I mean, let's get down to it. I'm aghast! I'm appalled. They drugged you! Why? But why?"

"Dunno," Rathman replied sheepishly. "Sport?"

"Oh, you're articulate when you want to be."

Zoia got him out quickly. Quick as a whistle. Then, when the helioplane was racing at speeds nearing 1660 kilometers per hour, she couldn't contain herself when she thought of the ways she was going to chew Jug out.

Of course, first, she had to put Rathman under ice, pack him up under wraps. Two crazy men...one she didn't love, and one she did.

Chapter Forty-Two

"YOU SAID HE WAS CRAZY?" Jug said in a defensive voice. "He didn't seem crazy before he departed."

"Oh, nonsense," Zoia said. She frowned off into the distance. She sighed and added, in an acid-like voice, "Well, I guess he could have been crazy, mind you, a typical, garden variety of craziness, if I could have quieted him down a bit first—while he was drooling, moaning, and acting out like a creature that was stark raving mad. You're not going to smooth talk your way out of this one, Jug."

"I didn't want to know what his condition was," Jug replied. "He asked me to help him. Do you realize he was completely out of money? Did he explain his financial difficulties to you?"

"It's going to take a lot more than a charm attack to wiggle yourself off the hook on this one," Zoia said, deflecting the question. "No, he didn't tell me. I suppose he was too proud."

"If he was acting peculiar, and I'm not saying he was, but if he was, I might have thought it was because he was broke. I've seen that have a bad effect on men before."

"I've heard Jason is no longer in your service."

"Where did you hear that?"

"From him."

As much as Jug tried to put on a stern, cold front, it was as if he started disassembling in slow motion in front of Zoia's eyes.

"He spoke to you?" Jug asked.

"Of course. Do you want to get your story straight now, or do you want me to figure out some sort of stratagem to sweat it out of you?"

"Sometimes I act like a complete idiot. Sometimes not. But one fault I don't have is jealousy. Just like one fault you don't have is envy."

"Oh, so you weren't the instigator. You were just the opportunist. Is there something about power that makes people like you think you can get away with murder, or murder by proxy, or murder by accident? It's only because Rathman *does* know how to handle himself that he didn't go completely under, no thanks to you. You sent him to Cannibal Land! Because he had an idea stuck in his head?"

This time there was a really long silence before Jug replied.

"All right," Jug said. "I'll atone."

"You're going to do a lot more than that," Zoia said.

"I'll abase myself."

"I came here with the intention of hurting you. Really harming you. But I'm not going to do that. I'm just going to humiliate you. You can report your newly reformed behavior to my father. Why have I chosen him for that role? I'll tell you why. I don't want to see *you*. At least for a good while. And then he'll tell me—make his assessment, and give me a full report. And we'll watch and make periodical reassessments as we go. You're under watch."

"You don't expect me to completely change, do you?"

"I expect you to fly straight. We're not negotiating terms here. If you ever expect to see Rathman and me again, *ever*, you'll think hard on this. You'll think really hard on this."

"So, you're staying with him?"

It was only at this moment that Zoia realized that the circumstances were far worse than she had initially thought. She wondered what it was about her that caused her to have such a hold on this man, *this strange man*. There was something pathetic about Jug, and pathetic about the whole situation that they all had fallen into.

"You can start reporting to my dad. Say two months from now. Don't call us. We'll call you. I mean it. Don't contact us. Gosh, maybe this will be the best thing that ever happened to the people of Eccles."

"You wouldn't consider...you wouldn't think..." Jug started to ask.

"Redemption through suffering? Not a chance. Actually, that's asking too much of you. How about redemption through service, as in service to others, someone other than yourself. No me or myself or I operating here. In the mean time, until we see evidence of change, we'll continue to call you not Jug, but Juggernaut. If your father's goal in life was to make you into a juggernaut, this falsity and self-delusional duplicity will serve as an example of how *not* to conduct yourself. Now that I've thought about it, I have an even better idea. Don't contact my father. HE'LL contact YOU. You'd better be prepared to give him a report, something in the nature of the redemptive."

Chapter Forty-Three

ZOIA THOUGHT that it was a silly idea, but she also knew that it would have been even more silly to interfere.

To find a cure that would work, to expunge the darkness out of himself, Rathman insisted that all he needed to do was take long walks outdoors in nature, like he was—to use his own words—"a Pleistocene man."

He said to Zoia, "I walk. I don't run. Because I have far to go."

"Is this your new religion?" Zoia asked.

"Yes. Yes. Walking is my new religion."

Rathman started walking 15 to 20 kilometers each day, beginning and finishing at more or less the same time, starting at 7:00 or 8:00 a.m., completing his journey by 12 noon or 1:00 p.m. He walked by the Gatetar Tower, and into Pleasure Park, and completed the journey by coming back walking along some of the major thoroughfares and boulevards of Eccles. Eventually he was walking 25 kilometers a day.

He always tried to time his walks so that when he passed by Gatetar tower he could see the young woman who cleaned the bathrooms of a hash house just across the plaza, carrying her buckets, scrubbers, and mops. After a week or two, he asked someone who worked in the hash house about her and was told she cleaned the bathrooms of five or six small eating establishments in the area daily. He was told she was from the border of the Outer World. He guessed she was trying not to starve, undoubtedly barely eking out an existence, functioning just under the radar because she had no papers. He realized that she probably looked upon herself as "no account to the world," living on the edge of an alien world, she coming from a people who were "nothing people," their lives ensnared by abysmal failure, anguish, or bare survival. But why couldn't she be seen as heroic? Just like any other person who was depicted in a classical epic was heroic?

At some distance when they caught a glimpse of each other their eyes met momentarily, but they did not speak. After a time Rathman began fantasizing that someone should write a novel about her. But he knew that no one would. Still, the idea of someone writing a great and grand story about her became an obsession with him. Rathman thought that regardless of one's station in life, why would one person's story be any less important than any other's...?

Then, for a week, he didn't see her. He wondered what had become of her, he was worried, hoping she was okay, hoping that nothing untoward had happened to her..

And on the eighth day he sat across the street from the hash house on a long, low wall in the shade, hoping that she might walk by.

And she did!

As usual she was carrying her buckets, scrubbers, and mops, and, for the first time, she waved at him. And he knew that he might have written a novel about her, if he knew how to write one. But he didn't, so he couldn't. But with a great feeling of thrill, he waved back at her.

After about two months of walking, the route grew boring for Rathman, so he decided to vary when and where he chose to take his walks. That way he would catch the light at a different angle as he viewed the world of Eccles around him.

Sometimes he walked at daybreak, sometimes at mid-morning, sometimes later in the morning, sometimes early in the afternoon, sometimes just before dusk, and on occasion, even after dark. If he walked at daybreak, he noticed the little things. Like the heavy dew in the early morning, a light-brown and lime-green leaf lying on the grass, beads of water looking like beads of sweat sitting on the back of the leaf, glinting in the light of the early morning sun. As often as six or seven times every block he saw small gardens where rows of younglings of green plants were climbing toward the sun: Corn! String beans! Sunflower seeds!

If it was just before dusk or after dark, his favorite walking paths led to Pleasure Park. Sometimes Rathman walked in the opposite direction toward Mount Eta. And sometimes he chose the busiest routes, passing by the seemingly endless rows and blocks of electronics factories and the long apartment blocks, most of them 10 stories high, some of them 20.

He loved to follow the undulating and winding parts of the natural creeks, but also liked those sections where the creeks had been straightened into channels. In those cases Rathman had to go underground, inside the concrete walled and roofed tunnels where the natural bends of nature had been altered to mirror the gridiron streets, the gridiron of the city above.

In one walk at midday, after a heavy storm the night before, Rathman discovered a two-thirds meter-long Chinook salmon that had apparently swum about a three-quarter kilometer distance up Gaia Creek from the bay. Rathman found the large fish belly up in barely three inches of water, what was left after the storm waters had dissipated. Was the fish there because its homing instinct had gone haywire, or was it there because a deeper, ancient memory overwhelmed it's normal spawning instinct? Just 25 meters downstream from the fish was a snowy egret, standing guard proudly and securely. The sight of the creatures, one dead, one alive, filled Rathman with joy. Such a recovery after thousands of years!

Sometimes Rathman walked all the way to the bay, getting his feet wet in the saltwater marshes. During shrimping season he watched the boats come in and go out, meeting on occasion with the shrimp boat families who slept on thin mattresses in tents or in the backs of vans, surrounded by their drying nets. Or he watched the boats from a promontory overlooking the waters where Gaia Creek ran into the bay.

Once Rathman saw a minnow slither down the throat of the long, long neck of a snowy egret, serenaded by the sing-song cawing and cackling of seagulls and other spirited birds.

Seagulls would sit, unprotesting, not ill at ease even when he stood just five or six feet away from them. But if it were the nesting season, they would make convincing dive bombing feints if he came within a half kilometer of their eggs or their recently hatched young.

He saw flocks of pelicans streaming across the horizon, in groups of seven and 12 and 15. He saw two collections of pelicans, seven in one group, 10 in the other, apparently feasting on the schools of tiny fish. Sometimes all of their heads faced the interior of a circle. Sometimes one or two of them would break away and leisurely dip their beaks into the water, and then bring their beaks up and use the muscles in their gullets and gravity to send a silver-shiny fish down into their stomachs.

He saw a pair of stingrays two feet long, including one-and-a-half foot tails, sliding just below the surface, the tips of their flattened "wings," just breaking the surface of the surprisingly clear saltwater.

On one walk the air was so clear he could see across the bay to a "mountain" of calcified, rock-hard salt, reputed to have been deposited by men in the time before the Fall.

Sometimes he walked toward the foothills, where there were a number of parks filled with redwood groves or stands of oaks and sycamores. He would watch the young deer and raccoon come down to the salt licks. And sometimes these walks led to one of Zoia's favorite places, the Rainbow cemetery.

Sometimes he walked in tight circles, never traveling more than two kilometers or so away from his home base, walking the four points of a box or the five points of a star. But most of the time he preferred walking in longer, more linear stretches of the valley.

When the skin on his legs or his arms or his back itched, he had his fingernails to scratch away the discomfort. How could you get anymore basic than that?

He told Zoia that he could have been walking in the middle of a primeval forest, or on the playa of a high desert, or in Eccles, and the walk, from his mental point of view, would not have made any substantial difference.

How could that not be good for him?

From all appearances, Rathman's general mental state was improving. And as he was the beneficiary of Jug's beneficence, his money worries were gone.

Zoia asked Rathman, "Do you bring any gadgets or boxes with you on your walking strolls?"

"No. I eschew that. Eccles is Eccles, but I eschew that."

"As a matter of principle?" Zoia asked, trying to get Rathman's goat, trying to bait him into espousing his strange and Un-Eccles-like values formed at the edge of the Outer World.

But Rathman wouldn't rise to the bait. "No. It's just a matter of pride and a matter of cultivating certain sensibilities. When I take my walks, my skin and hair are exposed to the elements. Absent clothes and shoes, I am Pleistocene man." And then Rathman laughed at himself—at the outrageousness of his own comments. And to Zoia this made him like the person he was when she first met him.

Zoia said, "Anyone who can successfully find nature smack dab in the middle of Eccles can't be totally loopy in the head. Let nature take its course."

Zoia was more or less happy when she could see Rathman was content, happier when he indicated no interest in pursuing the story of the Time Repairer, and no interest in studying the subject of the 2,500-year-long Darkness, and no interest in visiting the Kafkaesque-like places or anything similarly outre.

After six months, all signs suggested that Rathman had recovered, even though it was never established what exactly had ailed him. He had dropped out of the Rhetoric Department a week after the two of them had returned from Cannibal Land, but he couldn't convince Zoia to do the same.

"The problem is my father," Zoia explained. "Unless I replace my studies with a viable alternative, it would be such a disappointment to him. I couldn't possibly do that. U. Presbyr to him is what Gaia is to Pius. And I love him."

One thing Zoia insisted on was that Rathman never go out barefoot. She promised that if he didn't walk around Eccles unshod, she would not call him "Cowboy" anymore. And she figured that since he had withdrawn from the Rhetoric Department, no one had the right to call him by that unsuitable moniker.

Only one time did something happen that reminded Zoia of Rathman's illness. Rathman woke abruptly. He rose from the bed and stood in the center of the room. He looked possessed, yet also, strangely himself. Was he sleep-walking? Was he awake? Then he started reciting:

"In the light — it has no meaning.

In the darkness — it has meaning.

Only in the darkness does this come to us.

Only through the darkness the deformed light comes to us. Our future lies in memory. In memory our future lies. Meaning is all."

And then he returned to the bed and in a robotic, automaton way he stretched out and went back to sleep before Zoia had a chance to interrogate him about the nature of his "dream." Within no time he was snoring soundly.

All Zoia was certain of was that when she first met Rathman he was an enigma.

It was now barely more than a year before the asteroid would either pass by or impact the Earth. Zoia had eyes in her head, and ears too, and was well aware there was only a one in 95 chance that one individual out of a population of 1.5 billion would survive beyond the first year of an impact. Which side of the globe you happened to be on mattered, but the scientists didn't expect anyone to survive more than a year. A growing segment of the population was demanding that the scientists cease and desist from making calculations and then broadcasting them. They didn't want to know. Jaime months before, when the odds had jumped from a one in 27 chance of surviving the first 90 days to a one in 439 chance, stopped making his prognostications. If the asteroid's impact occurred in the water (which was the most likely possibility), a very tiny number of people might have survived 10 months. But in the event of a land collision the ultimate outcome was going to be the same. Extinction.

Chapter Forty-Four

THEY NAMED THE SPACESHIP the Sea of Tranquility. Even while they were still in the process of constructing it, Jaime had come up with the name and the project leaders had agreed.

The Sea of Tranquility was the place on the moon where men had first walked 2,700 years before. It was hoped that the name would connote success, and would have a calming affect on the two crewmembers.

"Names affect how people look at things," Johnny observed. "Sea of Tranquility suggests lunar ambitions. LUNAR AMBITIONS! As in, crazy ambitions. How is being trapped inside a teensy-weensy tin can in space supposed to make us tranquil? Especially when you consider the crew."

Frankie looked at Johnny with an expression of bemused condescension. She still liked Johnny. She rarely gave him any external approval but she secretly enjoyed Johnny's offhanded displays of humor, as long as they didn't stray too far from the bounds of propriety and decorum. As for his irreverence, well, that was Johnny.

Auger was selected by the head of the space program to promote, stimulate, and inspire the two member crew. (To the space program's other leaders this decision struck them as odd, but the times were so strange and unusual oddities were occurring all the time.)

It was Jaime's idea. Auger had his druthers, but, of course, he accepted the task graciously. He had to travel all the way to the space program center itself, located 400 kilometers south of Eccles.

Once the two astronauts had been assembled, Auger began. "You two carry the weight of what will be a grateful planet," he said. "Do this for the planetariat!" ('Planetariat,' an unused term hitherto, came to Auger in a sudden flash.) "I think back at great moments in history when a tiny number of people engaged in acts of human sacrifice that turned the tide of history, and turned it not just for a generation or two, but for thousands of years. For example, the brave 300 who held off the Persian army at Thermopylae Pass. That's an example from the earliest beginnings of the *Westernized* Upanishads—5,000 years ago. The brave few in A.D.1940, when England stood alone against a foe in benighted pursuit of a darkness called Nazi German totalitarianism. For only a brief period of time, approximately a year, the glorious fighter pilots fought for Albion. To secure freedom. But I think of the best one, so near to home. I think of Kimmel, the simple genius who rediscovered the arcane secrets, the hidden mysteries, and enigmas of electricity. He brought us all back into the light of day after the long darkness of night. I think of his will, his sacrifice, his singular devotion to his vocation, living in rags, living in a state of extreme poverty and neglect, never himself seeing the results of his grim determination and his devotion to labors unrewarded."

Johnny scratched his head. "Well, I don't know anything about this stuff. From the Upanishads? The what ifs? It's all Babylon to me. But I do remember being taught about Kimmel. His bowls of thin soup and thinner gruel. Doing everything he could to prevent himself from freezing to death in his lonesome shack in Newfield. That must have been a time. Before he brought us so much to light. As young students we were taught that he was a great hero. The dynamo of our times."

Frankie thought of saying something, but this was one place she knew that any comments she might make would be deemed out of place and irrelevant.

Auger smiled. "You know the Gaia encyclopedia board have repeatedly requested from me a short piece on the subject of Kimmel. For the encyclopedia. Mind you, they've never requested any material from me on the brave 300 at Thermopylae, or about the Spitfire pilots of ancient England. Readers in general are not interested in the *Westernized* Upanishads. It's a lot easier for me to write a book on Kimmel than it is to condense it down, boil it all down, to 750 words. One time they had me do a 250-word piece on Gunter Gatetar. So recently deceased, and surrounded with so many controversies, he is a difficult figure to capture with even a patina of impartiality or objectivity. As a writer and historian, that's the hardest thing for me to do. Condensation."

Frankie burst into a thunder of laughter. "Jaime is a hero for discovering the asteroid. And I know he recommended you to be our...chaplain? But really...honestly. How important is history?"

"Now, isn't this, oh mighty historian, where you're suppose to say, 'Go with Gaia?'" Johnny stuck his tongue out, and gave Auger his standard, served-up-for-order, disingenuously loopy look.

Frankie gave Johnny a *look*, the one she had perfected during their years together when Johnny strayed over the boundary of what was considered permissible.

"You don't need me," Auger said freely, laughing at Johnny's pose and antics. "You need someone like my daughter. She should talk to you. She's the smart one. I'm just a cipher. She's the deep thinker. I'm the lame one. Go in peace."

Chapter Forty-Five

FOUR MORE MONTHS passed and Rathman was healed. Zoia celebrated her 19 1/2 birthday, and within a week Rathman celebrated his. (For reasons unknown, between the ages of 18 and 22, Gaians celebrated their half years as well as their years—it was known as the time of acceleration.) Jug celebrated his 34th birthday.

Rathman sprang it on Zoia. "I have a plan."

He explained it to her.

"You went to Jug without first consulting me?" Zoia asked. "Why did you do that?"

"Well, I didn't think he would be amenable to the idea, so why bother mentioning it to you? Without his active go-ahead, it would be a pipe dream, an impractical hypothetical."

"Let me guess..." Zoia said. "And what did Jug say?"

Zoia could see by the expression on Rathman's face that he was deeply serious about this, that this would be the fulfillment of a dream that he had held for a long time, that this was something that he had been thinking about—nonstop—since he started taking his long walks.

"Jug said, yes," Rathman said. "In fact, he was adamant, energetic, enthusiastic about it. He said he was perfectly willing to move very quickly on this. Expedite it was the expression he used. We could be there in a month, Zoia. We can go look at it any time we want."

"Small wonder," Zoia said. " Well, he's still trying to get himself out of the doghouse with me, isn't he?"

"Look, I may not know him as well as you do, but I do know him," Rathman said. "He's sincere."

Zoia nodded her head. "You know this corresponds perfectly with all the things my dad has been saying to me about the guy. The new Jug. Save the Earth, Jug. Explore the universe, Jug. Serve the people, Jug. I like to keep a healthy distance, a hearty skepticism, especially about the last one. Serve the people? Does that sound like Jug to you? But my dad goes on and on about how Jug has turned a corner. One thing I've learned about Jug. Maybe it comes with all that power and money he inherited, but if Jug can do anything, he can surprise."

Rathman was on tender hooks as he awaited Zoia's position on the proposition.

"Well, all right," Zoia said in a neutral, non-committal way. "There's no harm in looking at the ranch. You want to check it out? I'm willing to." As Zoia was speaking, she was thinking: this may be the way out, the way out for all of them. She was more positively inclined than she let on. But without knowing more of the facts, she was thinking: Why be premature? Why be forced to disappoint Rathman later on?

The expression on Rathman's face was one of irrepressible relief.

"This is good," Rathman said.

"Well, okay," Zoia said. "This is good. Let's look. But trusting Jug? That's another thing." Zoia shook her hand back and forth in a gesture of uncertainty. She felt like she was being forced to trust a barometer that had a history of being unreliable. "It can go poof, you know! All of it! If Jug has changed his mind once, he can change it again. That's all I'm saying."

"All I'm saying is..." Rathman started to say.

"Yeah, I know what you're saying. Let's check it out."

Chapter Forty-Six

"This is one of the most beautiful places on the edge of the Outer World," Rathman said. "Look at it."

"Well, it's a damn sight better than Cannibal Land, I'll grant you that," Zoia said defensively.

"The ranch was built when old-man Gatetar was young and took vacations out here with his first wife," Rathman said. "Back then it used to be 80,000 acres in size, including tongues of land stretching up to the Iona River. A very large ranch, really three ranches in one. Enough to run 800 head of cattle, given the sparse rainfall, dry climate, and difficult terrain. But now the ranch has been pared down to 17,000 acres. The main ranch house is long gone now, everything except its foundations had been dismantled more than 25 years ago. That's where we're standing right now. But there is still a derelict house up there." Rathman pointed to the west. "That's where we're going. It used to be called—before the Fall—the rangeland above the San Pedro River. Now it's called 'the rangeland above the Iona River.' Legend has it that Iona and her group of rebels came through here on their way to the Colorado Plateau after they fought the armies of the Gaia-Domes. This happened even before the world was divided between the Inner World and the Outer World, years before our great-great-great-great-great-great-great-grandparents were born. The river flows from the far edges of the Outer World into the Inner World just 50 kilometers north of here. That's been the border ever since Eccles annexed Albu. I'm going to bring in a strain of half Ethiopian highland and half Sub-Saharan, West African Borgu, I think."

"Bring in what?"

"A crossbreed of ancient highland Ethiopian cattle, lean and thin, mixed with a genus of West African Borgu. I know where I can find these crossbreeds. Both breeds, the Ethiopian more than the West African, are drought-resistant."

"You're going to raise cattle?"

"I know where to find them. Outer World. I know how to bring them in. Got a tip. Fifty kilometers away. In a place like this, with a slightly drier climate and similar rugged terrain. Even with the threat of a drought we can run 100 head safely. We can grow the herd 25 percent, maybe up to 50 percent. There's an underground river and it never dries up, we just have to find places where it bubbles up. Oh, what a grand experiment this will be."

"You've got it all figured out, haven't you, Rathman?" Zoia asked.

"Yes. A dream come true."

They drove north in a rugged terrain vehicle, later switching to a pair of loaned horses that they had tied to the back bumper. They followed a wash for 10 kilometers to where an underground river surfaced below sheer red and ochre-colored rock walls, hundreds of feet high. The river made a perfect pool in the middle of the desert, adjacent to a patch of grass in the shade of a small grove of cotton-woods. Nearby was a semi-derelict, three-room ranch house, with a small shady porch and a still-functioning, serviceable cistern. A solar-paneled generator that had only been out of use for two years could provide electricity to power the appliances, once the machine was repaired and serviced.

"Does the house have indoor plumbing?" Zoia asked.

"Of course," Rathman said. "But we're not going to use it. Uses up too much water. We will have to conserve. Once the genera-tor's repaired we'll have just enough juice to run a small refrigerator.

Maybe power up a lamp for a few hours a night. Maybe two lamps."

"That's comforting," Zoia said.

In spite of her privileged background in Eccles, and in spite of her personal predilections, Zoia felt strangely drawn to this place of spectacular, Outer World isolation. She didn't think she was going to like it, or feel that it could be a home. But she did. The sheer, utter remoteness made her feel it might be the perfect antidote and exquisite anodyne to being overly connected, overly *present*. If Eccles represented anything, it was the overly connected. Taking risks, jumping off the face of the world, wasn't that what life was about? But that wouldn't have been enough to get Zoia to give up her creature comforts, to give up her special relationship with her father, to give up all that she had been accustomed to. There was an added incentive. There was one more thing that could make the deal, if such a deal could be made. If they were going to face possible extinction, what better place to face it than here. Where you are all alone, and the person you are living with is only there to remind you that you are essentially alone?

That's what the darkness was all about that Rathman had discovered in Cannibal Land, Zoia realized. That was the secret.

"Wait until you see the Mesquite Tree, Zoia. Then I know you're going to be hooked on this place," Rathman said in a voice brimming with confidence. "I'll show it to you later. It's farther up, just below the cliffs. Everybody's going to face the unknown in their own way...everybody. Let's face the unknown here."

"You think Jug will keep his promise? Letting us stay here indefinitely?"

"Of course he will!" Rathman said in a voice filled with confidence. "That I'm certain of. That's the beauty of being the orphan. That's the beauty of going somewhere where nobody else wants to inhabit the place...at least, nobody from the affluent parts of Eccles. That's why it's been sitting here. Alone. Naked. Torn. Spent. Ever since Jug's father sold off the other parcels of rangeland, ever since they knocked down the main house with its modern conveniences.

You see the reason why nobody that Jug knows wants to stay here? The isolation is brutal. It's a primitive isolation. Unless you know how to cope. And we will know how to cope. I, the barefoot herder, will teach you. This will be the perfect place for us to be alone."

"All right, Rathman, but are there going to be any neighbors at all? Just tell me that. That's my last question."

"None," Rathman said. "Well, just one. You might even get to know her. She'll be coming down for water every now and then, but she won't be coming down for purposes of communicating with the rest of the world. Because she doesn't do that. But with you, she might make an exception."

Chapter Forty-Seven

THEY SWEPT THE FLOORS, swept out the corn crib, swept everything out. Mended the roof. The large three-foot-wide gaping hole in the living room floor was going to take much more work, but it was fixable. The refrigerator was very old and battered, broken beyond repair. But Rathman was able to fix the generator. He replaced the water filter with a brand new one, improvising with a couple of gadgets and a gizmo as he went. The sun was going to provide all the energy they needed, since they would require so little energy *living off the grid*.

Seven days after they arrived Rathman made the trip to the rock wall. On the mesa above the wall, smack in the middle, was a depression: one hundred feet deep that looked exactly like a bowl. This strange natural anomaly harbored a hut that was the life-long home of their only neighbor, Bruja.

Bruja met Rathman at the gate. Streaks of white and gray hair were mixed in with a whirlish mane of deep black-colored hair, worn waist-length. Though her face was wrinkled with age, she looked incredibly fit—thin, with a wasp-like waist, not an ounce of fat except in the thighs and chest. She moved with great agility, making her look even more fit. Like a new-born spider, she appeared to live on next to nothing. Rathman couldn't see the goats, but he could see evidence that they were there. Twenty of them, maybe as many as 25 or 30. Where were they at that moment? Grazing? This was the "it" in practice, the peasant's science of appearing to have fewer animals in their possession than they actually did.

When it was dry, Bruja watered the goats below. Even the old man Gatetar never interfered with Bruja over the business of the goats' watering rights. It was better to appease Bruja than to oppose her. Who in their right mind would want to fight with a force of nature like her?

"You going to bring them in?" she asked abruptly.

"Bring what in?"

"Cattle."

"Yes."

"One hundred head will do. Land can't handle more. You going to breed?"

"You think I should?"

Bruja remained silent. No offer of hospitalities, not even shade. She was making sure he knew who was invading whose space. Rathman got the message loud and clear.

Bruja nodded her head in a positive way. "You have electricity? Very few of us do. Unless you have some influence with the Inner World thugs, or you're one of their political puppets. Won't see those types out here. They stay in towns."

"I know," Rathman said.

"Solar-powered generators are the best pieces of machinery Eccles ever made. Just a small number of moving parts and the Sun. Keep that generator hidden."

Rathman nodded his head.

Bruja closed her eyes, as if she was experiencing a vision. "I see it now. As a child you lived on a ranch, on the outer fringes of the Inner World. Hard place to live all year round. Harder place to live during a drought." She opened her eyes and closed them again. "No electricity."

Rathman nodded his head. "No electricity or indoor plumbing. Everything came from the ground or from the animals straight and direct to the kitchen table."

"You're going to be the new lord and master around here, aren't you?"

"Do I look like a lord? I can fix the floor. I can mend anything. I can fix nearly everything. Everything just needs mending, or winding up, everything except the refrigerator. Which is broken. But I have a more important task. How do I get through to my love's heart?" Rathman asked.

"She's from Eccles?"

"Yes."

"While you're fixing the floor and mending all the other stuff, buy her a refrigerator," Bruja said. "Give me a second, will you?"

She proceeded to bring out a bowl of fresh water and a bowl of fresh grain morsels. And she set them down about 10 feet away from the hut—in the dust and the dirt.

As Rathman watched, two cats came around from the other side of the hut and started nibbling on the food and lapping up the water.

"You have so little," Rathman said. "Why are you taking care of these creatures?"

Without looking up, staring out into space, Bruja replied, "Because I've lived 78 years and six months on this accursed planet, on this despised Earth." Bruja stepped over and adjusted the bowl of water so that it would just barely rest in a bit of shade. "Because I've found that feral cats are more dependable than men."

Chapter Forty-Eight

"THE WHIG INTERPRETATION of history," Pius said to Auger snidely. "Progress? Reform? Improvement? Even if the improvements are piecemeal, and are desperately slow to be implemented, and are barely incremental, they still do happen. Even if it is a dance where it's two steps forward, then one-and-three-quarters steps back. Did you see what happened?"

It was another argument about history. Auger and Pius's millionth one. And again it was about history so ancient, so utterly unconnected to the lives of ordinary people in present time, that Auger didn't see the point of it. He was in a foul mood.

"Oh, you stoop to conquer. Obscurantism? Rank, rank, rank obscurantism... As a value? As a goal? Is this leading up to something? Pius, please. Tell me something relevant."

"The human race really messed up! BACK THEN! That's all there is to it!"

"In all of Eccles, perhaps you, I, Zoia, and Rathman are the only ones who really care about what happened 2,700 years ago. And I shouldn't even include Rathman. He's not really interested in studying history. All he wants to do is praise his ancestors, to venerate them." Auger started to walk out of the room.

"I'm thinking about the issue of releasing the Lloyd the Special Magister's documents, Auger," Pius said. "I'm reconsidering it."

"Really? That would be a reversal on your part. You've always been opposed to it."

"I know I've been stiff-necked about it. But don't push me too hard. Step back and give me some time. I won't need a lot. But I'm thinking about releasing the papers. All of them."

"To the public?"

"Yes, of course. To everyone."

Chapter Forty-Nine

FRANKIE AND JOHNNY were ordered to go on tour. They both hated this assignment, but Johnny hated it even more than Frankie did. No matter how talented he was, Johnny viewed himself as just a humble servant, a humble mechanic. To him, the tour carried a note that was falsely pitched, something that was laboriously grubby and overly grandiose at the same time.

They traveled separately, with completely separate itineraries. That way they were able to cover more territory and cover it in a shorter period of time. Frankie was assigned the northern and central route: Isistay, the new Portland, Grennier, and a dozen other points. Johnny was assigned the southern and central route, Grassley, Turboland, Episla, Albu, and a half dozen other communities.

Frankie had to spend four weeks on her tour. That was her mission. Johnny was lucky, he had to go out for only three weeks. Frankie had to go farther out, after all she was the commander, pilot, and navigator, and Johnny was not.

The star-struck crowds at these "whistle-stops" were ecstatic. Nevertheless, the astronauts would have done anything to get out of going on what they referred to as "The Save the World Tour." It was far more difficult than training, and training was all they wanted to do.

Shortly after beginning his tour, Johnny was forced to wear a spacesuit at most events. He abhorred and resented this practice, it made him feel like he was a monkey on display but he managed to maintain his loyalty and obedience to the greater cause (barely), by keeping his mouth shut on the subject. That in and of itself was an accomplishment.

After they arrived back in Eccles, they met at the Gatetar tower, for the grand finale. After the reception and dinner there was a huge fireworks display and they both got a chance to shake hands with Jug Gatetar. There were loads of photo ops. The rest was just feel-good promotion.

Chapter Fifty

THE VERY FIRST THING Jug did to try to redeem himself in the eyes of Zoia was to revise and extend his protection of a large constellation of World Heritage Sites located on five continents. For Jug this was an easy call though expensive. There were originally 51 sites; Jug added 20 to that number, including three spots associated with September Snow and Tom Novak.

Jug announced that he was doing this "to preserve the memory of humanity's past."

Preserving history was the be-all and end-all in the eyes of Auger, and thus he was filled with delight upon learning of this bequest. If Jug, by his actions had left a positive impression in anyone's estimation, it was in the estimation of Auger.

Knowing that Rathman and Zoia had chosen to deliberately isolate themselves from Eccles, when Auger came to visit the couple three months later, he reported the news to Zoia.

"How did you come to know this?" Zoia asked. "Did he come to tell you this in person? Or was it something that you learned about in the news? Too often, Jug likes to make a big splash in the news. So he'll make a big impression in the public eye. Sometimes that's his only motivation."

"First, before any press releases were made, he came to tell me in person," Auger said. "Well, three days later, as you apparently suspected, there was a huge press release. You do know him then, don't you?"

"I don't *know* him," Zoia said. "But sometimes I know why he acts. He loves archeology, therefore logically, he loves heritage sites. Of course that left a good impression on *you*. If he wants to impress me, he's going to have to do better. Tell him that, Auger. At least in his past calculations, he's always been looking for an angle in accomplishing news splash or reputation laundering. Next time, when he wants to do something good for humanity, tell him to do it anonymously. That way I'll know he isn't acting with ulterior motives."

"Unless he's changed?" Auger asked diffidently.

"Yes," Zoia said abruptly. "Unless he's changed."

Auger was happy to change the subject of the conversation. As he began to speak, Zoia interrupted him.

"Oh, I forgot to mention!" Zoia said. "By the way, Rathman and I are married."

"Who performed the ceremony?"

"Bruja."

"Well, congratulations," Auger said. "Bruja? Isn't she an old medicine woman who lives up on the mesa? You mentioned her several times in your letters. Is she—a stranger—more important to you than your own father? I could have given you away or even conducted the ceremony."

"She's no longer a stranger to me father, and don't worry," Zoia said. "Yes, we are going to have a great celebration. A celebration you've never seen before. I'm so glad you're here. And so is Rathman. It's hard living here. But it's the best move I've made in my life. If you want to get out of prison, sometimes you have to go to extremes."

Auger smiled.

"You see you're so liberated I knew you wouldn't mind that Rathman and I just slinked off and got ourselves hitched without telling you or anybody else about it or anything. It's none of the business of the world what we do."

"Your mother would have approved," Auger said. "I'm sure of it."

"Mary Wollstonecraft would have approved also, father."

"You still think about very obscure figures from very ancient history. At the very least, that's a backhanded compliment."

When Rathman had proposed marriage to Zoia, Zoia said, "I've seen women who've married and found that the man they married was horrible. I've seen men who married, and at the end of it all, they were the more worse for wear."

The hardest thing for Zoia was to get Bruja's approval. After that, she didn't worry about anyone else. She knew Auger approved of Rathman. Even from the day they'd first met, when Rathman had brought the manuscript of the *Time Repairer*, Auger had been fond of him. He had even come to love him, too.

Chapter Fifty-One

A FTER AUGER left they brought the cattle in to the ranch, sixty head, a mixture of two and three-year-olds, and some older bulls, eight years and older, along with a few breeding cows. They were brought in by a barefoot herder, a boy who was barely twelve years old. He carried with him a dark brown bindle and kept in his hand a long, stout stick which he used for minding the herd.

The boy was deaf and mostly silent, though he was capable of rudimentary speech. He preferred to use facial gestures and tics and sign language to communicate.

Rathman had paid for the herd in advance and had been told it was not necessary to pay the boy anything. He just needed to mark the paper the boy carried with the number of head that had been delivered, and initial it, to indicate that the delivery had been made.

The boy was fed and spent the night with Zoia and Rathman. Before he left to return home, Rathman gave him something special. It was a large amount of money (by Eccles's standards it was actually a very small amount of money—just barely enough to cover the cost of three month's rent for Rathman's closet space,) but it was five times more than any piece of money the boy had seen in one place before. The boy's eyes widened as Rathman thrust the bills into his hand.

For once the boy spoke. "Too much," he said. It wasn't clear to Rathman by his remark whether the boy was saying the gift was so large that it was incomprehensible and he was just expressing his amazement, or that the amount was understood to be, 'too large.'

"I can't accept this," the boy then muttered, with an articulation that made Rathman suspect that his deafness was more feigned than real, a ploy the boy might use to keep himself out of trouble and dodge potentially dangerous situations. Deaf-mutes often handled cattle, they were renowned for it. There was nothing unusual in that. But they didn't handle large sums of money. *Ever.*

"Yes you can," Rathman said. "This is between you and me." Rathman looked at the boy with a huge smile on his face. "It's a secret. Between you and me. Do not tell anybody that I have given this to you. Not your employer. Not even your mother. Hide the bills in your shorts, next to your scrotum. It is for you to choose what to do with them, when you choose to do so. If you ever manage to get out of your predicament and prosper, pay it forward. And keep doing the mute bit; it's marvelous. Nobody is going to suspect you of having money."

The boy was expressionless.

"Look, I know how dangerous it is out there," Rathman said at last. "And I had figured that out even before I ended up in the orphanage. All of my family—my sisters, my mother, my father— were slaughtered—and they lived on the *good* side of the border."

The boy nodded his head vigorously in affirmation, and then he was gone.

Rathman felt that this was the best thing he had done in a long time. When he told Zoia, she insisted that he tell Bruja. Upon hearing this she replied, "Well, I guess my decision to let the two of you stay here was the right decision after all. You might even see the boy again. Rathman is a good man."

After the sixth visit Zoia made to see Bruja, she returned with a message for Rathman. "Bruja says you suffer from a disease that afflicts too many of the marginal in Eccles."

"What's that?"

"Thinking too much."

"How is thinking bad?"

"Thinking is good. Thinking is necessary. But too much of it can lead to depression or something even worse. She said you have too much time to repair."

Upon hearing this, Rathman looked confused. "You mean you told her about my studying *The Time Repairer*?"

"No, no. I didn't tell her anything about that. She just came out with it." Zoia thought for a moment. "Maybe Bruja meant by her words that you can't repair the past, only the future. And that's the unintended message of the past, the long, long, long distance past. Makes sense. That's why I love being here. Everything seems to make more sense. Everything is so less complicated!"

"Okay..." Rathman said. "Go on."

"And she added," Zoia continued, "*and these are her words:* 'I have to say, thinking it through vigorously, whatever else you say about Rathman, he's no ordinary vaquero.'"

Chapter Fifty-Two

UPON AUGER'S RETURN from the ranch to Eccles, the issue of whether to release all of the papers of Lloyd the Special Magister that were found in the jar buried in the Manhattan-subway-tunnel-cut came to an abrupt head. Auger, and in fact the entire World History Department, had been pressing Pius to release them. Pius had strongly resisted a full release because he felt that the documents made a mockery of Gaia theology, portraying September Snow as not a goddess but a mere mortal, and asserting that September Snow and her rebels were locked in a life-and-death struggle with the Gaia-Domes, and that every ounce of their energy was expended in pursuit of defeating the Domes, not a reform of the Gaia faith. But when Auger talked to Pius this time, he realized he was talking to a new man.

"What made you change your mind?" Auger asked.

"I've come to realize that I'm NOT fighting against heresy, I'm fighting against a method of inquiry. Everything we find from the past should be revealed in the present. The consequences? Let the chips fall where they may. I'll catch hell for this later on, of course... The world deserves to hear the truth. There is no such thing as unholy or forbidden information, Auger. It's all just information. We make of it what we will. You've won me over to your point-of-view, completely."

"I'm overwhelmed," Auger said in a modest voice.

"Well, don't be," Pius replied. "Of course I'm going to catch hell for this from the leaders of the Obsidian Order. I've come to the conclusion that they are the most hidebound, the most unthinking part, of the order. They are the ones I have to worry about. And they'll resist me. Things have changed so much, especially with the younger generation. For the first time younger members are thinking independently. But the order is not a democracy, and the old conservatives are still very powerful. Their power is ebbing and they know it. Just in the last six or seven years things have changed radically. So they're desperate. But I say let's bring this matter to a head now, once and for all. I'm a proud and obedient son of the order, and always will be. But I'm a historian first."

Four weeks later, the papers were released.

Most of the public could not have cared less. To them Gaia was Gaia, regardless of what had happened thousands of years in the past. They were much more concerned about the asteroid. One absolute and fervent believer in the Gaia religion wrote an editorial that went viral: "*It happened so long ago. Can't we just call September Snow a goddess, even though we really don't mean it. Or we can mean it—because all it takes to mean it is to believe it. The "true" story is still just a story. September Snow is a goddess to me; how could she be anything else?*"

But the leadership of the Obsidian Order went ballistic. The fact that Pius had not even conferred with them before the release made them even more bitter, estranged, and angry. To them, it was as if Pius had committed a crime that was tantamount to him being a traitor to everything they believed in.

Pius wanted to put the editorialist on a pedestal. To him, this was the right way to approach the heresy issue. That's what the religion was all about anyway. The belief, the faith, to the thing, *to the thing*.

Papers included many *so-called* travesties and blasphemies, most importantly, they proposed the axiom that September Snow was a flesh and blood creature, and nothing more. In the words of Lloyd the Special Magister, September Snow and her followers were "committed and dedicated secular revolutionaries, though more and more frequently they were forced to channel this revolutionary ardor into the nascent Gaia religion. This merging of sacred and secular, sacred and profane, accelerated among the movements' 'chosen people,' who became increasingly primitive in their thinking. By 2075 A.D., conditions had grossly deteriorated, as the economy outside the Gaia-Domes had been in a state of complete collapse, and the environment was becoming starkly unlivable, especially after 2095 A.D. In this, mother and daughter were products of their disrupted, chaotic world, with hearts to make them ascendant, feet of clay to keep them grounded. In other words, they were a mother and daughter team, plain and simple..."

Thousands of years later, it was the word revolutionary more than the word secular that was perceived as being most damaging to the heart of the faith, at least as seen through the eyes of the religious conservatives.

Auger and Pius waited for the deluge, but only among the zealots and the fundamentalist true believers was there a hue and cry. And when the leadership of the Obsidian Order issued their public condemnation, only the zealots and fundamentalists took the bait. To their chagrin, the old guard of the Obsidian Order found itself out of sync with the Eccles' zeitgeist.

In the eyes of millions and millions of Gaians, it was a tempest in a teapot. They had other worries and concerns.

And that realization, more than anything else, wounded the old guard of the Obsidian Order the most.

For the Obsidian Order did not relent. To further their cause, the order issued a bulletin of excommunication against Pius. Pius ignored it. When that didn't work, they doubled down with a second round of public denunciations and condemnations. But this backfired, too. To the public, Pius was already a sympathetic figure. Something that hitherto would have been considered unthinkable, parts of the public started referring to him as "the historian," as if his "no account" profession was somehow at least as important than that of an accountant, a carpenter, or a plumber.

Pius broke his silence by at last preaching in a public forum. "People can believe anything they want! People have the right to *believe* anything they want. Let truth reign. The truth may always be far away, but with theological absolutism, it is even further away."

In this way, he was allowing for paradox, ambiguity, leeway in interpretation, uncertainty.

Two weeks later Pius received a note from a large group of young acolytes, which read: "We will not break our vows of silence nor will we break our vows of obedience to the Obsidian Order. But, confidentially, we want you to know that we are with you. Please burn this note after reading. There are spies everywhere. But we want you to know that Xanus is sharpening his knives. He's made it clear that he wants to annihilate your influence any which way he can."

Sure enough, the old guard made another appeal to the public. They issued a bizarre statement claiming that "if the asteroid destroys the human race, Pius's blasphemy may have had a part in it. Gaia is fragile, and irresponsible ideas and dangerous thoughts could have catastrophic outcomes. In these times, can we risk such acts of impiety?"

For more than two centuries the scientists had been hard pressed not to enter into any theological argument or dispute, and to a large extent they had succeeded. But in this case, the absurdity was too flagrant. "Pius the historian's statements regarding events that happened thousands of years ago have nothing to do with whether we will succeed or not succeed at our attempt to eliminate the threat of the asteroid. The day science and religion are put at odds with each other is a day we should not readily welcome. Civil discord is a far greater threat to the welfare of Eccles than any supposed impiety."

Jaime, though a member in good standing of the Forandi Order, and a firm believer in the Gaia religion, had also come to Pius's defense in the controversy.

Xanus, Chair Intellectual Supreme of the Obsidian Order, and Pius's chief adversary, was furious that a prestigious figure in the Forandi Order *publicly* broke ranks with the Obsidian Order. In every step he had taken to bring Pius down, he had been thwarted. Worse than that, he was being made to look like a fool.

Then Pius received a dire warning: "Leave Eccles. You're in peril. Go into exile. Wait until things cool down. It was signed, "a friend."

But out of stubbornness, or maybe out of arrogance, Pius refused to take the anonymous advice that had been given to him.

However, Auger was more concerned. "You know, making yourself scarce, and by that I mean thousands-of-kilometers scarce, somewhere deep into the Outer World, will hurt you not at all. I know that Jug will help you make the journey. In fact, he can make an exile easy and convenient. I'm certain he'd be willing to bear all costs. You have dropped a bomb on your religious order, and the fallout hasn't stopped. Even a secular man like me can see that this is a major, one-of-a-kind dispute. At least until this blows over, just disappear. This would entail only a minor inconvenience. After all these years I'm not even sure you like Eccles."

Pius refused. He viewed such a course of action as tantamount to cowardice. Maybe it had been his plan all along to bait Xanus and take the consequences, but events had just swung out of control. Pius decided to take a profoundly passive attitude to it all. This troubled Auger.

Pius ran out of time. He had gotten another tip explaining to him his life was endangered. He did not go to the police with this piece of controversial information. Instead, he just waited for his pursuers to attack, almost as if he were inviting them to do so. He knew they would come that night. All the warning signs were there. But he had come to muse about the past, and he thought maybe that was where he should be. That to him was the most important thing.

"Time is a fiction we cannot live without," Pius said out loud to himself. "Therefore, not in the name of Gaia, but in the name MOM, Memory Of Man, history. Does it matter in what name we die? Doesn't matter in what name *I* die. It only matters that, in the community of memory, I keep alive the story of September Snow. Our Goddess..."

Pius smiled. "There is only one Goddess, but she is a parody of a human being that once was. The documents prove it. All the documents, with the sole exception of THE BLESSINGS OF GAIA DOCUMENT, tell the truth, shout it out to the rooftops. The human being, the real one, *was* September Snow. Just a woman." Pius shrugged.

He knew that in the opinion of the Gaian Obsidian Order he had committed a grave blasphemy, but in his heart he knew it wasn't so.

Why did the lights flicker off fully, then come back on, Pius wondered. Then he witnessed something that was truly bizarre, but his eyes could not deceive him. It was true. How long had it been since they pulled one of these? One hundred and fifty years before? Before their great-great-grandparents were even born? Was that the last time? Rornar's definition of the time barrier was 150 years. Nobody thinks further back than that, she used to say.

Dressed in oddly antiquated uniforms, with matching white and red hoods, the very young men moved stealthily, quickly, and while the historian had his back turned they attacked. They grabbed his arms, pulled them taut, and bound them behind his back. From behind, they grabbed his hair and thrust his head back. It hurt. The knife edge was poised at his neck, but the attacker seemed to hesitate. Apparently changing his mind, he lowered his hand and came around to present himself in full view.

It was Xanus.

Xanus meticulously folded the blade on his knife, then gently placed the instrument of death in his pocket, the folds of his cloak swallowing up his hands as he did so. He then gently clicked his heels, almost in a buffoonish way.

"Yes, it is I," Xanus said.

"Not you," Pius stammered. "Chair Intellectual Supreme of the Obsidian Order! Sir! You can't demean yourself by doing this to a colleague in such a manner!"

Xanus nodded his head, then nodded his head to the others, and a rain of blows and hacks descended. Pius did not cry out. More thrusts came down. The attackers were surprised at Pius's resilience and endurance, they didn't expect such a display of physical strength. So, as a group, a little amazed, they stepped back. It was clear they had not done this kind of thing before. Their actions had not been properly orchestrated or rehearsed. Their movements were halting, robotic, uncertain. The attack had the look of a poorly choreographed encounter, instead of a professionally conducted murder.

Pius swayed. He was on the verge of saying something, wanting to say something, but no words came out. Then he slipped in a pool of his own blood, and died.

Chapter Fifty-Three

AUGER SHOWED the papers to Jug.

"The upshot is we're broke."

"You mean the entire World History Department is bankrupt? How can that be? That hasn't happened in my lifetime...or in my father's lifetime."

"No," Auger said. "Worse than that. Almost every department in U. Presbyr is bankrupt. Or nearly so. Rhetoric, Philosophy and Fine Arts, Post-Humanoid Studies, Post-Oral, Post-Writing Critical Theory, even the Gaia Religion and Earth Theology Departments, all of us, have run out of money," Auger said. "The only department that isn't broke is SOC. They've always had a gift for money. They always seem to be able to find customers looking for their primary product which is social statistics. They're basking in the one thing most academics desire: the trust of their most treasured customers. Apparently powerful people in Eccles have it in their heads to go deep in the human behavior prediction business. It's as if manipulating numbers makes life more explicable. If you can't count it, doesn't count. Count it, it does."

"Well, thank Gaia I'm in the business I'm in," Jug said. "And not in academia. But, all the same, it's an interesting theory." Jug faked a groan and then started laughing.

"Should we be looking outside for funding?"

Jug smiled. "Depends on how much you need?"

"Well, to tide us over for the next eighteen months, about D 26,000,000. We still have some collateral left for loans but, eight months from now, definitely 10 months from now, the hammer's coming down."

"No, I mean altogether."

"You mean till the end of the year?" Auger asked. "Or you mean till the end of next year?"

"No," Jug said. "I mean for the next twenty."

"Twenty years? Who can do that?"

"For one, I can," Jug said. Auger expected Jug to break into laughter, but he didn't. He didn't skip a beat. "Of course I'll insist that it'll have to be done anonymously. Isn't that what Zoia would have insisted upon? Right? So no one can say I have ulterior motives. But there is just one catch: no studies of Gatetar Industries, or the Gatetar family, or me. But other than that, no strings attached. Jason, my recently rehabilitated ex-employee, will administer it all. He knows all the ins and outs of cut-outs, fake fronts, false flags, you name it. It will be anonymous."

"None?" Auger asked.

"None. No strings attached. Except the one I mentioned. Auger, with the important exceptions of the World History Department and SOC, and maybe Philosophy, I look at these departments as intellectual brothels, shams, or shambles. They are boutique entities, thin as models, fashionable as robotic models, but nothing else to hang a piece of cloth on. And in that spirit, I want to add three more fully funded departments to the roster of the U. Presbyr: a Beautician School, an Interior Decorating School, and The Thomas Jefferson School for Social Science. The first two speak for themselves, as reminders that others shouldn't be so arrogant. The last one I see as competition for SOC, and to a lesser extent, competition for World History and Philosophy, as being, I don't know, an in-betweener. I'll pay for them all, of course. These will give Eccles color. You don't even have to put my name on the side of any buildings. In fact, I insist you don't! Thomas Jefferson's name on a building would be plenty good enough."

"A name from 3,000 years ago? Okay. But Beautician School and Interior Decorating School, sure, they can be located near the campus. But they'll have to function under a separate administration from U. Presbyr. For appearances sake."

"All right."

"Anything else?" Auger asked.

"I do insist that you tell Zoia about this immediately," Jug said. "Tell her about the one proviso, too. No studies of Gatetar, past or present. I want *everything to be out in the open.* With her, that is, not with the rest of the world. Also, be sure to tell her that Jason will be administering the program. In fact, tell her that Jason will be administering all of my gifts to the world from now on. And there will be more gifts. Many more."

"All right," Auger said. "I'll tell her."

"Oh, and tell Rathman..." In mid-sentence, Jug paused. He seemed to be searching for something. If Auger didn't know better, he would have thought that Jug looked lost. "Tell Rathman I'm sorry about what I did to him."

"I don't know what you're talking about," Auger said. "Shouldn't you be telling him that yourself?"

"Yeah," Jug said. "You're right. I should talk to him in person."

"Do you think they are going to move the asteroid out of the way?" Auger asked, wanting to change the subject. "And do it in time? It's driving the world crazy. I do know it drove Pius crazy. Willfully or not. he made himself a martyr. This is the worse intersection of science, reason, history, and religion that I know of."

"I don't know anything about this Pius," Jug said. "I do know he didn't like me. Business and religion don't mix. But the asteroid? Of course, they will succeed. They're pouring everything they've got into the project. I don't let things like that upset me. Or worry me. Why am I so certain? That's just how I think. Technology will prevail. Therefore, the space program will prevail. Therefore, humankind will prevail. I'm going to pour so much into revitalizing U. Presbyr because I'm certain that it's going to prevail too."

Chapter Fifty-Four

THE CIVIL AUTHORITIES agreed to let the Obsidian Order handle the murder of Pius internally. Xanus cashed in all his I.O.U.'s with the government to achieve that, but Public Safety insisted that any more bloodletting would have to involve the police.

In the Obsidian Order there was a circle of 10 dissidents who met in secret. They headed a larger group who had sworn an oath with their own blood that they would be willing to take risks— including giving up their own lives: to seize control of the Obsidian Order from the old guard. They believed that Xanus and his followers should be exiled to a far corner of the Outer World. They might eventually be permitted to come back, but that would depend on how well the new order was able to take root. This rebellion was unprecedented in Gaian history.

"Pius has opened the door for us, now all we have to do is cross the threshold and enter," Yana the youngest and boldest of the 10 rebel leaders said.

Spieling shook his head. "Half of our group is hot, but half is only tepid." Spieling was one of the older members of the order and had been a student with Pius when they were both young. "Altogether we are two-thirds of the membership. But if Xanus pushes back, there will be slippage. Maybe a little, maybe a lot. We have been trained to be subservient, fearful, and cowardly. It's easier to be courageous when you're standing with a large group of people and all that's asked of you is that you raise your hand and swear an oath. Your Obsidian brothers are not even used to the idea that their opinions matter. How long will it take to change that? Longer than a few months or even a few years. It'll take decades."

"The half who are not with us are cowards," Yana said. "What we need now is bold action."

"They're not cowards," Spieling said, "they're just being exceedingly cautious. Why shouldn't they be? Why risk the spilling of blood if all humanity is going to die when an asteroid crashes into our planet? That's all they want, more time. More time to think. They want to wait until the celestial fireworks are over. Do you blame them? Xanus is a cornered man. We don't know how he'll react. True, these are dangerous times. But he's so out of touch with the modern world it's ridiculous. I firmly believe this must be a peaceful change, or we'll risk further cracks and fissures in our Order. Even if we can afford this change once, can we afford it twice? Even those who want change want it to be built on a solid foundation. That's why change of this magnitude has happened so rarely in the past. There wouldn't be an Obsidian Order if stability wasn't our prized central tenet."

"The Forandi Order is with us—they are with us 100 percent—but only if the transition is peaceful and absolutely nonviolent in nature. Look at how much more we can accomplish if we have them on our side. And I need not mention how important it is to have the public on our side as well. The huge majority of people of Eccles don't know, much less care, what this dust-up is all about. Getting the history right from 2,700 years ago? Allowing people a broader scope of thinking with regard to what they believe?"

"But if we act now we have surprise on our side," Yana said. "If we wait until after the asteroid is nudged out of the way of the Earth's path, we'll lose all element of surprise. And by virtue of losing that, we'll lose our momentum. Xanus is a monster. We are his prey."

"Yes," Spieling said. "And let's make sure you, Yana, don't become a monster too. Surprise? What surprise? The cat's already out of the bag. We'll win because we are responsible and thoughtful, because of our superior numbers, and because we will be willing to die for our cause. But we shall not kill for our cause. Think how favorably the public in general will look at us if we keep it that way."

"That's what Xanus wants," Yana said. "That's what he's counting on. He's counting on us to be weak."

"I'm not afraid of Xanus," Spieling said. "He has already suspected me of being one of the ringleaders of a secret rebellion, if not *the* ringleader. If he decides to kill me, I will behave exactly the same way Pius behaved. We all must act the same way. Pius set an example. We know he didn't resist his attackers. He is our role model."

"Do you think Xanus will give up peaceably?" Yana asked.

"He'll do what is in his self interest. And if it's in his self interest to capitulate, he will. I'm banking on it. Xanus may come to see a cushy exile as better than what may await him here. Maybe we can peel away some of his support if his followers come to see the merits of accepting a generous reprieve. With them, we can afford to be very lenient. Mitigating circumstances, waywardness of misguided youth, we'll give them every chance to turn. They never wanted to kill Pius, I'm certain. They were just led on."

The vote was six for Spieling, four for Yana.

They took the vote to the larger group in secret rooms provided by the Forandi Order, and the vote was 142 for Spieling and 82 for Yana. The majority had come to the opinion that by conducting affairs this way, the other half of the rebels would surely join them, standing together in strength and solidarity.

They agreed to a postponement of four months, and that if future decisions were not made in a democratic way there would be no point in making any attempt of reforming the Obsidian Order. And if any of them were to die in the interim, they would die. They all agreed to this with a solemn raising of their hands. Goddess or no goddess, September Snow, saint or no saint, Iona, were still their two most beloved and venerated ancestors. Would they, as a mother and daughter team, have expected anything less of the sons of the Obsidian Order?

To those who still doubted him, Spieling declared, "Even Xanus would agree with this sentiment: piety professed actually requires piety extended. Think of the example of Pius. Piety professed, piety extended."

Even though Yana suspected he was losing ground even among some of his core supporters, he insisted on holding one more vote.

The outcome of the second vote was even clearer: 168 for Spieling, 56 for Yana.

After the vote, after the supporters and non-supporters alike left the room, Spieling took the note out of his frayed pocket and unfolded it. He had been carrying the note around with him for weeks. Whenever he thought he needed his resolve strengthened, he would take it out and reread it. So he took it out once again, and read it, as if for the first time.

My dear Spieling:

We've talked about this so often in the past. I go now. I did not seek martyrdom. I only sought the truth. And the sharing of truth. Xanus will crush us if given half the chance—I was never made of the stuff to be a leader—too much the scholar, too much the remote thinker. More importantly, too much the boring academic. All those quirky expressions of thought just so I could more effectively cover my tracks. If the membership of the Obsidian Order can be moved, especially the younger generation, I think you'd make an excellent leader. Why do I think that? Because you have stores of common sense and stores and stores of experience. Also, there has been no better a consensus builder, perhaps in the history of the Obsidian Order, than you. Xanus always feared you more than he feared me, and in this late hour of the day I can see why he'd think that. If you succeed in instituting the changes we have both dreamed of for so many years, you'd be the best candidate for the leader of the Order. I'd vote for you in a heartbeat. Also, I'd mount a serious campaign to encourage others to do likewise. But you must obtain this honor, should the opportunity arise, on the basis of your own merits. Therefore, I forbid you to show this note to anyone. I don't want to be

*seen as a kingmaker. The die has been cast. I know that I will be dis-
patched soon—they'll kill me—I just don't know exactly the place and
time. Thus this note. Maybe we'll all go quickly in four months time, if
the asteroid does its job. Best of luck. As a historian of long standing, I
believe part of what makes history happen is luck—kismet, chance, fortune. Surely we can be riders on one of these strange ethereal creatures...
horses... Xanus might call them, in one of his absurdly devotional and
fanatical frames of mind. The Four Horsemen of the Apocalypse? (I
know how much you love some of the Pre-Gaian religious tropes—apparently Matthew of the Forandi was into the Christian religious themes
and tropes too. If there ever was a tomb-robbing, grave-stealing thief of
ideas from the past, it was him!) Could we not be one of those horses or
one of those riders? Oh, that's right, I was talking about another subject.
I was talking about the Four Horsemen of the Apocalypse. If we don't
try, we'll never know, right?*

*You think I'd edit this before sending it to you so untidy and broken
up. I'd send you a corrected version but I'm jumpy and I don't care
much about the rest of it. Read between the lines...I can't help it, that's
how stupid they are. This might be one of the strangest things you'll ever
imagine me saying, but I'm saying it now: viva activa, viva long life.*

Love and affection, Pius

The letter had two different levels of meaning. Spieling figured
out by 'reading between the lines' that two of the horses Pius was
referring to were Ayre and Planifor in the Obsidian Order, one back
East, middle level, one in the Midwest, very high level. That was
Pius's opinion, but Spieling could choose his own lieutenants, Pius
knew that.

Thank Gaia, Spieling thought, few could penetrate all that Pre-
Gaia arcane, so it was the perfect blind. "Did he really think I was
going to follow his advice, though?" Spieling thought.

And then he placed the rumbled slip of paper back into his shirt
pocket and looked wistfully away.

Chapter Fifty-Five

ZOIA RECEIVED NEWS from her father, which included all the details of the terms Jug had proposed for purposes of economically saving U. Presbyr.

"Not good enough," Zoia said, nodding her head.

"Not good enough?" Rathman parroted, surprised. "You realize how much money Jug is going to pour into the university? You'd think as a good businessman, you'd think with the uncertainty of the asteroid mission, he'd wait. But no, he acts. You love U. Presbyr. You love it almost as much as your father does. What's there not to like about the deal?"

"We'll see what he comes up with next," Zoia said with a provisional smile. "Making the gift anonymous is the best part," she conceded. "It clearly means Jug is no longer as concerned as he was with receiving plaudits and esteem from the world. Every penny spent can't always be about making the name Gatetar glitter. I'm sure Jason will work great with dad, regardless of whether the obstacles that will present themselves are institutional in nature, administrative in nature, or even just logistical in nature. Jug must have had to put ashes on his forehead, wear sackcloth, and walk on his hands and knees across the many floors of his mansion to get Jason to agree to come back on board. With Jason, Jug will perhaps even have a greater sense of vision. We'll see what he comes up with next. Whatever the gift may be, it had better be given anonymously."

"I've completely forgiven Jug," Rathman said in a quiet voice. "After all, in my opinion, all he was guilty of was having given me exactly what I asked for."

"But that was when you were crazy as a loon."

"Maybe he didn't know I was crazy as a loon."

Zoia smiled. Rathman knew that Zoia didn't believe that. But Rathman could also see that some of Zoia's defenses where coming down. Not all of them of course, but some of them.

"You know," Rathman said, "by helping to change Jug's behavior, you're changing the world. At least in some small ways."

"Small potatoes," Zoia scoffed. "People who talk about fixing society are quieter about their own involvement in what's broken. The only thing better than controlling money and power is to control the efforts to question that distribution of money and power. It's difficult to convince a man to understand something if his wealth and power is based on not understanding it. Don't you think that fits Jug? Fits him, wouldn't you agree?"

Rathman thought so. Zoia knew how to express herself. She always had the right phrase, perhaps even the most perfect phrase. And her description of Jug was spot on.

"You know, I love it here," Rathman said, anxious and eager to change the subject. "I think Bruja has it right."

Zoia smiled when Rathman mentioned her.

"When I think about the Subversion of Technology Commune," Rathman said, "I realize that the members had a skewered understanding of the hazards of technology because it was taken from an over-reading—actually a secular over-reading—of the religious-oriented BLESSINGS OF GAIA DOCUMENT. I don't know if any of them ever had an occasion to read the Time Repairer, we didn't discuss that. But if any of them had, it would have been an over-reading, an over-reach, as well. In hindsight, I know I over-read the Time Repairer. I'm completely certain of that now."

"At last," Zoia said rejoicingly. "The past is the past. And I was going to ask you how you were feeling about the asteroid. But why even ask that question? You're hopeful! You're so wonderfully, wildly hopeful! Look at you. Just look at you. Bulls! Cows! Calves! No darkness! I just can't believe the change that has come over you."

Chapter Fifty-Six

THE PICTURES THAT CAME BACK from the first unmanned probe, four years earlier had been fairly accurate, but far from perfect. Camera one and camera two both shut down before they could get close enough for a detailed survey. Fortunately, a small core sampling attempt did work. As far as they could tell, the asteroid was made of rock and lots of metal.

The pictures that came back from the second unmanned probe, taken when the asteroid was much closer to the Earth, eighteen months after the first probe, proved to be perfect, close to immaculate.

They revealed that the asteroid was oblong and 6.5 kilometers in diameter and indirectly confirmed there were high concentrations of metal. In terms of having a negative impact, that was as bad as the news could have been. (Prior to the probes, there had been a forlorn hope, at least on the part of some of the more speculative scientists, that this was not the case, the asteroid might have been composed of looser debris and gaseous ice that could be broken up easier. That was the problem. If they blew it up, some of the fragments could very well continue on the same path and hit Earth anyway. So a "hard"—rather than a low-density—asteroid might actually be better, no fragments.

Jaime called it, "A hard, dense rock with high concentrations of metal. A fist. Nothing soft about it."

An object of any mass that was that large would be catastrophic, but now any talk about human extinction was not just speculative or questionable, it was real and nearly foreordained.

When that "unfortunate-turn-of-phrase" hit the airwaves, it made even more people everywhere jumpy, cranky, disquieted, and unhappy. Which motivated Jaime's most loyal supporters and devoted followers to convince him to shut up. Which, being the good Forandi brother of a Gaian Order that he was, Jaime did, saying apologetically, "I'll never again let a description become an unintentionally weaponized idea."

The "armed" trip to the asteroid was to commence in five weeks. It was going to take the two person spaceship 61.5 days to travel the 75 million kilometers, which was approximately 200 times the distance to the moon. The three proton bombs on board would each be detonated 1,000 to 2,000 feet from the asteroid, packing several times the wallop of a nuclear bomb. Carefully aimed, staggered several days apart, these devices would slow the asteroid down at least enough so that the people of Earth would not have to worry about it being a threat for millions of years. That was the plan.

Chapter Fifty-Seven

T HE ROCKET WAS more than 400 feet tall. It was fitted together with the precision of an ancient mechanical clock, carrying all the equipment needed for propulsion, guidance, supervisory control, gyroscopes for stabilization, steerable thrusters, an imager, a spectrometer, sensors, communications, proton-bomb platform and payload, food, accommodations, spacesuits, and survival for two. At the program's height, 500,000 people worked on the mission, signifying an array of professional networks that included contractors and consultants. All the people involved were driven by an ethos of collaboration. In the memory portion of the one-cubic-box that was the "brains" of the mission—the guidance computer—there were 988,546 wires, each of which had been threaded by hand, (yes, a little primitive), though the screens and viewing apparatuses were touch-tone and therefore even more modern. The mission was to put two persons on top of the equivalent of 14 million pounds of explosives, aim them at the incoming asteroid, light the fuse, and after finally achieving HeliosX4 speed, and after completing the mission, return to Earth.

A few minutes before launch time, a launch status check took place. The launch manager asked: 'Go' or 'No Go.' 'Go' was the word from 29 of the 29 desks of the control center.

"Sea of Tranquility, this is the Launch Operations Manager. The Launch Team wishes you good luck and Gaia speed."

"Ready to implement," Frankie replied.

The countdown was sounding off at Supervisory Control at 120 seconds, but Frankie and Johnny weren't listening to it. They were watching the numbers on the Flash Board.

The count hit zero.

The rocket disappeared into the sky. Four minutes later, Frankie was talking to the ground controllers as a matter of fact, as if she were driving a car in the old section of Job, heading toward downtown in Eccles. "We are away," Frankie said. "And this is an all-clear. Thank you Supervisory Control."

They were already several hundred kilometers from where they started.

After unplugging the supports on her suit, Frankie got out of her chair, and Johnny turned on his wrist gadget and started reading from a short script that was highlighted on the screen. "No words can convey the slightest idea of the terrific sound! An immense spout of fire shot up. With great difficulty some few spectators obtained a momentary glimpse of the projective victoriously cleaving the air in the midst of the fiery vapors."

"We're in the tin can," Frankie said. "Sounds like how things may have looked from the perspective of down on the ground." Frankie spoke with her typical paradoxical mix of verbal jousting and cerebral arrogance.

"What I said comes from the middle of the 19th century of the ancient calendar," Johnny said. "It's not from now, it's from our ancestors. You see, you're mistaken, I wasn't describing what just happened. It's a quote from Jules Verne. He was the *first* science fiction writer at the end of the Westernized version of the Upanishads. The first. I thought you might be impressed by that."

"I'm going to check the warheads," Frankie said dismissively.

"You don't have to do that now," Johnny said.

"I want to get away from you," Frankie said.

Frankie descended down the ladder to the bomb platform.

Suddenly there was a stream of music coming through the sound system—which reached all sections of the ship.

It was the psychedelic instrumental opening of an ancient song from 1965 ancient calendar, (100 years after Jules Verne), a song that had been among the recordings preserved among the Antarctica documents. Frankie had not only never heard the unusual song before, she had never known that such a piece of music existed. The title was called Eight Miles High, written by the guitarist Roger McGuinn, of the pop musical group the Byrds.

Frankie became suddenly angry. With only a cursory examination of the proton bombs, having descended to the lower platform, she squeezed through the 30 feet of the middle section of the ship. On the other side of the thin wall were the sleeping quarters, holding bay, tubes for the three proton bombs, and the proton bombs themselves, one above each bed, and one above the toilet, which was located next to the warehouse. She got back up to the top of the ship.

By the time she got to the entrance of the cockpit the song had been playing for 30 seconds. Immediately she confronted Johnny. Face to face, with her face contorted in a near-state of furious rage, she shouted, "Knock...that...shit...off!"

Johnny immediately flipped the song off.

"You need to relax," Johnny said. "We need to act like we know what we're doing. Remember during the training session when we..."

"Your point is well taken," Frankie said. "I just wish you'd let me know when you're going to do something—you tell me about it—in advance."

"Things are going to happen that we are not going to know in advance," Johnny said. "I'll let you select the song next time."

"Will you check the oxygen gauges."

"I'll do that right now," Johnny said.

"And I want you to let me know the minute when we've achieved HeliosX4 speed. The moment. We're still an hour away from slingshot..." *Slingshot* was not exactly the scientific term. More accurately it was "gravity assist," but it was a good description.

"Right away."

Was Frankie still angry with Johnny five minutes later? No she wasn't. She realized he was right. But she hated the song.

Chapter Fifty-Eight

"I got the news from your father," Rathman said. "Jug has recruited thinkers to help him dream up potentially dreamy philanthropy projects."

"Plutocratic ideas that eventually result in greater commodification?" Zoia asked.

"Please, Zoia," Rathman said gasping. "We need to steer clear of that rhetoric. Gatetar people aren't partial to that kind of turn of phrase. We need ideas that are friendly to the victors and winners of the age. Ideas that are useful, that is to say, results-oriented—results that could turn a profit down the road. He wants something that might give him a glow of heroism. Change making! A mission! A cause! Well, they've been given certain parameters. Jug wants something where the ideas go down easily. Snappy ideas. That don't hurt."

"Oh, and what have they come up with?" Zoia asked. And she quickly added, "Oh, and by the way, ideas that don't hurt *whom?*"

"Look, I'm just reporting to you what your father told me, that's all," Rathman said. "Imagine a search for a philanthropic idea that approaches an ideal. How about something that lights up part of the darkness of the Outer World? Wouldn't that be a worthy project?"

"Lights up part of the world?' Zoia asked. "What do you mean?"

"Electrification," Rathman said. "Direct it at the most needy of people. In the smallest places. In the most difficult places. In a place where no one's been able to make money at it so far. Start with a small island. Move on to a larger one. Wouldn't that be heroic? Eventually light up whole continents. End some of the darkness. Wouldn't that be a worthy project?"

"Well, that would be something truly interesting to see," Zoia said, "I admit it. There would have to be protocols, solutions to problems that his current methods have been causing."

"Do you want me to pass that on to your father?" Rathman asked.

"Of course I do," Zoia said. "Pass it on. Maybe Dad can get through to him. What about the money Jug is willing to give to keep half of the elite part of Eccles's higher education going?"

"Seven of the eight departments of U. Presbyr you mean?" Rathman asked. "What are the terms of the agreement? They can't study Jug. That's no big deal, he's boring. But they also can't study Gatetar Industries either."

"That's like telling them they can't study nearly half of the world."

"A quarter of it," Rathman said. "Let's be fair. Don't exaggerate."

"Okay. Have it your way. If Gaia is synonymous with the world, Gatetar is a quarter of it."

"You're taking on the whole world, Zoia," Rathman said at last.

"No, just a quarter of it."

Chapter Fifty-Nine

FOR THIRTY-ONE DAYS Frankie and Johnny had the odd experience of living in a spaceship that was hurling itself through space. When Frankie wasn't working, she was exercising: harsh mental tests (math calculations, physics puzzles), and severe physical tests (sometimes as many as 16 kilometers a day on the running board), to keep her wits sharp and her body fit. Johnny acted in the exact opposite way, doing only the minimum that the space team said was required which was *still* a significant amount.

"Lighten up, Frankie," Johnny said. "We're in chimp mode. You know the new history claims that September Snow was a crackerjack helioplane pilot. In her day, the very best. Let's say piloting a spacecraft like ours is similar to piloting a helioplane 2,700 years ago. You think you're as good as September Snow? I mean, not as a goddess, but as a pilot?"

Frankie gave Johnny a 1,000-kilometer-long stare. "You want to fight? Why are you baiting me?"

"Remember the night you thought my love-making was so brilliant?" Johnny asked. "I mean, to be making love to a goddess, my goodness..."

"Oh," Frankie said, knitting her brows. "Which night? There were so many. So long ago... Remember the time I hit you over the head with a book? Want me to do it again? A book of physics? A book of calculus?"

"Oh, that's a setup if I've ever seen one," Johnny said beaming. "Time for the occult mysteries of the Tang Dynasty and the Teflon Query-land," Johnny said. It was a private joke about ancient space programs.

"Want to check the bolts, how about the welds?" Johnny added. He broke out into a very large Cheshire Cat-like grin. "You know Eccles makes the best welds of all! Even better, want to check time itself? Time itself! Whoa! When's the last time you saw the sun rise? You like the artificial lighting? Want to adjust it—there isn't day and night? Want to check your life rhythms and your neural-bio rhythms and your time rhythms? See if they're all in sync?"

"Uh?" Frankie asked.

"Want to check the clocks?" Johnny asked, but he spoke in a way that suggested he was already bored with the subject and wished he could move on. "Want to check the accuracy of the time indicators on board? Without clocks we have no notion of where we're at. Do we even have a clock to check our clocks?"

"Of course we do," Frankie replied. "Back on Earth via radio."

"But what if we lost that connection?" Johnny said. "In that event, there are numbers. And there is space."

"I know where we are," Frankie said. "We are in a vast expanse of darkness. A vast blank nothingness. A silent, immutably infinite space, but we have an invisible string attached to us so we can get back home. Are you still testing me?" Frankie asked, smiling. She knew exactly what was going on.

"You have to rely on so many people," Johnny said. "What if somebody didn't get it right. What if we've been sent up with no other purpose in mind but to test us? I mean, what if somebody got the math wrong and we end up five million kilometers off course? Or ten million kilometers off course?"

"This line of questioning seems vaguely familiar. But it escapes me."

"Just doing my job, commander," Johnny said. "They should make the questions better, or less philosophical. More realistic. I know it's stupid. Just doing my job."

"Put the report in an encrypted code that I can't open. I'll send it back at the end of the week with the charge codes."

Five days later, Johnny caught Frankie eating between meals. "Ha, ha, ha!" Johnny exclaimed. "You thought I wouldn't notice? Sneaking it on the side? Is it pouched jam again? Banana puree? Sweetened nutrients? That means less for you later. Bad girl. Naughty girl. What is the matter with you?"

Frankie smiled, and said in a non-guilty tone of voice, "I only do my jam busts as a reward *after* I run my maximums. No banana puree. Yes, I'll have less jam on the return trip." Frankie squeezed another bit of the jam from its pouch into her mouth.

"Look at me, I follow the rules," Johnny laughed. "Maybe that's why they hired us. Because we can eat under such extreme conditions, even when we're upside down for a goodly period of time, we don't throw up. I can perform surgery on myself. According to the tests, I can perform self-surgery better than you or anybody else. Stitching a garden variety wound—stitching a tummy-tube three inches deep gash in one or two of the larger tubes in the viscera of my guts—all the same to me! No difference! I'm quite relaxed about it. Look, I'm literally a space cadet. Not a figurative one. I'm literally one. Eat whatever you want. I don't care. I won't tell. I got some brain matter going on this stuff too, you know! I don't believe for a second any of this breath-takingly ludicrous, drill-a-hole-in-your-skull hokum about colonizing other planets. Why do they keep pushing this stupidity-manufacturing malarkey? It's worse than baby food for people with full-grown teeth. Candidates that are close to us—the moon, Mars, the moon Europa of Jupiter, the moon Titan of Saturn, four or five other moons, are close— or candidates that are still a goodly distance from our teensy-weensy corner of the galaxy—either way—it's like they're trying to use really bad science to make up a new religion. It's humanity's childhood hoax, perpetrated by people—including billionaire technocrats, who should know better. What about high-energy radiation and ultraviolet light and the Iron Laws of Nature? Thinking that if we can go one percent

of the speed of light would mean we can get to the nearest star in 400 years. That's the closest gap between our sun and the nearest star. Even with HeliosXfour speed, we can't go a fraction of that speed. It'd take 80,000 years, but multiply that by a 100, by 500, by 1,000, to a livable, or not livable, planet. Lots of ping-pong paddles, ping-pong balls, ping-pong tables, lots of tuna fish sandwiches, tuna fish salads, hamburgers made of algae. One would need a food-producing apparatus, one has to lug up with one like it was creating the equivalent of a 400-car-long freight train in the form of an elongated picnic basket, for each person on board living a stupendously improbable number of lifetimes. Then eight million years later, or 16 million years later, or 32 million years later, give or take, you see the horizon. Ah! the sky the color of pale, blushing rose—clouds instead of floating—swimming spirals in the sky, or gold on gold, or gold on blue, or just blue? The Collapse and the Fall put to rest these incredulous fables that made the Dark Age absurd nonsense seem—in comparison—down right endearing, elegantly charming, and even plausible—marine animals that can talk, both desert and mountain winds that can sing, and trees that contained within themselves memory that goes back 6,000 years. During those times, and before those times, the Gaia religion—as I understand it—messed up plenty of things. My extremist nephew and my less extremist niece used to say Gaia beliefs created a millennia of sorrow. They exaggerate. They exaggerate many things. After all, they're young and one is extremist and one is less extremist. But one thing the Gaia religion got right—in spite of the many things it got wrong—is this: 'We've only one planet to save.' There's no science—no matter how falsely used, no matter how crudely and fraudulently pursued—that can dispute this absolute core: 'We've only our planet to save...'"

"You certainly have a way of saying things," Frankie said. "You talk as if September Snow were shouting in your ear. What is happening to you in you sleep? Are you still in touch with reality?"

"Stop it, now," Johnny said. "Now... I'm warning you."

"Have you been listening to Beethoven's *Ninth Symphony* too often? I catch you often. Are you being visited by a ghost? By an apparition? September Snow perhaps? Are you being visited by a very important guest, or a very important ancestor? Do you have to get some distance away from Earth for this to happen? In your dreams? Stop! Think!"

Johnny frowned. "Okay. Stop it. Stop making fun of me. But I'm saying that from 37.5 million kilometers from Earth, Frankie, you have to go back 2,700 years to find another small group of monkeys like us—posing as human beings—going out into outer space. We're going at least a fifth more—than *that* distance. We'll be out farther than anybody has, and that's less than a month away."

"It's almost like you got just a little bit too much of the old time religion in you, don't you, Johnny? Got you all wound-up, like a clock, or a top! Are you drunk on it? I'd never guess you were the type. Is the darkness getting to you? Something *religious* stirring inside your swear-by-science, atheistic bones? Outside our tin can? What do you see? We've been cooped up here for a while. Cabin fever?"

"Stop making fun of me."

"Oh, touchy. Thirty point five more days to go. Shall we check the electrical devices on the proton bombs again? And again? And again? Shall we check the imager, the spectrometer, the sensors, the communications again? I don't even have to order you around anymore. You're on automatic. You're an automaton."

"You're doing a *psych proof* on me?" Johnny asked. "Aren't you? Come on! Come on!"

"Well, it can't be a duplicate of yours, can it? I just do this... Time? Distance? Let's just keep with the program."

"What if we switched our profiles and sent them back that way," Johnny said with a leering, mischievous grin. "Nobody's done that before... As far as I know. We'll switch yours with mine and vice versa. Change the names. Change the dates. Do it on a lark. Wouldn't that perplex them? I mean, there's really nothing they can do about it, is there?"

"Only when you joke about it do I know *how* serious you are,"

Frankie said. "As you know, that could only happen if you were commander. Kill me, then you can do it."

"That's getting too close...," Johnny said.

"Too close to what?" Frankie asked. "Oh, so you're the only one who has the right to make a joke? No, I think, when you say, we've only one planet to save, it *is* beautiful. It is gorgeous. We hold on to that, there's nothing inside or outside this tin can that can rattle us."

Chapter Sixty

A BREAKAWAY GROUP of 15 people, a sub-group section of a larger formation of Gaia pilgrims, came through on their desert trek. Having started four hundred kilometers to the south, they were now following the course of the Iona River flowing north from the depths of the Outer World. In advance, Rathman and Zoia knew they were coming. Even in their section of the Outer World word traveled. They had heard they would be in want, and it was reported that they were on the verge of running out of food. When they had progressed just the distance of 20 kilometers away, Rathman decided he'd come down from their ranch to the valley below to greet them.

As Rathman walked he was surrounded by red rock, towering saguaro cacti, and mesquite. During the course of his long morning's jaunt, a jackrabbit ran out in front of him, as did a roadrunner an hour later. Between short stretches of walking, there were small groups of lizards that could be seen congregating or scurrying around. It was an exceptional day, more than on one occasion, in the distance, Rathman could spot a raven, a hawk, and a vulture working the sky.

Finally Rathman could see the pilgrims' camp beside the river. At that time of the year the Iona River wasn't more than three feet wide and barely a few inches deep.

As he approached the camp he made a clear sign of his intentions by raising his hands above his head, palms out, indicating he was friendly. A little girl playing in the dirt on the edge of the camp eyed him warily, then without saying a word nodded her head. She was telling Rathman to follow her.

"When did you break away?" Rathman asked the leader of the group.

"The main group threw us out just south of the ancient site of the old town of Nogales. The point of our pilgrimage was to pray to our Goddess September Snow, and to the saints, Iona and Tom Novak."

"We jumped the gun," the leader said. "We think Tom should be seen as a part of our religion and that makes us heretics. We believe that if we pray fervently to him, and make proper sacrifices to Mother Earth Gaia at the holy places, it'll guarantee that Tom will help the astronauts deflect the asteroid out of the way and save the world. And so two weeks ago they told us to leave and take our prayers to Saint Tom with us. We're moving up a parallel valley, to the east of them, even though we know Tom didn't travel up this way."

"You're hungry," Rathman said.

"We're out of food," the leader admitted.

Rathman thought back to his youth, when his father taught him how to survive in terrain very similar to where they were standing. He spent the next six hours gathering edible plants and roots from the desert floor, looking especially for fruit-bearing prickly pear and cholla. His father had taught him that the desert was rich in protein, every several acres had enough food to feed a dozen people, even in a drought. Remembering his Gaia studies from his days in the orphanage Rathman said, "I bet Iona did something similar when she was alone crossing the Forbidden Zone. Of course, because of the experiments, that zone must have been many times more forbidding than this land is now. It was a blank space, a horror, more desolate than desolate..."

"Are you a man of the Book?" the leader asked.

"I was obligated to study it just like so many others were," Rathman said. "My wife Zoia, a skeptic, thinks parts of THE

BLESSINGS OF GAIA DOCUMENT are great and rich literature!"

Rathman knew that pilgrims could have strange beliefs, even stranger ways of living. And this was a renegade sub-flock of pilgrims that had been exiled by an even larger group of pilgrims. His curiosity got the best of him. "When you're doing pilgrimage, what do you mean when you say, sacrifice?" Rathman asked.

"For every 50 kilometers we walk, we walk 250 meters on our knees. I had a vision."

I bet you did, Rathman thought. No wonder they're so hungry. But out of respect he didn't make a comment.

"They have to walk 50 kilometers so there's enough time in between for their knees to heal," the leader confessed. "Sometimes we have to cheat. Sometimes we have to carry the children, but when we're carrying them, we can walk upright."

Why make rules at all? Rathman thought. But he did not express his opinion, remembering how much his father had *enjoyed* quarreling with the idiosyncratically religious, and how the subsequent bouts of enmity often had unhappy results.

Rathman wondered if the leader whipped his own children, Rathman's father had seen plenty of that happen before.

When Rathman returned two days later, the group was already struggling again. The group didn't have the best handle on desert-floor foraging. They were skilled enough to trap a good many scrawny jackrabbits, and they knew how to find water, even from the underground pools. But originally being semi-urbanites they were only able to scrounge the most obvious in-the-wild edibles. When they were with the larger group of pilgrims, they had traveled in a more decent and civilized manner, with all parties contributing to the commons, which included a cook, a cook's tent, and a transportable tent-like mess.

So under these conditions, how far could this group proceed? Especially at their pace? They'd just completed their 250-meter-long walk on their knees, resulting in lots of very sore and bleeding knees. So feeling sorry for them, and wanting to be more tolerate than his father, Rathman brought a cow down and told them to slaughter it. "This should keep you fed until it's time for you to move on. You can dry some of the meat and take it with you. So 50 kilometers from here, you can walk on your knees again."

"You are most generous, sir," the leader said. "We'll pray for you. As we'll pray for the astronauts' mission."

"When you get to the border with the Inner World, are you going to continue north?" Rathman asked.

"If the authorities let us. By then it will be only a couple of days before we know the mission's outcome. Do you think, if we're on pilgrimage, they'll let us through?"

"Good luck. I'm from Eccles, but before that I was from the border area. Ask for help from the Forandi Order. You'll have much better luck with them than you'll have with the Obsidian Order. They'll get you farther on. Maybe everyone will be celebrating then. What a time to be on the border between the Inner and the Outer World, huh!"

After this encounter, Rathman spent time describing to Zoia the peculiar ways of these odd Gaia pilgrims. The two were standing in their house in the dining room area, where Rathman had filled and repaired the huge gaping hole in the floor, and it was here that he discussed with Zoia the pilgrims' strange religious practices and beliefs.

After hearing him out on the subject, Zoia replied: "Gaia pilgrims come in many sizes, shapes, and forms. Oh, you think they're something, have you heard about the Neverists?"

"The Nihilists?" Rathman asked. "What?"

"No, not the Nihilists. The Neverists."

"Are they related to the Neverlanders?" Rathman asked.

"Rathman," Zoia said. "Listen to me. You're talking to an expert on cults. Neverlanders died out more than 50 years ago. Although there are legends that suggested some managed to escape to the mountains of Ghat, and made a home there, otherwise they're impossible to find. No, I mean the Neverists. Of all the subjects Auger and Pius tried to do a joint study on, the topic of the Neverists was the only one they ever managed to complete. Their study on the Neverists was the only collaboration they ever penned. You haven't hear it all until you've become familiar with the Neverists."

Rathman smiled. "Well, elucidate!"

"All right," Zoia said. "The Neverists live exclusively in the Outer World. They believe that the asteroid crisis is a hoax, and that the Earth was never in danger. Furthermore, they believe that the Earth could *never* be in danger because that would contradict the principles of Gaia as the Neverists understand them. Their belief system is so strong that there is a taboo on even talking about such an event."

"Neverist doctrine holds that time is an illusion and that everything happens simultaneously. In fact, separate events are also an illusion. Past, present, and future are one, as well as many. They speak to each other using a bewildering mix of verb tenses that is meant to merge the past/present/future continuum. 'Did you will be taking that trip now?' one might ask another. The rejoinder: 'You could have said that, yet I won't.' If someone were to tell one of them to 'live in the moment,' that person might retort, 'Which one?'"

"Studying the Neverists also resulted in my dad investigating writings of the Before-the-Fall-time author Kurt Vonnegut. Vonnegut was a general fiction writer and a science fiction writer. Dad studied him because in at least five of his books he made references to the Tralfamadorians. Tralfamadorians? According to this author, they were an alien species who apparently experienced time the same way the Neverists do. So the Neverists revere Vonnegut as what they call a Venerable Descendant or a Special Ancestor. To them he is something like a saint, only without all the moral baggage. In fact, they regard the fictional Tralfamadorians as an actual race that hasn't been contacted yet due to the imposition of some sort of temporal quarantine."

"Pius's part of the paper specialized on the Neverists doctrine called Time's Boomerang," Zoia continued. "It involves a conflation with the Australian Aboriginal idea of Dreamtime, or the Dreaming. The Aboriginals believed that the entire world was made by Ancestral Beings at the beginning of time. During Dreamtime the sky, land, waters, plants, animals, and humans were created by the spirit ancestors (not gods). They understood the Dreamtime as a beginning that never ended, a period on a universal temporal continuum. To those who say that backward time travel is impossible because the past cannot be altered, even by God, the Neverists reply: 'Denying Gaia power over the past equates to denying Gaia power over the present and future. And this is blasphemy.'"

"For the Neverists, Gaia lives in an eternal everywhen during which matter can neither be created nor destroyed. Furthermore, if the event is to happen it has also already happened, so why worry or try to change it?"

With Rathman in tow Zoia flowed in from the living room to the kitchen nook to stir a pot of beans simmering over a fire. "Hungry?"

"Yes...but not yet."

"It's hot."

"Later. Corncrib first. Got to keep watching. So far no rats, fortunately. But blight? Rot?" Rathman eyed the uncovered pot. "Something to look forward to."

Zoia banged the heavy wooden spoon on the rim of the pot and covered it. "You know a Neverist theologian once said that if logical consistency is a requirement for validity, meaning, rationality, and truth, we're all in big trouble. Rational exploration is all well and good, he stated, but irrational exploration is equally meaningful. He went on to extol *dialetheism,* the belief that there can be true statements whose negations are also true. Such 'true contradictions' were called by the Greeks dialetheia, or nondualisms. It follows from this belief that conundrums and paradoxes are not philosophical problems to be solved, but rather truths to be embraced."

"That theologian was reviled and banished by the Neverists for, as they put it, 'making too much sense.' But his observations are still worth considering in the context of Neverist thought. Or not, as the case may be."

"Auger and Pius's paper on the Neverists runs 65,000 words. If you're interested, I..."

"You've got to be kidding!" Rathman exclaimed.

"There is more than one path one can take for one to think that one has arrived at the doorstep of eternity," Zoia said. "Many things may disappear in the future. As long as there are humans, religion is very unlikely to be one of them."

Chapter Sixty-One

THE DRABNESS AND MONOTONY of the routine finally got to one of the astronauts about 52 days out.

Johnny was trying to "bump" or "jump," as if he were a rabbit, but with his bright red counter-weightlessness shoes, there was a delayed action. Once aloft, his weightlessness caused a midair, high-leg kicking movement in slow motion, and having achieved that, Johnny screamed, "Earth to Frankie! Earth to Frankie! Earth to Frankie!" He desperately pointed at his chest, trying to draw Frankie's attention. "Earth to Frankie! Earth to Frankie! Look at me."

Frankie didn't respond. Still reading her physics scroll, yes, Frankie had to go back and reread the same sentence again, but without looking up, still looking down, she murmured, "I can't tell if you're bored or you're just trying to freak me out, Johnny."

"Earth to Frankie!" Johnny repeated is a desperate sounding voice.

Frankie didn't look up. "Okay, is your heart beating very fast? Are your hands feeling clammy? Are the bottoms of your feet tingling, like the blood isn't circulating well at your extremities?"

"Earth to Frankie! Earth to Frankie! Please, Frankie... Look..."

Finally Frankie put her book down. She looked. The expression on Johnny's face suggested a look of a clown, but not a malevolent one, rather a kindly, elfish one."

"Okay, so you're just bored. Or perhaps crazy."

Upon hearing the words '*perhaps crazy*,' Johnny became happy. Hearing that, he ceased performing his bizarre antics, as if he had achieved some sort of bizarre victory over Frankie.

Johnny was complaisant and passive for the rest of the day, indeed, for the rest of the trip.

Four days later, Frankie and Johnny were now 56 days out. They were focused. They were in a thoughtful and serious mode. They had to use sensors and thrusters to get exactly on line, but all the equipment functioned exactly as it was supposed to. It took only a few hours to complete the course correction. The computer did the calculations, but this part of the mission was so critical, separately, Frankie did the calculations too. They were correct.

The asteroid was where it was supposed to be. The Sea of Tranquility was where it was supposed to be, in relationship to the asteroid.

They contacted Earth. All was 'Go.'

Following the procedure that they had rehearsed a thousand times, Frankie and Johnny shot the first proton bomb. It traveled at exactly the correct speed for several hours, and detonated 1,725 feet from the asteroid. They sent a message to the command base on Earth and waited the four minutes for it to arrive and the time it took for the message to be composed and returned. The message was brief. "Aces. On top. All in the affirmation. We salute you."

At intervals of 12 hours, 24 hours, 36 hours, using multiple telescopes to triangulate, the command base on Earth was able to confirm and reaffirm their measurements of the asteroid's location, movement, trajectory, speed, and distance. Yes, they estimated that the 'nudge' had worked exactly the way they thought it would.

"So far, so good," Johnny said. "We'll be back in time for the Gaia Day parade at this rate. Can you just see it? Can you imagine us on display in the very first limo in line behind the marching platoons of jolly coppers in blue and winged-footed motorcyclists, with a bevy of helioplanes flying overhead, confetti by the bucketfuls being tossed down from the upper floors of the buildings of Eccles? Even if they dress me up in a formal suit, I'm going to have my helmet on my lap. Although I'd prefer it if you were on my lap."

"Oh, as if I am waiting for the arrival of some tender mercies," Frankie said. "I shouldn't have expected that we'd get this far out without my ex-boyfriend saying something exceedingly unseemly. You take the cake, Johnny."

After completing the first strike, it took them a 40 hour cycle to set up for the second strike. This they did. Sensors and thrusters were apparently working optimally. The second proton bomb was released.

And was also completely successful, although there was a momentary vibration in the exit portion of the release tube that came and went so quickly it was barely detected. The asteroid had responded to the 'nudge' again, precisely the way they had anticipated. The numbers were coming back exactly the way they were supposed to. It was as if math and reality were sharing the same space in the vast emptiness. Frankie and Johnny were basking in a state of exuberance. They really felt like they were a team. They sent a message out and they received a congratulatory message back again.

'Aces. On top. All in the affirmative. We salute you. We applaud you."

Frankie and Johnny spent the evening having a special celebratory meal, which included, between them, two steaks, two potatoes, four beers (Johnny had 3 beers to Frankie's one), spinach salad, a sort of green-glammed jello, and glace marinated cherries.

Frankie and Johnny were as happy as two peas in a pod. Johnny was so exuberant he jumped up—and in the process—he'd momentarily forgotten to calculate the effects of his own weightlessness—to such an extent—it took a brief moment to readjust himself by adjusting his counter-weightlessness shoes.

Frankie, ordinarily so proper, serious, and somber, cried out with sheer joy. She excitedly clapped her hands, and laughed at Johnny's struggle to escape his predicament. If only for a brief interlude, perhaps for an hour or two, the burden of their cares and responsibilities seemed to drift away.

And then, in his capacity as the spaceship's electrical engineer, Johnny found the fault.

"What are the chances of a failure?" he asked Frankie.

"We've had a number of them," Frankie said. "Let's see, reliability specifications failures you're talking about, you know this involves things that we may never have to use in the course of the voyage. Or can be rerouted. Most of the time we reroute. You'd know this too. We've had 30. So far, on a nearly half-completed voyage, that's almost five times better than models tell us we might have. So, on the basis of that, we're actually doing extremely well. Thanks to the people who put us up here. Thanks to you as well. By far the majority of our operations have a reliability requirement of 0.99998, which means we have two failures in 100,000 operations. You're the mechanic! If it's a system's failure, that makes any *difference*, that is to say, could jeopardize the mission, or our lives, or both—a small number—three? Out of 30? An example? We lost a very small amount of food. Vapor pack failure. Big deal. So what?"

"Three cases," Johnny said.

"Three cases," Frankie repeated. "First the one I mentioned. Food. Then ventilation. Then, radiation-deflection shields. You're the mechanic! Why? Why do you ask, Johnny?"

"Just to make sure my memory is correct," Johnny said. "We've had a failure."

"So." Frankie nodded. "Okay."

"No, you don't see," Johnny said. "Not like the others. We've had a *significant* failure. A big one."

"Okay."

Johnny looked suddenly downcast. "The first part is electrical, Frankie. Seems small, doesn't it? It is. But it isn't. Because it involves a mechanism involved in the release of the proton bomb."

"That's not electrical."

"No, you're right, it isn't. It's the lever in the tube of the proton bomb that's the problem. The electrical, that's relatively easy. But the lever has been literally sheered off! Repairing it means it needs to be done in a shop. Not up here! Or at least, not with my skills. I've never seen anything like this before, even in simulations. I don't even know how it happened. *Why it didn't blow the ship up, I truly don't understand!*"

"Replace it."

"How simple a problem can there be? A simple lever. Well, I can't solve it. Not 75 million kilometers from Earth I can't."

"Repair it."

"Like I said, I don't know how to go about doing that."

"Reroute it."

"You know that's impossible. It's the lever governing the release of the third proton bomb. It would be easier to build a whole new tube! Striker might have been able to. She had an uncanny way of devising..."

"Stop it, shut up," Frankie said.

"I can't fix it. But we can still do the detonation. But we have to use the Sea of Tranquility—the spaceship—the delivery vehicle, as part of the weapon. We have to detonate the proton bomb when the spaceship is somewhere between a 1,000 and 5,000 feet from the asteroid. Preferably *less* than 2,500 feet of course, but 5,000 feet will do. We can do that."

"You can do that?"

"Yes."

"We have to call Earth Command."

▶▶▶

Frankie sent the message. "We've had a failure in 2144573," she said. "It cannot be repaired. I repeat, the problem cannot be rectified. We cannot launch the third bomb. We have to deliver it ourselves. We have to take it to the asteroid in the ship. We await your orders."

They waited for a response. It was going to be an eight minute turnaround wait, plus the time it would take for a ground conference, including the time to compose a reply. Frankie and Johnny knew what the response was probably going to be.

Strangely, uncharacteristically, as they waited, there was a period of complete silence between Frankie and Johnny.

Finally, Johnny couldn't resist saying, "You should have done what I said. You should have broken the rules. That one time. If you had switched the dates and names on the psych proofs, they would surely have called us back by now. 'Turn around and come back home. Don't worry. You've done enough.'"

"You know," Frankie said sarcastically, "your sense of humor has been a boon on this voyage, Johnny. It has contributed to the success of our mission."

"Every voyage that involves a collective needs a comedian," Johnny said. "If the comedian is a hero too, now, that's a two-for-one. When we become heroes, what do you want them to name after you? A high school? A university? Oh, I've a better one. The Winnebet Center of Science. Your father, grandfather, even your great-grandfather, studied there. Go back between your father's time, and your grandfather's time, 50 years ago, didn't let women in. *You* studied there. Now, your name is on it."

Frankie refused to answer the question. "What do you want them to name after you?" she asked Johnny in a flat, emotionless, fatalistic voice.

"Change the name of Eccles to Johnny. No, name a continent after me. No, name a tiny stream after me. No, name an inter-city dog-pooping fenced-in corral after me. The Memorial Johnny Dog-Pooping Center. No, in the worst, toughest, crummiest part of Eccles, name animal protection after me. Once reviled street dogs get a chance at a better life, uh? Animals for Gaia. Pet hotels. Cafes up on the new snobbery. Grooming emporiums. Spaying and neutering service centers. Get them off the street. Give them a better life. If they don't have one yet, they should make one. Then after they do, they could name the place after me."

"No, seriously," Frankie said. "You know we're going to send one more message before we die. What do you want? They're almost certain to give us our heart's request, you know. I mean, assuming we succeed, how could they refuse us?"

"They should give our names to the two extreme points of the city of Eccles," Johnny said. "They would be—what? 80 kilometers—90 kilometers—apart? With the heart of Eccles in between. Therefore, first, they should rename the Love Observatory on Mount Eta after you. That'll cover the south. Second, they should name the San Francisco Game Reserve after me. That'll cover the north. Think about it."

"I'm serious."

"I'm serious too!"

The message finally came back. It simply read, "You know the answer. Proceed. You have to do three. It has to be done."

"I know why you're a navigator," Johnny said. "Your father taught you how to navigate by the stars. In the forest. In the desert. In the city? Before you even dreamt of becoming a pilot."

"No," Frankie said. "*Not the city.* There were always too many lights, and always some atmospheric pollution. But, in the forest, and in the desert, yes, it worked. In the case of the forest, find a clearing, that's all you had to do. I was eight years old at the time. It wasn't as if it was a life-and-death struggle, mind you, it was more like a simple game. That's how my father looked at it. A game. There were always the stars. That's how he taught me. I think it had less to do with a survivalist's strategy and more to do with having a curiosity about the world. A cold, emotionless, fatalistic curiosity. My father taught me never to be emotional about navigating, or anything else, for that matter."

"You know how I got started?" Johnny asked.

"Started in what?" Frankie asked. She grinned weakly.

"This business of ours of course," Johnny said. "When I was young my mother read to me a passage from one of the great classics, Jay Zehennie's *Gold Across The Horizon*. I know you know the work. For so many children of her generation, and children of other generations, Jay Zehennie was a favorite author. *Gold Across the Horizon* was my mom's favorite book. I know the quote by heart. Can I recite it to you?"

"Of course. Why not?"

Johnny cleared his throat and began to recite. "We've been stuck here since before I was born. We'll be stuck here long after I'm gone. I was born a prisoner. I'll die one. We're forced to live our lives on a perennially fog-encrusted sea, with slabs of white ice, gleaming oblong blocks of ice, splintered, clunky chunks of ice somewhere in color between light-blue, light-green, and white, holding us in, bobbing up and down, swirling all around us, forever and ever, churning year upon year. But, maybe only once in a lifetime, we may be able to catch a glimpse, a faint sliver, of the shore of an otherwise perennially—*forever*—cloud-shrouded, fog-choked land. Like Earth... There but not there. The hidden place of energy. The land coast of memory. The land coast of mystery. If...in this darkness... this can carry you through the darkness."

"I don't know why," Johnny said, "but my mother liked that quote so much. So positive, even in it's negativity! 'If...in this darkness...this can carry you through the darkness.' I didn't know what it meant! My mother said it meant: 'darkness is horrible. But sometimes it's just inscrutable.' Something about that frozen, darkened seascape and the close—so tantalizingly close—but still unobservable landscape. Mariners! Such yarns. When I was down in the mouth, she loved to quote the Arctic ice slab scene to me. And now it's mine. Like the place we are now is."

"It's beautiful," Frankie said. "You're a romantic, Johnny."

"It was my mom who got me interested in the space program. Now, you didn't know that, Frankie, did you?"

Frankie shook her head. "No. You talked about so much in your life. But you never talked about that."

"My dad never bothered, or had an inkling for me to be in space or in science," Johnny said. "It was my mother who got me started. With a book. Written by a blind woman. Jay Zehennie. A woman who never made it past the age of 35. I bet you didn't know that, did you?"

Chapter Sixty-Two

SEVENTY-FIVE MILLION kilometers away from Earth, they were in space. The farthest away any *manned* spaceship had ever gone. Ever. In old mystic time, or in the new times.

"Here comes the goose," Johnny said. "Here it comes! We should be fighting over it. We should be fighting over something that's worthy of fighting over, don't you think? How did they get us to this place? How did *you* get us to this exact point of intersection so exquisitely, so perfectly? Frankie! Look! There's the asteroid. It's big! It's ugly! It's cruel! You're the perfect pilot, Frankie. September Snow can't hold a candle to you. You're my goddess."

Johnny put the proton bomb detonator timer on the meter-gauge and waited for the "go" sign to appear. Then they waited. They stared at each other. It was now 65 seconds before impact. They didn't verbally count it down, but together they watched the numbers tumbling down on the screen. Thirty seconds. Twenty seconds. Fifteen seconds.

"We need to make sure we do the blast before we hit it," Johnny said. "Even if we're still 3,000 feet out."

"Maybe we should get serious," Frankie said. It was kind of strange. Who, among a world of fatalistic pilots, was considered to be the most fatalistic of them all? Fatalism made a good pilot better. Fatalism made a great pilot near perfect. With slightly trembling shoulders and strained, tearless, emotionless eyes, Frankie stared at

Johnny, she stared at her mechanic, one last time.

"Oh, I think it's too late for that," Johnny said.

Johnny hit the timer and there was a huge explosion. It was happening now, but it would take Earth, or at least those who were tracking the asteroid and the ship, four more minutes to learn about it.

Chapter Sixty-Three

EIGHT WEEKS LATER, Auger arrived at Rathman and Zoia's ranch.

"The asteroid missed the Earth by 219,000 kilometers," Auger said. "More than the astrophysics experts had anticipated. By almost 27 percent more than they had anticipated. Give it three million years and it'll miss the Earth—very conservatively—by at least 199,000 kilometers. That's what the numbers people say... The one that got away. What a success. It's like a miracle. It's like a fairytale, isn't it?"

"It is," Rathman and Zoia said.

Auger, the humanistic secularist, couldn't resist making the additional point. "There are some extremists who say that by deflecting the orbit of the asteroid we have altered the will of Gaia. You can't make everybody happy."

"Oh, we had a visitation from some Gaia pilgrims," Rathman said, "Zoia labeled them primitive religionist. They became, in the course of their pilgrimage, very peculiar in their beliefs, to say the least. The paranoia of this asteroid business, I think it only encouraged the irruption of irrational impulses followed by superstitious responses. The pilgrims left here a couple of months ago, heading north. I wonder if the border guards protecting the Inner World let them pass? In and of themselves, they were quite harmless. But crazy. With the success of the asteroid-interception mission,

I wonder if they stopped walking on their knees? Did walking on knees make the mission succeed? Oh, the power of belief!" Rathman paused. "Speaking of beliefs, you must tell us what happened with the Obsidian Order after Pius's death."

Auger nodded his head. "Pius surprised everybody, didn't he? Perhaps his contradictions were adaptations to circumstance. He was a good man. He died for truth. Which meant he died for freedom. I thought I knew Pius better than anyone. But honestly, I didn't know he had it in him. He gave his life. Truth...? Freedom...? *For what exactly?*"

"Anyway, Pius would be glad to know that Xanus has been sent into exile. That was the one place where the insurgents in the Order were successful. What has not been determined yet is if his exile is going to be permanent or not. That's important. The hierarchy of the Obsidian Order has not been altered. The old organization is intact. The old order has been overthrown by a new generation, but the institution itself has not changed."

"But, that's not entirely true. Something has changed. Pius, for the Obsidian Order, and Matthew, for the Forandi Order, have been canonized as saints in the official Gaia religion. In importance, there are only behind Iona as a saint, and September Snow as, now only metaphorically speaking, 'a goddess.' Spreading the sainthoods around will maybe make people less touchy. Tom Novak is now seen as a pre-Gaian guide to the new Gaia religion. All the writings, thoughts, and ideas, and the experiences they were all derived from, whatever we have left from the past, will never be proscribed again by the Gaia faith—official or unofficial, orthodox or unorthodox."

"Pius would have been proud of that outcome," Zoia said.

"Pius wasn't killed by modernity," Auger said. "He was killed by reactionary fanatics in his own religious order. Gaia, I miss him already. I wish he were alive to see his accomplishments!"

The three of them, Zoia, Rathman, and Auger, sat around and relaxed. They ate their meals in a pleasant way, taking their time. Rathman showed Auger around. He took him to see the cattle as they lowed and drank water. He took him to see the mesa. He took him to see the Mesquite Tree.

At the Mesquite Tree, Rathman told Auger the story about how Zoia brought Bruja to celebrate a picnic with her at the Tree. Rathman explained to Auger that the hardest test Bruja gave to Zoia was for her to prove that she wasn't a stereotypical, over-privileged, entitled, affluent resident from the city of Eccles. Once Zoia had passed that test, Bruja welcomed her with open arms. Also, at the same time, she told Zoia that the Mesquite Tree should be seen by me as being a sacred place. Bruja said to Zoia: 'This is a totem for Rathman. It's a place for him to sleep. It's a place for him to dream."

"Do you know what she meant by that?" Auger asked.

"No," Rathman said. "I just take it at face value."

At the conclusion of Rathman and Auger's talk, as they began to depart, Rathman stuffed a piece of paper into his father-in-law's pocket. "Do me a favor, will you? Next time you see Jug, give this to him."

"What is it?" Auger asked.

"It's something special. It's a map for a 25-kilometer-long walk in Eccles. Tell him to take the walk. On the exact course I've specified. Just as I've laid it out. No slipups, no shortcuts, no detours, and no add-ons. Tell him he must do it without the accompaniment of any gadgets, boxes, or flips. *Tell him he is not to let his own people know about it.* Tell him he must walk the entire course alone. Tell him to not take any money with him, except for something small, perhaps enough for bus fare. He should be incognito. He can talk to people along the way, but he can't say who he is. Tell him he must complete the journey in one go. Tell him to start no later than 10:30 a.m. and to finish no later than 6:00 p.m. He can stop along the way, but he can't alter *anything.*"

"Okay," Auger said. "But why, if you don't mind my asking?"

"He's never done anything like that before in his life," Rathman said. "That's enough. That's why."

Rathman looked carefully at his father-in-law. "Remember when

I was talking about Bruja?"

"Your neighbor?"

"Yes. She started coming over to see us. And then she started, well, you know, being with Zoia. Teaching her things..."

"What kind of things?" Auger asked.

"How should I know!" Rathman replied in an irritated voice, throwing his hands in the air. "They keep everything to themselves. All I've heard of is this: 'reality in the form of modernity and modern-ness is overrated.'"

"I'm just an historian," Auger replied. "I don't know what that means."

"It's not for me to say, either. It's not meant for me to know," Rathman clarified.

"Oh."

"I think it's always like that."

While Rathman and Auger were visiting the Mesquite Tree, Bruja made a short visit to see Zoia. When Bruja saw the two men slowly coming down the hill, she left through the back door and quickly disappeared. She didn't want to meet them.

When the three of them were together again, eventually they got around to the subject of Jug.

"Well, here's my report," Auger said.

"Saving the best for last, no?" Zoia asked.

"Well, hear me out." Auger smiled. "You might be surprised. Jug found someone who was able to use solar and wind power to set up a decentralized electrification system on an extremely remote island in the Outer World. With a fairly limited amount of infrastructure, the system can bring electricity to even the poorest and most remote parts of the island. Using this model system as a prototype, Jug wants to devote one quarter of all Gatetar's profits to electrify, first, the rest of the islands in the group, then, step-by-step, to electrifying other places. Eventually, he wants to power up the entire Outer World. Small decentralized installations, but on a massive scale."

"No strings attached?" Zoia asked.

"Not as far as I can tell," Auger said. "Once the whole system is up and running, it will be owned and controlled by the public on a non-profit basis. Jug will do it anonymously. He wants to do the entire thing for the public good. If everything he's saying is true, it will be amazing. By the way, he is going to put Jason in charge of the entire operation. And Jason has agreed. He wanted you to know about this, Zoia."

"How long will it take?" Zoia asked.

"Eighteen to twenty-five years."

By the look on Zoia's face, they could tell she was impressed. "Promising is different than spending. Until I see it with my own eyes, I'll still maintain a healthy skepticism."

"Aren't you being a little hard on him?" Rathman asked. "Come on, Zoia. His goal is a good one. He wants to bring light where there is darkness."

"Do you think I am being too hard?" Zoia asked. "We'll watch. We'll keep an eye on him. Oh, this world is strange. But you know you can't judge him by the same standards as we judge other people. He's used to getting his way too much. Ultimately, Juggernaut must thread the needle between two dehumanizing extremes. Men first feel necessity, then look for utility, next attend to comfort, still later amuse themselves with pleasure, debauchery, and decadence, thence grow dissolute in luxury and privilege, and if they do not reverse this trend, or at least moderate it in some very important way, they finally go mad and waste their substance. Juggernaut can choose the dangerous delusion that he is capable of his own redemption and salvation, and that a few more super-technological wonders will do the trick. But he will live in a despondent state of apathy, born from quiet desperation, which is his world now whether he knows it or not, or he can choose to muster the courage for a genuine concern for the meaning of his humanity. If we have learned anything from history, Father, we must be acutely aware of the dilemma that scientific-technocratic civilization has always faced."

Rathman turned to Auger and said, "Look at what Zoia's marvelous education has produced! Aren't you proud of her? I'm proud of her. She has an absolutely one-of-a-kind education. No one else in all of Eccles has an education like hers."

"Yes, well, some of this I've learned from Bruja as well," Zoia said. "Father, have we not learned anything from the history? From our ancient times? Equally important, have we not learned anything from the sacrifice of Frankie and Johnny?"

"Zoia is riffing," Rathman said. "All that education. Coming to something. The Sallow singers have adopted Zoia for a reason. They call her their History Daughter! Maybe she is the History Daughter for us all! Maybe she does have a special line on truth?"

Zoia just shrugged her shoulders. "It's simple. In shorthand, it's the lesson of Frankie and Johnny. And that lesson is this. It's easier to unite the world in a fight against a malevolent force coming from outer space and threatening the entire world, than it is to unite the world against practices of liberty and freedom which—because they've become *unsafe*—too quickly, too violently, morph into practices of anarchy, repression, and chaos, threatening not just order, but life itself. To be an 18 year old or a 19 year old in the year 2022 A.D., the year of the birth of September Snow, and to face that! That's what the history lesson has taught us, Father. If Juggernaut follows through, tell him that I will stop calling him Juggernaut. I will call him Jug. I will not love him. But I will tolerate him. And if he gives further proof of his sincerity, integrity, and honesty, then and only then will I extend my permission for him to come visit us. With my blessing. That's my message."

Chapter Sixty-Four

JAIME'S PROJECT.

Underground. Twelve enclaves beneath the surface of planet Earth were created just in case the mission failed and the asteroid crashed into the Earth. The creation of the underground depots and their locations were kept secret from everyone but a choice group of need-to-know people, or "next-of-kin" people.

The banks, the financial institutions, the largest corporations, and the military, lobbied hard to influence the choice of who'd be allowed to enter the lottery that would determine those who would be sheltered underground. But the science administrators agreed by unanimous vote in their insistence that the Forandi Order would select the personnel, and half would come from the Inner World, and half would come from the Outer World. Not a single member of the Forandi Order could be in the group. Jaime insisted on that rule, as a condition before the Forandi Order would participate in the program.

Twenty people were selected for each of the twelve locations, *ten* females, *ten* males, *four* children, *four* teenagers, *four* young adults, *four* middle aged, and *four* elderly. Aside from the ideas in their heads, no history, no written records would be kept. Each enclave was outfitted with oxygen-creation machines, food, water, and protected shelter for everyone, to last a minimum of 12 years. Half of the placements were located in abandoned deep-shaft mines, a quarter were buried under shallow water, good for insulation, a quarter were buried under forests or steppes. The experts knew that the odds of any of the participants surviving were very thin. Should such an unlikely event occur, those who did manage to survive would come to the surface, and bringing only their memories with them, try to reestablish human habitation on the surface.

They were not selected on the basis of their skills, or their intelligence, but they all had to have achieved a high level of fitness and general good health. (The Forandi insisted on that.)

Jaime greeted each of the participants, who, of course, were delighted and happy to learn the good news about the success of the asteroid mission.

Traveling around the world, speaking to each individual as he or she came out of the pits, 12 locations, 140 people, Jaime said exactly the same thing to each one, addressing them separately: "When you save one, you save all."

After Auger had delivered Rathman's instructions to him, Jug took them to heart. He walked 12 kilometers for several days, then 20 kilometers for several days, as a form of preparation before he attempted the 25 kilometers sojourn Rathman had prescribed.

"Zoia would be pleased," Rathman had written at the bottom of his note, and below that he wrote, "Zoia is softening. But she's not there yet. See other side of paper."

"By the way," Rathman wrote in a lovely scrawl on the back, "In his research, Auger found that the word in ancient Greece for

'assembly' was 'ecclesia.' It had, apparently, nothing to do with
the word 'Ecclesiastes,' which is the word for which 'Eccles' is an
abbreviation. How about that? Not one dude, an assembly. When
you think Eccles, think ecclesia, Jug. That's the point of the walk,
too."

Following Rathman's instructions, Jug walked to the Rainbow,
the cemetery where Rornar, Zoia's mother, had been buried, and
that brought back many memories, his attempt to woo Zoia and his
failure to do so. Then per Rathman's specific instructions Jug walked
north along a hidden creek that ran through a tunnel underground
for six kilometers—and he loved it. The route took him all the way
from the lower-middle neighborhood of Eccles to the shores of the
bay. By the time he turned around and headed back in the direction
of the tower, Jug realized by looking at his distance measurer he had
already covered 18 kilometers.

When he got near one of the entrances to Pleasure Park, he took
a brief break. Feeling fatigued he stopped at a cafe and drank two
cups of coffee which he realized had been a mistake when he felt
nervy-ness and over-stimulation. Walking more, more walking, miti-
gated that. Five kilometers to go. Following the map, walking three
streets south, he tried to find a young 'undocumented' woman who
apparently earned her living cleaning toilets, sinks, whatnot. Rathman's directions said she would be carrying her signature parapher-
nalia, a bright red plastic bucket, a long-handled mop, scrubbers.
She would be wearing blue rubber gloves and a plastic hairnet that
looked glossy and white. But as hard as he tried, he couldn't find her.
And then he realized Rathman's point had been that he search for
something that he had never bothered looking for before.

Then Jug was in it, the worst, the most notorious slum of them
all, the Favela Shantytown East. This was the place where Zoia had
first made the acquaintance of the outlander group, the group that
Zoia helped name, *Opium and Raw Pork*.

Jug remembered the newsflash. The three member women's band had been deported to Delos. They had been warned on no less than five occasions, but they kept singing the songs that were proscribed—songs that had been written in the Outer World, songs that were considered dangerous, and they publicly refused to comply with the authorities' edicts. They could sing their hit songs all they wanted, including their supreme hit song, *Back to Nature*, but they couldn't sing a brand new song by *Flee The Angry Strangers*, for example. This song was considered too risky.

When they were sent back to Delos, they were instantly hailed as heroes.

There had been some protests in Eccles over this decision, scattered protests, scattered here and there. Even the Rhetoric Department put on a little show of rebuke, which, of course, was completely ineffective. But otherwise, everybody went about their business. Otherwise, not much of a fuss. Songs, especially from the outside world, didn't have the same license as speech, which was still mostly free. People had their own short, complicated lives to live. You could still listen to the songs on velco recordings, you just couldn't hear them performed live.

New musical groups replaced the old musical groups in Eccles with great alacrity, very quickly, as swiftly as new kinds of gadgets replaced old ones.

Jug discovered that he was more exhausted than he had realized. He didn't like being in this slummy place, especially without a flip, or a gadget, and with no one knowing were he was.

Now, it was just starting to get dark, the sun had just passed behind some tall buildings. He had never been in a place like this before, under such circumstances. *This experience was unique.*

And then he felt it. There was a pain. First in the right leg. Then in the left. At first it was a throbbing sensation. Then it really hurt. Jug was in good health, but he had a history of rheumatism that occasionally weakened his left leg. But when that happened, he always managed to just limp along. At the same time he was also struck by a stiffness akin to arthritis, nearly incapacitating his right leg. By now the sun had gone completely down, it was getting dark, and everything started to close in on him.

Jug started to panic. He could barely move. He reached into his pocket and there it was, the small sum of money Rathman had told him he had permission to carry, only enough for a bus.

But as he stood at the bus stop, at an intersection, the bus sped by—not stopping. He could see that the bus was full and so he figured if he just waited long enough another bus would follow behind.

The smell hit him first. A figure sidled up to him. Like him, waiting for the bus. The young man, pavement dweller, beggar, maybe even worse than that, was wearing clothes that had not been cleaned for an eternity. There had been an accident in his pants that had occurred perhaps a week ago. The smell was stunningly powerful. This was disgusting. With the young lad standing immediately behind him, Jug waited 25 minutes for the next bus to arrive, and he was perfectly aware of exactly how long it took to arrive.

And when Jug got on the bus the young man followed him, taking the empty seat behind him. Jug was overwhelmed again by the powerful smell. Then Jug just started laughing, laughing out loud, as hard as he could.

Such a detail could not have been in Rathman's plan, Jug knew that. But he realized Rathman had figured out that something of that nature was bound to happen at some point. Rathman was a friend, he thought.

Chapter Sixty-Five

AND SO everything had become—more or less—settled.
Jug was out of the doghouse with Zoia, but just barely, and only provisionally.

In accord with the memory of the Obsidian Order, Pius was now considered a saint.

The Love Observatory was renamed after Frankie, and the San Francisco Game reserve was renamed after Johnny. With these memorials, Eccles was imbued with a powerful aura that would last for many generations to come.

Jaime retired early, and entered into an extreme state of obscurity that he was only too happy to embrace. In this, he was thoroughly and absolutely a Forandi, and he was one until the day he died.

Auger taught history. Like his antecedent, Ubaar Suwiot, not dreaming of an alternative, he stayed on in his job until very late in life, when he transferred his chairpersonship to a very young woman.

Rathman and Zoia tried their best to keep the ranch going.

And Bruja, like a ghost, hovered over all of it.

For Rathman and Zoia life at the ranch grew into a routine and the longer they lived together the more the routine became settled. They lived a successful life and a richly rewarding one.

"What can Jug really do to make it right with you?" Rathman asked Zoia.

"He could sell off all the Gatetar land. Especially the huge tracts of land that his family owns in the Outer World. Give the money away."

"Including the ranch?" Rathman asked. "That would be part of the deal?"

"Yes. Of course."

"Would that satisfy you?"

"It might."

"Would it satisfy Bruja?"

"Oh, that would only be starters for her!"

"Does Jug know what he's up against?"

"Oh, I'm sure he hasn't a clue."

But after eight years living on the ranch, something started creeping up from behind. Rathman started having them again. They got worse. Then they got better. Then they got worse. Then they got better. They were dreams.

Although there were some powerful nightmares, the best dreams were about what Rathman presumed—without certainty of course—was the nature of his ancestors.

Zoia understood that Rathman loved his deep-time ancestors, although it was a mystery how he *knew* them. Whenever she could, she encouraged him to think. Was it ancestors, from the time of the darkness, who kept him out of the darkness, Zoia wondered?

Bruja kept out of it.

Rathman and Zoia brought a picnic basket up with them to the Mesquite Tree. After an elaborate lunch, Rathman fell asleep. The first dream he had was of a woman of indeterminate age grinding mesquite pods in a mortar to make grain flour. The next dream was of a man of indeterminate age seated in a rundown place surrounded by books, perhaps it was a ramshackle scriptorium, and in the dream the man was reading an old manuscript by candlelight. Aside from the light emitted by the single candle, there was darkness inside and out.

As often as three or four times a year, Rathman had dreamt about the poet Ulm. These were at least dreams that could be placed in time, from the time of darkness, 2,000 years before.

Zoia quizzed Rathman on his two dreams. The woman grinding mesquite pods. "Old or young?" Zoia asked.

"Neither. Both."

Zoia was assuming Rathman was going to say he had dreamt of Ulm. "You've been eating, drinking, sleeping, so of course the man with the books was Ulm."

"But I wasn't dreaming of Ulm," Rathman said. "I was dreaming of a man who loved Ulm's poetry. There's a difference. In the dream, the manuscript the man was holding in his hands, the section he was apparently reading, was *The Time Repairer.* I could see the title at the top of the page. I've never had this dream before."

"The man who loved Ulm's poetry. Old or young?" Zoia asked.

"Neither. Both."

"Well, it's a good dream," Zoia concluded.

Rathman thought of the names of the ancestors from the Oral Tradition that his mother had whispered into his ear so many times when he was young: the mother, the father, the three daughters, the son: Telia, Pallas, Aura, Teanna, Vivianna, and Pontus.

Rathman just shook his head. "This dream? I don't know what it is. I don't know what it means. I'll never know what it is. But when you don't have knowledge, or at least comprehensive knowledge, all you have is belief. And so I'll keep worshipping the ancestors, as my family taught me, told me, to do so."

"I've always hoped that it was true that meaning and life were the same thing," Zoia said.

"The will—the wish—the dream—for a purposeful existence?" Rathman asked. "How much more can a specimen of human being-ness aspire to?"

"Yes. Can a specimen aspire to anything more? Yes. That's the question." Zoia thought long and hard on this. "Do you think, Tom Novak, perhaps near the end of his days, had an answer to that question?"

Rathman scratched his head. "Don't know. Was Tom religious? No. Tom was not religious. *We know that.* 'Let not man come extinct?'"

"Yes," Zoia exclaimed. She nodded her head. She let out a peal of laughter. "Yes. Let not man come extinct! Yes! We could call that a religion. Maybe with—and maybe not with—Gaia. But what would Tom Novak have called it? He didn't believe in Gaia, of course. I know!"

Rathman had a relaxed expression on his face. "The breath I inhale and the breath I exhale when I think of you. Ah, so lovely..."

"I've really had only three other men in my life, Rathman, and they were my father, his deceased friend, and Jug," Zoia said. "Two of three of them spent their lifetimes getting all passionate about people who lived thousands of years in the past. And now one's dead and the other's surprised that no one cares about what he spent a lifetime thinking about. Look, I'm a freak! I don't know why Jug's crazy about me."

"Jug's trying to find his worthiness—through you—in relation to the world," Rathman said. "As long as that lasts, it's a good thing."

"They said that Homer was a blind poet," Zoia said. "But Bruja taught me that there might have been a host of blind poets before him—women singers, songwriters, poetesses, one and all, *in* the age before writing, before reading. Of all the Homeric Hymns, 'To Earth, Mother of All,' hymn # 30, says it all:

'Gaia! Allmother will I sing! Revered
Firmgrounded nourisher of everything on Earth.
Whatever traverses holy earth or the seas
Or climbs the air enjoys your dispensation.
From you sprout fine fruits and offspring;
Lady, you have power to give mortal men life
Or take it. But happy those you care for in
Your heart: all is generously present to them.
Fields thicken with lifegiving nourishment,
Herds at pasture multiply, houses fill with
Splendid things. Right and law rule in the city
Blessed by plenty and wealth among women beautiful.
Children beam with youth and joy, gleeful girls
Dance the ringdance, their hands all blossoms,
Leaping on flowery carpets of meadow.
Such pleasures your servants enjoy,
Goddess sublime! Generous divinity!'

"There is one thing we can count on," Zoia said. "Beginning almost 6,000 years ago, when a procession of generations, blind or otherwise, recited those lines. And 6,000 years in the future—if we are lucky—they'll still be reciting them. And maybe 12,000 years from now, when much more of the Earth returns to the old normal, and 50,000 years in the future, *it is so speculative,* when virtually all of the world returns to the old normal, Gaia will prevail. But for how long? Did the ancient Greeks really worship their goddesses? Or were they just impishly pretending?"

THE END

Auger's Touchstone (2021) is the Book Four of
THE BLESSINGS OF GAIA SERIES
Book One: *September Snow* (2006)
Book Two: *Runes of Iona* (2010)
Book Three: *Embers of the Earth* (2016)

Reader please note: *Auger's Touchstone* can be read as the first book in the series. Indeed, it's a pre-read for Book One. Though the books can be read in their natural sequence:1, 2, 3, 4, if reader wants alternative: try 4, 1, 2, 3! That'll work too! All books also stand alone.

The Invention of Fire

by Christopher Bernard

One day I heard on a street of this city—
billionaire ville of high tech and IT
cultured pearl of Silicon Valley,
capital of the twenty-first century,
San Francisco of the crazed and crazy—
a man laugh out, "Whatever you do,
or think you can do, there's one thing you can't do:
you can't disinvent technology!"

But, darling, what if we could, you and me,
undo the long gold chain of human
marvels and practical disasters, back
to the wild dawn of it all? What if we could
unpave, unpollute, unpoison the world
that we are destroying with our civilized life,
that Frankenstein's monster of silica and code?

— The cell phone suddenly melts in my hand
like a Milky Way bar left too long in the sun.

The laptop wrinkles like an autumn leaf,

the desktop goes up in a puff of smoke
at the sparrow's pass of a magician's wand,
goes up with a smell of burning wood.

Servers curdle like bottles of milk.
GPS goes out like a light.
Monitors line up like dead fish on the sand.

Abruptly vanishes the World Wide Web
like a spider's cobweb catching humans like flies.
and with it the stranglehold of the internet.

A wind picks up over the empty land:
it blows forests of sky dishes away,
flocks of radios, stereophonic herds,
the clotted brainpans of obsessive nerds,
landfills clogged with wireless TVs,
movie cameras, projectors—not those!—yes those
too—molten flash drives and CPUs,
busses and rockets and snowboards and skis,
rollerblades, Velcro and nonstick pans,
silicon chips reduced to sand,
rare earth metals melting down with smartphones,
the burnt-out husks of intelligent homes,
trains and steamships and telegraphs and sails
crossing the seas like clouds of white whales,
skyscrapers and skylights, iron alloys and glass,
the first lawnmowers smelling of cut grass,
and the central beast at the heart of the wheel:
the million-headed Hydra, the automobile;
the casket elevator, the pick, the spade,
the tackle and hook of a cable of braid,
the IUD, pill, the condom, bidet,
vaginal rings and penis pumps
(the tech of pleasure isn't spared its lumps),
Glocks and anklets, in vitro wombs,
water-sealed coffins and virtual tombs,
robosoldiers, RFIDs, ebola bombs:

the wind of time in reverse sweeping away
everything we invented: the plough, the clock,
the spectacles on the pimpled nose of a monk,
dreadnaughts, all dreading, at long last sunk,
pencil, parchment, typewriter, quill,
propeller, salt cellar, egg-beater, scythe,
horseshoe nail and dentist drill,
uncool change lane and cool Swiss knife:
everything that fell from the war of life
into our far too-clever brains
that are never satisfied and never tire,
back to the beginning of everything until
we lie down again in the mud of the cave
and, snuggling together, as we know best,
disinvent the one we can blame for the rest:
the two sticks that first rubbed together into fire.

See? All gone! It couldn't be done?
We've done it, you and me, in the course
of a little fantasy and, with apologies, verse.
But then, I never needed any of it.
I have needed you, deep as I am in the mire.
Each time we embrace, we invent fire.

ABOUT THE AUTHOR

Robert Balmanno retired from the Sunnyvale Public Library after 32 years of service. He has been a trade union activist for more than 40 years. He earned his bachelor's degree in Political Science from the University of California, Santa Barbara, and did some post-graduate work at the University of Edinburgh in Scotland, and the University of London, King's College. More importantly, he is the author of three novels, *September Snow, Runes of Iona* and *Embers of the Earth*. A semi-Luddite, that is to say, ambiguously oriented toward — and at times suspicious of — technological advances in communication, Balmanno lives in Silicon Valley surrounded by Facebook, Apple, Google, Yahoo, and others.